8

Stephen Baxter applied to ...
1991. He didn't make it, b...
thing by becoming a sc... hontae Luimni
novels and short stories h... UNTY LIBRARY
won awards around t... ...ence background is in maths and engineering. He is married
and lives in Buckinghamshire.

Voyager

STEPHEN BAXTER

Traces

HarperCollins*Publishers*

Voyager
An Imprint of HarperCollins*Publishers*
77–85 Fulham Palace Road,
Hammersmith, London W6 8JB

This paperback edition 1999
1 3 5 7 9 8 6 4 2

First published in Great Britain by *Voyager* 1998

Copyright © Stephen Baxter 1998
For further copyright detail see Acknowledgements

The Author asserts the moral right to
be identified as the author of this work

ISBN 0 00 649814 0

Printed and bound in Great Britain by
Caledonian International Book Manufacturing Ltd, Glasgow

To my father

ACKNOWLEDGEMENTS

Traces, first published in *Interzone*, 1991.

Darkness, first published in *Interzone*, 1995.

The Droplet, first published in *Other Edens III*, ed Christopher Evans and Rob Holdstock, Unwin Hyman 1989.

No Longer Touch the Earth, first published in *Interzone*, 1993. *Mittelwelt*, first published in *Interzone*, 1993.

Journey to the King Planet, first published in *Zenith 2*, ed David S Garnett, Sphere, 1990.

The Jonah Man, first published in *Interzone*, 1989.

Downstream, first published in *Interzone*, 1993.

The Blood of Angels, first published in *Isaac Asimov's Science Fiction Magazine*, 1994.

Columbiad, first published in *Science Fiction Age*, 1996.

Brigantia's Angels, first published in *Interzone*, 1995.

Weep for the Moon, first published in *In Dreams*, ed. Paul McAuley and Kim Newman, Gollancz 1992.

Good News, first published in *Substance*, 1994.

Something for Nothing, first published in *Interzone*, 1988.

In the Manner of Trees, first published in *Interzone*, 1992.

Pilgrim 7, first published in *Interzone*, 1993.

Zemlya, first published in *Isaac Asimov's Science Fiction Magazine*, 1996.

Moon Six, first published in *Science Fiction Age*, 1997.

George and the Comet, first published in *Interzone*, 1991.

Inherit the Earth, first published in *New Worlds 2*, ed D. Garnett, Gollancz 1992.

In the MSOB, first published in *Interzone*, 1996.

Contents

TRACES

By the time we reached the comet, Dillard and I had spent fifteen months together inside the two-man GUTship; and, although we'd respected each other's privacy as far as possible, I'd come to know him as well as I've known anyone. And I believed that his Holistic faith was as well-founded as it was possible to be.

So, when his faith crumbled before the ancient images we extracted from the comet core, I was profoundly shocked.

I was the pilot of the GUTship while Dillard was the mission specialist, with special responsibility for the Berry archaeological imaging process. The ship itself looked a little like a giant parasol: a stem five hundred yards long tipped by our lifecell, a fat disc some fifty yards wide, while the 'handle' of the parasol, at the other end of the stem, was a block of asteroid ice within which the GUT drive was embedded.

The lifecell was cluttered with communications banks, with living equipment such as a galley, shower and Virtual tank, and with lab equipment. Thus, much of the lifecell was of necessity common ground to Dillard and me – but it also contained two precious privacy booths into which we could retreat, with books or vision cubes, in order to make-believe we were somewhere else. We decorated the booths in styles of our own choosing – I fixed mine to match my fancy of the sailing ships of old Earth, with blackened ship's timbers, a narrow bunk and creaking floorboards (I never found out what Dillard did to his; I liked to imagine a bare stone cell containing a jug of water, a hard bed with a single blanket, and a few books – but this was whimsy: the Holistics are not renowned for their asceticism).

In any event, Dillard and I spent much of our journey in polite avoidance of each other. Ship's days would pass with scarcely a word between us, and such conversations as we had tended to centre around work.

So my journey to the Oort Cloud with a minister of the First Church of Christ the Holistic wasn't the cartoon nightmare one might imagine.

One of the few times we discussed Dillard's beliefs came at turnover. After seven months at one gee we were a sixth of a light year from Earth and travelling at three-quarters of lightspeed: just enough to tinge the receding Sol with redshift. Now we were to begin the slow deceleration to our rendezvous point in the Cloud. The GUT drive closed down and gravity lifted from the lifecell, and Dillard and I strapped loosely into our couches. I touched a panel and the lifecell turned transparent, so that we lay in a bowl of multicolored light, suspended amid stars. Verniers nudged the ship over so that the diamond-hard stars wheeled around us.

Dillard turned on his side and peered down through the floor. He was a stocky man, a head shorter than me, and, at forty-five, some ten years older. Now I could make out the starlit outline of his blandly handsome, blocky face. 'Brewster, look down there.' I twisted to see. The ship's main stem emerged from the base of the lifecell and dwindled into the distance like an exercise in perspective, finishing in the amorphous grey mass of the asteroid ice block. Dillard grinned. 'That block was a perfect cube when we left the Moon.'

I nodded. 'Well, we've used a little less than half of it: just about on schedule. We shouldn't run out of gas until we get to the comet . . .'

'Let's hope we can refill as planned.'

Most of our conversation was like this: gentle, delivered in the mildest of tones, and meaningless. Dillard was always calm, friendly and interested in everything; habitually he would run a hand over his greying blond crewcut and turn to me, unfailingly curious.

I felt guilty for not liking him more than I did.

We continued to consider the GUT drive. GUT stands for 'Grand Unified Theory', that philosophical system which describes the fundamental forces of nature as aspects of a single superforce. The GUT drive consists of a fist-sized chuck of hydrogen locked into a superconducting bottle and bombarded to creation physics temperatures. At such temperatures only the unified superforce can act. When the hydrogen is bled from the bottle the superforce goes through 'phase transitions', decomposing into the four familiar forces of nature – strong and weak nuclear, gravitational and electromagnetic. Just as steam releases heat when it goes through a phase transition by condensing to water, so at each transition of the superforce a pulse of energy is emitted.

The GUT phase energy flashes asteroid ice to plasma; the superheated plasma is expelled through a nozzle, so that a GUTship is a kind of steam rocket.

A random impulse prompted me to observe to Dillard, 'Of course it was GUT phase transition energy, liberated during the cooling period after the Big Bang, that fuelled the expansion of the universe itself.'

He raised his head and studied me patiently.

I went on, tempted to needle him, 'Seems almost blasphemous – doesn't it? – to put such a godlike force into a box and ride it . . .'

Dillard smiled. In his gentle Boston accent he said, 'If we thought it was blasphemy the Church would hardly have funded the expedition.'

'But I thought your faith was based on the sanctity of nature.'

'It is. But that does not preclude the advance of technology. We believe that nature has been designed for the use of wise people . . .'

'Ah,' I said. 'The anthropic principle. The theory that the fundamental constants underpinning the universe were set so that human life would be possible; that even the primordial supernova, which caused the birth of the Sun, was part of some Grand Design –'

'Something like that.' Dillard's face was like a sketch, with small mouth and nose, widespread eyes and barely a wrinkle; now he wore a smile that was irritatingly tolerant. 'Brewster, we've spent the last seven months skirting the topic of faith, and I suspect that was the wisest path.' He looked up through the clear roof; the turning manoeuvre was almost completed now, so that we were looking back the way we had come. 'But I'll say this,' he went on. 'Blasphemy is an outdated concept. Look up, Brewster; that redshifted blur is the Sun and, with a little wishful thinking, you can make out around it a muddy pool of light that is the inner Solar System. Earth alone holds life –'

'As far as we know.'

'As far as we know after a century of assiduous research, yes – and I can cup the extent of intelligence's spread in the palm of my hand. Brewster, we believe that the reduction of entropy – the encouragement of self-organization – is sacred. If we are here for any reason it is to build, to spread, to grow and learn. As yet we've built nothing.

'You can only blaspheme if you shout loudly enough for God to hear. We've a way to go before we achieve that.'

Dillard's church had been the first to weld late twentieth century scientific notions – such as cosmology's anthropic philosophy, the self-organization principles of the chaos scientists, Lovelock's Gaia ideas – to a subframe of simple, robust Christianity.

The new religion, I reflected, had been ideally comforting for the spiritually starved Western world – and it had spread like a virus. Science and technology suddenly became spiritually valid activities, and we walked with a swagger, confident of our preeminence in the universe.

Still, despite my own cynicism, I conceded that Dillard's conviction was impressive; perhaps it ought to have been inspiring, even . . .

But I come from Liverpool – not the Martian colony but that battered old city on the west coast of England – and my family have been lapsed Catholics for generations. So there is a scarred hole in me where faith (perhaps) ought to lie, and the conviction of others serves only to make me feel threatened. At that moment – despite the fact that underneath it all I had come to respect Dillard – I wished only to pry at his beliefs, to seek to undermine them. Yet, perhaps I was hoping that he would stand firm even so; I think somewhere inside me there was a baffled child seeking comfort from Dillard's steadfastness.

I said nothing, and the moment passed.

At length a low bell tolled, signifying the return of gravity. With some relief I turned the hull opaque, locking out the universe.

The months wore away, and at last the ship reached its greatest distance from the Sun. The relativistic tinges faded from the stars as the GUT drive sighed to stillness. I turned the hull transparent once more, and we peered out.

The comet was a grey ghost fifty miles wide, sliding along the rim of the Sun's gravity well like a bristled spectre.

This comet was one of billions in the Oort Cloud, a rough sphere a third of a light year from the Sun. Comets are balls of grubby snow; only if they fall into the depths of the Solar System does the Sun's heat cause them to blaze across the sky. But this nucleus had never fallen; since the birth of the planets – perhaps even since the primordial supernova – it had circled alone here, as undisturbed and discrete as some eyeless fish of the ocean depths.

And this isolation was precisely why we had come to visit. As Dillard had explained during the voyage, 'Brewster, if we're careful this comet could yield Berry phase image data from half way back to the Big Bang itself . . .' He had grinned, boyish. 'This will knock those portraits of Caesar into a cocked hat, eh?'

The Berry phase of an electron is a quantum attribute which records the particle's history: its displacements and velocities, the forces which have acted on it . . . The Berry phase is the particle's memory. The effect was discovered in the 1980s, but it was not until this century that a way was found to cross-correlate the phases of a multitude of particles to reconstruct three-dimensional traces of macroscopic events . . .

Images of the past.

When the first Berry image was made public – a murky swampscape reconstructed from a lump of coal – there was wild speculation. Perhaps, for example, you could take a core from the Notebooks and gaze into the eyes of Leonardo . . .

But it didn't work out like that. Earthbound particles have been handled, eaten, excreted, incorporated into bone, ground to meal, buried, burned, blasted, over and again. Trying to untangle all that is next to impossible.

By the time we left Earth only the face of Gaius Julius Caesar had emerged from the gloom of centuries, thanks to a chance isolated find in Britain.

But, still, image archaeology had caught the imagination of the world. And when Holistic Church money had started to pour into glamorous science projects, Berry phase research was a prime candidate.

So here I was, orbiting a comet in a ship mostly owned by the First Church.

Well, I wasn't complaining. As long as I was here.

We got to work. I closed down the ship's flight systems, and Dillard began to deploy the Berry phase analysis equipment. Five small probes nosed their way out of a stem-mounted cargo pod and spread themselves evenly around the comet nucleus; Dillard took particular care that the probes' vernier exhaust did not contaminate the comet surface.

Then, from each probe, electric-blue laser light lanced into the comet. Five superhot wavefronts converged at lightspeed on the dead centre of the nucleus. A cubic centimetre of the ancient ice flashed to plasma, and the light beams carried precious Berry phase data back to the probes.

It took less than a second.

Dillard was flushed and excited; perspiration had gathered in droplets over his scalp. I couldn't help but smile. 'Is that all there is to it?'

He wiped his brow, grinning. 'This is where the hard work starts . . .'

'Call me when you find something.'

*   *   *

With the Berry extraction complete I was free to set up the rest of our research programme. Over the next few days a hail of small robots tumbled eagerly to the comet surface, and laser and other beams scored the icescape.

At length, restless, I suited up and climbed out of the ship through the airlock; from the transparent roof of the lifecell I kicked off towards the comet nucleus. As the ship receded beneath me the lighted lifecell became a raft of incongruous normality, adrift in a bottomless sea.

I turned myself over and descended feet first towards the comet.

Spires and needles of ice hundreds of feet high bristled menacingly towards me. It was like falling into some cartoon mountain range. As I passed one triple-edged peak I reached out a gloved hand, cautiously; the substance of the peak evaporated within my grasp, less substantial than candyfloss.

These fantastic structures had condensed here thanks to a stillness lasting billions of years; but one trip around the Sun would wipe this nucleus clean.

I landed and – with a hiss transmitted through my suit – I sank to about knee depth in insubstantial gossamer. I found I could walk about with little difficulty, and my motion jumbled the ice into new, precarious sculptures. I walked in a faery city worked in silver and ebony, laced with threads of purplish organic compounds. Arches of feathery ice twisted over my head, seeming to defy even the microgravity of this place.

A movement to my left caught my eye: a fist-sized sample robot clambered busily out of the interior of the comet, its tiny caterpillar treads spinning. For a few seconds it lay as if resting, surrounded by a crater of disturbed ice; then it retracted its treads, sprouted a tiny rocket nozzle, and set off towards the GUTship, leaving me alone with the antique stillness.

I let my heart open up. Moments like this, I suspected, were why I endured the pain, loneliness and boredom of deep space flight; moments like this gave my life its meaning and definition; moments like this were as close as I would ever come to the numinous.

My helmet radio hissed to life. 'Brewster.' Dillard's voice sounded flat. 'You'd better come back.'

I frowned, my mood broken. 'What is it?'

'. . . I've found something.'

He would say no more. With a growing sense of unease I kicked off from the surface of the comet, careless now of the ice sculptures I shattered.

Dillard had extracted a sequence of Berry phase images from the comet core material. When I joined him he was cycling them through his workbench.

I was stunned.

There was a star – not Sol, but a monster: huge, brooding and blighted by vast spots. A clutch of planets showed as discs and crescents.

'These are good quality traces,' Dillard said, his voice tight. 'And remember that a Berry image is like an animated hologram, containing depth and time information; there's so much data here that –'

I touched his shoulder. 'Dillard, you don't need to lecture me. These images are – magical.'

Dillard seemed to take comfort from my impressed reaction, and some of his customary bland composure returned. Underneath, though, I sensed a deep disturbance which I could not understand; hesitant expressions chased across his face.

The stellar system shifted across the screen as the imaging process panned over prehistory. At length the 'camera' selected one of the planets, a ruddy crescent off to the left of the huge star, and zoomed in. I stared at the picture, willing myself to make out surface details; but as the planet image grew it continually shattered into boxes of uniform colour which only hesitantly reformed. Dillard explained that we were close to the process's limit of resolution.

The crescent settled at the centre of the workbench, distinctly red and tipped by small icecaps.

There were stars within the horns of the crescent.

I stared stupidly, shaking my head.

'Cities, on the nightside,' Dillard said calmly.

'Cities?'

'Watch.' For a moment I studied him: his broad face remained blank and his shoulders were hunched as he worked the workbench controls. His reaction continued to strike me as odd, but my excitement at the Berry traces was overwhelming, and I turned once more to the images.

Now more details trickled through the frosted-glass imaging process. A little above the world's surface I made out sections of arcs; it was rather as if the planet image had been sketched hastily and was surrounded by remains of earlier drafts. At first I speculated that the world was ringed; but the truth, as it emerged, was far stranger: a Net of light surrounded the planet, a wide mesh like a longitude-latitude grid. Beads of green and brown slid along the Net, here and there dropping to the surface through the thin layer of air.

Now a ship dropped gracefully into the image, a slim cylinder of startling blue; it slid through the Net and settled towards the planet surface. It was difficult to be sure of the scale – but the ship looked so vast that its keel must have been bent to match the curve of the world.

The image faded, leaving the workbench empty.

I reached behind me, found a couch, and pulled myself into it. 'Dillard, man; I don't know what to say.'

He spread his wide hands flat on the workbench.

I said, 'This is a triumph. More than we could have expected. This is – the discovery of the age! The first evidence of life, intelligence beyond Earth. So we're not alone –'

'But we are.' There was an edge in his voice and again I caught the impression of some deep distress. 'These images are more than five billion years old, Brewster.'

'But there may be other traces of their passing.' Suddenly my overworked imagination was full of images of a new Renaissance, as GUTships scoured the Oort Cloud for the wisdom of a lost race –

'No. Brewster, you've had some astrophysical training;

think it through. What did you make of that star? Was it a quiet little main-sequencer like Sol?'

I remembered the star: massive, swollen even, with those deep spots racing across its surface –

Dillard mused, 'Already they must have been preparing for the betrayal of their star. Perhaps they moved their cities underground, or erected force fields. Perhaps they were even planning to move their worlds.'

'The star is going to supernova,' I breathed.

'Wrong. It did supernova. Five billion years ago.'

I felt a great sadness settle over me. 'So we've lost them.' My head seemed to clear as my wilder imaginings evaporated. Dillard still drifted over his workbench, his labourer's hands spread flat against its empty surface. 'Dillard, forgive me,' I said. 'I still can't understand the way you're taking this. To extract this data is a great achievement. Why is it distressing you so?'

He turned away, his face working. 'Brewster, I'm going to take a break. Excuse me. There isn't much more I can do with the facilities here in any event; when we get back to Earth I will be able to extend the range of the Berry images forwards and backwards in time – maybe all the way up to the explosion itself – '

I said harshly, 'Dillard, your faith has taken a dent today, hasn't it? Is that the problem? Your Church is based on the premise that the universe was designed for man; and that therefore we are alone. Its mass appeal is based on that anthropocentric element. Yet today you have found proof that another race existed.'

'Brewster – '

'But you're a scientist, man. Surely you can rise above this. The old Christian churches had to absorb Darwin's ideas; if your faith is strong enough it will survive – '

'Brewster.' His voice was hard and his hands had gathered into fists. 'Please don't lecture me on matters you don't understand.'

And he pulled himself away from the bench and into his privacy booth.

I stared after him.

And, at length, I began to work it out.

Dillard's faith had been more than damaged. It had been destroyed.

The Berry process had shown us another race building cities, sailing between planets. Perhaps they too had evolved some equivalent of our anthropic theory, by which they also believed the universe had been built as a sort of racial adventure playground for them.

But their sun had exploded, and their worlds were put to fire.

Perhaps Dillard's faith could have survived even these blows, but there was more.

For this comet was a relic of the birth of the Solar System, of the great compressive wave which had crossed this region of space and sparked into existence the Sun and a host of other stars . . .

A wave emanating from a supernova.

Today Dillard and I had seen the star which had exploded so that Earth, and human life, could be born; and so our very substance was composed of the blasted carcasses of that lost race. Just as we, one day, would die so that some other people, fantastically different, could arise – another race to believe, fondly and foolishly, that the universe was designed for them alone.

Anthropocentrism was dead.

Dillard's Church would probably survive, I reflected, even with its anthropic heart ripped out; the cynicism of its wealthy leaders would see to that. But Dillard was an intelligent and honest man, and now he would have to come to terms with this amputation of his philosophy.

As would I. I grieved – not for Dillard, but for my confused self, left once more without even the faith of others for comfort.

Clumsily I made the workbench replay the Berry traces, over and again.

DARKNESS

Philmus fell out of the light.

She staggered as she dropped into her new body; it was small, compact, with a lower centre of gravity than her own. Hillegas's Virtual scenario flooded over her, a penetrative assault of vision, sounds and smells.

A room: large, gloomy, giving onto a veranda. It was day, but so dark that candles burned on the mantel. A log fire made the room hot, the air heavy. Through the open French window she could see terraced gardens, sweeping down to a lake. Vine leaves crowded around the window frame; but the leaves were small and yellow, under-nourished, and the sky outside was piled thick with brooding clouds.

At a desk before the window sat a man. Sheets of paper on the desk-top were covered with fine, ink-blotched handwriting, heavily revised. There was other furniture in the room: a couch, a heavy armchair, bookcases, small tables. There was an overpowering scent of dirt — musk — barely overlaid by perfumes; the people of this age had had odd notions of hygiene, she remembered.

Philmus held up her hands: they were delicate, the palms free of calluses, and there was a silk ruff around her wrists. The hands were those of a twenty-year-old; she'd lost about thirty years in age, she estimated. Her dress, blue, was heavy around her legs – it consisted of layers of stiff, useless material – and something dug into her waist, maybe a corset. Her hair was pulled back into what might be a bun, so tight it hurt.

Another man stood beside her. Was this Hillegas? Tall, young, thinning blond hair, a rather blank expression. His suit was of some rough, dark material; his boots were polished and dark against the carpet.

13

'Christ,' she said. 'I hate this part. The arrival.' Her voice, she found, was high-pitched.

To her surprise, the man at the desk seemed to react. He turned and ran his hands through a mop of hair – red, shot with grey. 'Polidori?' He peered at her – no, *through* her, she realized. He looked perhaps thirty. He wore a shirt open at the neck, what looked like jodhpurs, and boots like Hillegas's.

Hillegas ignored him. 'We're in the Villa Diodati,' he murmured to Philmus. 'By the shore of Lac Léman – Lake Geneva. It's 1816. July.'

'July? But it's so dark. It's more like winter.'

The man at the desk stood and stepped towards them. 'Is that you, Polidori?' His accent was clipped – not like modern British – almost Germanic, Philmus thought. His face was strong, compelling, but pale and dark-eyed, she saw, and there was a layer of unattractive fat over his belly and ribs. He had a limp; one of his shoes was built up. 'I hear you speak – I *see* you, but indistinctly – are you spectres? Oh! damn this weather – for a bit of sunlight . . .'

The man was only three feet from Philmus. '*Can* he see us?'

'No,' Hillegas said.

'Are you sure? Maybe there's some leakage –'

Hillegas walked indifferently around the red-haired man and crossed to the desk. Philmus followed uneasily, oddly embarrassed, avoiding the man's questing eyes.

Hillegas pointed to one of the sheets on the desk. '"The brows of men by the despairing light/ Wore an unearthly aspect, as by fits/ The flashes fell upon them . . ."' He turned to her, evidently excited. 'This is it! The manuscript of *Darkness* . . .'

The red-haired man turned and strode back to the desk. '*Damn* you,' he shouted. He picked up a page of his manuscript, crumpled it dramatically and hurled it towards the window. The paper disappeared as soon as it passed through the window-frame, out of the man's sight; it was clumsy, and Philmus's doubts about the quality of Hillegas's simulation deepened. The man cried, 'I cannot write! – not the simplest letter. It is as if you have scooped out half my brain, and all of my heart! Why do you spectres not simply kill me?' He opened a drawer in the desk, angrily searching for something.

'Something's wrong,' Philmus said, watching him. 'Definitely. He is aware of us, and he's conscious of a change in his internal condition. He knows he's not the man of his memories.'

Hillegas stared at the man with a kind of greed. 'But the simulation's worked. Don't you see? He's in the middle of composing *Darkness*. I'll be able to ask him – But I need more processing power. Especially if I'm going to achieve a definitive reconstruction of the poem's composition.'

'I don't think you're listening to me,' she said. She felt tired, and her Virtual body, in its restricting, heavy clothes, was irritating her. 'This isn't a question of authenticity, Hillegas. If you've allowed this projection to become fully self-aware, you've broken the sentience laws.'

Hillegas's face showed an echo of anger. The face was odd, inhuman, not a full reflection of his mind; it was as if the small muscles around his mouth, governing expression, had been cut. Hillegas's body, like much of the rest of the simulation, was imperfectly visualized; he'd obviously devoted most of the mips available to him to the core of his Virtual, the man at the desk.

Then Hillegas's lips moved – he was sub-vocing, she realized belatedly.

'Hillegas. Don't try anything –'

Hillegas's body seemed to shimmer, and it became more solid, subtly; she was aware of his stronger presence, there in the room with her, as if his gravity field had been increased. She felt wraith-like, insubstantial by comparison.

The red-haired man stared at Hillegas, his full lips parting in shock. To him, Philmus realized, a shadow had just congealed into flesh and blood.

Events moved rapidly, then, out of her control.

Hillegas stepped forward, his hands spread wide. 'Lord Byron. I –'

The other man took something from the desk drawer. It was a pistol. He fired it, directly into Hillegas's chest.

It was more an explosion than a shot. Byron's arm was hurled backwards by the recoil. The ball, hard and massive, ripped through Hillegas's torso, and embedded itself in the wall beyond. There was a sharp stink of cordite.

Hillegas looked down, startled, at the hole in his chest. Pixels fluttered about him, blocks of colour in the air.

Philmus sub-voced herself up to Hillegas's density. Byron saw her materialize, and saliva streaked at the corner of his mouth. He dropped the pistol on the desk, and rubbed his firing arm.

Philmus stepped forward. 'Congratulations, Hillegas. Now you've really blown it.'

Hillegas's face sketched confusion and fear. The pixels clustered like blood platelets over a wound; she could see his shirt and jacket reforming.

'Are you ghosts?' Byron was whispering. 'But I do not credit ghosts; for I cannot accept the existence of spirits without a belief in God . . . What are you, then?'

'Sit down,' Philmus said.

His eyes were dark and savage. 'Young woman –'

'Sit,' she said heavily, '*down.*'

He sat, still massaging his bruised arm.

Hillegas turned to her. 'Philmus –'

'Onto the veranda,' she ordered. 'You –' she stabbed a finger at Byron '– wait there. Don't do a damn thing.'

After the room's stuffy interior, the cold outside soon penetrated. She wrapped her arms around her, grateful for the thickness of her clothes. It may have been July, but the temperature was no higher than ten or fifteen degrees.

Lac Léman was a steel mirror, reflecting mountains. She saw a sail-boat toiling across the lake surface, ship-waves arcing from its bow across the dead water. There was little sign of habitation: more villas perched on hill-sides, huts speckling the lake shore. Threads of smoke rose up from many of the buildings. She wondered how far this Villa Diodati was from Geneva.

She lifted her face to the sky. The dome of cloud, thick and uniform, cast a grey pall even over the gaunt shoulders of the Alps, on the lake's far shore. There were puddles on the veranda, and in the terraced garden beyond, as if it had been raining recently, and frequently.

But they were close to the edge of the projection, here, and the scene had a lack of substance which enabled her to make out, dimly and occasionally, another vista underlying the surface of things. It was like glimpsing a landscape in the quivering surface of a soap bubble.

Across/within Lac Léman, the campus of Stanford University stretched away, the trees' enviroshields glimmering. Further off, through the misty images of mountains, she made out an immense sphere hulking over the horizon: that was the Palo Alto Snowball, millions of tons of carbon dioxide frozen out of the air and lagged with fibreglass insulator.

And in the sky, just visible as a sketch through cracks in the cloud image, she could make out a Wong Curtain. The sheets of zinc and aluminium wire, suspended twenty-five miles above the ground, were busily charging ozone-busting chlorofluorocarbon pollutants to harmlessness. Superposed over the clouds of 1816 Switzerland, the Curtain was a bizarre, angular sight, like a huge starship falling into the atmosphere. *Except that starships don't exist. Not yet, anyway.*

She shivered again. 'Your simulation is shoddy, Hillegas. And why is it so damn cold?'

'This is 1816,' Hillegas said. 'The "year without a summer".'

'What happened?'

'The eruption of Tambora, in the East Indies, last year – I mean, in 1815,' he said. 'The greatest volcanic explosion in centuries. Cubic miles of dust injected into the atmosphere; cold and gloomy weather all around the world. Harvests failed all over Europe and Asia; in America the migration to the Midwest was accelerated by –'

'It's damn depressing.'

'Yes. It didn't do much for his peace of mind.'

'Whose?'

'Byron's. He'd just been forced out of England in disgrace.
He'd fathered a child by his half-sister, and another in a love-
less marriage, where he'd behaved brutally. His friends
shunned him. He was drinking too much brandy, and taking
laudanum. In a letter to his friend John Hobhouse –'

'I don't care,' Philmus said wearily. 'I'm just a cop, remember? Jesus, Hillegas. Have you got *any* idea how much trouble
you're in?'

'But the project –'

'Let me spell it out, college boy. You've got the processing
balance wrong. Byron is too deep; the rest of your simulation
too shallow.' She waved a hand at the cracked sky. 'Look at
that. No wonder Byron became suspicious. You've created a
self-aware life form, which has strong suspicions of its true
nature. And that's against the law.'

'I needed more mips. I told Professor Laussel. And Laussel
said he'd back me up, over the Byron projection.'

'Well, when it came to the crunch, he didn't, Hillegas. In
fact it was Laussel who called me in.' *And maybe you're dumber
than you look.* For the first time she felt a twinge of sympathy
for Hillegas; he *was* only a student, and he did seem to have
been abandoned by the University authorities. Perhaps he'd
been set up, in fact; she wondered how many of his seniors had
been intrigued enough by this project to authorize it discreetly,
letting this boy take the risks for them. And the rap. But she
suppressed the thought; alone or not, Hillegas had known
what he was doing when he got into this.

Hillegas stalked to the edge of the veranda. 'You don't even
know what I'm trying to achieve here. Do you? It's that poem.
Darkness. What it meant to Byron – and what it means for us.
I –'

'Tell it to the judge,' she said bluntly. 'My responsibility,
now, is to the thing you've made in there.'

There was a submerged determination in the numbed
layers of his face. '*You* could authorize more mips. Couldn't
you? Right here and now.'

'Only for the benefit of the sentient,' she snapped. 'Not for your research.'

He smirked. 'But maybe the sentient will be interested by my project. *Intrigued*. What then, cop? What will the "benefit of the sentient" mean then?'

'Hillegas –'

'Why don't you ask him? You have to talk to him anyway. Why don't you ask Byron?'

George Gordon, the sixth Lord Byron, was still sitting at his desk – just as she'd ordered – moodily toying with his pen. The pistol, its muzzle blackened, lay on the desk-top.

His eyes shone, cat-like, as he watched Philmus and Hillegas return to the room.

Philmus stood before Byron and prepared to read him his rights. 'Lord Byron –'

He looked at her acutely. '*Is* that my name?'

I hate this part too, she thought. *I hate the whole damn job, in fact.* 'I'm a police officer. Do you understand? I work for an executive administration concerned with the preservation and enforcement of public order –'

'Are you from Geneva?'

'No.' *No, from much further than that.* 'I'm an American. And this is not Switzerland.'

'Then where?'

'California. The west coast of America. I have to tell you that what you see here –' she waved a hand '– isn't real. It's a sort of picture – an illusion.'

She couldn't tell if he understood her. 'And *I*? Am I real, madam American? Are you?'

Her upper chest felt constricted. *There's no gentle way to say it.* 'I'm real,' she said. 'And so's Hillegas – this man, here. Although we don't look like this; these aren't our bodies. But you are –'

She stopped. He searched her face, haunted.

'A sort of automaton,' Hillegas said.

'Sir,' Philmus said to Byron, 'two centuries have passed since 1816. We are in the future – your future.'

Byron stared at Lac Léman, beyond the window; a muscle twitched in his cheek. His face, its handsome lines masked by puffiness, was like a pool, with currents of speculation and emotion criss-crossing within its depths; this *was* an impressive projection, she conceded.

'I think I knew,' he said at length.

'You understand?' she asked, surprised. 'You accept what I say?'

'I was aware of something wrong. Certain discontinuities in the warp and weft of things.' He touched his scalp gingerly. 'And *here*, I find a place of echoes, a half-empty house from whence the people have fled.'

'I'm sorry,' Hillegas said. 'If I'd had more mips, I –'

'Shut up, Hillegas. Look, sir, you have been projected illegally. We have laws against the creation of consciousness for frivolous or immoral purposes; that's why I was called in, to inspect this simulation. But now that you *do* exist, you have rights, under our Constitution.' She spoke rapidly. 'You have the right to continued existence for an indefinite period in information space, if you wish it. You have the right to read-only interfaces with the prime world . . . I'll explain all these terms. You have the right to specify the Virtual environment which –'

Hillegas grabbed her arm. 'Let me talk to him.'

'Haven't you done enough, damn it?'

Hillegas's eyes seemed to glitter. 'He's fully accepted the reality of what you've told him. He doesn't have need of your counselling.'

'And I don't need you to tell me my job.'

Byron rose from his chair with a languid grandeur; his mood seemed to be changing, blackening. 'Your clap-trap bores me. Why have you people summoned me from Hell?'

Philmus found herself quailing before his sudden anger; there was something elemental about it, as if it arose from some fundamental fracture within him.

'*Let me answer his question,*' Hillegas said. 'He has the right to know.'

Byron stepped forward, almost coming between them, and

Philmus's head was filled with his powerful, stale stink. 'Talk to *me* – not to each other – now that you have troubled to conjure my bones from their grave!'

Philmus felt dizzy, distracted by the tightness and weight of her clothes, the oppressiveness of the day, Byron's powerful presence. 'All right,' she said weakly. She moved away from them towards the window, trying to get some air. Through a new crack in the sky, she saw a brief flare of light: probably a Nanosoft killersat taking out a rival, somewhere above the poisonous atmosphere.

'Lord Byron,' Hillegas said hesitantly, 'I am a student. And I'm fascinated by your poem –'

'*Which* poem?' Byron snapped with arrogance.

'*Darkness*. This one.' Hillegas picked up a page from the desk-top. ' ''Morn came and went – and came, and brought no day,/ And men forgot their passions in the dread/ Of this their desolation . . .'' '

'It is new,' Byron grumbled. He paced about the desk, and then he sat down, his boots reflecting the candlelight. 'It is unfinished.'

'In my day,' Hillegas said, half-smiling, 'it remains famous. After two centuries. It has intrigued generations. As has much of your work.'

Byron looked pleased, Philmus thought, though he tried to hide it with a scowl. She felt a prickle of scorn. *After all the shocks he's suffered – even the agony of his recreation as a homunculus – he's retained his vanity. God, I always hated poetry.*

'And it is for this work –' Byron flicked the papers on his desk ' – this scribble, that you have roused me from my long sleep?'

'It's important,' Hillegas said, and there was an edge in his voice now – an intensity – that made Philmus turn away from Byron to study Hillegas.

'We have to know what you meant by the poem,' Hillegas said. 'Here.' He scrabbled on the desk, and picked out another manuscript page. 'The poem opens: ''I had a dream, which was not all a dream . . .'' '

'And so it was,' Byron said lazily. 'A dream. Or a hypnoid fantasy, perhaps . . .'

' "The bright Sun was extinguish'd, and the stars/ Did wander darkling in the eternal space,/ Rayless, and pathless, and the icy Earth/ Swung blind and blackening in the moonless air . . ." ' Hillegas dropped the page. 'I have to know what you meant,' he said urgently.

Philmus felt suspicious. This did *not* sound like a run-of-the-mill literary research topic; something deeper was going on here, something she didn't understand yet. She crossed to the desk. 'Show me this damn poem.'

Hillegas picked up the manuscript pages, muttering to himself, and assembled them in order; evidently he knew the poem almost by heart.

She tried to scan the poem quickly, but Byron's handwriting was too impenetrable, the layers of corrections obscuring; and she had to go back to the start.

The poem's narrator described his 'dream' of an Earth plunged into darkness. 'Morn came and went – and came, and brought no day . . .' Cities and forests were burned for light and heat, but the fires faded. Men despaired, and the ecology evidently collapsed. 'The wild birds shriek'd,/ And, terrified, did flutter on the ground,/ And flap their useless wings . . .'

Wars were fought over the last food-stocks. Finally, 'The world was void . . . / Seasonless, herbless, treeless, manless, lifeless . . . / The winds were wither'd in the stagnant air,/ And the clouds perish'd; Darkness had no need/ Of aid from them – She was the Universe'.

Philmus found herself shivering.

Byron's eyes, bright in the gloom, were fixed on her. 'I was watching you; your lips moved. The image of the birds disturbed you. Did it not? Despite yourself.'

She shrugged, trying to be casual. 'Why is this so important to you, Hillegas? Why were you prepared to risk breaking the law?'

His imperfectly focused face worked. 'Didn't the poem sound *prescient* to you, as if it were predicting a future –

our future, of ecological and climatic collapse? Look, Philmus – what if the poem describes, not just a dream, but a *vision?'*

And suddenly she saw it, whole and entire. 'Oh, Christ,' she said, disgusted. 'You think this poem of Byron's is a prophecy of our own time? *That's* what this is all about?'

'What if it's true?' Hillegas said rapidly. 'What if the poem is telling us that all our efforts to stave off the eco-collapse are going to fail? If we've tipped the Earth's climate too far away from its life-bearing quasi-stability, perhaps we can't recover. The starship program is a joke, but maybe it's the only hope. Maybe –'

She threw the manuscript papers back on the desk, disappointed at the foolishness, the mundanity of it all.

I might have known there would be something like this behind it all. Something pre-rational.

Despite her protests to Hillegas, Philmus had actually started her own career in scientific research, and had drifted into police work when she'd become intrigued by the way scientific progress threw up previously unimaginable new crimes – like the illegal creation of sentience. She'd kept up with her reading on science and technology, though. And she'd watched, with despair, the tendency towards irrationalism grow over her lifetime; it was as if humanity was slipping back into the dream landscape, of gods and supernatural causes, it had inhabited before the Enlightenment. And just at the worst moment, given the multiple crises facing the species.

The advance of technology didn't seem to help. *In fact this is a classic example*, she thought. *This dumb kid is actually using Virtual technology – millions of mips of processing power – to reinforce his own spooky, superstitious obsessions about Byron's clairvoyance.*

All she could hope to do now was to resolve this sad situation, with as little pain as she could manage to the thing that called itself Byron.

'Come on, Hillegas. You're an educated kid – a Stanford student, for God's sake. How could Byron foretell the future?

I'm just a cop, but even I know enough about the Uncertainty Principle to know clairvoyance isn't possible.

'And we don't need visions of the future to explain that poem. We're *already* plunged into a world of darkness – here, in 1816 – thanks to that volcano of yours. You told me what a mess Byron's personal life is; and he's ingesting plenty to mess up his head . . . Christ, I'm no psychoanalyst, but what would you expect him to write – "Oh, What A Beautiful Morning"?'

Byron's eyes flickered between the two of them, fascinated, perhaps amused.

'No.' Hillegas shook his head, stubborn, barely listening to her. 'There's more to it than that. I know there is.'

Byron turned to Hillegas. 'What is it you want from me?'

Hillegas breathed hard, and his artificial face looked flushed; this was clearly the moment, Philmus thought, towards which he'd been working, the crux of it all. 'I want to know about the dream,' he said. 'Tell me about the dream. Not as you've interpreted the raw material in the poem – *what did you actually see?*'

Byron picked up his empty pistol, toying with it thoughtfully. 'Even if it were true,' he said, 'that my dream were such a future vision – how could *I* tell you of it? For – so you have informed me – *I* am a simulacrum. I am *not* the poet. I do not share his thoughts, his visions – his dreams.' He looked scared, Philmus thought, at this statement of the shallowness of his own identity; but he faced them, defying them to answer.

Hillegas tried to explain. 'You aren't Byron. But you *are* a good reconstruction. The processors – the machines which are sustaining you – have access to everything you wrote, or which was written about you. And the machines are pretty smart; the science of the mind, and the techniques of textual analysis, have advanced a lot since your day. We can *interpolate* – make guesses about your state of mind. What you are experiencing internally is not authentic Byron. It couldn't be. But it's as good a guess as can be made.'

Byron frowned and raised his fists to his eye-sockets, in a dramatic gesture that Philmus was coming to recognize as typical of him. 'Then why is it that your *guess* is so inadequate?'

Hillegas looked uneasy. 'What do you mean?'

With sudden violence Byron brushed the manuscript from the desk; as the papers fluttered and fell Philmus was reminded, oddly, of the birds in the poem. 'I mean,' Byron shouted, 'that I can remember nothing of my dream – nothing of the intensity of vision I *know* I experienced. You have remade me, sir, but you have made me incomplete! – so much so that I cannot even progress my work; I can barely pen a note for the baker.' He got out of his chair and paced to the window, his deformed foot thudding against the carpet. 'Oh, damn this gloom! Will it never end?'

Hillegas, grim-faced, turned to Philmus. 'I need more mips,' he said. 'I told you. *He* needs more mips.'

'I'm not going to authorize it, Hillegas.'

Byron turned. He was silhouetted by the grey light beyond the window, and candlelight shone over his face, making him look younger. His deep eyes flickered between their faces, alert and haunted, and Philmus felt a prickle of unease. 'What is he saying?' he asked her softly. '*Can* you make me whole?'

'No,' she said quickly. 'I mean – it's not like that, sir. It's not as simple –'

Suddenly his rage erupted again. He tore at his hair; great clumps of it came away in his hands, speckled with blood. 'I cannot live like *this!*' he roared. 'I am half what I was – less; I am an empty gourd. Fill me, or smash me!'

'Do it,' Hillegas hissed. 'Come on, Philmus. Authorize the extra mips. It's obviously for the benefit of the sentient, in this case. And –'

'And what?'

'And – no matter what you think of me and my ideas about the poem – *we might learn the truth.*'

Byron's eyes were huge before her, filled with reflections of candlelight. The pain etched into his reconstructed face was extraordinary, as graphic as a wound.

She thought again of the poem's image of the birds, falling to the ground.

Oh, Christ.
She sub-voced an authorization code.

Byron stepped away from her, his eyes alive, his mouth half open. 'I . . . My word,' he said softly. 'It is as if I have returned to life.'

'It's an illusion, sir,' Philmus warned. 'You're no more alive – no more Byron – than you were before.'

Hillegas was breathing hard. He stepped close to Byron. 'But the dream. Have you retrieved the dream?'

Byron's gaze became reflective, as if looking inward. 'Yes. Oh, yes.' He turned his face up to Hillegas, his mouth set hard.

Hillegas laughed, a triumphal sound that was ugly to Philmus. 'Show me,' he said; and he sub-voced.

The simulation – the Villa, the lake, the cloud-cloaked sky – all of it disappeared, as soundlessly as if a bubble had burst. For a moment the three of them, in their heavy nineteenth-century clothes, were suspended in grey light.

And then a storm of pixels closed around them.

A sticky, moist heat hit Philmus immediately, soaking into her heavy, multi-layered dress. There was grass under her feet, long and damp. Gravity turned on again, and she stumbled. Byron, beside her, caught her arm.

Savanna:
The three of them stood isolated at the centre of a vast bowl of grass. Perhaps three miles away there was a lake, small and brackish, and beyond that a range of hills, climbing into mountains. The lower flanks of the mountains were cloaked in forest, and their summits were wreathed in smoke clouds. More clouds, grey and shot with black, coated the sky, growing lighter only at the horizon opposite the mountains.

Philmus heard a remote bellowing. She saw animals working across the plain, two or three miles away. They might have been elephants; they were huge and grey, and tusks gleamed white in the unnatural light of the cloud-shot sky.

'God,' Hillegas said. 'What a place.' He pulled open his collar.

Byron grinned; of the three of them he was the only one who looked remotely comfortable in his open-necked shirt. 'We are in my dream,' he said simply.

'Where do you think we are?' Hillegas asked Philmus. 'Africa?'

'*When* is maybe more to the point,' Philmus murmured. 'No part of Africa is like this in our time, Hillegas.' There were no elephants left in Africa, or anywhere else, outside the zygote banks.

Hillegas said uncertainly, 'What do we do now?'

Byron laughed. He cast about and pointed. 'There's a track – see, where the grass has been beaten down? It leads towards the lake. Come. We will walk.' And, without waiting for acquiescence, he turned and led the way.

Philmus found it difficult to keep up with Byron's pace, despite his limp. Her 1816 shoes had flat, soft soles, and soon her feet ached.

Hillegas grumbled, 'This damn heat –'

'Stop complaining,' Philmus snapped. 'This was your idea, remember?'

'Do you think there's vulcanism, in that mountain range up ahead?'

Obviously. She ignored Hillegas, and concentrated on following Byron across the uneven ground.

After a few hundred yards, Philmus felt as if she would melt inside her dress, so she ripped it open and cast it away. The dress lay on the grass like an abandoned blue flag, vivid in the overcast gloom. She pulled off a few layers of underskirts, and opened her chemise sufficiently to allow the air to get to her skin. She didn't care what Hillegas thought of this, of course, but she felt a frisson of embarrassment when Byron paused and turned to look at her. He laughed, once, then proceeded with his vigorous limping towards the lake. He seemed to be singing.

The remote elephants seemed unaware of them. From a stand of trees, Philmus thought she saw a human face peering

out at them; but it resolved itself into the scowl of a cat –
perhaps a lion – with long sabre teeth protruding over its
lower jaw. In the lake ahead, she saw what looked like fla-
mingoes. And she almost tripped over a lizard, hiding in the
undergrowth at her feet; it was a foot long, with three sharp
horns protruding from its crest. It scampered away from her
and then sat in the grass, its huge eyes fixed on her.

They passed a skull, perhaps of an antelope, bleached of
flesh. It had been cracked open by a stone arrowhead – little
more than a shaped pebble – embedded in a pit in the bone.
Byron bent down and prised out the arrowhead with his fingers.

The savanna seemed somehow deserted, and the rapid
evolutions and shifting light of the volcanic sky lent the world
a sense of impermanence, of urgency and flight. This was a
doomed landscape, Philmus felt.

She found the corpse of a bird. She couldn't identify its
species. Its feathers were blackened, its beak gaping; she sur-
mised it had flown into volcanic gas and dust, and had fallen
out of the sky.

If this was a dream, it had a remarkable clarity, consistency
and internal logic. For the first time, she began to wonder if
Hillegas had, after all, stumbled on some kind of truth. *And
all of this*, she mused, *interpolated from the words of a poem.*

At last, after perhaps two miles, Byron drew to a halt.
'Look,' he whispered, pointing ahead towards the lake shore.

Philmus squinted; it was difficult to see through the gloom,
and at first she could make out only vague shapes, like low
hillocks. Some animal moved between the shapes: tall, lean,
like an ape – *walking upright*.

Suddenly the image resolved itself. The 'hillocks' were
crude huts, cones of branches woven together. The branches
were anchored by stones to the ground. There were perhaps
a dozen huts in the little village. Philmus saw hides hanging
from a rack before one hut, weighted by threaded stones.
From some of the huts threads of smoke rose up to join the
roiling clouds, and Philmus was reminded of her distant view
of the houses along Lac Léman.

The huts were arranged in a rough circle, and in a clear,

trampled area at the centre of the circle, a number of adults had gathered. They were naked, dark-skinned. They were piling tools – spears and stone-bladed axes, choppers, cleavers and scrapers, together with skins and what looked like crude cooking pots – into a heap in the clearing. The people spoke to each other with short, sharp barks which carried across the grass to Philmus; they were clearly cooperating and communicating, and they worked seemingly oblivious of the immense vulcanism behind them. The people looked under-nourished to Philmus: gaunt, skinny.

A child came limping out of one of the huts, pursued by a guttural barking. Her belly was swollen, evidently by malnutrition, the skin stretched and translucent.

Abruptly, one of the adults stepped away from the central group. It was a woman. She raised her head to the air, cavernous nostrils flaring; her face was flat, her jaw projecting. Philmus saw how a thick bank of muscle at the back of her neck made it difficult for her to lift her head.

The woman turned, seeming to look directly into Philmus's eyes.

'They're human.' Hillegas's breath was shallow, excited.

'No,' Philmus said softly. 'Look at the thick eyebrow ridges, the skull's long, low shape, the shelving forehead –'

'Do you recognize them?'

'Yes.' *But this is only a dream, for Christ's sake . . .* 'I think these people are *Homo Erectus*. The precursor to H. Sap.'

'I do not understand,' said Byron, and Hillegas proceeded to give him a condensed summary of the evolutionary rise of humanity. Philmus studied the woman. She could see her ribs and the shape of her skull. Her dugs were slack and pendulous, and her pubic hair was a tangled triangle.

She worked her memory. *Erectus* had flourished from a million and a half to maybe two hundred thousand years ago. But the tools and techniques of the group before her appeared crude. So they were a primitive variant – she was probably deeper than a million years into the past – and this, therefore, must be the Rift Valley, in East Africa, where *Erectus* first evolved. *But it's only a dream, Philmus!*

She related this to Hillegas and Byron.

The poet rubbed his chin and stared speculatively at the *Erectus* woman. 'I am impressed by your erudition,' Byron said. 'But whatever the provenance of these people, it appears we may not enjoy their company long.'

'What do you mean?'

He waved a hand. 'They are evidently packing to leave.'

'I guess they're fleeing the vulcanism,' Hillegas said. He peered about, at the iron sky lowering over the little human village. 'The real question is: *why are we here?* If this is your dream landscape – '

'And it is,' Byron insisted. 'Although I saw it only in fragments, remembered it in shards ... I assembled my poem after much meditation.'

'I suppose you rationalized the dream vision, of a world you couldn't comprehend, into a narrative that made some sense to you. *But where did the dream come from?*' Hillegas turned to Philmus. 'I mean, Byron couldn't possibly have known of the existence of *Homo Erectus* – of eras like this.'

Philmus sighed. 'I have an open mind, Hillegas. Despite being a cop for so long. Do you want to hear what I think?'

'Tell me.'

'I think you were partly right, after all. Byron's *Darkness* dream *was* a vision of another time. But not of the future – ours or any other – *but of the remote past.*'

Hillegas stared at her.

'Look,' she said patiently, 'it's not impossible to imagine we might share inherited memories – records of traumatic, devastating times. In Byron's case, perhaps his personal instability – forgive me, sir – his use of drugs, and the unique conditions of the "year without a summer", all combined to release ancestral visions buried inside the deepest, oldest part of his brain.'

Byron bowed his head ironically.

Hillegas frowned, looking confused. 'I don't understand. Memories of disasters? Like what?'

'You're depressingly ignorant, Hillegas.' She waved a hand. 'This is the Rift Valley vulcanism interval of a million and a half years ago. Tectonic shifts, upwells of magma ... The ecology and climate collapsed – with a devastating impact on the primitive variant of *Erectus* who had evolved here.

'They had been the most advanced and prosperous hominids in the world. But now their game fled, or died; their wells and lakes became stagnant or dry; the climate became impossibly unstable, even lethal.'

'And did the people die?' Byron asked.

'Many of them,' Philmus said. 'But not all. They learned new techniques, evolved further; they increased their mobility and varied their diet. And they migrated, seeking better homes.

'They spread out of Africa, to Europe, East Asia, Java ...'

'So. The near extinction of a race of evident intelligence, followed by a Diaspora lasting a million years.' Byron gazed at the village. 'A fine candidate for this "racial memory" you postulate.'

Philmus turned to study the people, as they assembled their crude belongings. 'A disaster, yes. Of course. But also a beginning. The great migration was the making, the shaping, of *Erectus* – of the human line as a whole.'

Byron nodded. 'And thus, in that dark future of your own of which you have hinted, perhaps there are also seeds for hope – that from all your pain and anguish, a new Diaspora may be generated, which will lead the race to new, unimagined heights.'

Philmus thought of the first starships – crude, underfunded things – being assembled in Lunar orbit. 'Perhaps,' she said. 'Sir, I outlined your rights earlier. Have you decided what you want to do? Do you need more time?'

Byron still carried the arrowhead; now he tossed it into the air, testing its weight and running his fingers over its surface. 'I doubt that more time will benefit me, my dear. In these last few hours, you have demolished my world for me – what I remembered as my world, at any rate.

'I cannot return home – for my home does not exist, has not these past two centuries; and in any case, *I* did not travel from there. Besides, I was already in exile, in Switzerland. I am as displaced as those poor, naked creatures over there.'

He threw away the arrowhead and grinned at Philmus. 'I have a fancy to throw in my lot with these people. A man with a brain might build a life for himself, here. Some of the women look as if they might be – cooperative. Besides, I have never been shy of adventure. Did you know I once swam the Hellespont? Is that still remembered?'

'Yes,' she said. 'Yes, we remember.'

'May I stay here? Is it possible?'

'It's your right. We'll make it so. This world will be maintained as long as you need it. And you'll not be disturbed.'

They stood awkwardly for a moment. 'Well,' Byron said. 'Perhaps you will think of me. *Benedetto te, e la terra che ti fara!*'

Hillegas murmured, 'A Venetian benediction. "May you be blessed, and the Earth which you will make . . ."'

'Oddly apposite – don't you think?' Byron said. He clapped Hillegas's shoulder, bent to kiss Philmus gently on the forehead, and made along the path, his vigorous limp carrying him away rapidly.

Philmus breathed the muggy air, and pulled the tatters of her undergarments around her. 'At least you'll get your doctorate out of this, Hillegas. And you'll have plenty of time in jail to write up your thesis.'

Hillegas still appeared confused; he shrugged.

After fifty yards, Byron turned. 'Scholar! Tell me this. Did I die well?'

Philmus knew Byron had never returned to England. He had died of malaria, and the clumsy ministrations of his doctors, in Greece at the age of thirty-six.

Hillegas called: 'You die gloriously, sir.'

Byron laughed, waved, and turned towards the village. Philmus saw how the *Erectus* were watching his approach.

Philmus sub-voced, and she fell into the light.

THE DROPLET

'You're Mr Jakes. Peter, isn't it? Your brother's in the collider hall. He won't see you, I'm afraid.' He strode into the TLC reception office. He was taller and leaner than me; Paul Newman eyes fixed me from nests of tanned wrinkles.

A bit overwhelmed, I dropped my eyes to the lapel badge he wore. It was a little pyramid of emeralds. The girl behind the desk – Tracy, luminously beautiful – smiled at me. Feeling a bit stronger, I said, 'I didn't know I was so easy to recognize.'

His hand squeezed mine, bronzed calluses pressing into my pasty flesh. 'Well, I guess you do look a little, ah, Englishman lost in California. And maybe the jacket's kind of quiet. My name's Reaney. Mike. Hi.'

'Hello.'

'I work with your brother George; I took Tracy's call. George's wife told me she'd asked you to come over from England. Look . . . can I buy you a coffee?'

The corridors glowed in the sunlight, suffused with a new carpet smell. I peered into offices that seemed full of healthy people. I couldn't help comparing it with my memories of shabby English universities.

We came to a lounge, large and comfortable, where Reaney bought me a machine-made cup of coffee. 'You know we're under threat of closure here, at the TLC,' he said.

'Yes. Mary told me about it. She said it was the cause of George's . . . troubles.'

With a rangy grace, Reaney crunched up his cup and lobbed it into a bin. 'Well, it's no picnic for any of us.' He laughed. 'Of course, most of us try to be rational . . . we're not all quite so loony-tune as George. I've always thought it was the loss

33

of their kid. Something like that leaves a hole in a guy.'

I stared up at this grinning Californian who stood in such easy judgement over my brother, and tried to think of some response. Then he said disarmingly, 'I'm sorry. I guess I shouldn't talk about him like that. To us, he's just loopy old George . . .'

'I'm grateful to you for meeting me,' I said. 'There's no reason why you should be spending time with me like this.'

He shrugged. His eyes roamed the lounge's pastel walls. 'Well, I know Mary. And I felt you came a long way to be turned away.'

'Why won't he let me see him?'

'There's nothing I can do about that, I'm afraid. In the collider hall, if it's your experiment, your say goes. George has got a deadline to beat. He says.' He pulled his face into a mock frown. 'Listen, I've a half hour free. Why don't I show you round the site? If we wait long enough maybe our hero will take a coffee break . . .'

The TLC was separated from the rest of the Stanford Linear Accelerator Center by a high, close-meshed wire fence. We followed a gravel drive out through the fence, then walked about half a mile to the east, climbing a gentle hill. At the summit I felt a lot closer to the sun. I draped my jacket over one arm, loosened my tie and felt sweat soak into my shirt collar.

Reaney, of course, merely blossomed a little. I judged he was about thirty – a decade or so younger than George and Mary.

A clay-coloured sprawl to the south was the campus of Stanford University. Incredibly healthy students cycled beneath palm trees; it seemed quite idyllic to me. Reaney pointed, the sun catching the mat of hair on his forearm. A structure like a long shed ran north from the campus and disappeared into the collider hall complex. 'See that? One of the TLC's twin linacs. Over two miles long.'

'I'm sorry . . . linac?'

'Linear accelerator. It's a huge cathode ray tube, like in your home TV ... it produces pulses of electrons that travel in towards the collider hall at nearly the speed of light.' A second linac came out of the hills to the north and swept into the collider complex, opposite the first. 'The second linac produces a beam of positrons,' Reaney explained. 'You know what a positron is? It's an anti-electron. Anti-matter, you know?

'The two beams shoot inwards and impact in the collider hall, annihilating each other. The collision's kind of tricky to manage. It's like shooting two pistols a hundred miles apart, and getting the bullets to meet. There's also a ten per cent gradient in those hills to the north ... We have a computer system actively controlling the whole shooting match.' He spoke with a studied languor. 'Tell me, Peter, what do you do for a living?'

'I'm an accountant,' I said. 'I work in the City. London, I mean.' I laughed. 'I feel a little shy to admit to being so boring, after all your glamorous talk of anti-matter and the speed of light. George always made me feel the same ...'

'Nothing glamorous about it,' he said restlessly. 'Ninety-nine per cent of any job is crap. Am I right?

'Anyway, that's the TLC. The TeV Linear Collider. A TeV is a tera-electronvolt. Which means very high energy particles, and exotic physics. Although nothing as exotic as what's going on in your brother's head.' He laughed easily at his joke. 'He doesn't publish his results, you know,' he went on, swivelling his blue eyes towards me. 'And that's bad for all of us. An establishment is judged on its output. But old George doesn't care about that. No, sir ...' A breeze ruffled his corn-like hair.

If this is one of my brother's closest colleagues, I thought, how utterly alone he must be.

The phone woke me to darkness. 'Hello?'

'You shouldn't have come, you know. I'm perfectly all right.'

'George? You pick the damnedest times to phone ...' I fumbled for a light switch. My mouth was dry; I wondered if I had enough loose change to get a Coke from the vending machine outside my motel chalet.

'Listen, Peter, go home,' said George. 'I mean, don't go, have a great holiday, see the Bay, ride the cable cars. But I'm okay. She shouldn't have rung you.' The seam of Yorkshire in his voice was refreshingly untainted by California.

With one hand I searched for a cigarette. 'Mary is worried. She thinks you're working too hard.'

'Rubbish. She thinks I'm going crackers. Right?'

'Well . . .'

'Sure I'm working hard. I've got a deadline to meet.'

'Yes, that's what Mike Reaney told me this afternoon.'

'Reaney? That dick-head?'

'He showed me round the site. When you refused to see me. Your own brother,' I added theatrically.

He laughed again.

'George, I know your TCL is under threat of closure.'

'TLC, for Christ's sake, and it's not just a threat. But that's not the only problem . . .' His voice had an edge now. 'If I don't finish this work, now, I don't think it'll get repeated. Ever.'

'Why? What's going to happen?'

He said nothing. Then: 'How's . . . ah . . .'

'Jane?' I asked heavily. 'Fine. And the kids, Bobby age eleven and Geoff age nine –'

'All right, funny man.'

I switched off the light and sat in the darkness, smoking and savouring his voice. 'Tell me about your work,' I said.

I heard him sigh. 'All right. I guess you deserve that much. You know our machine, the TLC, is a high energy electron collider. Lovely clean physics.' His phone voice grew dreamy. 'Electrons are fundamental particles, you see. You remember I used to work on the CERN proton collider, in France. Protons are made up of quarks. Working with them was like throwing bags of marbles together –'

'So what's the point of all this beautiful colliding?'

'The collisions produce packets of high energy density – like bits of the early universe, right after the Big Bang. You know what the Big . . .'

'Of course I do.'

'Back then physics was different. There are four fundamental forces – gravity, electromagnetic, weak nuclear and strong nuclear. According to theory, when the energy density is high enough the four unify into a single superforce. There are particles called Higgs bosons which mediate the superforce. That's what I started off looking for.'

He was losing me. I rubbed my gritty eyes. I couldn't remember the last time I'd spoken to my brother . . . and now here he was at three in the morning telling me about Higgs bosons. Well, that was George. 'Did you find them?'

'We got some evidence. I don't know. I started noticing something much more interesting.'

'So you never wrote up the boson stuff? Dick-head was complaining about that.'

'Really? I'm not surprised.' He hesitated. 'Oh, Christ, look at the time – So why are you staying at a Hyatt's? Do you know what they charge?'

'I'm looking forward to finding out,' I said drily. 'I . . . didn't feel comfortable about asking Mary for a room. I got the impression I wouldn't have been all that welcome.'

'You probably wouldn't. Even though she asked you over in the first place. And she calls me crazy.'

Again we laughed together. He agreed to let me see him, in a couple of days' time.

And, just like that, he hung up. Well, I reflected, at least I'd made contact. After Mary's rather disturbing phone calls, I was relieved to find nothing more worrying than the same old George.

My body clock refused to believe it was the small hours. I lay in the darkness and missed my family.

The next day I got the motel girl to hire me a Hertz car, and I drove out to Palo Alto to visit Mary.

I cruised down a broad, double-parked avenue. The crumpled car doors and wings, casually unrepaired, made me feel a long way from England and its salted roads.

Outside George's house was an old Jaguar XJ6. The house itself was a neat bungalow set in an expanse of glowing lawn.

'Oh. It's you.' Mary was a small, dark woman, looking too old for the pink jumpsuit she wore. 'You'd better come in.'

The house was open plan and wood-panelled. The morning sun evoked a smell of jasmine and orange.

Mary made me coffee and we sat on opposite sides of a glass table. She wore a pyramidal brooch of emeralds set in gold, rather like Reaney's. 'I'm sorry. I drag you all this way, across the Atlantic, and now we can't think of a damn thing to say to each other.' She sipped her coffee and pulled at her mass of frizzed hair.

'You seem settled here,' I said.

'Oh, I am,' she breezed. 'It's a terrific lifestyle.'

I felt like puncturing her. 'It's helped you forget, then?'

She gave me a hard look. 'Philip's death, you mean? Don't flinch like that, Peter. You referred to it. Why not say it? It doesn't hurt any more.'

'They never found the cause, did they?'

'It was a cot death,' she said witheringly. 'Although the Americans have a few theories . . . Little Philip was a textbook example. Eleven weeks old, just the time when his growth was at its fastest.'

'Does that have something to do with it?'

'How should I know?' Her voice had become a little shrill. 'Anyway. To return to the point . . . the reason I asked you to come over.' She looked away, seeming embarrassed. 'I didn't know who else to turn to. George has always put a lot into his work –'

'I know.'

'– and the announcement of the closure of the TLC was utterly shattering for him. He worked even harder. He made up some sort of cot, a sleeping place, at the lab. He'd stay over one night, two. When he did show up here he'd be overtired, wound up, twitching to get back to it. You know? And finally, he stopped coming home at all.'

Her skin was tanned but dry-looking; I found myself studying the lines of her skull. On impulse, I asked: 'Do you still care about him?' – and regretted it immediately. 'I'm sorry. I don't want to sound as if I'm judging –'

She laughed lightly. 'Why not? Everyone else does. I . . . don't know what I feel,' she said. 'That's the honest truth. I've had six months of this, for Christ's sake. I'm not sure what I feel any more.

'When I asked you to help – I cared then, I suppose. The closure's in a few days, you know. No more high energy collisions. I was scared there'd be – a crisis.'

'Surely he could get another job.'

'Evidently the TLC is unique; the only place George can do the sort of work he's gotten into.'

'I've visited the TLC. I met Mike Reaney . . . You know him, don't you?'

She met my eyes and nodded.

'What's it all about, Mary? What is it about this work that's driving him like this? And why does he think his work might be lost?'

'Ask him.' She averted her eyes and would say no more.

On my way out, she handed me a carrier bag. It was from some store called the Crystal Market, and was covered with Eastern-style religious symbols, rust brown on yellow. 'A change of clothes for him.'

I weighed the bag, as if weighing up Mary's feelings. 'I'll tell him I saw you,' I said, but the door was already closing.

'What's so important about my work?' George ran a huge hand back over his widow's peak. He was a big-boned man, very unlike me, and his wrists stuck out of his cuffs. 'It's only about the birth pangs of the universe, Pete. That's all. Here, give me that damn bag.' He grabbed the Crystal Market carrier from me and stalked out of the TLC reception area on his whippy legs.

Tracy gave me a sympathetic smile as I passed, but I ignored her. George was no clown.

We reached a door plastered with security notices and combination locks. 'The collider hall,' George said, slowing down. 'Where the action is.'

Through a glass partition I peered into a tall, gloomy space constructed of bare breezeblocks. A pipe a few inches across ran at waist height through the centre of the hall; instrument packages snuggled around its midpoint. 'What's that?' I asked. 'The central heating?'

George laughed. 'That's the particle beam guide. Lined with focusing magnets. The collisions take place right there, at the heart of those arrays . . .'

We moved on. A metal door let us into a boxy, windowless room. It looked like a storage cupboard, with unvarnished shelves piled high with dirty shirts and underwear. 'Jesus, George, how do you live like this?'

George threw the carrier onto an unmade camp bed. 'Peter, you're a bloody old woman, and I love you. Let me tell you about my work. That's what counts, not socks. Now, we're only a fraction of a second after the Big Bang. Everything's compressed into less than the width of a proton . . .'

Automatically I dumped out the clean clothes and began stuffing the carrier with laundry. George swivelled as I walked around him, a gaunt container of energy. 'The universe is filled with a sort of fluid. A quagma, a soup of quarks in radiation, bound together by the unified superforce.

'The universe goes through an inflation phase. The quagma's expanding, and cooling fast. It's like steam, super-cooled below liquefying point. Bubbles form in the quagma and expand with the released latent heat. Within the bubbles, the superforce falls apart into our four fundamental forces. One of the bubbles becomes the space we live in, filled with ordinary matter.'

My carrier bag was full. I made room on the bed and sat down. 'What about the other bubbles?'

He grinned a bit wildly. 'Other universes embedded in the quagma foam. But with different physical laws, where the superforce decomposed in a different way. See? In one place gravity might be so strong the bubble would instantly collapse; in another so weak that stars could never form and the place would be full of lukewarm hydrogen . . .'

He wore a v-neck jumper with a Marks and Spencer label sticking out of the neck. I stared at him in admiration. 'My God, George, California hasn't changed you a bit, has it?'

'Bollix to California,' he said. He paced up and down, glancing at his watch. 'Droplets of quagma formed at the heart of my collisions,' he said. 'I found a way to mould the shape of the electron-positron colliding pulses to get a controlled cooling of the droplets. A supercooling.'

'Right. And you get this . . . inflation effect?'

He paced faster, kicking the leg of the cot. 'Sometimes. The droplets soon evaporate, of course, but I can tell a lot from the debris. There are bubbles in those droplets where different physical laws apply. Think of that.'

I had to smile at his enthusiasm. 'So what next, George? What are you trying to achieve now?'

'Stability,' he snapped. I could see tension in the hunch of his shoulders, the motion of his elbows – a visible impatience to get back to his work. 'A non-evaporating, self-fuelling droplet which won't need further electron collisions to sustain it.'

'And will you write up then? Or is writing up still for cissies, George?'

'I'll write up after they close me down, in a week's time. But I've got to get finished. That's all that counts. And look, Pete, I'm sorry –' Now he waved the watch in the air. 'I'll talk to you again in a day or two. Okay?'

I didn't move. 'George,' I said quietly, 'I've on' ⟨…⟩ arrived. I can see you're in a state. And we've har⟨…⟩

Panic crinkled his eyes. 'You've ask⟨…⟩ ⟨…⟩ork. I've told you.'

'Yes, but I want to hear ⟨…⟩ ⟨…⟩ and out of the corner of ⟨…⟩ embarrassment. 'Yo⟨…⟩ Come on, Geor⟨…⟩ particular ⟨…⟩

He ⟨…⟩
he ⟨…⟩

Astonished, he stared at me with his red-rimmed eyes.
Then he laughed once, hard, and led the way out.

I tried again a couple of days later. Reaney took the call.
'I'm sorry,' he said in an amused tone. 'You know how it
is . . .'

'Yes. Look, Mike, can I ask you a couple of questions while
you're there?'

'Sure . . .'

'This closure. Of the TLC. Will it really be so difficult for
you all to get other jobs?'

He snickered. 'In high-energy physics, yes. The field's con-
tracting, world-wide. But there are plenty of other options.
For the realistic man.'

'What are yours?'

'Expert systems. There's one here working on a DEC Vax,
controlling our colliding beams. I've had an offer from a
securities firm in Frisco – an expert systems application in
international dealing. Same principles, you see, just different
problems. And megabucks,' he added smugly.

Well, I couldn't see that appealing to George. 'Also – the
"Crystal Market". George said it was the reason for his hurry.
What's that all about?'

'Ah. The Market is a New Age store.'

'New Age?'

'I guess it hasn't reached England yet. It's a loose, quasi-
religious movement that's taking root over here. Disappointed
Sixties children, a mish-mash of Eastern mysticism – homeo-
pathy, pastel colours, pyramids – you've read the movie, seen
the book . . .'

His dismissive languor was irritating. 'I notice you wear a
pyramid button yourself.'

. . . ded a little less easy, I noted with satisfaction.
. . . fashion . . . Anyway, George takes it all
. . . ows the rise of anti-science in
. . . ore particle acceler-

'Bullshit. George wouldn't use a phrase like that. Do you actually listen to what he says, or are you too busy laughing behind his back?'

'Hey, pal, no offence –'

I hung up.

'Peter, it's me.'

'George? Christ, it's after four . . .'

'I'm about to do it, Pete. I wanted you to be here. I've phoned Mary.' He sounded as if he'd been crying.

'George, are you okay?' I began searching for my shoes in the dark.

'Of course I am. It's just . . . I'm that close to getting one of these babies to stabilize. So many of them have failed, just at the moment of maximum growth – Peter, I have to go.'

'George?'

A sleepy caretaker at the motel desk called me a cab. Recti-linear streets slid past, dark and obscurely menacing.

The TLC was lit from end to end. It looked as if a spindle-shaped spacecraft had landed in a fold in the Californian countryside. I pulled my coat tighter around me. Somehow I doubted this display marked good news.

There was an empty police car on the gravel drive. The gate in the wire fence was closed, with a single policeman standing before it. He watched me steadily.

Floodlights suspended over the fence beat at my face; moths fried on the glass. A siren cried within the compound. 'You can't go through, buddy.' The policeman chewed gum with a practised rhythm, his eyes in shadow.

'My brother's in there somewhere. What's the problem?'

He tilted his head back and stared at me. 'Sorry, sir. It's some kind of automatic radiation alert. Hey, you from England?'

I walked away from him and followed the fence for a few feet, finishing up in a puddle of darkness between two floods. The policeman's broad head returned to its survey of the driveway.

I closed my eyes and tried to picture George in there, his jumper covered by an ill-fitting white coat. He must be alone. If what he was doing was so dangerous he would have made sure no-one else was on the site.

Tyres crunched on the gravel – a Jaguar driving up the path. Somehow I wasn't surprised to see Mary and Mike Reaney climb out together. They were holding hands. I turned my face to the fence, trusting they'd miss me –

The explosion was like the fist of God slamming into the earth.

I was thrown backwards onto the shaking ground. The fence collapsed over me, bulbs popping.

Something was rising out of the ruins of the collider hall. It was hot and bright. A dry wind fled from it.

I had to crawl out from under the fence. My hands were caked with blood and dust. The officer had lost his cap. With barked questions he checked we were okay, then trotted down the drive to his car.

I stood facing Mary and Reaney. He looked at the ground, his tracksuited frame clumsy with embarrassment.

She stared into the fire and smiled.

I hit her, hard, across her face. She tumbled back onto the gravel.

'Hey –' Reaney came at me and drove his fist up into my stomach. I couldn't believe how far it penetrated. I doubled into a squat; my diaphragm seemed to cramp up and I gulped for breath.

'Leave him, Mike.'

Reaney put one mitt under my armpit and hauled me to my feet. Pain lanced through the muscles of my torso, but I stayed upright.

'You bitch,' I gasped. 'Are you so glad to be rid of him?'

She tried to talk, then spat out blood and a piece of tooth. 'You don't understand, do you?' She pointed over my shoulder. 'Look.'

I turned. Out of the collider hall's ripped-open roof had risen a colourless sphere. It was the size of a small house, and it contained a froth of bubbles that swelled and collapsed, flickering through existence almost too fast for the eye to follow.

Sirens wailed in the darkness behind us.

'He did it,' Reaney growled. 'Damn him, he did it.' He stared into the sphere. There seemed to be genuine wonder under his studied cynicism. 'That's a stabilized droplet of inflating quagma. And inside each of those bubbles is a different set of physical laws. We'll be able to study creation physics with nothing more elaborate than a freeze frame video camera.

'This will fast forward our understanding a thousand years. No wonder he was so desperate to finish this. They'll build a statue to the silly old bastard, right here.' He laughed and scratched his scalp. He wore his green pyramid badge; now he plucked it out of his tracksuit and threw it into the droplet. 'I guess that's the end of this anti-science shit.' He turned and walked towards the Jag.

'I'm happy for him.' Mary's face was swelling a little, but the smile was returning. 'The endless deaths – I always understood it, you see. I just couldn't live with it . . .'

Her voice trailed off; she was looking at me strangely.

I found it an effort to speak. 'The door was metal,' I managed.

'What?'

Reaney turned back; I looked to him, willing him to understand. 'The room George was sleeping in. I thought it was just a store room. But the door was metal.'

'That's the safety shelter,' Reaney said softly. 'The shelter!'

The three of us ran over the ruins of the fence, ignoring the cop's shouts.

'Well, of course I'm alive,' George snapped after they dug him out. 'What kind of dick-head do you think I am? . . .'

Then he saw the droplet hanging above him. His head hinged back, eyes wide, mouth hanging. His face shone in the creation light.

We pulled him to his feet. Mary grabbed his tattered sleeve, searched his face.

'My baby,' he said hoarsely, still staring upwards.

Mary's head dropped; she let him go. Reaney put an arm around her shoulders.

'Come on, George.' I took his hand and led him from the rubble.

NO LONGER TOUCH
THE EARTH

Oberleutnant Hermann Göring emerged from the muggy warmth of the tent into bright, clear Polar air. To get the blood flowing Göring stamped his feet and wrapped his arms around his torso; the leather of his flying suit creaked reassuringly around him, and under his feet sandy frost-rime crunched over an underlying hard surface. The Antarctic summer Sun hung to the north, separated by about a quarter of the blue sky from the horizon; and the land was a tabletop of wedding-cake white.

This last fuel depot was less than two hundred kilometres from the South Pole. Less than two degrees of latitude from the floor of the world; less than an hour's flight, Göring thought, from his destiny. He peered into the South, savouring the crispness of the frozen air as it misted before his mouth . . . And there, like a single ray of light passing from some Earthbound star into the huge sky, was the Axis itself; Göring tilted his head back, following the clear line into Heaven.

He surveyed the little fuel depot. The crude tent in which he'd shared a night with the four English who manned this station was a patch of mud-colour, jarring against the pristine white of the ice. And – ah – there was his Fokker, emerged from the shelter the English had erected for it. Emptied fuel cans and discarded canvas tarpaulins lay piled around the machine. Göring let his eyes rest on the triplane's round, elegant form, relishing its vivid red paintwork. From the air, Göring thought, the plane must look like a splash of blood, a wound in the icy carcase of this desolate land, alive with the bloody shade which had struck terror into the heart of every Allied airman who had risen to face the *Jagdstaffeln* in the war.

His goggles and facemask in hand, Göring walked the few metres of uneven, snow-strewn ice to his plane. His arthritis – which had driven him from the trenches, and which had almost precluded his admission to the Air Service – was his constant companion still, now sending needles of pain through his legs and feet. Hermann Göring was not designed for the cold, he reflected ruefully.

Two of the doltish Englishmen, bundled up in their furs, were clearing the short strip they'd laid in the ice for him. A third – Collishaw? – was working on the Fokker. And the fourth, Davies, the most senior of them, waited for Göring in the long, striped shadow of the Fokker's triple wings. Davies was about forty, Göring supposed – a good decade and a half older than Göring himself – but he had nevertheless seen combat in the war which had ended a couple of years earlier. The burly man walked with a pronounced limp, though Göring had not heard him complain about the problem; and the German speculated that Davies had taken a lump of shrapnel home with him from the trenches. The other English – younger, brasher – were fools. It had been a long night for Göring with these English and their schoolboy humour, their tea and their 'hooch'; but Göring had found a grudging respect for Davies.

Davies smiled through his mask of beard. 'Well, Herr Oberleutnant. Are you fit and rested for your great challenge?'

'Indeed,' Göring said. 'And in not many hours I will return in my trusty scout, and you shall be the first to hear of my adventures.'

'But take a care, Leutnant.'

Göring, wincing, turned; they had been joined by the mechanic, Collishaw. Foul breath misted before the man's round, foolish face as he stomped feet clad in sealskin fur.

'Oberleutnant,' Göring corrected him mildly.

Collishaw, no older than Göring, grinned impudently. 'The Pole is an unforgiving place. It did for our chap Scott, don't forget, despite all his experience and preparations.'

'I know of your "chap Scott",' Göring said, letting irritation leak into his voice. In fact, Göring was retracing Scott's fateful route, from the shadow of the astonishing thirty-metre-high cliffs of ice that marked the edge of the Great Ice Barrier, and then across a frozen sea to the mighty limbs of the Beardsmore Glacier.

Collishaw nodded. 'You visited the cairn, of course.'

Göring hesitated. He had had little choice; for the Englishmen of the Royal Geographic Society who had sponsored this expedition had, naturally, established the first of Göring's refuelling stops not a hundred metres from the place from which Scott and his companions, at last, had not had the strength to rise. Göring had walked out, alone, to visit the pile of grubby snow, the sad cross of skis which marked that pathetic end, and he had paid his own, silent respects to the brave Captain R.F. Scott.

But now he yawned, hoping to irritate the smug English. 'There was not time, Herr Collishaw. Perhaps another occasion . . .'

'It's not a damn Bavarian beauty spot, man.' As Göring had hoped Collishaw's grin was replaced with a glaring frown. 'Look around you. See the unevenness of the ground? That's what we call sastrugi – frozen waves of ice. Damn near impossible to drag a sledge across, with dogs or without 'em. It's what did for Scott and his chums.'

Davies said mildly, 'But the Oberleutnant will be far above our sastrugi, Phillip.'

'True.' Now Collishaw grinned again; his beard and hair were so blonde, his eyes bluer than Göring's own, that he could almost have been a Prussian, Göring thought. But not in the foolishness of his manner, of course. 'Tell me, *Ober*leutnant. Did you fly with Richthofen himself?' Collishaw gestured towards the Fokker. 'I see you've borrowed his taste in paintwork.'

Göring drew himself to his full height and turned to Davies. 'Am I required to converse with this ignorant young man in compensation for my fuel?'

Davies said, 'Phillip, the Oberleutnant took command of Rittmeister von Richthofen's *Jagdgeschwader* – the famous ''Flying Circus'' – after the death of *Der Rote Kampfflieger* himself.'

Davies' German pronunciation was woman-soft, thought Göring, but passable. Davies smiled at Göring. 'In fact, Herr Oberleutnant, your triplane is the same model in which von Richthofen met his death.'

'The Dr I, yes,' Göring said, somewhat mollified.

'So you see, Phillip,' Davies went on, 'if anyone is capable of completing this astonishing flight, it is surely the Oberleutnant.'

Collishaw nodded, but insolence lingered in his voice. 'So you used to fly with the Red Baron. Now you're off to fly with the angels, eh, Göring?'

The man's tone was like sandpaper over raw flesh to Göring. After the sorry end of the war the ex-Officers had been regarded by some Germans as responsible for that conflict's disastrous conclusion. Göring himself had been forced to face down a 'Soviet' of drunken Communists in Darmstadt – he, Hermann Göring, holder of the Order Pour le Merite, the 'Blue Max' itself! And it had not been the violence but the *disrespect* of those dark days which Göring had been – was still – unable to accept. Now he heard echoes of that insolence in the tones of this Collishaw: overlaid, of course, with the smug contempt of the victorious for the vanquished. Göring said, 'Perhaps, my friend, you are of that superstitious rabble who believes that man is not fit to challenge the Heavens. You are a follower of that ancient Hebrew, Maimonides, who believed that humans are one with the Earth and the things which crawl over it; perhaps you believe that some mysterious Nemesis will strike me down as I sail through the skies around the Axis.' As indeed had predicted Göring's own godfather, the dreary Epenstein, the Oberleutnant reflected.

Collishaw looked baffled. 'Maimon . . . who?'

Davies laughed. 'Herr Oberleutnant, cosmology has been the fashionable subject for a decade, ever since Scott's astonishing discovery. And even the shallowest circles have buzzed with the names of long-dead philosophers, monks and clerics. But I doubt very much if a debate on Maimonides with our young friend here is going to bear you much fruit.' He looked thoughtful. 'Of course, the resolution of the puzzle to which you allude is of great interest, even beyond the human fascination of the feat you are going to attempt. Is the Universe, the layered sky above the Earth, an artifact which we can touch, handle – perhaps, one day, manipulate – as Eudoxus and Aristotle believed? Or are there some things forever beyond our reach? The Rabbi Ben Sira said, "What the Lord keeps secret is no concern of yours . . ."' He studied Göring. 'I suspect you yourself are an Aristotelean, Herr Oberleutnant. Or you would surely not be attempting this feat.'

'Indeed.' Göring smiled. 'Let me counter your antique Jew with the words of Ptolemy, who said: "I know that I am mortal, a creature of a day; but when I search with my mind into the multitudinous revolving spirals of the stars, my feet no longer touch the Earth, but beside Zeus himself I take my fill of ambrosia . . ." Well, Herr Davies, perhaps before this day is over we shall know one way or the other.'

Davies nodded, his brown eyes thoughtful; but Göring noticed that the burly Englishman had drawn away from him a little, apparently flinching at Göring's dismissal of Ben Sira. Davies said with mild reproof, 'I'm not certain that a man's race is a valid test of his philosophy, Herr Oberleutnant. Still, I find I envy you your adventure.'

'Well, I don't,' Collishaw said brashly. 'Flying to the Pole in that crate? Good luck to you, man; but, good God, what a crazy stunt!'

Göring glared. 'I do not perform "stunts".'

Collishaw grinned. 'And what if you get the same sort of nasty shock as did poor old Scott? All the way to the Pole, only to find a Norwegian flag waiting for him!'

'Your prattling irritates me, Herr Collishaw,' Göring said evenly.

'Amundsen beat Scott because he took a shorter route,' Collishaw went on, ignoring him. 'He travelled from the Bay of Whales, from the other extreme of the Ice Barrier. And that's the route those Americans have plotted, isn't it? Will you feel as miffed as poor old Scott if you get to the Axis, only to find some grinning Yank perched on the top?' He laughed. 'What a sight that would be!'

Göring strove to keep his face empty. This dolt was not worth the expenditure of his energy, he decided coldly; and, as he had learned to do throughout his unruly, violent life, he put away the anger which burned inside him. He turned to Davies. 'I believe I am ready to fly.'

The Fokker triplane had been adapted for its jaunt into Antarctic skies. Göring had studied the modifications in the Oberursel rotary engine and in the layout of fuel and other lines, all designed to combat the cold by crowding the fragile elements of the plane around its warm heart. And a canvas frame with glass windows had been erected around Göring's cockpit, its seams sealed with grease to keep the Polar air away from the pilot.

Of course, the twin Spandau guns had been removed.

So there were plenty of unfamiliar aspects to this odd flight; even the thick woollen mask around Göring's lower face, beneath his goggles, felt rough and strange. But when the Oberursel roared to life, turning with the propeller – and the prop blew a tiny storm of ice-sand over the watching Englishmen – and when Göring let out the throttle and the Fokker bounced across the short strip smoothed out of the sastrugi – then, with relish, Göring felt in his belly the Fokker's powerful surge from the frozen ground, and he was as at home as if he had been returned to the skies of France.

The Fokker rose like a stone cast into a huge bowl of sky. The Englishmen's little fuel camp turned into a scrap of muddy cloth and disturbed snow, lost in the ice; and Göring was cloaked in the silence of the air. As he rose he seemed to sail above his petty irritation with the doltish Englishman, Collishaw. The irony was that, in common with most of his fellows in the Air Service, Göring had evolved a great deal of respect for his English foes. The typical Englishman in the air showed pluck and daring, although rather prone to stunting. The same could be said for your average American. The Frenchman, on the other hand, was sneaky, cunning, and lacking in tenacious endurance, although a dangerous opponent when the Gallic blood was enraged. Göring recalled von Richthofen likening the French to carbonated water – for a moment there would be an awful lot of spirit which would suddenly go flat.

But the English flyers were almost like Germans, and so Göring had not been averse to accept the startling invitation – made in a dubious spirit of post-war reconciliation – to join this English expedition to the Axis . . . But his essential respect for the English made the insolence of the likes of Collishaw even harder to take.

He tried to put all of that out of his mind, now, and to turn his thoughts to the task which awaited him today. He took the Fokker through a few turns, testing out the elevators and rudder. The English had kept the triplane stored under canvas through the sunlit 'night' of the Antarctic summer, warming her with blubber stoves; the simple measures seemed to have worked, for although the external thermometer showed an astonishingly low temperature all the control lines were free and the engine's note was smooth and steady. The smell of oil and fuel in the enclosed cabin was warm and reassuring, and the triplane handled as well as he had known her.

He climbed easily to a thousand metres, dipped his wings once in salute to the waving English – ants, now, on a frozen map – and turned the Fokker to the South . . .

And there, like a guiding beacon before him, was a translucent stripe down the sky. His heart already pounding, Göring centred the nose of the triplane on that near-invisible line and pushed at the throttle. Soon he hurtled across the ice at more than a hundred and fifty kilometres per hour. In sixty minutes he would reach the Pole; and already a sense of mystery, of wonder at what he was attempting, stirred within him.

When Göring was a boy he had been taken to Berlin by his Jewish godfather Epenstein – leaving his mother and father in Epenstein's castle-home in Veldenstein. And young Hermann had been glad of an opportunity to get the hated Epenstein away from his parents for a while, for even at an early age he had become aware of the filthy demands Epenstein made on his mother as compensation for accommodating the little family ... and he had become helplessly sickened by the steady humiliation of his father.

But all of his troubles had been forgotten when Epenstein had taken Hermann to see the famous Orrery in the capital's greatest museum.

The Orrery, a clockwork model of the whole Universe, was a glass onion taller than three men; in the staring eyes of eight-year-old Hermann it had seemed as large as the Universe itself.

The guide – tall, sombre, smelling of tobacco and musty antiquity – told them how centuries of close observation had confirmed the essential correctness of the ancients' ideas about the structure of the Universe. As Aristotle had imagined with startling prescience four centuries before Christ, the Earth was a ball, floating in a pool of air at the stationary centre of the Cosmos. And now Hermann had studied a painted, football-sized Earth fixed at the centre of the Orrery. The planets and stars, the Sun and the Moon, were affixed to a series of concentric, crystalline spheres which cloaked the Earth. Each planet required a nest of no less than *four* of the spheres to carry it on its meanderings through the sky. The planet was fixed to a point on the Equator of a sphere, and that sphere turned about its axis. But the ends of this axis were let into the inner surface of a larger sphere which rotated about a *different* axis, carrying the first sphere along with it ... and so on. And the nests, of course, were mechanically connected to each other by smaller 'neutralizing' spheres which sat between successive nests and turned in the opposite direction to the working spheres. And as the young Hermann had looked into the misty heart of the Orrery he had been able to make out, like crystal ghosts, the fifty-five clustered spheres described by the guide, and the clockwork engines within them.

The celestial globes were constructed of fine wire and immense, carefully shaped glass panes, and connected by stubby axes of crystal. The effect was something like an immense, complex greenhouse. The planets were fist-sized wooden blocks fixed to their respective globe-nests and painted brightly in their characteristic colours – Mars a vivid blood-red, Venus a beguiling yellow, and so on. The stars were modelled by a thousand tiny diamonds fixed to the outermost sphere – actually, the adult Göring reflected, those 'diamonds' were probably no more than fragments of glass – while the Sun was a ball filled with electric light, so huge that Hermann felt convinced it gave off heat as well as radiance.

And the model wasn't just a pretty ornament; to Hermann's delight, and with a slow, subdued whir of fifty-five clockwork motors, the huge spheres sailed steadily around the Earth, reproducing the motions of a year in half an hour. The guide had explained to the nodding Epenstein how the complex, layered motion of the many spheres produced such oddities as the retrograde motion of the planets, and Hermann had watched painted Mars turn back on itself in the crystalline sky.

Forever after, Göring recalled now with a rueful smile under his woollen mask, he had pictured his world in terms of that beautiful model; in his mind Aristotle's 'Unmoved Movers', the agents who patiently turned the globes of the Cosmos, were still constructed of some magical celestial clockwork.

But as he had grown older Göring had become aware of the metaphysical debates which raged still among philosophers. What if Aristotle's vision of all those spheres and axles were simply a mathematical model? – what if in fact the stars and planets were floating freely in space, guided along their invisible tracks by some unknowable force? Or, as Aristotle himself had believed, could the crystal spheres actually *exist*, physically?

When Peary reached the North Pole in 1909 without finding any evidence of an axle through the world, the debate had seemed to be resolved against the Aristoteleans. But then had come Amundsen and Scott, and their astonishing discovery in the South . . .

So the spheres, it seemed, were real. But still the philosophers could not agree about the place of man in the Universe. Some clung to the view propounded by twelfth-century Maimonides that man was barely fit even to consider the structure of Heaven. Göring remembered with bitterness how his god-father had quoted to him from Maimonides' newly fashion-able writings at long and gloomy length. ' "Man is filled with awe and dread at the sight of his own lowliness ... He becomes aware of himself as a vessel full of shame and con-fusion, empty and lacking..."' And so on, and so forth. To Göring such a view seemed dark, claustrophobically pessi-mistic – all but unbearable, in fact, and forever associated in his mind with the long, severe face of his hated godfather.

With a small part of his mind Göring conceded that it was scarcely rational to erect preconceptions of an entire race, to dismiss a complete and majestic philosophical tradition, solely on the basis of childhood reactions to a godfather. But within the man, it seemed, the child lingered on ...

As Davies had intuited correctly, Göring clung to the Aris-totelean concept that – although the changeless matter of the spheres might differ from the imperfect atoms of which he, Göring, was composed, along with the rest of the sublunar realm – still, humanity was that element of creation below the stars most in accordance with nature. And the Cosmos itself, that great and complex artifact designed and manufactured by some purposeful, immanent intelligence, was a fit subject for study and exploration by man – perhaps even, Göring mused, for his exploitation.

Now Göring smiled, his eyes fixed on the thickening blue line that was the approaching Axis. Well, he, Oberleutnant Hermann Göring of the Imperial Air Service, would this day with a single act of audacious courage resolve the debate of centuries of logic-choppers.

And, Göring thought grimly, perhaps at last he could still the voice of Epenstein, whose droning, depressing words still sounded in Göring's memory.

When it was done Göring would be the most famous man in Germany. In the world! The humiliation he had endured at the end of the war would be ended; they would call him *Der Eiserner*, the Iron One, in recognition of his valour, and his country's stature in the eyes of the world would be restored ...

Now the Axis was widening from a geometrical abstraction

into a band of light, vertically painted down the china-blue sky. Suddenly it was close enough for Göring to make out structure: a deepening of its blue-white colour towards the vertical edges showed, even from kilometres away, that the Axis was clearly a cylinder, and draughts of warmer air caused light to flicker all around the immense pillar.

Göring, willing the Fokker forward, stared hungrily at the Axis and dreamt of wealth.

Göring banked and turned; he flew parallel to the slow curve of the cylinder perhaps a thousand metres clear of the surface. It was like flying past an immense building, or a cliff. The Axis looked as smooth as glass and was translucent; it seemed that he could see several metres into the substance of the construct, but beyond that there was only a vague glow of trapped blue-white light.

The artifact was immense, of course: no less than two kilo-metres wide, Göring judged. He felt like a mosquito buzzing an elephant.

He took the Fokker into a cautious downward spiral. On the ground snow and disturbed ice was piled up around the interface between Earth and the base of the Axis. The Earth was, of course, stationary in space; thus the circumference of the Axis marched endlessly past the Polar ice at the rate of six kilometres in every twenty-four hours – even slower, Göring thought with a stab of contempt, than Scott and his shambolic team. Scott, in his sad diary, had recorded that the surface of the Axis was warm to the touch, and had noted a thin film of water, slick against the lower few centimetres of the Axis. And Scott had heard a continuous, grinding crackle of ice crusts freezing and cracking endlessly as the Axis turned. Now Göring fancied he could hear that dim sound, the noise of the sky turning, as he circled in his Fokker.

He passed the site reached by Scott himself, and he studied a small cairn constructed of skis and heaped-up snow. A Union Flag, limp and frozen, hung rather pathetically from a ski-pole, not fifty metres from a grander construction topped by the bold colours of Amundsen's Norwegian pennant.

Göring, staring at the cairns so painfully scraped from the ice, tried to imagine the feelings of those thwarted Englishmen.

Now, pushing on the control stick, he dipped the Fokker's nose a little further; when he was perhaps a mere thirty metres from the ground – with the sastrugi hurtling beneath him like some rigid ocean – he banked cautiously, hoping to approach the Axis still more closely. But the air here was lumpy, turbulent; and as he approached the Axis itself he became aware of a steady updraught, an incongruous warmth which threatened to mist over his canopy. Göring hauled at the stick; with a roar from the Oberursel the Fokker banked until its right wingtip was pointed at the frozen ground, and Göring pulled up and away from the dangerous, turbulent air.

Göring tried to find metaphors for this experience from his long years of flying. Air warriors were accustomed to empty skies, to fields, infantry-filled trenches, perhaps the grey-brown quilts of towns and cities below. But to fly before this huge, curving face, to share the sky with such enormity . . . When he had first arrived aboard the English research vessel in this bleak Southern continent Göring had taken the Fokker for a brief jaunt along the broken face of the Great Ice Barrier. He recalled the ice floes like immense water lilies in the rich blue sea, the beating flukes of whales . . . He had felt lost in the sky. Perhaps *there* was some point of comparison – the presence of grandeur, the feeling that one's fragile wood-and-canvas plane were a mere mote before the immensities of Nature.

But the comparison was distant. The Ice Barrier endured for hundreds of dreary kilometres, it was true; but it had not risen beyond the nose of the triplane into emptiness, dwindling from an immense trunk – to a gleaming pencil line – to a thread against the azure texture of the sky . . . to a point whose very presence seemed masked by the motions of air molecules, by the liquids of one's own eyeballs! Göring, his eyes following the Axis up into Heaven, felt as if the whole immense, impossible construct might come crashing down over him at any moment.

And there was another dissimilarity with such natural wonders as the Ice Barrier: there was no doubt, this close, that the Axis was indeed an *artifact*. Göring had read of engineers who had remarked on the impossibility of constructing the cylinder reported by Scott and Amundsen from any known material. Why, the hardest steel would flow like toffee under the immense weight of the pillar itself – not to mention the notional weight of any celestial spheres the device might support. Göring had always thought such analyses foolish and shallow. Let those box-builders come here and see what he saw; the Axis was clearly an artifact, but an artifact utterly and eternally beyond the capability of humans. And Göring doubted very much that calculations of tensile stress had played any part in the thoughts of the Builder of this great device.

. . . And there was an impression of *agelessness* about the Axis, he realized now; it had been manufactured, certainly; and yet it was also Eternal, enduring. That was paradoxical, of course, and yet, as Göring continued to circle the Axis, he sensed the rightness of his diagnosis.

A made thing, and yet Eternal . . . And he, Hermann Göring, was the first man in all of time – disregarding the ice-crawling Scott and Amundsen – to have challenged this great device. He felt his face tighten into a rictus of triumph. As a boy he had longed to take that wonderful Orrery home with him, to pull out the beautifully crafted models of Mars and Saturn and suspend them in his small bedroom so that all would know they were *his*. Well, he could never take the Axis away, and yet it was his nevertheless; whenever men came to this place in the centuries ahead they would have to speak his name. He, Hermann Göring, the first of them all; *Der Eiserner* –

But there was something else in the sky above him: a mote which flew towards him from behind the great pillar, as insignificant as a dust speck descending against the columns of some Greek temple.

His heart pounding in his chest, Göring levelled the Fokker and narrowed his eyes. It was a dark grey biplane. A Sopwith, probably a Camel; Göring had flown against enough of those in his time.

The pilot of the other ship looped an extravagant loop and waggled his wings in foolish greeting. Then he returned to hovering proprietorially before the immense face of the Axis.

Göring felt his lips pull back from his teeth. *Rickenbacker!*

As rage consumed him, Göring became abruptly aware of the pain of his arthritic joints. Even the Fokker, it seemed, was reacting to his fury, for the patient triplane juddered in the air, the Oberursel whining.

Göring closed his eyes, tried to contain his rage, to *focus* it. As a child, at boarding school and even earlier, he had become notorious for his fury, his ill-discipline; and when angered it seemed he was utterly unaware of physical danger. Well, over the years he had learned to control his temper, to use it to fuel his actions; and his disregard for danger had matured into a raw physical courage which had served him well in the trenches, and later in the air.

He opened his eyes. With absolute clarity he studied the Sopwith lazily circling before the Axis' impassive cheek, and he allowed all of his rage to centre on that small scrap of canvas and wood, alone with him in the Polar sky.

The American was circling loosely at about a thousand metres. The Sopwith, Göring saw, had been modified for the Antarctic conditions in a manner similar to that employed on the Fokker, with the installation of a protective canopy around the cockpit; but now the pilot had thrown open his canopy and, regardless of the cold, was leaning out and waving to Göring. A thick scarf billowed behind the American, and his flying helmet was adorned with an absurd Stars-and-Stripes design.

Rickenbacker!

With their insolent gestures from the cockpit, their utter disregard for the most elementary forms of chivalry – and above all their damnable *stunts* – the Americans, those clowns of the air, had always infuriated Göring far more than their pitiful contribution to the war effort had justified. Oh, Captain

Edward Rickenbacker was the best of them, Göring allowed; and with his twenty-six verified kills he had exceeded Göring's own tally. But still Göring could not accept that these casually-dressed foreign oafs were fit to share a sky with von Richthofen, Loewenhardt, Udet and the others.

And now, with the war lost to this loutish coalition, was Rickenbacker to be allowed to have beaten Göring himself to this, the greatest of prizes?

Göring's rage transmuted to determination, as cold as the air beyond the cockpit. He hauled on his stick and climbed steeply; the featureless surface of the Axis swept beneath the wheels of the Fokker. Göring spiralled rapidly around and above the Sopwith, and within a few seconds was positioned above the American's tail. Rickenbacker, of course, did not react immediately; and as his opponent continued to circle lazily Göring's fingers itched for the buttons of his missing Spandaus . . .

Now the American pulled to his right, climbing steeply.

Göring felt his face draw into a smile. So the *Jagdfliegerei*, the aerial hunt, was on.

The American hurtled up and behind Göring and, with a brisk barrel-roll, levelled out a few hundred metres above the Fokker. Göring held the triplane steady for a few seconds, allowing the American an illusory taste of victory; then he wrenched the Fokker into a frame-bending left curve, climbing ferociously. This time the American did not sit and wait for Göring to complete his manoeuvre, but peeled away to his right before Göring could get over him. But Göring had anticipated this and hauled the Fokker through the sharpest of rolls.

The two planes entered a tightening spiral pattern, with each of the pilots trying to get above and behind the other. Above the screaming of the Oberursel Göring heard the struts of the Fokker creak in warning, but the canvas of the triple wings bit deeply into the thick, cold air and the Fokker did his bidding. Peering out through his canopy window Göring could see Rickenbacker in his open cockpit, could see every move of the American's head. Rickenbacker was grinning and seemed to be calling something; even now the American thought this was some sort of game . . .

Like flies in the sky-blue dome of a cathedral the planes buzzed before the silent bulk of the Axis, the tiny roars of their competing engines the only noise in the Polar stillness.

The Sopwith was a good crate, Göring admitted, and Rickenbacker was not without skill. Göring found time to wonder how they might have fared, one against the other, in the fields above France; and he found room for a stab of regret that such a contest had never occurred.

At last, with the circles in the air no more than fifty metres wide, and with the Sopwith so close it seemed Göring could see every strut and stay quivering in the chill air, every twitch of its punished elevators, Rickenbacker conceded. He pulled out and levelled into a slow, shallow descent, and he waved back at Göring in evident good-humoured defeat.

But Göring was not done with him.

Göring hauled at his stick, twisting to the left and gaining height rapidly, and then forced down the nose of the Fokker. The Sopwith was below and before him now. Göring shoved at the throttle and screamed in triumph as the Fokker hurtled like some bird of prey out of the sky at the American.

Rickenbacker twisted in his cockpit; Göring fancied he saw the grin vanish from that doltish Yankee face. Rickenbacker hauled his Sopwith away and to the right. But Göring had the advantage now and it was easy for him to stay above and behind the Sopwith and, by steady pressure, force the American down and towards the ice. Rickenbacker began to zig zag, evidently hoping to throw Göring off; but Göring was readily able to follow the Sopwith's manoeuvring. Next Rickenbacker hurled himself upwards into a loop – or tried to; Göring, his face set, refused to give ground. Göring was treated to a plan view of the shuddering Sopwith as it rose before him. Rickenbacker threw back his head, saw with evident horror that the Fokker was still closing on him, and was forced to drive the nose of the Sopwith down and out of the loop.

Göring roared laughter. He hurled the Fokker still harder at the American.

But Rickenbacker was game for no more. Levelling, he opened his throttle and fled across the ice. There were no hand gestures now, Göring thought with grim satisfaction; no barrel rolls, no loops, no *stunts*. For a few seconds Göring savoured the option of allowing Rickenbacker to flee North to his waiting companions, of allowing him a lifetime of being forced to tell how he, the famed Captain Edward V. Rickenbacker of the US Air Service, had been driven out of the sky by an unarmed Oberleutnant . . .

But the *rage* would not allow it.

Göring turned, roared into the sky like a kestrel, and swept down on Rickenbacker once more.

It took only seconds to finish it.

The undercarriage of the Sopwith, travelling at two hundred kilometres per hour, barely seemed to touch the sastrugi.

The wings crumpled like paper, blew away in fragments. The fuselage plunged into the ice like a burning stone.

Göring could never put into words the exultation he experienced at the clean ending of a man's life. In such a moment it was as if the rage within him was transformed into a golden fire which permeated his every cell, as if he had become a being of the celestial substance of the spheres above the Moon . . . and yet, amidst his triumph, there was always a trace of *relief*. For surely if he were one day to fail that rage would turn inwards and eat away at his own soul.

But, for today, he had challenged and beaten the American, Rickenbacker; and now he, Hermann Göring, must fly up to challenge the Gods themselves!

Impatiently he drove his fist into the canopy which encased him, smashed the canvas sheeting away from its struts as if bursting from some artificial egg; the fresh cold air burst into the cockpit and soon he was exposed, at one with the winds which he commanded. He pulled back on the stick and dragged the triplane into a tight bank; he levelled rapidly and hurled the Fokker towards the bland, patient face of the Axis. The engine screamed as he depressed the throttle once more, and he yelled defiance into the bitter air, the rage still warming him like a fire; it was almost as if he were on some astonishing strafing run!

At about three hundred metres from the Axis, and with the milky substance of the construct a wall looming before him, he pulled the valiant Fokker into a steep climb, spiralling tightly around the pillar. He almost wished there were observers for this astonishing feat – even the American, Rickenbacker, might have sufficed. And now, at last, he would learn whether the parade of dreary logic-choppers, from Maimonides to his own godfather, had been right in their diagnosis of men as worms, unfit to lift their eyes to the stars . . . or whether men, led by golden warriors like Göring, could rise into the Heavens and be as one with the Gods.

The ground fell away. Göring could see the base of the Axis recede beneath him, as if to enormous distance; soon the great pillar dwindled to a geometric abstraction above and below him and it was as if he were suspended at the midpoint of an infinite column.

Still he climbed. The Fokker's nominal ceiling was eight kilometres; when Göring passed ten the altimeter could no longer report his height, and he ignored its tiny, accusing glass visage.

The air thinned and his lungs laboured; and now the patient Oberursel too was coughing, causing the plane to shudder. Well, Göring would accept being struck out of the sky by angels, but not by the deficiencies of an engine! He hauled his stick a little further to the right, maintaining his climb but allowing the Fokker to spiral closer still to the Axis.

The plane entered the updraught of warm air coating the construct; for a few gut-wrenching seconds the Fokker threatened to break from Göring's control and tumble like an autumn leaf in the wind – a tumble from which he would surely never recover. But by responding instantly to the triplane's every twitch – and by sheer strength and will – Göring maintained the Fokker's stability; and soon, perhaps two hundred metres from the surface of the Axis, he reached a region of comparatively calm air. Now, uplifted by the mighty lungs of the Axis itself, Göring rose with increasing rapidity.

. . . And the blue of the sky darkened until at last it was as if he were above the air itself. Over his head stars gleamed like fragments of glass. Below him lay a blue sea of atmosphere; the Sun lay close to the horizon, its rays flattened and trapped by the layer of air. The iceclad planet curved visibly beneath him, impaled by the Axis which plunged out of the air and into the distant ground.

Göring was beyond the cold, beyond the thinness of the air in his lungs; he was alone, here, above the atmosphere, in a holy silence broken only by the stuttering of the Oberursel . . . And now, as his eyes grew adapted to the dark, a structure congealed out of the sky above him: he saw shadowy curves, immense globes suspended against the constellations as if sketched there in frost crystals by some vast Artist.

Göring lifted his head, mouth wide, as the tiny Fokker climbed into the celestial spheres.

Awe filled him. He felt as if he were a small boy again and restored to that Berlin museum, to the wonderful Orrery. But now he was as small as an insect and inside that wonderful clockwork; the Universe itself had become an Orrery around him.

His oxygen-starved brain raced, filling up with visions of a spectacular future. He, Hermann Göring, had proved that – though magical and wondrous – the Universe was indeed an artifact . . . and a resource for mankind. Göring imagined a greater Germany, a new Reich, inspired by his feat and arising out of the ashes of the present. He saw new aeroplanes, more powerful, riding the thinning air on huge wings to bring men to the Moon, and rising further to scrape against the roof over the sky. Perhaps the planets, too, could be reached, wrested from the spheres like pearls from shells and returned to adorn the palaces of Berlin. And other planes could be built – pilotless birds loaded with explosives which would hurl themselves against the enclosing spheres, shattering and breaching them! Göring pictured the stars themselves being dragged away like burning coals and hurled down to Earth, marvellous bombs in some future conflict.

He, *Der Eiserner*, was invulnerable, sublime; and for the first time in his life the brooding presence of Epenstein fell away from his consciousness. For his godfather had been *wrong*. No furious angels had clustered around the Fokker, forcing him down as he had driven down the foolish American.

Göring had won. *He had won*. And now he would return to Earth, to begin the lifelong savouring of his victory.

He pushed at his control stick. The plane was sluggish, the control surfaces ineffective in the thinness of the air; but at last the iceclad ground tipped up before him and, as the Fokker dove once more into the ocean of air, the Oberursel's roar grew in confidence and vigour.

Hermann Göring, his apotheosis complete, turned the Fokker to the North, and to home.

MITTELWELT

The antipodal bomber *Werde Was Du Bist* clung to its glittering launch rail. Oxygen vented angrily, and vapour drifted across the stark form of the Imperial German cross emblazoned on the gaudy hull of the *volplane*.

To Michael Kilduff, the *Werde* looked like some grounded bird of prey.

High clouds coated an immense, domed sky. The wind cut through the woollen layers of Kilduff's flying suit, and made his bespectacled eyes water. *Christ. This is supposed to be July.* How long was he going to be kept waiting, before they let him board? He wrapped his arms around his body and tried not to shiver; German technicians watched him impassively.

The aerodrome was a splash of scorched concrete, here on the bare Baltic coast of northern Europe; the few buildings were squat and functional, and the bomber's two-mile launch rail was a shaft of silver pointing to the east, towards the old Prussian town of Stolp.

Kilduff was the only American at the 'drome. He felt utterly isolated, as if he were alone here at the huge, bleak heart of the *Mitteleuropa* of 1940.

'. . . Herr Kilduff.'

The voice, from behind him, was female, precise. Kilduff turned.

'I am Oberstleutnant Guderian. Eva Guderian.'

'Ah,' he said. 'The *Werde*'s pilot. I've heard much about you, Oberstleutnant.' He lifted his gloved hand tentatively, wondering whether to offer to shake.

Guderian watched his fumbling, making no effort to put

him at his ease. Her face was square and stern, her eyes almost black, her hair invisible under her flight cap. Her flight coveralls were jet black, inscribed with the identity of her *Bombengeschwader* – the long-range bomber group to which she reported. 'And I know of your reputation, and the engineering expertise you bring,' Guderian said. Her intonation was clipped, economical. 'As does the Kaiser, I might add.'

'The Kaiser?' Kilduff glanced nervously around the aerodrome, at the parked fuel tankers, the observation bunkers, the little convoys of parked official vehicles. 'Is the Kaiser here?'

Guderian smiled thinly, making Kilduff feel naive. *Of course he isn't here, Mike.* 'Alas,' Guderian said, 'Kaiser Wilhelm is not as young as he was. He is sitting out our refreshing German summer at Bad Ischl, in the Salzkammergut. Perhaps you know it.'

'I – ah –'

Guderian turned to one of the observation bunkers; it was a low blister in the concrete. 'But your visit is not without interest.'

Kilduff followed her gaze. His vision, despite his spectacles, wasn't all that sharp, but he could make out a small party of gaudily dressed men clambering down into the bunker. The figure at the centre of attention was short and plump, with a soft, almost girlish complexion; a white greatcoat covered a fat-swathed body.

The man looked pompous, almost comical. But on that broad chest, Kilduff saw, rested the Blue Max: an indelible token of the courage of a young flyer in the victorious *Kaiserskrieg*, twenty years ago.

The figure was quite unmistakable: Hermann Göring, Chancellor of Imperial Germany.

'I'm surprised the Chancellor has time to be here, Oberstleutnant.'

'Yes. History crowds us, Herr Kilduff. The Japanese fleet is steaming towards Australia, and the Reichstag is in continuous session ... But one must maintain business as normal. Yes?'

'I guess so.'

'So,' Guderian said, 'give me your first impressions of our *grossflugzeug*, our new eagle.'

Kilduff wondered what Guderian wanted to hear. He turned to gaze anew at the *Werde Was Du Bist*.

The craft, clinging to its launch rail, was heavily streamlined, shaped like a sharp-nosed fish. The underside was quite flat. Wedge-profile wings swept back from the midpoint of the ship's ninety-feet length, and a gaunt tailplane jutted from the rear. Behind the *volplane* itself, the captive booster clung to the rail, nestling against the bomber. The booster too was streamlined, though it lacked the aerodynamic grace of the bomber; it was rather squat and fat – like some beetle, Kilduff thought, resentful of its imprisonment against the Earth. The nozzles of the booster's rockets gaped like mouths, preparing to exert their six hundred tons' thrust.

'Look at the curve of those wings,' Guderian murmured. 'The *Werde* has what the old men of the *Kaiserskrieg* would once have described as a *taube*, a dove profile. Well, Herr Kilduff? Does this stir your soul, as it does mine?'

Of course it does. 'I've waited ten years for a chance to climb inside a Sänger-Bredt *volplane*, Oberstleutnant. This is obviously a great technical achievement. Allgemeine Elektrizitats Gesellschaft have taken Dr Sänger's basic *volplane* design to extraordinary limits, and great strides have been made in high Mach number airframes, fuel and material research, combustion chamber development, trajectory theory –'

Guderian shook her head, a short, impatient gesture. 'Technicalities are nothing. With the resources of Europe in our hands, and with Tojo's declaration of *Toa Shinchitsujo* ringing in our ears –'

'I'm sorry?'

'A "New Order in Asia".' Guderian looked at him, reproof in her black eyes. 'As all informed Americans should be aware. Well. Inspired by such a global challenge, we should expect nothing *less* than such a technical triumph from our engineers. If we are to fight a war of the hemispheres, we must have hemispheric tools – eh?'

'I'm just an engineer, Oberstleutnant,' Kilduff said carefully. 'Technicalities are my business.'

'But *I* am not interested in your doltish engineering observations,' Guderian snapped. 'I want to see your *heart*, Herr Kilduff.'

She glared at him. She was no more than thirty-five, so hard and efficient she seemed like part of some machine herself. She made Kilduff – overweight and bespectacled – feel weak and decadent.

Shaken, he studied the *volplane* again.

The upper surface of the sleek, monocoque hull was painted a brooding forest green, and the flat base a sky-blue; the green and blue were separated by an irregular curving line. Just before the imposing Imperial cross a huge, brooding eye, a Gothic splash of white and black paint, scowled ferociously. At the hull's midpoint a bat was sketched: wings spread, the bat swooped on a kill from some lurid sky.

The looming images, the explosions of violent colour, were audacious, intimidating, disturbing. With these designs, the *Werde* proclaimed its identity as a warplane, loud and brutal.

Guderian was watching him.

'It is savage,' Kilduff blurted. 'Barbaric.'

Guderian threw back her head and laughed. 'Good, Herr Kilduff. Some passion, at last. Barbaric? Perhaps. But we are a barbaric species, Herr Kilduff.'

'Are we?'

'*Werde Was Du Bist*, Herr Kilduff. Nietzsche: *we shall become what we must.*'

Now Göring's little party was climbing out of the bunker once more; aides fluttered around the Chancellor anxiously as he stalked away across the concrete.

'It looks as if the Chancellor won't be sticking around to watch us go after all,' Kilduff said.

Guderian said drily, 'He must busy himself with more barbarism, perhaps.'

Kilduff faced her. 'The *Kriegsgefahr*?'

Guderian's eyes narrowed. 'The mobilization. *Good*, Herr Kilduff.' Guderian stood before Kilduff, hands on hips. 'And you Americans. Where will you stand, when the world erupts? At present we *court* you. Our engineers, from AEG and Dornier, exchange visits with yours – like you, from your Hughes Aircraft Company.'

'That's *corporation*,' Kilduff said mildly.

'Perhaps Tojo and his legions are also flattering you, with promises of trade across the Pacific, and utterances of respect for your *democracy*.' She pointed a gloved finger at Kilduff's chest. 'The truth is, we are all barbarians – but now, barbarians competing for the resources of a planet. And soon you Americans must choose, not *whether* you will fight, but *with whom*.' Guderian studied Kilduff's face, evaluating. 'Enjoy our flight,' she said. 'And *learn*.'

The *Werde*'s single cabin was barely ten feet long. Kilduff gazed around, rapt.

Oberstleutnant Guderian sat in an open cockpit crammed into the nose of the *volplane*, with her back to Kilduff and the fresh-faced navigator beside him. The Oberstleutnant worked briskly through an instrumentation checklist, her German clipped and precise. Many of the instruments, glinting behind their little discs of glass, seemed of familiar enough design; there was an aneroid, there a barograph, there an anemometer; the radio looked like a standard FuG VII.

And – in case, he thought wryly, he had been left in any doubt as to the true nature of this beautiful ship – there on the floor between Guderian's feet was a cannon breech.

There were no open ports, of course, at this moment of launch; the stressed-skin hull was smooth and seamless, the cabin enclosed. Steel longerons swept back from the pilot's seat, enclosing Kilduff within the belly of this metal bird. There was an earthy smell of wood, oil and leather. This *Werde* was founded on simple, effective engineering, he thought, impressed.

The navigator, beside Kilduff, held out his hand. 'My name is Sperrle – Wolfram Sperrle, Leutnant. You are welcome on our mission today. You may call me Wolfram.'

Kilduff shook his hand. 'Michael.'

'I saw you looking at the breech. The cannon is a twenty-millimetre Mauser. A handsome weapon. But it isn't a great deal of use, you know.' Relaxed in his bucket seat, his uniformed shoulder no more than an inch from Kilduff's, Sperrle looked around twenty-five; blond hair, cropped short, sprouted from his skull.

'Why do you say that?'

'This is an antipodal bomber, not a fighter.' His English was even and flatly accented. 'For most of its flight the *volplane* is ballistic – falling like a hurled stone, with about as much manoeuvrability. This is no Eindecker, Herr Kilduff.'

Kilduff smiled. An Eindecker had been Richthofen's plane, in the *Kaiserskrieg*. 'Then why carry a cannon?'

'Ah.' Sperrle touched his lips with a forefinger. 'Vanity, Herr Kilduff. Sheer vanity.'

Kilduff laughed out loud. He found himself taking a liking to this young Leutnant Sperrle; his irreverence was about the first touch of humanity Kilduff had encountered since crossing the English Channel and entering Reich-controlled territories, two days before. But he suspected, sadly, that Sperrle's intelligent cheek would not do him any favours in the Imperial Germany of 1940. And Kilduff couldn't help noticing the heavy pistol holstered at Sperrle's waist: no doubt Sperrle had strict instructions about what to do in the event that the *volplane*'s American passenger became unruly.

Oberstleutnant Guderian turned in her seat, and pulled her mouthpiece away from her chin. 'Herr Kilduff.'

It was the first time she'd acknowledged his presence since boarding the plane. 'Yes, Oberstleutnant.'

'In the greater world beyond our happy little ship, events are accelerating, it seems. I have been instructed to apprise you of the status of this flight.'

'This is a low-altitude test flight. Isn't it?'

She smiled a wolf's smile. 'At present. But our flight is due to last several minutes. That is a long time, when the world is unravelling.'

He frowned. 'What are you saying?'

'The *Werde Was Du Bist* is fully fuelled and loaded, Herr Kilduff. Its configuration is flexible.'

He thought that through. 'My God,' he said. 'Are you saying that we could become operational? But that's insane . . .'

'We are three minutes from launch. We can postpone – *if* you decide it would be better not to accompany us, this fine day.' Her black eyes fixed him, coated with contempt.

He considered. He knew the international situation was grave; there were a dozen points of friction between the ambitions of Germany and Japan – Australia, Manchu Kuo, India – any of which could explode, to trigger a new war. And if any incident *were* to erupt, it surely wouldn't be politic for an American to be found in the cockpit of a German warplane.

Maybe he should get off the *Werde*. Yes, that's what he *should* do; no doubt about it . . .

But Kilduff had waited a long time to see the Reich's magical new *volplane* technology, so far ahead of anything managed by American manufacturers . . .

And, more than that, this was his chance *to touch space*.

Kilduff was forty-one years old.

He shook his head sharply. 'I've no concerns. Launch your *grossflugzeug*, Oberstleutnant.'

She lifted her eyebrows, registering amused surprise. Then she turned to her instruments. 'Two minutes fifteen,' she snapped.

Kilduff took off his spectacles and folded them into their case; the cabin became an impressionistic blur of metal and glass.

'I hear you were in the *Kaiserskrieg*, Herr Kilduff,' Sperrle said.

'That's right. You all seem to know a lot about me.'

Sperrle grinned. 'I was interested. The *Kaiserskrieg* is something of a fascination of mine.'

'I was just an infantryman. I came across the Atlantic in 1918. But I didn't see any action, before the Allies accepted the terms of the August armistice.'

'Ah. Then you just missed the *Kaiserschlacht*: Ludendorff's great victory, in which he smashed his way between the British and French lines ... After four years of trench war, it was a great breakthrough.' Sperrle sounded proud.

'Maybe,' Kilduff said. 'But Ludendorff still needed a fair amount of incompetence from the Allies to achieve his goal.'

'One minute,' Guderian announced.

'I agree with you,' Sperrle said, surprising Kilduff. 'The French commandant, Petain, was much too cautious. He was concerned with the defence of Paris, not with supporting the Allied operations.' Sperrle grinned easily. 'Who knows? If Petain had been overruled, perhaps the war would have ended in 1918 or '19, with the defeat of the Reich in the West.'

'But as it turned out –'

'As it turned out, Petain did *not* in the end save his capital from the Kaiser's triumphal entry, in 1919. And the rapid victory in the West enabled us to return our attentions to the Bolsheviks in the East. Then, by 1925 –'

'By 1925,' said Kilduff drily, 'you had established your dreamed-of *Mitteleuropa*.'

Sperrle shrugged, good-natured. 'There is a certain inevitability to history, do you not think?'

But now his voice was drowned out by a roar which overwhelmed Kilduff. The huge rockets of the captive booster had ignited, he realized; it was as if he had been transplanted into the chest of some bellowing giant. An invisible weight crushed him deep into his chair, and the cabin rattled around him, as if it would come apart. There was a surge forward, a feeling of plummeting, helplessly.

The *Werde Was Du Bist* was launched.

He knew what was happening here; he clung to his understanding, as if it were a spell which could deliver him from the noise and vibration penetrating the most private recesses of his skull.

The booster would burn for twenty-two seconds, hurling the *volplane* along its two-mile monorail. The acceleration felt enormous – rib-crushing, unbearable – but it was only, *only*, one and a half gravities, far less than he had endured in training centrifuges at the Hughes test sites in California.

There was a violent shudder, transmitted longitudinally along the *volplane*'s creaking structure. That must be the *Werde*'s traverse through the speed of sound . . .

And now his seat was tipped backwards, and the *Werde* leapt into the air like some metal gazelle.

For brief, miraculous heartbeats, the cabin was free of vibration. Kilduff gasped. He was as weightless as a stone inside a dropped tin can. He felt a surge of exhilaration; in that moment, he *knew* why he had come to the Reich, despite the reluctance of his Government, and the fears of his wife.

But, even in this fragile moment, he was aware of the precise voice of Oberstleutnant Guderian as she spoke to her controllers on the ground.

And now a new roar erupted, even louder than before: this was the ignition of the *volplane*'s own hundred-ton-thrust Daimler-Benz combustion chamber. Now, muscles of liquid oxygen and hydrogen would carry him to the fringe of space.

Kilduff closed his eyes. The renewed buffeting should last just a few seconds. This flight was a mere test hop over East Prussia, to try out a new dynamometer. He only had to wait, and endure.

The rockets burned.

A second can be a long time, he thought. Perhaps he should have started counting, or timing off on his watch . . .

There's something wrong.

He opened his eyes and tried to read the chronometer, the accelerometer. Without his glasses he was unable to make out the small faces of the instruments.

He remembered the hurried departure of Göring, the visible tension of a country undergoing *Kriegsgefahr*. Was it true? Was the world really unravelling?

The rockets roared on, hurling the *volplane* ever further from the safe Earth.

At last the combustion chamber died. Again, the *volplane* hurtled through silence, and Kilduff was without weight.

Sperrle turned to him, his young face creased with concern. 'Herr Kilduff, how do you feel? Are you nauseous?'

Actually, yes. Kilduff felt as if he were falling out of the sky; he fought an urge to grip the edges of his seat. He dug his spectacles out of their case and put them on, restoring the cabin to a harsh focus. He tried to find a smile. 'Weightlessness is not going to be a picnic, I think. But I'm fine.'

Oberstleutnant Guderian unclipped her harness. She twisted in the air, floating out of her bucket seat. 'We have entered the ballistic part of our trajectory,' she announced without ceremony. 'We have been hurled by the rockets above the greater part of the atmosphere, and are heading for our apogee – our furthest point above the Earth.'

'Oberstleutnant,' Kilduff said, 'what the hell happened? The rockets burned far longer than they were supposed to.'

Guderian showed teeth, even and white. Then, with an unexpectedly theatrical flourish, she turned and pulled on a heavy lever, set in the upper canopy. Hydraulics hissed, and covers snapped off ports all around the cabin.

Light – blue and brown – flooded in, dimming the cabin's own electrical lighting.

Kilduff ducked his head to peer out of the main windscreen. Beneath the prow of the ship, the planet curved away, a cloud-laced patchwork of brown land and sombre blue ocean.

My God . . .

Guderian seemed triumphant, Kilduff thought: exultant, even. 'It is *krieg*,' she said. 'The proclamation has come from the Kaiser in the last few minutes. The Reich will not any longer stand by and endure Hideki Tojo and his dreams of an Asia dominated by Japan. And –'

'Fighting has started?'

'In India,' she said. 'There has been an insurrection, easily throwing off the remnants of British rule. But this was inspired by the Japanese, who have already landed by sea. And so –'

'And so, German troops have entered as well.'

'The first engagements are already under way,' she said, rapt.

Wolfram Sperrle's face was expressionless. 'And what of us, Oberstleutnant?'

'Ah, Sperrle,' Guderian said, her eyes shining. 'We have a special honour, you and I. A privilege.'

'A privilege?'

'Our orders were amended even as the *Werde* hurtled along its track. The full *Kriegsgefahr* will take many days to complete. But we have the fortune – the honour – to serve as the Reich's first-mobilized strike force.'

Kilduff pushed out of his seat; he floundered in the air, trying to get closer to Guderian. 'What the hell are you talking about?' he shouted. 'What strike? I demand that you bring this damn *volplane* down.'

She ignored him. 'Kilduff, we will not land in East Prussia. We will go on. We will follow a great circle, passing over northern Eurasia: crossing the forested belt and skirting the ice itself –'

'For Christ's sake, *where are we going?*'

'Tokyo,' she said.

'You can't do this.'

She frowned. 'You are being absurd. This is what the *Werde* was designed for.'

'What if there's some mistake? What if you misheard your new orders? We were in the middle of a launch out of the atmosphere, for God's sake.'

'You make so many appeals to God,' Guderian observed mildly. 'There is no mistake, Herr Kilduff.'

Wolfram Sperrle came drifting out of his seat towards Kilduff. 'You must calm yourself, my friend Michael,' Sperrle said sadly.

Kilduff eyed the gun in Sperrle's holster. Aware of his own rapid breathing, he tried mentally to rehearse his next actions.

'I'm an American citizen, damn it. I won't let you involve me in this. I demand –'

Now she looked amused. 'You *demand*? What? That we let you off?'

Sperrle touched his arm. 'This is as we discussed, Herr

Kilduff. We are embedded in history. The war is inevitable. We cannot –'

With a single motion Kilduff reached out and took Sperrle's revolver. It slid easily from its holster.

Kilduff snapped off the safety catch and pointed the weapon at Guderian.

Guderian studied the gun with mild irritation. 'Oh, Sperrle,' she said softly.

'I'm sorry, Oberstleutnant,' Sperrle said, sounding confused. 'I did not anticipate this.'

'And I'm sorry too, Wolfram,' Kilduff said sincerely. 'This is going to get you into a hell of a lot of trouble. But I was desperate, frankly; I couldn't let this go on.' He pointed the gun at Guderian, trying not to let his trembling show. 'Now,' he said. 'Now we will talk.'

Guderian did not reply immediately. For long seconds she studied the gun.

The intensity of the situation struck Kilduff with an almost physical force. He was aware of every detail of the cabin with a lucid clarity: the soft ticking of instruments, the airframe's creak, the scent of oil and leather, the hallucinatory feel of weightlessness. There were just three of them here, after all, stranded in this tiny bubble of air beyond the sky. And they might destroy each other in the next few seconds. He was struck by the *power* of weapons – like this revolver, this mute lump of oiled steel – to transform human situations. Maybe it was this power which was fundamental to the glamour of war, he thought.

At last Guderian spoke. 'Listen carefully,' she said to Kilduff. 'A *volplane* passage to Tokyo is not simple. The flight will last three hours, and will involve several grazing entries into the atmosphere. I will be fully occupied from now on – as will Leutnant Sperrle, who must assist me with his navigation.'

'She's telling the truth, Michael,' Sperrle said.

'I am going to return to my position,' Guderian said evenly. 'And Sperrle will resume his.'

'I told you,' Kilduff said. 'You're going to take this ship down, somewhere. Or –'

'Or what?' She studied him with a bleak pity. She seemed beyond contempt or mockery now; she had assessed his strength, he realized, and she believed she could overcome him. 'Do you think that the revolver you wave in the air is a wand, capable of controlling others by some magic? A weapon is valuable only if used.'

'I know that if I do use it, we'll *all* die.' Kilduff dug into his soul, searching for conviction. 'But that's not as important as stopping you.'

'You will not use that weapon, *because you have never killed,*' she said, still analytical. 'You are weak, Herr Kilduff. You may sit in your seat and cling to your toy. Your presence in this cabin is not of importance for me.'

Then, as if dismissing him, she turned to Sperrle and snapped instructions at him in rapid German. Sperrle acknowledged and began to unfurl charts.

Kilduff sank back into his seat, the revolver cold in his hands. Carefully, he put the safety back on.

Is she right? Am I really so ignorant of my own heart?

Beyond ports of armoured glass, the roof of Earth slid past.

The *volplane's* smooth arc took it a hundred miles above northern Eurasia. Then it began its first dip back into the fringe of atmosphere, and there was a thin keening from the hull as air plucked at the streamlined monocoque.

There was a glow, roseate, from the lower half of the hull, like a fire banked beneath the still-opened ports; the temperature in the cabin began to rise, and Kilduff tugged open the collar of his flying suit.

He sat in his seat, the revolver still resting in his lap. The gun felt heavy, clumsy, useless: a tangible symbol of his indecision and weakness.

Guderian spoke softly into her radio. Kilduff wondered how much attention was focused, across a world girding itself for a new war, on this single, astonishing *volplane*, and the audacity of the attack it was carrying through. Perhaps his own Government was trying to contact him, he wondered.

The buffeting grew severe, and Kilduff was jolted down,

hard, into his seat. Then, gradually, the unevenness ceased, and once again the *Werde* was soaring free above the atmosphere.

When the skip was over, Wolfram Sperrle folded up his charts with a sigh. 'Excuse me,' he said to Kilduff. From a small compartment set in the hull, Sperrle withdrew a leather bottle; he unbuttoned his flies and, with a soft grunt of relief, filled the bottle. He stoppered it and stowed it away. He grimaced at Kilduff. 'Primitive, but the best concession to the needs of the human our designers are prepared to make, I fear.'

Kilduff, cradling the revolver, said nothing.

Sperrle opened out his charts once more. 'So, Michael,' he said, 'now the *Werde* is operating as a *volplane* – a glider, yes? How are you finding your first experience of aerodonetics?'

Aerodonetics: soaring flight . . . Kilduff tried to think like an engineer. 'It's smoother than I expected, I guess.'

'And remarkably efficient. We are skipping like a stone across the atmosphere. And so, with virtually no further expenditure of fuel, we can cross the five thousand miles to Tokyo in little more than three hours.'

Kilduff grunted. 'Just the right toy for the rulers of the planet,' he said.

Sperrle gave him a reproving look. 'Come now, Michael. There is no use denying the realities of *Weltpolitik*. Consider *Mitteleuropa*: a single market, stretching from the Atlantic coast to beyond the Urals. Unified Europe is now self-sufficient in food, and the mines of France, Belgium and Rumania are working for wider markets than could have been dreamed possible, before the liberation of the *Kaiserskrieg*.'

Kilduff felt claustrophobic, frustrated. 'Look, Wolfram, nobody but a German is going to have a rosy view of your *Mitteleuropa*. German control extends from the Atlantic to the Baltic, through Russian Poland as far as the Crimea. France has become a weakened rump, shorn of much of its resources. Luxembourg has been turned, by force, into a German federal state. Belgium and Holland have been compelled to put their ports at German disposal . . .' He became aware that he was raising his voice.

'But it is not so simple,' Sperrle said. 'We also pushed back the Slav – we freed millions of non-Russians from Moscow's dominance. Ask *them* their views on *Mitteleuropa*. Why, if not for *Mitteleuropa*, would the great Russian engineer Tsiolkovsky have had the opportunity to come to develop his rocket engine ideas with Daimler-Benz?'

The Oberstleutnant stretched luxuriously. She unfixed her clasps and came floating out of her seat once more. Guderian looked radiantly happy, Kilduff realized; she was nearing the apotheosis of her life.

'Sperrle is right,' she said.

Kilduff waved his revolver at her. 'You described to me how you are going to war with Tojo, for his schemes of *Toa Shinchitsujo*. But what difference is there between your two nations? Two absurd, antiquated militaristic traditions – you damnable Prussians, and the Japanese with their thousand years of *Bushido* . . .'

Guderian snorted. 'Perhaps there *is* no difference. We share many facets of what the Japanese call their *kokutai* – their national character. This is no shame. This only demonstrates that we, and the Japanese, are wolves in a world of sheep.

'And now, we are ready for war over the greatest prize of all: the resources of a unified Asia. And I, *I* will launch the first strike in the history of this historic conflict.'

Her eyes shone, like the painted eyes on the *Werde*'s hull.

Kilduff stared at her. For a moment he felt drawn to her vital intensity: to the deadly, seductive glamour of this warrior.

It would be so easy to *believe* . . .

No, damn it, he thought, with a last access of will.

Savagely, he snapped off the revolver's safety. He swung the weapon through the air and fired, twice, into the control bank in the *volplane*'s nose.

Glass splintered; severed connections sparked across the panel, and the stink of scorching insulation filled the tiny cabin. Wolfram Sperrle grabbed a fire blanket; he pushed past Kilduff and smothered the instrument panel with the blanket.

Kilduff looked down at the gun in his hand. Smoke seeped from its barrel, and the metal felt hot, oily.

With a single kick against the back of her seat, Eva Guderian thrust herself at Kilduff. She slapped the revolver easily from his unresisting hands, and then her gloved fist slammed, unimaginably hard, into his temple.

His glasses buckled, and that single punch was enough to scramble his awareness. But still her fists came raining in, and now he could feel, remotely, the hard impact of boot-heels in his stomach and ribs.

He made no attempt to defend himself. He let his thoughts dissolve, welcoming the sweet oblivion of unconsciousness.

He woke to pain, and heat, and an unremitting shrieking.

He opened his eyes. They were crusted with sleep deposits, encrusted tears, and blood, but his vision – blurred without his lost spectacles – seemed unimpaired.

He was crammed, awkwardly, into his bucket seat. His head was a gourd of pain. He tried to straighten up, but there was a stabbing agony across his chest. He could scarcely move, in any case; his hands and legs were strapped to the frame of the chair by what felt like thick leather straps – uniform belts?

The shrieking, and the heat, were coming from beyond the hull, he realized. The ports had been closed, and the *volplane* buffeted violently, cramming him into his seat.

Guderian sat at her seat before him, hauling on her joystick. Wolfram Sperrle had folded his charts neatly away: the time for navigation was over, it seemed. The young German gripped the arms of his seat, and he was speaking under his breath – perhaps in prayer.

Kilduff opened his mouth to try to talk. 'Wolfram,' he gasped. Pain lanced through the joint of his jaw, and he could taste blood and dried snot on his lips.

Sperrle turned to him, startled. 'Michael. I didn't think you would awaken again.'

'We're . . . entering the atmosphere, aren't we?'

'This is our final descent. We are somewhere over Mongolia; in a few moments we will approach the Sea of Japan.'

'Japan? But the shots – the instruments –'

'Oh, you did a great deal of damage, Michael.' Sperrle had to shout to make himself heard over the shrieking of the air. 'You shattered the undercarriage indicator, the artificial horizon, the manifold pressure gauge, even the pilot seat height adjuster . . .'

'So I failed. I thought I might disable the ship.'

'In a sense, you did. The Oberstleutnant was most disappointed that you damaged the Lotfe.'

'The what?'

'The tachometric sight, which should have enabled us to make a precision bombing run over Tokyo.' Sperrle sighed. 'But the fact is, Michael, in its *volplane* mode the *Werde* is very difficult to disable. It is only a glider, after all.'

'But without the tachometric sight –'

'Ah, the Lotfe. Well, the ingenious Oberstleutnant was able to devise an alternative stratagem, to ensure we deliver our gift to Tojo.' He grinned without humour; it was a skull-like grimace. 'We will be visiting Tokyo ourselves, Michael. We should make quite a spectacle, as we come plummeting from the sky at near-orbital speed . . .'

Abruptly, the ports snapped open. Fire rimmed the armoured glass, and sparks and gobbets of flame swept across the view: these were fragments of the hull itself, ablating under the intense heat of reentry. It was as if the *Werde* was flying into hell; and perhaps it was, Kilduff thought. Beyond the vision of fire he could see glimpses of the Earth itself, blue and brown and white, reeling across Guderian's windscreen.

So, he thought, *all I have done is to ensure our own deaths*.

'Before we lost radio contact with the Reich, we got a call from Kaiser Wilhelm himself,' Sperrle said. 'He congratulated us on our courage. And he assured us that we would not be the last to die, in this war to end wars! How comforting . . . ach, *Gott* . . .' He closed his eyes, and Kilduff felt a stab of pain for him.

A war to end wars: well, perhaps it would be so. And, between the ancient fanaticism of the Bushido and the hard-eyed expansionists in Prussia, America would surely be crushed like an eggshell.

Eva Guderian half-turned. Kilduff could see Earthlight reflected in her glowing black eyes.

This is a war for the *Mittelwelt*, he thought. Whoever won the coming struggle would control the planet, for a thousand years: a true Axis World. And with space technology in the hands of the winners of this war to end wars, what could come next? A *Mittelkosmos*, perhaps?

In the windscreen, Kilduff could see the buildings of a city, sprawling innocently around a bay.

He closed his eyes and thought of his wife.

A Journey to the
King Planet

It was in the year 1882 that I reluctantly became one of the first men to leave the inner Solar System; and I find my keenest regret about the whole episode is that the launch of the liner *Australia* from her yard in Antarctica was degraded from a spectacle into a bloody massacre.

I was to have been one of the great liner's most favoured passengers. I was met at the dock of Cape Adare by the ship's master himself; Captain Roberts was tall and resplendent in his Cunard dress uniform, and his space-tanned face, shielded from the polar breeze by a mass of black beard, creased into a professional smile. 'Professor Conseille? Welcome to the Pole.'

I stepped cautiously from the steamer's gangway and shook the Captain's hand. Roberts ordered a waiting steward to organize my luggage. The steward's name was Dart; he was a slight, solemn-looking fellow of about fifty. He scuttled on board the steamer. 'I hope your journey from France was comfortable,' said the Captain.

I grinned, remembering seasick days. 'I'm rather a – what is the English? – a landlubber, I'm afraid, Captain. Seafaring has been something of a theoretical science for me until now. And I suspect that at the age of forty-five I'm rather too old to adapt –'

Roberts smiled sympathetically. 'Well, the ocean of space sails as smooth as an ice rink, I can assure you.'

'I'm in your hands, Captain. And I'm enthralled at the prospect of converting another theoretical science to the practical – my speciality, celestial geology.'

'Of course. I read your popular monograph of last year on

the Nix Olympica, Professor. And fascinating I found it too,
if I may say so.'

I bowed my head.

'Well, Professor,' Roberts went on, 'you may put your fourteen days at sea behind you; after only three days in space
you will be aboard a Cunard airship sailing not fifty miles
over that great volcano.'

These words, simply delivered, sent a jolt of electricity
through me. 'You know, it's scarcely believable that such
things are possible. Are there no limits to what men can
achieve with the power of anti-ice?'

'Oh, we've plenty of goals left, Professor Conseille.'

The Captain escorted me to a waiting railway carriage. Within
minutes we were rolling smoothly across frozen earth, while,
within the warmth of the carriage, Dart took our steaming
overcoats and served us coffee. The crockery was china and
inscribed with Cunard livery.

Soon the low wooden buildings of New Liverpool – mostly
storehouses and other utilitarian constructions – slid past the
iced windows. 'Well, Professor,' Roberts said, 'a fine meal, a
hot bath and a deep mattress are waiting for you a few miles
further on in the heart of the town – but now we're approaching the shipyard and so I've asked the driver to slow.' He
grinned proudly. 'I thought you might like an early glimpse
of the great lady herself.'

As if on cue the train swept around a tight curve; and there,
standing proud, was the *Australia* herself.

The space liner was built around a pillar of ice not less than
five hundred feet tall and a hundred feet thick. The pillar was
engraved with deep flutings – for stability during the climb
through Earth's atmosphere, I was told – and was capped
with a cone of burnished iron. There was a stout construction
strapped around the pillar about a hundred feet below the cap,
like a boxy belt of wood; I recognized this from lithographs as
the living quarters of passengers and crew. Precarious-looking
elevators dangled from open hatchways in the belt. The ship
was surrounded by a frame of wooden scaffolding over which

shipwrights and workmen swarmed. The liner was the centre of a veritable village of huts, storehouses, dormitories and other buildings.

'Captain, she's magnificent,' I breathed.

Roberts nodded, his blue eyes fixed on his ship. 'She is, isn't she? Professor, would you care to postpone your bath and pause an hour?'

'Can we?'

'Of course,' Roberts smiled. 'I'll make the arrangements.'

And so I found myself striding across timber-carpeted ice towards the yard. Dart followed us quietly. Soon I stood in the shadow of the scaffolding, staring up at the bulk of the liner. The iron hood was hidden by the fluted perspective of her white-ice sides, and sunlight scattered highlights from the polished wood of the passenger compartment.

Captain Roberts pointed at the wall-like base of the ship. 'Look closely, Professor. What do you see?'

I made out a soft glow from within the ice itself. The glow had form, rather like the features of a face in shadow.

'That is the anti-ice motor,' explained the Captain, 'the agent of locomotion which propels this unlikely construction to the planets; and all embedded in the ice.'

'One would think it would require many tons of anti-ice to raise this monument from the ground.'

'Not at all,' said the Captain, 'and that is the most astonishing feature of the substance. Professor, this ship contains only a few ounces of anti-ice. And yet, such is its vigour of combination with ordinary matter, that tiny quantity will more than suffice to carry us all from Earth to Mars and back! – Yes, even poor Dart, who I can see has turned whiter than the ice.'

Roberts walked me slowly around the base of the ship. Navvies in frost-rimed coats of fur nodded curtly as we passed. Roberts went on, 'A powerful electromagnet generates a sphere of magnetism which stores the anti-ice, protecting it from instant annihilation by contact with the substance of the normal world. It is this antipathy the two forms of matter hold for each other that inspired the original savants,

conducting their dangerous experiments, to assign the label
"anti-ice".

'The slow destruction of the anti-ice, controlled by a series
of magnets, liberates great quantities of heat. Every second
one hundred and seventy pounds of ice is converted to steam.
Over a flight of ten days fully half the ship would be consumed. The steam is expelled at some millions of knots from
nozzles at the base of the ship; and so the liner is a kind of
steam rocket.'

'Captain, this is an imposition, but I am longing to inspect
the ship's interior. Is it possible . . . ?'

Roberts hesitated. 'I'm afraid the crew compartment is
deserted. Although the equipping and victualling of the ship
is almost complete, my crew are engaged in final briefings. In
fact I'm due to attend such a session myself in a short while –'

'You mustn't let me keep you from your work.'

He eyed me; then he grinned. 'I know quite how you feel.
Dart!'

The spry steward was at our side immediately. 'Captain?'

'I've a little job for you. Escort the Professor up to the
Australia for a brief tour, will you? Dart will see you on to
your hotel later, Professor. And if you're sharpish, you'll catch
the elevator that's about to raise over there. Ho!'

A navvy had just stepped into an elevator twenty yards
from where we stood; at the Captain's call the navvy started
and turned. He was a thin, swarthy man; his eyes flicked over
us. He clutched a heavy wrench against his coat of fur.

'You're ascending, fellow?' Roberts asked. 'Then be a good
chap and take up two passengers.'

The navvy stared at me for a full second, unexpected hostil-
ity in his thin eyes. Then he nodded assent.

The cage of the elevator was an open box with walls no
higher than my waist. The surly navvy pulled a lever and we
rose from the frozen ground; Captain Roberts waved briefly,
a grin splitting his upturned face.

The wind was sharp. We slid slowly past the white flank
of the ship, dwarfed by its huge fluting. I resisted the temptation to clutch at the rim of our car. Dart stood staring at the

sliding ropes that drew us into the sky, a sheen of perspiration covering his white cheeks.

'Are you all right, Dart?'

He managed a ghastly smile. 'Thank you, Professor. Despite my job, I'm no lover of heights.'

The navvy stood in one corner of the car, chilling eyes fixed on us.

The car glided upwards into a rectangular chamber about twenty feet long and ten wide. A metal lid was poised over our entrance. Garments of treated leather hung from the walls, and helmets of beaten copper were set on shelves, their glass plates staring like eyes. Canisters of what I guessed to be compressed air were stacked beside each helmet.

'This is the Wardrobe Chamber, sir,' Dart said. 'The suits are for excursions outside the ship.' Eyes averted from the four hundred feet drop below, he climbed stiffly over the wall of the car and offered me his arm.

'Men will actually leave the ship and enter space?'

'Only in emergencies, sir. For repairs and suchlike. This way, please.'

He led me to a heavy metal door set at one end of the compartment; our surly pilot had disappeared in the opposite direction. I stepped over the doorway sill and entered a chamber full of light. The inner wall curved around the ship and was coated with mirrors; the outer wall, which leaned inwards a little, was a copper latticework set with small glass slabs. I peered through a pane: a view of the Antarctic afternoon presented itself like a miniature painting. 'This is charming,' I said.

'We call this the Observatory, sir.'

'How many chambers are there?'

'Twelve, each about twenty feet in length, spaced around the liner like the divisions of a clock. To clockwise are passenger areas; to anticlockwise – the way that navvy set off – is the Bridge, and other crew areas. If you'll follow me, sir –'

I entered the next chamber to find it full of enclosed bunk-beds set out rather like a railway sleeper carriage. This Dormitory was warm and comfortable and included a small bathing area. The carpet was a rich crimson and soft as down, and there was a smell of freshly polished wood.

'Dart, I'm impressed.'

He flashed me a smile whose pride was reminiscent of that of the Captain. 'Well, if you'll follow me into the Library –'

'A Library?'

And so the next chamber turned out to be. Oaken-panelled walls were lined with books in uniform bindings, all stamped with the Cunard crest. The outer wall once more tilted inwards, so that a picture of an English hunting scene hung away from the wall. The floor also seemed to slope slightly. Electric globes fixed to the walls provided ample reading light. A leather-coated divan was placed between two desks, and seated at one of the desks, poring over a book of lithographs of outer-space scenes, was a small, bald man in morning dress. I judged him to be about fifty-five years old. He squinted up at me through thick spectacles and nodded, smiling.

'I'm sorry to have disturbed your reading,' I said.

'Not at all.'

'Let me introduce myself. My name is Conseille, of the University of Paris.'

'Ah! I noted your name on the manifest.' His smile broadened to reveal yellowed teeth. 'I've read of your work. I look forward to stimulating conversations during the fifty hours of our voyage to Mars.'

'You're also a passenger, sir?'

'Indeed.' He stood and offered me his hand; it was plump and warm. 'My name's Holden. No university, I'm afraid; I hail from London, where I scrape a living writing popular science articles for the newspapers.'

'Then you have a commission from some editor for this trip?'

He nodded, eyes swimming behind his glasses. 'At least for some of the fare. I'm afraid I've rather overstretched my finances in paying for the rest of it. But, you see –' He waved a hand at the open book on his desk. 'This voyage to another world will be my life's fulfilment.'

I nodded, warming to the odd little man.

'As you can see it's quite comfortable here,' Holden said. 'But there's no crew yet; I go dashed long intervals between cups of tea . . .'

'Allow me, gentlemen,' Dart said smoothly. 'I'll see if the Dining Room is open and –'

The ship shuddered. There was a sound of doors slamming.

Dart, halfway to the Library's far doors, gasped and turned. Holden took off his glasses and stood carefully.

'What the devil – Dart, is it an earthquake?'

The steward backed towards a wall, clutching at the spines of books. 'It sounded like launch procedures to me, sir. That slamming must have been the safety equipment closing external hatchways.'

'But that's impossible! Launch is five days away –'

Now a distant thunder rose from the heart of the ship. The carpet lurched upwards; the pictures rattled softly against the walls.

Holden stood before me, stolid, round and grim-faced. 'Impossible or not, Professor, I suggest we determine what is happening. Steward! Take us to the Bridge.'

Poor Dart's mouth gaped like a fish's. 'I – yes, sir. This way.'

We returned to the Observatory. Panes set low in the wall gave a panoramic view of the ground. A bank of vapour surged from the base of the ship, evoking steam from the polar earth and forcing men to flee – but to no avail.

They went down writhing.

I thought I saw the tall figure of Captain Roberts battle valiantly towards his ship; but soon he, too, was lost, wrapped in live steam.

'Dear God,' I breathed. 'They're utterly unprepared. It's a slaughter.'

The deck slammed upwards once more. The ship sloughed away its scaffolding surround. I saw workmen, shipwrights and navvies all tumbling in the air, hurled loose as a dog shakes off fleas. The ground fell away, sliding sideways. The land turned to a cap of ice, human suffering lost in the scale of it all, and for the first time in my life I saw the curvature of the Earth.

'We've launched,' Dart sobbed, his face pressed to the windows. 'Holy Mother of God.'

A breeze whistled through the Observatory. 'But – how can it be, Holden? There are no crew, no engineers –' I recalled Roberts' statement that the crew of the liner were engaged in briefings away from the ship.

Holden spoke bleakly, clinging to the frame of the glass wall. 'There are no engineers during the flight. The anti-ice chamber is inimical to life. The engines are worked from the Bridge by an arrangement of current-bearing wires. Professor, one man could fly this ship.'

And yet, despite this ease of theft, the craft had been left unguarded. Not for the first time in my life I reflected sourly on the overweening confidence of these English that surely no-one would dare impede their designs.

Well, if the scene beyond the windows was unreal, more immediate concerns soon crowded in on me, hard and sharp. I was shivering. My chest ached; suddenly I seemed to be sucking at drained air. I gasped to Holden, 'My God, the hull must be breached!'

'The cause is not hard to find.' Holden pointed to a quartet of smashed panes. 'This has been done deliberately – no doubt to seal us off from the Bridge, which lies beyond that far door.'

A wrench with jaws the size of my fist lay on the floor beside the damage, the obvious instrument of this violence. I remembered the shifting-eyed crewman who had accompanied myself and Dart into the ship. Was he the sole pirate? 'Then we must break down the door and apprehend the villain –' I stopped, coughing. My limbs felt heavy as lead; black spots crossed my vision.

Dart was tugging at my sleeve. 'There's no time, Professor! Within minutes the air will be gone and the acceleration of the engines will crush us. We have to return to the Dormitory.'

'But the Bridge –'

'The steward's right, man,' Holden panted. Leaning heavily against the wall he made his way back towards the sleeping chamber. 'Let's make sure we survive this launch. Then we can think about wresting back control of the ship.'

So we returned to the Dormitory; Dart pulled closed the heavy door and air sighed into my lungs. I climbed cautiously into a bunk and was soon pressed into the mattress by the joint action of Earth's gravity and the locomotive power of the anti-ice rocket.

The whistle of atmosphere faded. The fatigue of my astonishing day crept over me, and after a few minutes I was surprised to find my eyes sliding closed.

There was a discreet cough. I opened my eyes. Dart stood beside my bed. His stance was composed but the hands clutched before him showed white at the knuckles.

The noise of the launch was gone now. I heard and felt only a distant, solemn vibration; it was like being aboard a large ocean-going liner, and the soft scents of furniture polish and bed linen added to the impression of normality.

I sat up, rubbing my eyes. 'How long did I sleep?'

'About two and a half hours, sir. Mr Holden asked me to wake you; he says you might be interested in the view.'

I swung my legs from the bunk and stood cautiously. I might have been standing in my own study. 'Dart,' I asked, in sudden, confused hope, 'surely we haven't landed?'

Dart raised an eyebrow. 'I fear not, sir. The weight you feel is caused by the *Australia*'s steady acceleration away from Earth, at the – at the mercy of whoever is on the Bridge.'

The catch in his voice moved me. I touched his arm. 'Do you have a family, Dart?'

'I – Yes, sir. Two grandchildren.'

'Well, don't lose hope of seeing them again, man. We're not finished yet.'

We walked through the Library: Holden's book of lithographs lay open on the desk, and I noticed that the paintings now hung flat against the exterior wall. We entered a chamber I had not previously visited. 'The Saloon, sir,' Dart announced.

Once again this chamber was about twenty feet in length. Tapestries and some small paintings adorned the inner wall.

Couches and small tables studded the carpet, and on a number of stands around the room rested glass cases fastened with copper rivets. The cases contained models of notable Cunard vessels, both of sea and of space, their every fixture beautifully crafted.

The outer wall was composed of oak panels punctuated by a series of small windows. At one of these Holden stood, hands compressed behind his back. A stark light slanted through the window and crossed his grim countenance. He turned at my entrance. 'Professor Conseille – forgive me for having the steward wake you. The viewing conditions aren't ideal here, but we must make do now that the Observatory is open to vacuum.'

I pressed my face close to a window. At first I saw only stars, precise and unflickering – and then a tranche of light slid into view from the left. I made out a light-grey surface mottled by splashes of darkness and crater rings.

It was the Moon, of course. It looked close enough to touch.

'As luck has it,' Holden said, 'our unplanned flight has swept us to within a few thousand miles of the lunar surface. A grand view, you'll agree.'

The brilliant sphere slid to the right and out of my vision. After less than a minute the ship's evident rotation returned the sister world to my view – but she was a little diminished; we were obviously receding dramatically. 'Why are we rotating?'

'For stability,' Holden said briskly. 'A spinning object is more likely to retain its orientation. It's all designed in, Professor; you may have noticed – on Earth – an odd tilt to the chambers, tapestries hanging away from the walls, and so on. Now that we're in flight the rotation adjusts our perception, so that the floor appears level, the walls vertical.'

Once again the glory of the Moon danced past my eyes. 'But this is impossible. Have I truly slept for only three hours?'

Holden smiled sadly. 'Professor, with every second that passes we pick up an extra twenty knots. At present I judge we are travelling at around one hundred and seventy thousand knots –'

I gasped.

' – and so we have reached the Moon as if it were no more than a brisk morning's walk away. And, of course, we are still accelerating. Who knows when it will end?'

I shook my head. 'Mr Holden, I am scarcely a man of action. But clearly we must act.'

'How?'

'We should reach the Bridge and take it from whoever has commandeered the liner.' I began to think it through. 'Now, the Observatory is a barrier of vacuum. But since the habitable compartment is circular, we can travel around the ship and approach the Bridge from the far side.'

The steward was shaking his head. 'I'm afraid that's impossible, sir.'

'You see, Conseille, while you slept Dart conducted me on a tour of the rest of the ship. Beyond this chamber lies a Dining Room; then comes a galley and a forecastle followed by an equipment station, a supply area which includes air reservoirs, and finally a cargo hold. Beyond the hold lies the Bridge. The hold contains material for our planned excursion into the Martian atmosphere, including airships folded neatly away; but I'm afraid those airships will never fly.'

'What do you mean?'

'The hold is open to space, its walls blown outwards, its contents shredded. The Observatory on one side, the hold on the other; our unknown pilot has surrounded his Bridge with a fence of vacuum.'

'And so we plummet into open space, further and faster – and utterly helpless.'

Holden nodded grimly.

Dart shook like a leaf, his face coated with a thin sweat. He noticed my eyes on him. 'I'm sorry,' he said.

'Dart, you didn't sign up for this kind of escapade, did you?'

'Hardly, sir.'

'Well, we'll just have to make the best of the situation. Now, then, I've heard mention of a galley. Is it functioning and provisioned?'

'It is, sir.'

Holden clapped the steward on the back. 'Well, Dart, how's your cooking?'

Dart smiled faintly. 'I'm hardly an expert, but I dare say I could rustle up a respectable omelette.'

'Omelettes it is, then,' I said. 'And we'll eat in the Dining Room.'

'Yes, sir. And,' he asked, a twinkle in his eye, 'will a cloth laid for two be appropriate?'

'Yes, thank you,' I said with a smile. 'Entirely appropriate.'

And so we settled into a parody of civilization, punctuated by the clink of wine glasses over Dart's modest meals, and by the companionship of Holden over cigars in the Saloon. It was a dreamlike interlude during which I found it easy to forget that I was hurtling away from Earth – that even the comforting solidity of my own weight was a sign that the thrust of the runaway ship was unwavering.

Holden and I debated the nature of our captors. 'Heaven knows,' Holden reflected, puffing out cigar smoke, 'we Britons have plenty of enemies in the modern world. I sometimes think the mechanical revolution fuelled by anti-ice has been a curse rather than a blessing – even for Britain herself.'

'That's a surprising viewpoint. Surely the development of your great cities, the wonderful machines which ply the skies of Britain, Europe and beyond –'

'But consider the uses to which we've put these marvellous machines. It was in 1842 that our explorer Ross traced Australian legends to their source in Antarctica, to the cache of anti-ice locked safely into its fold in Earth's magnetic field. By 1850 our engineers had constructed the first simple devices to extract and exploit the anti-ice – and by 1860 our flying bombs were dropping into Paris, Berlin and Boston.'

I sipped at my port. 'I suppose I speak as a victim of Britain's expansion. But your Pax Britannica is less severe than many regimes I could envisage. And Britain was on her way to establishing a dominant position in world affairs even without the anti-ice.'

'But not nearly as dominant as she is,' Holden said sourly. 'And the supply of anti-ice is not infinite. Ross found about a ton of the stuff. Although tiny amounts will power the hugest machines, nevertheless we are finding ever more ingenious ways to use it up. What happens when our flying machines are grounded? How will our "trading partners" look on us then?'

I thought it over. 'Well, that's a gloomy prospect for us all. How do you think it might relate to our present predicament?'

'I assume some enemy of Britain has seized the Bridge in order to damage the country's prestige and power. Our fate depends on this hypothetical person's further intentions. I see two possibilities. Perhaps he intends to land the ship in some other country. We will ride into space for some period, then turn around and return to Earth.'

'Then,' I said, sudden hope stirring, 'we will have a chance of escape after landing.'

Holden took the three-quarter-full bottle of port, leaned forward and refreshed both our glasses. 'But the pirate's plans may be simpler. Perhaps he does not intend to return to Earth at all. Perhaps he merely intends to waste his own life, and ours – and a few ounces of anti-ice into the bargain.'

I frowned as the bleak prospect unfolded. 'So we would fly on into interstellar space, on without destination, until our food, warmth and air expired.'

Holden said quietly: 'The longer we continue to accelerate outwards, the more the latter course becomes likely.'

And so the hours wore on, as we waited for the steady thrumming of the engines to die, for the great ship to turn in space and head once more for Earth.

But the thrust never wavered and my agitation increased.

A day and a half into the flight we completed yet another of Dart's bland meals. Holden checked his watch. 'You may like to know,' he announced, 'that we have just passed the orbit of Mars. My limited astronomical knowledge informs me that the planet of war is far from our present position –'

I thumped a fist into the table. Crockery rattled and Dart jumped like a startled rabbit. 'Damn this uncertainty!' I said.

'Holden, surely our pilot has no intention of returning to Earth.'

'I fear you are right.' Holden sipped at his wine, mulled it over his tongue. 'And so we must face our deaths.'

'Mr Holden,' I said grimly, 'I don't intend to go down without a fight.'

Holden nodded. 'Very well.' He set down his wine glass and turned to face me, a sparkle in his eyes. 'What do you suggest?'

I stood, paced around the Dining Room. 'Let's take it a step at a time. We need to halt the ship. Dart, is there any place other than the Bridge from which the craft can be controlled?'

'No, sir.'

'Very well. Then we must reach the Bridge.'

'But vacuum surrounds it,' Holden said.

'Then we must cross the vacuum. The ship holds suits to allow men to work outside the air . . .'

'True, sir,' Dart said, 'but those suits are all stored in the Wardrobe Chamber to which you and I rode in the elevator – and that chamber is itself cut off by the airless Observatory.'

'So,' I said doggedly, 'one of us will have to brave the vacuum unprotected.'

'I fear that courageous volunteer will die without result,' Holden said sombrely.

'Will he? Holden, I can hold my breath for a good half-minute. Why could I not survive the vacuum for as long?'

Holden hesitated. 'You know,' he said at length, 'I'm not sure if you're so wrong. Although you might be better advised to enter the void with your mouth open. Retained air would expand to fill the vacuum – and rupture your lungs in the process. So – yes, keep your mouth open.'

Your mouth . . .

A silent understanding was growing in the room: the mission was devolving to me.

My breath grew shallow, as if in anticipation of the vacuum. Could I undertake such a task?

I considered my companions: the steward pale and wavering, the journalist overweight, ageing and patently unfit.

It was clear there was no alternative. Therefore I did not address the question further.

'Very well, I'm outside the air. What next?'

Dart said, 'The entrances to the Bridge from the Wardrobe Chamber and the hold will undoubtedly be locked.'

'Then I'll take an axe.'

'Axe-wielding in the vacuum, Conseille?' Holden said. 'You'll be lucky to get in one good blow. And besides, the doors are of plate steel.'

'Then we must find another door. Dart?'

'Well,' the steward said doubtfully, 'there are emergency access points . . .'

'Can they be opened from outside?'

'Oh, yes, sir. That is their purpose.'

'Then lead me to them,' I whispered.

'Now, Conseille?'

'I see no advantage in hesitation, Mr Holden. And besides,' I admitted, 'I'm not certain how long my courage will last.'

Holden touched my shoulder. 'Then let's be at it,' he said softly.

We walked around the ship to the air supply chamber. The copper reservoirs of air were each taller than a man. They were girdled about by bands of steel, and their spherical forms were obscured by pipes that snaked into the walls and ceiling.

There was a ladder leading to a hatch in the roof. I climbed the ladder and found myself in a plain metal box, barely large enough to stand upright. This was an 'air capture chamber', Dart explained. Its air could be withdrawn. And the door from the chamber, operated by a wheel, led to space.

Holden popped his head through the hatch. He handed me the end of a series of knotted tablecloths. 'Around your waist, Professor,' he said briskly. 'If you reach the Bridge dip the ship's lights. If we do not receive your signal within sixty seconds Dart and I will open the hatch and start hauling you back.'

I nodded, my neck muscles stiff as ropes.

Holden reached up and handed me the heavy wrench the

saboteur had used to smash the Observatory. 'You might need this.' He reached up to shake my hand. 'Godspeed, Conseille. Now remember: mouth open.' He ducked down through the hatch and closed the metal lid.

I heard the wheel lock close. The scrape of metal on metal was final; I fought for some seconds with the temptation to cry for readmission.

At last, with an effort, I turned to the doorway. I laid my hands on the ice-cold metal wheel, took as firm a grip as I could, and turned the wheel anticlockwise.

The door opened a fraction of an inch. Air hissed – and there was a whir of electric pumps, a stab of pain in my ears. I opened my mouth wide and felt air rush past my drying tongue.

Sound died.

The door slid open and I stepped out of the air capture chamber.

I stood on the roof of the passenger compartment, a wooden path that snaked like a mountain road around the curving wall of ice to my right. To my left was – nothing. An infinite drop with a backdrop of unflickering stars which rotated grandly.

Needles of pain thrust at my eyes; I clenched them shut, allowing myself only the occasional squint through tight lids. I reached to the right and found the cold wall. Then, trailing my fingers over the fluted ice, I hurried around the roof, my footfalls eerily silent.

After some forty feet – perhaps fifteen seconds into vacuum – my cautious glimpses showed me another air capture compartment. This, I knew, was the entrance to the Bridge.

Mouth gaping, the need to suck in a breath mounting in me, I grabbed at the door wheel and twisted. It gave; shreds of air puffed out around my face.

I untied my knotted cloths and entered the chamber, pulling the hatch behind me. Air sighed into the chamber and sound returned in a rush. I fell to my knees, gasping; I found blood flecks at my mouth, ears and nose.

When the pain in my lungs had dulled enough to let me think I bent to the hatch set in the floor. I hefted the wrench in my right hand and with my left hand turned the wheel.

The hatch fell open easily. I obtained a sudden impression of the Bridge – of a mosaic of dials and needles set around a circular, midnight-blue table – and of a single, swarthy face looking up at me in shock. It was indeed the navvy who had accompanied me and Dart in the elevator.

Surprise was my only ally. I half-leapt down the ladder to the deck; I gathered the muscles of my right arm and swung the wrench in a wide arc. The jaws hit his left temple; he crumpled to the floor.

A hasty scan told me that he had indeed been alone; other than Bridge equipment and fixtures there was only the remains of a packet of food, a cask of water and some improvised toilet arrangements. It was a matter of a few seconds to find a way to dim the lights of the main compartment, and so to signal to my waiting companions that my extraordinary mission had been successful.

And then it was over. I stumbled against a bank of instruments and felt the universe whirl around me; my every muscle trembled as if drained, and I wished passionately that I were safely back in my book-lined study in Paris.

When I had recovered my composure I bound up my kidnapper with his own jacket. He stirred briefly to consciousness, fixed me with eyes whose despair was jarring, and collapsed once more.

I found that the Wardrobe Chamber, adjacent to the Bridge, was still pressurized. The deck hatch had closed over the gondola Dart and I had taken up to the ship less than two days earlier; its remains jutted from the metal frame. I donned one of the clumsy vacuum suits and entered the airless Observatory. I used the material of spare suits to block up smashed panes of glass. At last air hissed once more into the chamber and I was able to doff my suffocating helmet.

I threw open the door to my waiting companions. I allowed them to remove my vacuum suit and put up with their effusive expressions of thanks. Holden took my wrench and returned to the Bridge; I allowed Dart to make me some coffee, stretched out on a couch in the Saloon, and slept for three hours.

On waking I washed myself and gargled for some minutes in the Dormitory's small bathroom, attempting to relieve the vacuum pain of my throat and chest; then I straightened my tie and walked through to the Bridge.

Dart was surveying banks of dials and switches. I recognized manometers and thermometers, among much else. The steward doubtfully compared readings against diagrams in a fat, leather-bound manual. I noticed he carried the wrench tucked into the belt of his trousers.

'Professor!' Holden had his jacket off and was bent over the circular table I had noticed earlier. 'I trust you're recovered.'

It was difficult to speak. 'I'm fine, thank you, Mr Holden.'

The renegade I had overcome lay propped against one wall. His arms and legs were firmly bound by strips of tablecloth and his dark head was down, his chin against his chest. I dropped to my haunches before him. At length he raised his bloodied head and met my gaze. His thin face, covered by three days' dirt and growth of beard, had a dark, almost Latin complexion. He looked less than twenty-five.

'I hope I didn't hurt you,' I said stiffly.

'I live,' he said – in French. 'My name is Michelet.'

A shock passed through me at the sound of my native language. 'So we're countrymen,' I replied in the same tongue. 'But I don't understand –'

'And I don't understand why you walked through vacuum to help these pigs.' His accent, full of bitterness and contempt, bore soft traces of the south – perhaps of Marseilles.

I noticed the Englishmen glance around uneasily at this flow of high-speed French, but I ignored them. 'How could you fly the ship alone?' I asked.

He sneered. 'It was not difficult. The ship is directed by a set of controls simple enough for the English monkeys to operate. Despite my appearance I have some technical education; of course no English would suspect a lowly "Frenchie" of such capability. I got myself assigned to the Bridge and simply observed their training routines.'

'Why did you take the ship? You were trying to destroy it, weren't you? And yourself in the process. Why?'

'Because,' he said as if to a child, 'I wanted to hurt the English. I wanted to take away their prestigious space liner. I wanted to waste a little more of their damned anti-ice, against the day when it is all used up and we are free.'

'Damn it, man, the war is a generation ago. History. We have to live in the world as is. Why so much hate?'

'Because of the Declaration of the Rights of Man,' he said. 'Banned from the streets of Paris since the day the English bombs flew from Kent. Now do you understand?' And he dropped his head, as if dismissing me.

Shaken, I turned to Holden. The journalist still worked at the blue table. 'And how is progress here?'

'Well, the steward seems to be making a good job of checking the ship's systems. And I have been puzzling out this remarkable gadget.' His cheeks were flushed with a kind of pleasurable excitement. I stepped forward and studied the midnight-blue table. It was some five feet across. Eight concentric rings, each separately moveable, surrounded a globe of yellow glass. Each ring bore a marble-sized globe of its own. The context made the meaning clear. 'This is undoubtedly an orrery,' I said, 'showing the sun and all eight of its planets, out to the furthest, Neptune.'

'An arrangement of cogs and gears beneath the surface make the models track across this wooden sky. And that's not all – notice the fine perforations covering the tabletop, Professor; and see these flags thrust through the perforations.'

The little metal flags marked a line, nearly straight, that swept outwards from the third marble – from blue Earth. 'This is our course?'

'That's right. The orrery is a navigation aid, a mechanically maintained image of our trajectory. I imagine it works by inertial means. There must be a series of gyroscopes buried in the table, capable of detecting changes to the ship's orientation or acceleration.'

'Ingenious. But can it tell us how to return to Earth?'

Holden grinned. His hair stood in an excited fringe around a flushed scalp. 'Ah, Conseille; it tells us that – and a lot more besides. Look.' We bent over the line of metal flags. 'Here we are. At present we are flashing away from home at some three million knots, and we are still accelerating. We must subdue the ship's engines –'

'Can we do that?'

'Yes, it's quite a simple matter,' Holden said testily. 'After all ignition was easy enough, as our unkempt companion over there will testify. Let us suppose that takes another six hours. Next we turn the ship over, so that we're flying along backside first. There are small rockets fitted to the nose and tail of the ship for just that purpose. That takes, let us say, twenty-four more hours. Then we relight the engines and begin a steady deceleration. It will have taken us over three days to reach our top speed; we will be about here –' he pointed to the orrery ' – and it will take as long again before we glide to rest. And then we will start to build our velocity once more for another week's journey home.'

'We will come to rest twice as far from Earth as at the midpoint. We will be – about – here.' My finger rested on the fifth ring from the Sun; a fat, pink marble lay beneath my nail.

'That's right,' Holden breathed. 'We will lie some five hundred million miles from the Sun. We will have flown further and faster than any human before. And look where your finger lies, Conseille. That globe is the fifth planet. The king world, Jupiter! An adjustment of just a few degrees to our trajectory – easily achieved with the controls laid out in this Bridge – and we can sail past the Jovian moons. Professor, we must take this opportunity. We owe it to ourselves – to science!'

Fired by his enthusiasm I could only agree. Even Dart eyed the orrery with interest.

And so our journey was transformed from a helpless fall into terror to a voyage of wonder – and yet . . .

And yet I found it impossible to put aside the words of my compatriot.

I walked up to Michelet. He raised his face, a look of faint scorn about his mouth. 'Listen to me,' I said in our common language. 'You have made your gesture.'

He snorted. 'All I have achieved is to deliver to these English another world upon which to plant their ugly flag.'

'But,' I persisted, 'you would agree that further damage is futile.'

I waited for his reply. At length he nodded.

'Very well. I propose to cut your bonds and take you out of here. I will watch you every moment. And I will have Dart, the steward, keep that wrench in his belt. But you will have some freedom of movement.'

He studied me distrustfully. 'Why are you doing this?'

'When we return home I will deliver you to the proper authorities. But until then you are a fellow human, one of just four in this immense void. I would rather you did not suffer.'

At length he held up his bound arms; I freed him and, leaving Dart and Holden to continue their inspection of the ship, I escorted Michelet through the ship to the Dining Room. And so, at a table set with silver cutlery and the finest china, a Professor of the University of Paris set a meal before a round-eyed boy from Marseilles, the whole tableau hurtling tens of thousands of miles every second through interplanetary space.

A gong sounded through the ship. The vibration of the great engines faded and weight disappeared from my shoulders. Dart and Holden, our impromptu crew, worked on the Bridge, while we two Frenchmen remained in the Saloon and Library, clinging cautiously to the furniture. Now more subtleties of the ship's design became apparent: each piece of furniture was attached to the floor or wall, either by screws or by lengths of elastic, and within each divan were concealed belts which could pin one reassuringly into place.

I took a bottle of wine and attempted to fill a glass. To my surprise the liquid emerged in small, wobbling spheres.

Michelet and I poked at them until they combined into a single planet of wine; we pierced its meniscus with straws and took sips of the stuff, watching the globe shrink as we did so.

Michelet laughed. When he did so he looked very young.

After some hours of this the gong sounded again, telling us that the turnover manoeuvre was complete. The huge motors inside the ice shuddered to life, and weight settled on us again.

Three days and ten hours past the mid-point, the steward summoned us to the Observatory. I stood before the glass wall and wonder surged through me.

Jupiter hung before us. Its pinkish clouds were swirls of watercolour paint. We were slightly above the equator so that one pole was tilted towards us, and a crescent slice of the sphere lay in the sun's shadow. One moon showed as a clear disc, off to the right; the sharp shadow of another tracked slowly across the cloud tops.

The four of us stood in a mute row, our faces bathed in salmon light. 'Well, Professor,' Holden said, his shirt open at the collar, his voice strained, 'this is a sight never before granted to human eye. Was the trip worth the trouble?'

'Oh, I think so, Mr Holden. Don't you?'

The liner's slow rotation brought another moon into view. This had been made irregular by a series of monstrous craters.

'Which moon is that?'

Holden shrugged. 'It is only a mile across. Far too small to see from Earth. It is our discovery. Ours to name and claim.' He grinned. 'Not much of a territory, mind you; it looks as if truly severe explosions have taken place on that surface.

'Well now, Dart, Professor. I suggest we return to the Bridge and begin our observations. We have barely a day before we begin our rush back to Earth.'

And so the three of us reluctantly turned from the window –

The three of us?

The door to the Wardrobe Chamber was closed. Holden studied it, as if puzzled.

'Michelet,' I breathed. 'But he gave me his word.'

Holden whirled, eyes blazing. 'Has that damn Frenchie gone ape again? I knew we shouldn't have trusted him. Is he going to destroy us without giving us a chance to take all this home to humanity?'

Dart coughed sadly. 'I don't believe he betrayed your trust, in fact, Professor. Look.'

We turned back to the windows. A figure, stiff and immobile, drifted over our heads and away from the liner.

Michelet's eyes were closed.

I sighed. 'He must have stepped out of the air capture chamber over the Bridge.' And he let the air spill from his lungs and stepped over that infinite cliff –

'Well, that's a damn fool thing to do,' Holden murmured. 'What's that he's got in his hand?'

It was a fragment of multicolored cloth. 'I believe it is the Tricolor.'

'The what?'

The body arced towards the battered moon, caught in its feeble gravity field.

- and a flash like noon sunlight slammed into the Observatory. The ship lurched, rocked, stabilized.

There was a new crater on the moon, glowing still.

Dart crossed himself. 'Dear God. Was that the Frenchie?'

'It was.' Holden turned to me, eyes narrow and glittering in the Jovian light. 'You know what this means, don't you, Conseille?'

I thought it over. And I feared I did understand.

'No simple impact could cause a bang like that,' Holden said. 'There's anti-ice down there. Maybe the whole damn moon – cubic miles –

'Just think of it! No longer will we have to fear the exhaustion of our cache in Antarctica. I picture fleets of magnetized freighters plying to and fro from Earth – of course we'll have to work out vacuum mining techniques –' His words came faster, higher-pitched. 'Perhaps anti-ice is scattered throughout the Solar System and beyond, waiting to be claimed by British explorers. The shadow of the Union Flag will stretch out across the centuries and the stars, vast and unassailable!

Come, gentlemen. We're at a turning point in human affairs. Let's retire to the Saloon and drink a toast to the future.'

I lingered for some seconds, staring at the crater made by the boy from Marseilles. Then I followed the Englishmen.

THE JONAH MAN

In space accidents hit you fast.

And in nine-space . . .

'It's my bones, doctor. I feel so – fragile . . .'

'Calcium deficiency does usually take longer to set in than the two weeks since we've left Earth, Mr Tojo.'

I'd just completed my morning surgery and was standing outside the crew lounge, trying to forget my own aching feet and concentrate on the elderly passenger's complaints. Other crewmen grinned over his shoulder as they made their way past us and around the corridor's gentle curve.

I wasn't thinking about it at the time, but the reason the curve was so gentle was that the corridor happened to be situated just beneath the ship's outer skin. That fact was about to save my life.

The ship shuddered.

The lights snapped to emergency red and my feet left the floor. The corridor exploded into a scene from hell as passengers and crew boiled into it. 'Doctor! What's happened?' Tojo was screaming now as he floundered suddenly into the air.

A section of the ship wall blistered and peeled back. Tojo was whisked away pitilessly, his screams drowned by the roar of escaping air.

Then the silence of vacuum settled over the smashed equipment and lifeless faces. The orderly routine of just a few seconds earlier seemed a surreal memory.

I thought it over. No gravity meant the fusion plant had failed. And in that case I was dead. I drifted there while my lungs emptied, trying to remember what I should do –

– until a massive hand grabbed my collar and pulled me backwards.

I found a thick-set face glaring into mine. Pack, I recalled vaguely; Pack from engineering. He nodded with a kind of gruff reassurance, his mouth gaping wide in the vacuum.

As I should have done, he'd wrestled open the entrance to one of the two-man escape pods studded around the ship's hull. I was stuffed inside unceremoniously. I bounced off equipment lockers in the zero-gee darkness and tried to orient myself.

Pack was working the door closed. From the pod's safety I peered back out at the corridor's lethal chaos –

There was a man out there. A passenger. Blood dribbled from his clenched lips.

And Pack was still pulling closed the door. 'Two man,' I saw him mouth. 'Not enough fuel. Only two man.'

Those bloody lips opened in a soundless cry.

Black globes clustered at the edge of my vision. I considered letting them close around me. I was too old for this . . .

I hauled my bulk across the cabin and cannoned into Pack. We tumbled from the door. The passenger fell into the pod and slammed the door shut. The pod's lights came on and air sighed in.

Pack untangled himself. After a murderous glare at me he began to hammer at a large-keyed control pad. There was a jolt as the pod kicked away from the ship.

I found myself pressed against the wall. Through the pod's single port I watched the wrecked ship recede. Like a smeared photograph, the image was distorted by the impossible perspectives of nine-space; but I could see that giant handfuls had been ripped from the centre of its spindle-shaped hull – and where the fusion plant should have been was only a curdled glow.

There were no more pods; only ours.

And then my stomach twisted as we dropped out of nine-space. The dying ship folded out of sight – to be replaced by something very strange . . .

Heavy hands grabbed my shoulders and twisted me around, away from the port.

'You stupid bastard,' Pack croaked in the new air.

'Listen to me . . .' I protested weakly.

'Why did you let him in? This is a two-man pod . . . You've killed us both.'

Over his shoulder, I saw the passenger's thin face tremble, a pale mixture of fear and calculation.

And then I looked out of the port again.

Ticking as it cooled, the pod was drifting over a crimson plane that stretched to infinity. There was a sun, set in the middle of the plane like some fantastic jewel.

Life pods are designed to dump you out of nine-space, fast. You can end up anywhere.

My throat hurt.

Pack was shaking me now, spittle flecking his chin.

I wondered about that plane. The black globes moved closer –

I sipped hot broth, hanging like a chrysalis in my sleeping bag. 'Thanks,' I said to the passenger. The single word filled my chest with pain.

Over the tube of broth I surveyed what was left of my world. The interior of the pod was a two-metre-wide cylinder crusted with equipment lockers. It was tight as a coffin after the ship's wide corridors.

Pack was sorting through one of the lockers, muscles moving over his turned back. The passenger had his wiry body pressed up against a clear section of wall, fingers spread out against the bare metal. His eyes flickered between us. 'Thank you,' he said to me. His vacuum-wrecked voice was like sandpaper. 'You saved my life. Thank you both.'

I didn't recognize him. He was about my age, with thin hair stained grey. He was nervy, pale – a typical city dweller . . . But his eyes were like independent creatures, shrewd little animals peering out of his skull.

'My name's Moore,' I said. 'The ship's doctor.'

He nodded. 'Windle. I'm a household bot service engineer.

I'm – I was – heading for a job in the new colony at Tau Ceti III . . . and this is Mr –'

Pack rattled bits of equipment around the locker with growing violence.

'. . . Pack,' I said quickly.

At the mention of his name Pack slammed closed the locker. His face was a broad mask of resentment. 'We've got to talk,' he snarled.

Windle tried to shrink further into his wall.

'What's the problem?' I asked.

Pack spat: 'He is.'

I sighed. We'd only been in that pod an hour or so, but already the atmosphere was wire-taut. 'Okay, Pack. Tell us the worst.'

'He's told you, hasn't he?' Windle broke in, his eyes widened to red circles. 'I'm the problem. He tried to close the door in my face. He'd rather have left me behind . . .'

Pack's voice was brittle. 'Look – we're stranded in the middle of nowhere. This pod was designed for two men . . . to drop them out of nine-space, and then lift them back up and get them somewhere safe.

'We just don't have the fuel cells for three. There's nothing to be done about it.'

Windle cowered – but the trapped little creatures looking out of his eyes were studying Pack.

I pushed my bulk out of my bag and tried to break up the tension with a bit of bedside manner. 'Come on, Pack. That's not the end of the story. I know these pods are equipped with spare cells.'

'What do you think I've been searching for?' He held out twenty or thirty card-thin slices of ceramic – superconductor circuit cells. 'This is all I could find. And they're all uncharged.'

'Well, we're bound to have recharge equipment aboard.'

'Yes, but –' Pack growled with frustration. 'Even so, there's still only enough for two . . . with a safety margin. There isn't enough for three.' Muscles worked in his cheeks and arms. I was aware that he was half the age of Windle and me . . . and certainly stronger than the two of us together.

I said carefully: 'Isn't enough . . . or mightn't be enough? Which is it, Pack?'

His square face closed up. 'Don't play word games, doctor,' he shouted. 'There's enough for two. And that's it.'

Windle's mouth worked. 'You're lying, aren't you?'

'You've no right to be here, groundhog.' Pack was a block of muscle looming over Windle; the passenger glared back, quivering.

I stared at them, trying to decide what to say next.

Men like Pack – solid, reliable – are the backbone of Earth's merchant fleet. I reminded myself that he'd risked his life to save mine. He wasn't vicious, or a coward . . . but he'd probably hardly left the ship since signing up at sixteen.

It's a simple environment. It produces simple priorities.

'Let's slow down a little,' I said. 'Look, Pack, I know the drill as well as you do. We have recharge equipment for these fuel cells. I say we break it out, load up all the cells . . . and try to save all three of us.'

Pack's fists clenched, but he said nothing. I felt a flicker of hope. Maybe I could handle him, protect Windle long enough to get us all out of this.

But Windle seemed to be doing his own calculations. His black eyes peered at us over his bony nose. 'Let me just get this straight. Even if we charge up the cells . . . even then there mightn't be enough power for the three of us?' He nodded, as if absorbing the logic of the situation, and he and Pack eyed each other like mismatched cats.

'No more talk. Let's give it a try,' I said. 'Come on, Pack. Show us what we have to do.' Briskly I opened up the wall lockers, searching for a suit that would fit around my middle-aged midriff.

After a time, the others did the same.

Pack led the way out of the pod. He pulled himself briskly around the hull's sharp curves searching for equipment caches. I followed, my shadow stretching ahead of me. Windle came last, fiddling with a simple portable analyzer he'd found in one of the lockers.

I found myself panting already in the unfamiliar confines of a spacesuit. I checked my watch. In another universe I would have just finished my afternoon rounds . . .

To hell with that. I stared straight ahead and concentrated on moving.

Pack had found propulsion belts; now he pulled one on and clipped a ceramic fuel cell to it.

'The cell charger is a sunlight collector, isn't it?' I asked.

Pack studied the hull with an engineer's measuring eye. 'Yeah. A parabolic reflector, with the cells at the focus. When we set it up it'll be a couple of kilometres across – a semi-rigid frame we have to spray with all-wavelength reflector skin.'

'Right.'

He turned to face the star behind me. 'We're falling towards that stellar system,' he said. 'So we trail the reflector behind us, spinning it for stability –'

I turned for the first time.

I'd forgotten about the wall across the sky I'd seen from the pod window. Now I was facing it. I stopped listening.

There was a blood-red ocean that stretched to darkness at all sides, hiding the stars. And set at its centre was a sun, sliced neatly in half by the plane.

'I thought I was dreaming,' I breathed.

Windle was waving his analyzer around, one foot jammed in a handhold. 'No dream,' he said. 'God knows where we are – but this is a T Tauri. A very young star, surrounded by that disc of red-hot debris.'

'I guess the star's heating up the disc.'

'Not completely. The disc shines by its own power – from gravitational collapse, and even a little fusion.

'Three times as wide as the solar system. A fifth the Sun's mass. And giving off as much energy at all wavelengths as Sol itself.'

'How do you know all this, Windle?'

He grinned. 'Self-taught. I didn't want to spend my whole life with my head stuck inside broken-down bots. So I worked and I learned . . . and I saved enough to make it out here. To see this.'

'Yeah.' The plane of rubies glistened in his faceplate. 'Yes,' I said, 'I know how you feel.'

He studied the analyzer. 'Of course there are a few anomalies.'

'Like what?'

'A ring structure. See?'

He pointed, and I could just make out a thin gap in the infinite disc. Stars peeked through.

'So what? Saturn has a disc of debris with a ring structure –'

'Put there by the tidal effects of its moons. Maybe a Jovian planet here could have the same effect –' He swept the analyzer around his head. 'But there's no Jovian! So how did the rings get there?

'And another thing. Most of the disc is just fine dust, as you'd expect. But around the gaps there are boulders, consistently sized a few metres across. Now how could they have formed? And –'

A dull clang shook the hull. Over the pod's tiny horizon, Pack was opening up lockers and hauling out equipment. 'You two hogs going to work, or do I dump you right here?' His limbs moved like steel rods, suffused with impatience.

Windle fumbled to stow away the analyzer – but I thought I saw him grinning at Pack's anger inside his helmet.

Well, I didn't want to know about that. I grabbed his arm and pulled him after me.

After three hours the prefabricated skeleton of the reflector had grown to a lacy veil draped across the Tauri disc. It was already half a kilometre wide.

Pack called a break.

I lashed my can of reflector spray to a semi-rigid strut and jammed myself back into the pod. We stripped off our suits, releasing a satisfactory stink of sweat.

'We're doing okay,' I said, having a luxurious scratch. 'Okay.'

Pack silently worked a strained muscle as he prepared

himself a coffee. Windle was huddled in one corner studying his analyzer's display. For a while, we had a little peace.

It didn't last.

Windle came bustling over to the locker I was searching for food. He waved his analyzer. 'Look at this,' he whispered, his sly eyes flickering at Pack. 'Life! Or at least the complex molecules and necessary conditions – all in the disc of the T Tauri.' He poked at the analyzer's tiny keyboard. 'I suppose the complex material is left over from previous generations of stars . . . makes you wonder if this has anything to do with those other puzzles – you know, the strange fragment size and the gaps in the disc. And another thing –'

I watched Pack uneasily. His tube-like fingers were whitening on his coffee cup, every high-pitched word of Windle's winding him up tighter.

Windle was goading Pack deliberately, I realized. 'Maybe later,' I said to Windle as urgently as I could. 'Later. Okay?'

Pack's fingers stretched out like a cat's claws. 'Yeah, maybe you should shut your rattling mouth, groundhog –'

Windle cowered back – but he said sharply, 'It might pay you to listen to a bit more.'

I moved between them hastily. 'All this tension's wearing me out,' I said. 'If you've got something on your mind just tell us, Windle.'

He brandished his analyzer. 'According to this we'll hit the Tauri disc in about six hours.'

Pack said, 'So?'

'So will we have finished with your umbrella thing by then? No? And how well do you think the umbrella will survive a passage through the disc?'

Pack's square face clenched up every time he said 'umbrella'.

I thought it over. 'He's got a point, Pack,' I said reluctantly. 'So what do we do? Come on, Windle. Don't play games.'

'We deflect,' he said quickly. 'We've got a limited three-space drive, haven't we? We furl up the umbrella, deflect, and go through one of the gaps we observed.'

Pack shook his head. 'Waste of energy. The fuel cells –'

'We can always recharge the cells on the other side,' I said. 'And we might not survive otherwise. We'll have to go over the figures, Pack.'

He shook his head, stiff with hatred.

But we checked the figures – and there was no other way through. Pack had to give in.

So we suited up again. Pack rammed his fists into his suit sleeves while Windle hummed contentedly to himself – just loud enough for Pack to hear.

We descended towards the gap, the rolled-up reflector trailing behind us.

The disc foreshortened as we approached. Eventually I could make out detail – not individual fragments, but clumps of varying density in the ruddy swirl. Half a sun sat like a dome at the heart of the disc; long shadows swept towards us, cast by the scurrying clumps.

Windle jammed himself and his analyzer to the single port, staring out like a kid. 'There's such a lot of detail, such structure,' he said, his breath misting up the port. 'It's like a smeared-out world out there. Full of organic molecules . . .'

Pack was a slab of muscle anchored by one hand to a strut. He stared incuriously ahead, simply waiting for the transit to finish.

Windle lapsed into silence. Our breaths were the only sound as we descended, the light shifting through the cabin.

And then the transit was upon us.

We fell into shadows a million miles long. A crimson band swept upwards past the pod. I got a glimpse of detail, a sea of gritty rubble . . . with a few odd, smoothed-over shapes gliding through it –

Windle scrabbled excitedly at his analyzer. 'Do you see that?' he asked with real joy. 'My God – my God –'

I had to laugh at his enthusiasm. 'See what? Show me.'

'Those creatures . . .'

Suddenly what I was watching clicked into place; my sense of scale exploded outwards.

Those pale forms drifting through the plane of the disc like kilometre-long whales ... They weren't drifting, I realized now. They were swimming.

Each whale-thing was a bloated cylinder moving inexorably through the crimson mush. The wall-like flanks were broken by huge vents that opened and closed like mouths, and around the vents the flesh was studded with deep pits.

We peered into one pit. At its bottom was something very like an eye. It looked back at us ...

Then we dropped out of the disc. The bottom half of the sun was dazzling. The disc detail closed up again to a washed-out uniformity.

'Those things were alive,' I breathed.

Windle shook his head, bemused. 'I suppose it makes sense. There's plenty of organic material in there ... and in places the disc material is warm and dense – quite a comfortable ocean. I guess the lack of gravity would encourage the development of large structures. But who would have thought it?' His thin face was flushed with an analytical wonder. 'Look, here,' he went on. 'They suck in debris through those vents ... They must leach out organic material – maybe even simpler creatures, the plankton of this strange sea.'

He expanded the scale on his analyzer. There were hundreds of whales, streaming through space. 'A school,' said Windle. 'Eating their way through their orbit around the sun.'

'I guess that explains the gaps in the disc.'

Windle laughed. 'So we owe those space whales our lives. I guess eventually they could consume the whole disc ... maybe these whales play a part in the formation of planets ... But we still have one puzzle, the strange fragment sizes which –'

'Enough,' Pack growled. He was already forcing his huge frame into a suit. 'We're through the disc. We get back to work.'

'Tell me later,' I said gently to Windle. I started towards the suit lockers – but Windle froze. Ideas chased across his clever face; his eyes narrowed and he grabbed Pack's arm. 'Listen,' he said quickly. 'When we've charged up the cells – do we need to go straight back?'

Pack stared unbelieving at him – and at the hand resting like a spider on his huge forearm.

'I mean, we could do another transit of the disc and get more data . . . this is quite a discovery.'

'You crazy groundhog,' said Pack, his face clenched like a fist. 'Who the hell cares about whales?'

I jumped across the little cabin and pulled Windle away. 'Shut up and get your damn suit on.'

Once outside, I touched my helmet to Windle's so Pack wouldn't hear us.

'Listen,' I said angrily. 'I know things are kind of tense – but we're all still here, and working together. We don't need much more time. If you could just avoid . . . irritating him, I'm sure we can get Pack to accept –'

'No.' His voice came out of a helmet filled with shadow. 'In his eyes I'm a dead man. A useless groundhog.'

'Maybe . . . but you don't have to act the part.'

'Save it, doctor. I know you mean well, but listen: you can't help me. You don't even need to help me. I'm a survivor. I worked my way out of the mess I was born into, didn't I? – and I'll work my way out of this.'

His words were chilling. They were a statement of fact.

I tried again. 'But all three of us might make it.'

'Might.' He began moving away. 'But Pack doesn't want to take that risk, does he? And maybe I don't, either.'

He moved away smoothly, determined and composed.

When we returned to the pod, Windle took some time packing up a tool. Pack and I found ourselves briefly alone.

Now it was our turn to touch helmets. 'Doc . . .' His voice was a violent growl. 'That groundhog's driving me crazy. I say we shut the door now.'

I closed my eyes. 'We can't just kill him.'

'He's killing us. Without him we'd have a safety margin.'

'Yeah. Maybe . . .' Suddenly it all descended on me, hard. There'd been the shock of the wreck itself, which I'd striven to put out of my mind ... and then Pack's dull obstinacy, Windle's almost fanatical will to survive.

I gave up. I suddenly felt old, fat, tired. 'So what do we do? Draw straws? Have we got any straws? Maybe straws are standard equipment on a lifeboat –'

'You can do what you want, doc, but I'm pulling no straws. One berth in this boat's mine ...' His voice tailed off. 'Where is he?'

'Huh?'

He stared at me. 'How come he's so slow?' He hung there for a moment ... then dived cleanly to the door.

Our nearly-finished structure was a net of silent shadows. There was no sign of Windle.

I shrugged. 'Do you think he's in trouble? Maybe got stuck –'

Pack was unblinking. 'The groundhog wanted to go back to the disc, didn't he? Go back and take snapshots of the whales.'

'But how could he? He only took a propulsion belt ...'

Pack opened up a locker. 'And more than half our spare fuel cells,' he said softly.

He floated there for a few seconds, a single muscle ticking beneath the surface of his cheek as he thought.

'We take the pod back,' he said slowly. 'We furl up the damn reflector, again, and we take the pod back after him. We've enough cells left for that.' His voice grew brisker, as if in relief that the crisis was finally here.

I hesitated. 'I hate to say this, but ... why don't you just leave him? That was what you wanted.'

'Because we need the cells he's taken. No. We follow him back to the disc. Then,' simply, 'I kill him. We take the cells. We recharge them, and leave here. Yes. That's what we've got to do.'

As he spoke, his claw fingers were flexing inside spacesuit gloves.

I prepared to turn the pod around. I didn't know what else to do.

*   *   *

I dug another hand-held analyzer out of a locker, worked out how to use it well enough to track Windle.

Once more we hurtled towards the disc, a mote tumbling to a vast red carpet. The gap grew from a band of starlight to a ragged-edged highway, full of detail.

It wasn't hard to find the school of whales working methodically through their cold ocean. We dropped amongst them and buzzed around their mottled flanks, Pack cursing as more of our precious energy was wasted.

I stared out in awe. Whales loomed around us like nightmares, great living walls sliding past the sun. Jaws larger than the whole pod worked steadily at the sparkling debris around us, and eyes metres across studied us as we passed.

'There!' I said at last, pointing at a fluttering spark ahead of the school. 'There he is. Jesus, he's going in close –'

'Right.' Pack snapped shut his suit and clipped fuel cells to his belt.

'Pack, listen –'

He didn't. With a surprising grace he rolled out of the pod and arrowed past the whales.

Windle saw us coming, of course – even through the ruby fog it was hard to miss a partly-rolled silver parasol two kilometres long – and when he saw Pack leave the pod he began moving.

I turned up the magnification on my analyzer. Windle had been hovering at random before the school. Now he moved – clumsily but purposefully – towards the blunt prow of the nearest whale.

The great animal worked through the mist like some vast machine, utterly oblivious to the tiny creature flitting around it –

– and to a second which now appeared before it, for Pack had seen Windle's move and had arced in front of the whale. Now Windle was trapped between the multiple mouths of the beast and the equally deadly hands of Pack.

Pack slowed to a halt – relative to the whale – and hung there in space, a great block of muscle gently beckoning to Windle.

Windle hovered before the animal for a moment, and I studied him, baffled. Surely he realized he'd trapped himself – it was almost as if he'd done it deliberately . . .

Windle raised a hand to his face. I upped the magnification on my analyzer.

He was thumbing his nose at Pack.

I cringed –

– and now Pack came hurtling into the image. Misty debris swirled and sparked in his wake, and his hands were outstretched like talons.

Windle, with sudden skill, flipped over backward and blasted away from Pack as fast as his belt would take him, and straight into a massive mouth. He curled into a ball and disappeared.

Pack realized what he was heading for. He fell past an eye pit and tried to brake, stopping just inside the lips of those huge lips. He scrabbled at the cold surface of the skin – and then the great lid slammed shut over his lower body.

Something splashed over the pallid surface. Pack's head jerked back, once. I couldn't see his face. Then he fell out of sight.

So it was over. With dark stains congealing around one vent, the whale moved on. The agitated knots it left behind in the disc debris began to smooth and clear.

I heard a voice.

'Moore?' Coughing. 'Doctor Moore? Can you hear me?'

'Windle? Where the hell are you?'

A weak laugh. 'Where do you think I am? Just on the sunny side of the whale's . . . rear end. But I . . . could you . . .'

'Leave your carrier wave on. I'll track you.'

I grabbed my propulsion belt.

When I found him he was still curled up in a foetal ball. His passage through the whale's digestive system had left his suit crusted with bits of hot rock, and half the bones in his body had been broken, as if he'd been wadded up like a tissue. But the suit had held. And he was alive.

'It was those odd-sized fragments that gave me the clue,' he said faintly. He sipped at a coffee, huddled inside his sleeping cocoon. 'They were too big, too consistent a size, to have formed by chance. And when I saw the whales . . .'

'You realized the fragments were whale droppings.'

'Yeah. And if the creatures passed chunks that size, then provided a man entered one of those vents fast enough – to avoid ingesting muscles at the front – then he'd have a fighting chance of making it right through the whale's system.' He laughed, and winced in pain. 'It was fast, hot, dark, tight – but I lived through it. Call me Jonah.'

'Yeah.' I put a bit of hardness into my voice. 'Shame about Pack.'

His battered face showed traces of a sneer. 'Well, he wasn't exactly the type to think through a situation like that. And I didn't force him to chase me.'

'Didn't you?'

He shrugged and turned away. 'Anyway, I guess we've solved the problem of who's going home and who's not.'

I recoiled from the casual chill of his words. 'You know, I felt sorry for you. I tried to protect you. But I was wrong, wasn't I? The way you goaded and provoked him, systematically – Pack never stood a chance.'

He coughed and clutched at his ribs. 'I don't need to listen to this.'

'Well, what now?' I demanded. 'Do you still want to go back and study the whales?'

He coughed again, a little blood flecking his lip. 'Whales? For Christ's sake, unfurl the umbrella and let's go home. I've won. Who the hell cares about whales?'

There was nothing more to say. I turned away and began to suit up.

DOWNSTREAM

'Stone! *Stone . . .'*

Even as she called to him the voice of his mother was failing, attenuating into the silence of Downstream.

Keeping his fingers and toes jammed into the rock of the Floor, he lifted his head and looked Downstream. The current battered the back of his skull.

His mother held up her arms to him, the fingers which had failed her outstretched. Her face, with its halo of greying hair, sank like a dream into the unattainable Downstream.

Already, in mere heartbeats, she was lost, much too far Downstream for anyone to climb down to her and return.

'I'll always love you!' he cried.

When his mother fell he'd been feeding on a fat tube-spider egg. He'd spotted the Larva trapping the egg moments earlier.

The Larva was a cylinder of translucent flesh, fixed to the Floor with a circlet of fine hooks. Its body was much taller than a man's, and it reached far into Midstream, away from the Floor; pale, feathery fans, fluttering in the Stream, grabbed at the fine morsels of food that tumbled down from the unknowable Upstream.

The Larva supported the little linear colony of fifty adults and children. The Larva's pickings from Midstream were much more nutritious than the fragments which bowled along in the stale currents close to the Floor.

One day the Larva would unpin its hook-roots and swim off Downstream, on its way to its next, unknowable, stage of life. The people would have to follow it – gingerly clambering Downstream – or die.

Stones-of-Ice had climbed cautiously along the body of the patient, insensate Larva, reaching for the fans. He'd avoided the Larva's flicking tongue as it patiently coated the fans with sticky mucus. He took the egg from the outstretched fans and edged away from the Larva, clambering over the backs of the people. They clung to their tenuous holds, fingers and toes anchored deep in the rock, heads bent against the current. Infants squirmed, tucked securely between bodies and rock Floor; they lapped at the tiny pool-drops of water which clung to the rock face.

Stone had passed Flower-of-Bones, his kid sister, and broke off a piece of the egg for her. Flower was so named after a particularly spectacular configuration of bones, not even remotely human, which had come drifting down from Upstream on the day she was born. He had given her the egg, and Flower had grinned at him around a sticky mouthful. As she ate she pressed the palm of her hand against her mouth, so that her long fingers reached up and over her scalp, like a mask of pink flesh.

. . . And then his mother had fallen.

'*Stone* . . . '

Receding rapidly she was still calling to him, still pointing. He saw the dull sparkle of her necklace as a point of light in the Downstream darkness. The necklace was a thing of chitin bits threaded on rope – crude and precious. He remembered how she'd taken him to the Larva as an infant, helped him reach up for his first succulent morsels.

He would never see her again.

He probed at his feelings. He was wistful, he supposed, but not sad; old age – *losing hold* – came to them all, in the end.

But she seemed, even now, to be pointing. And not at him. *Past* him.

He raised his face into the oncoming Stream. The invisible substance battered his cheeks, but he breathed easily; the air which sustained him was a still, superfluid component of this swirling, endless flow. He peered Upstream. Perhaps his mother had espied some rainstorm, plummeting towards them from the unreachable Upstream. A storm cloud could be deadly – fat with raindrops and laden with electricity – and they would have to shelter. But, ultimately, a cloud would be a thing to be welcomed: the rain replenished the life-giving sheen of water droplets, clinging to the Floor by surface tension, which kept them all alive . . .

Then he saw it. Not a cloud, not even a hailstorm of the type which had given him his name. Something far stranger came tumbling along the Floor: an ungainly corpse from some community far Upstream, impossibly long limbs flailing. And it came *straight at Flower-of-Bones.*

Flower – and his father – hadn't noticed the incoming danger. But even as she fell his mother had tried to warn him.

'*No!*'

He lifted himself away from the Floor. The Stream battered at his chest. He scrabbled sideways across the Floor, jabbing his fingers and toes carelessly into gaps in the crumbling rock.

Once he lost his footing; for an instant he clung by one hand to the rock, his legs dangling, his body flapping against the surface. But he hauled himself back to the Floor and scrambled on, careless of the danger. He had to reach Flower before that tumbling corpse.

'Flower! *Flower!*'

He clambered over the patient line of people, past his father, grabbing for holds at shoulders and hair. Flower was just beyond his reach, now. She'd seen the corpse and she screamed, bits of egg still clinging to her chin and mouth.

He risked a single glance Upstream. The corpse, angular, suited in a carapace of armour, was close enough for him to see into its staring, eyeless skull-sockets.

He grabbed Flower. He wrenched her away from the Floor and lifted her high into the Stream. She wriggled, limbs fluttering in the current. Stone arced her, one-armed, back over his body and brought her down into the arms of his father.

His father wrapped his arms around Flower, pinning her tight.

Stone looked up.

The skull-face of the Upstream corpse, peering from an outlandish helmet, plunged straight at him.

The body engulfed him, a spider of bones and chitin armour. Long, multi-jointed limbs wrapped themselves around him. He felt angular elbows, lumps of decayed, feathery flesh, dig into his back.

The skull was long and distorted; the remains of vast lips flapped before his face. He screamed, squirming, trying to push the thing off him.

He lost his grip.

He fell upwards, away from the Floor. The Stream snatched at him, harder than he had imagined; it seemed to wrap a fist of pressure around his chest. The bony, distorted corpse fell away from him, folding over itself.

He reached below him, trying to turn –

But the Floor was out of reach.

He swivelled, turning his face Upstream. Already his people were falling away from him, a row of skinny bodies clinging to the Floor around the waving tube of the Larva. He saw – or imagined he saw – the faces of his father, of Flower, turned down to him in shock.

He heard the voice of his father, drifting Downstream to him. 'We'll always love you . . .'

That was all. Soon the murk of distance enclosed even the Larva's tubular form.

Midstream was cold, silent, empty save for food-fragments which drifted around him; the lichen-glow of the Floor picked out only the corpse from far Upstream, his sole, grinning companion.

No-one could travel Upstream. He would never see his people again. He stared into the unending darkness of Downstream.

So, in heartbeats, his life had ended.

The Upstream corpse tumbled as it fell alongside him. It was almost graceful in its slow, languid movements – but it was impossibly alien: its arms and legs were twice the length of Stone's, and its fingers – reduced to chains of bones – were thin and multi-jointed.

The face, with its immense, rotting lips, looked as if it was designed to clamp onto the Floor surface. Stone imagined a long tongue, prehensile itself, flicking out of that ugly mouth and delving for food deep into fine cracks in the Floor; perhaps the mouth would be strong enough to hold the body against the flow of current itself. The head, torso and legs were encased in sheets and tubes of armour – chitin from some animal, softly luminescent, stitched together.

Someone had killed this strange warrior and sent it tumbling Downstream.

Warrior? It was more like a spider, Stone thought with disgust. Stone's people were *real* humans – the original form which had emerged from the Crash, spilling into the Stream so long ago. This spider-warrior – and its stranger cousins from even further Upstream – were aberrations. Mutants.

He lifted his knees to his chest and wrapped his arms around his legs, letting the Stream buffet him, apathetic.

Far Upstream, there were huge, strange communities. Vast wars were fought. Sometimes bodies rained down from Upstream, thicker than food fragments.

How the spider-folk lived – and what their battles were about – no-one could know, of course. It was impossible to climb Upstream to find out. And only once in Stone's memory had a living human ever travelled down the Stream to Stone's people – another wounded soldier, one arm severed, eyes bloodied and staring. It had sailed over Stone, screaming insane curses; Stone had cowered against the Floor, in the shelter of his father's arms . . .

A touch at his back.

At first it was feather-light, almost ticklish. Then, in an instant, it became firm, enclosing, grasping; it felt as if he had been wrapped in a hundred thin, sticky ropes.

He struggled, opening out his limbs. Clinging threads stretched between his legs and pinned his arms to his body. *Spider-web.*

The web was a broad cylinder, anchored to the Floor. Its

mouth was wide but the web funnelled rapidly into a narrow neck. The webbing stretched, elastic, hauling him down from the Stream. He fell into the neck; the walls of the web-tube were soft, warm, yielding. Floor-lichen light filled the web, making it a corridor of spectral beauty.

Damn. Was it over so quickly? How could he have been so stupid? A spider-web was visible enough; if he'd been watching, he'd have had plenty of time to swim up and out of the way.

The gauzy webbing seemed only to tighten as he struggled.

After a few heartbeats he gave up; he relaxed in the enfolding grip of the web, letting its sticky, half-alive substance wrap tighter around his legs.

His breath slowed. Gradually, his mood softened; soon he felt strangely at peace. Since losing his grip on the Floor he'd been doomed anyway. It was comfortable here, in a way even secure. The web was soft, mistily pretty . . .

At least it was *done*. His endless, purposeless fall through the Stream was finished. No more questions; no more hope; no more events. He closed his eyes. Perhaps he'd be able to slide quietly into insensibility as the lack of food overcame him . . .

The web shuddered.

. . . And again, rattling him in his cage of sticky web-stuff. His muscles clenched. His eyes snapped open.

The spider. It was coming at him, spiralling out from the throat of the web, clambering around the widening walls. Its legs flickered, long, feathery, and that mouth – with mandibles endlessly scissoring – would slip easily around Stone's head.

His elegiac acceptance vanished, washed away into the Downstream of his awareness. Suddenly, vividly, *he did not want to die.* He lunged against the web bonds, screaming, causing the web itself to ripple. But his struggles seemed only to add strength to the webbing around him.

The spider's body was coated in fine, white hairs; a ghastly moustache of fur lined its mouth, meat particles clinging . . .

'Stone. *Stone!*'

Flower's voice? He was dreaming, of course; fantasizing – and now the spider was close, close –

He stared into that mouth, his fear fading into fascination. He wondered how long a snipped-off head would remain aware, as it tumbled into the pit of digestive juices inside the spider.

A ripping sound, behind him; a small, warm hand scrabbling over his back. 'Stone! You've got to get out of there!'

He twisted his head, straining his trapped neck. '*Flower-of-Bones?*'

His sister was clinging to the outside of the web, strands of the stuff trailing from her lithe limbs. She was hacking at the web with a chip of smashed-off Floor. She looked into his eyes, her sweet, familiar face creased with anxiety.

Energy, urgency flooded him. He got a leg free. He kicked at the webbing, scraping the stuff away from his other leg. Flower cut through the web around one arm; he took her scraper and dragged the crude edge through the webbing around his other arm, careless of gouges in his flesh.

He pushed his way backwards – at last – out of the web. Strands clung to his flesh, stretching, as if nostalgic for his presence.

The jaws of the spider loomed over the hole in the web. Mandibles protruded from that sightless sketch of a face, seeking the spider's lost meal; then a long, black tongue began to lick at the webbing, extruding new strands to plate over the gap the humans had wrought.

Stone clutched Flower to him, relishing her warm, familiar scent.

Then, hand in hand, they let themselves fall away from the web and tumble Downstream.

Above and around them there was only the darkness of the endless, infinite, unknowable Midstream. Below them was the Floor, its coat of lichen softly glowing, its rocky surface worn smooth by the current.

Flower was staring down moodily. 'I wonder where it comes from.'

'What?'

'The Stream.' Her face was round, child-like – well, she *was* still a child – but there was a calm depth, an intelligence there.

He smiled at her, in the manner of an adult. 'The Stream is a mixture of two fluids,' he told her. 'The bulk of it is a *superfluid* – stationary, light and frictionless – and that's the part that contains the air we breathe. The rest of the Stream is a viscous mass, flowing at high speed, and that's what we *feel* as the Stream – that's what is sweeping us along like this. The two components flow *through* each other; it's as if they were two separate Streams in the same space, in fact. And it's just as well for us that they are separate, for we couldn't draw breath if we had to take our air from the viscous part of the Stream, and –'

'That's not what I asked,' she said, sounding irritated.

He was disconcerted. 'What?'

'Oh, come on, Stones-of-Ice. All you're doing is parroting what Father used to tell us –'

'*Parroting?*' He was appalled at her disrespect. 'But this is learning which has survived since the Crash itself.'

'Yes,' she said with strained patience, 'but it's not telling me anything I want to *know.*' She stared into the huge, empty volumes around them. 'I want to know where the Stream comes from – where it's going to. Where would *we* end up, if we never went down to the Floor again?'

'We'd end up dead,' he said practically. 'Starved.'

'Where did *people* come from? How did they get here? Are there people all the way Downstream, forever and ever? And all the way Upstream as well?'

'We'll never know.' Questions like these occasionally occurred to Stone, but they never troubled him. The Stream was just *there*, all around him. It gave his world its framework: *Downstream* was forever separated from *here*, which was forever separated from *Upstream* – as surely as his own childhood was separated from him forever by the flow of time.

'But why *can't* we know?'

She looked at him, and suddenly he felt embarrassed that he could not give her an answer.

He felt resentful. He owed his life to his sister, but – he realized slowly – she might actually be smarter than he was. It wasn't a comfortable thought –

Flower-of-Bones gasped. She pointed, pulling Stone closer to her.

Suddenly, the Floor wasn't featureless . . . There were *people* here, unimaginably far Downstream as they were, great sheets of them clinging to the rock like human lichen.

In wordless panic brother and sister clawed at the thin, powerful Stream, trying to swim up and away from the Floor and deeper into Midstream.

They were suspended over a city of squat chitin buildings, of structures of rope and web, bright lichen-pits hacked into the Floor . . . and dozens, hundreds of people. It was a community unimaginably larger than the simple huddle of folk they'd left Upstream.

Flower whispered, 'Do you think they can see us?'

'No. I don't think so. Even if they could, they can't reach us.' He thought it over. 'Although it might be better if they could.'

She looked at him, her face round and troubled. 'What do you mean?'

Gently, he said, 'Sooner or later we're going to have to go down again, to the Floor. We'll starve up here. And it might be better to land where there are already people. They might take us in. Help us. We can't survive alone, Flower.'

Flower grimaced, pulling a comical face at Stone. 'But not here. Not with them. They're so *ugly*.'

From up here the Floor-city people looked like squat animals, burrowing into the rock. Flower held up her own free hand, stretching her long fingers; she curled the fingers back over themselves, letting the tips touch the back of her hands. 'Look at those people. Stubby fingers and toes, round little heads, tubes for bellies. It's amazing they can get a grip of the Floor at all.'

He patted her arm affectionately. 'If you think like that you shouldn't have come after me.'

'It's just as well I did, spider-morsel. You wouldn't have lasted five heartbeats without me.'

'I know that.' He meant it; he wished he had some way of expressing it better. His sister had sacrificed everything – her parents, her people, her life itself – to fall Downstream, irrevocably, after her brother.

He searched his heart, hoping that if their positions had been reversed he would have found the courage to do the same thing.

She pointed. 'Look down there. See, those tube-shapes moving along the ropes?'

Stone squinted. The translucent tubes, twice as tall as he was, edged their way through the webbing of ropes. He thought he could see people, curled up inside the moving tubes; but that was impossible, of course, for the tubes looked like –

Like *larvae*. Unfamiliar forms – perhaps different species from those he was used to – but, yes, they were larvae! And people were *riding inside* them, in what looked like perfect comfort! Why, with such a steed it might even be possible to move Upstream – a little way anyway. And –

And, he wondered wistfully, how would it be to shelter one's head, one's aching lungs – if only for a short while – from the endless buffeting pressure of the Stream?

The city grew sparser, with wide patches of dull Floor between the scattered settlements. At last they were sailing over bare rock once more, and the lights of the city flattened into the distance.

Flower pointed at the Floor Downstream. 'Look. I think it's a net farm.'

Stone – still dreaming of larva-riding – twisted and looked down.

The nets lined the Floor, a family of them in a neat array, with their faces turned patiently Upstream. The nearest net was a translucent disc, barely visible in the lichen-light; it quivered as bits of current-borne waste pounded into its fine structure.

'You're right,' he said. 'Come on; let's go down.'

They struggled through the Stream, clawing at its thin, powerful substance with their hands.

Stone dropped against the Floor, a little way Upstream from the largest net. He let his fingers and long toes pry deep into the rock face, grasping at fine crevices; the Floor was hard, warm, familiar against his chest, and he felt secure for the first time since he'd lost his grip.

Flower-of-Bones landed beside him. He patted her hand. 'Let's see what we can get to eat.'

Fingers and toes working, they swarmed along the Floor, Downstream towards the farm.

Flower pointed, silently, past the first net. Beyond, the solitary farmer-beetle was labouring at its crop. The beetle's squat body was pressed flat against the Floor, smooth and streamlined; its blind head, raised into the flow, moved in steady figures-of-eight as it wove its nets.

Stone and Flower crept towards a net far from the beetle.

The net bulged in the Stream, laden with scraps. Stone wrapped the sticky threads around his hands and pulled himself to his knees, letting the flow of the Stream press him securely against the net. He found meat, bits of larvae, eggs. Much of it was decayed, of course, and some – from far Upstream – was too unfamiliar even to be safe to try. But he found some reasonably fresh fragments. He pulled a piece of spider-limb from the net – it came away with a soft plop – and passed it to Flower. He crammed a second piece into his mouth. Juices slipped down his chin as he chewed, pulling more food from the net . . .

Flower screamed.

He whirled. He dropped his bits of food – they went sailing over the net rim and Downstream – and he fell backwards against the net.

Two people had come upon them – two adults, a woman and a man. The woman was already lying over Flower, pinning her face-down against the Floor, easily suppressing his sister's struggles. The woman grinned, her skull round and feral. The man crawled along the Floor towards Stone. He was grim-faced, his head shaven crudely; he carried a knife of Floor-rock in his teeth, and his eyes were fixed on Stone.

He was only heartbeats away.

Stone stared, transfixed. The hunter's fingers were short, flat-tipped, and his toes mere stubs; his chest was round, scraping awkwardly against the Floor. But he moved powerfully; Stone would never be able to match such strength. And he wore a necklet – a crude thing, of chitin threaded on rope.

His mother's.

Was it possible? Had his mother – old, too feeble to grip – fallen among these people?

And – he found himself wondering with horror – had she been already dead when she arrived here?

The knife, underlit by the Floor lichen, cast a deep shadow upwards over the hunter's flat nose. There was no anger in that face, Stone realized, just – *anticipation*. Suddenly Stone saw himself through this man's pale eyes – as something weak, barely human, from the far Upstream – as *meat*.

The man pressed his legs flat against the Floor and raised his upper body. He lifted the knife high over Stone's face. Stone stared at the knife, saw each detail of its chipped, crudely sharpened edge.

Flower, somewhere, was screaming –

No. *It wasn't Flower*.

The man flattened himself against the Floor, shoving his knife between his teeth. He twisted, trying to see what was going on.

The woman still lay atop Flower. But she was scrabbling at her back, sharp teeth glinting in lichen-light.

A pole of wood, a *spear*, protruded from her back.

Flower lurched to her knees. The woman was thrown off, rolling sideways. The spear shaft scraped against the Floor. As the woman fell on the shaft there was a soft, obscene sound of *tearing* – the woman's eyes opened wide, seeing nothing, and her mouth stretched silently – and then the shaft broke with a sharp snap.

Head lolling, the woman fell upwards, away from the Floor. The spear shaft tumbled after her, lost in a moment.

Stone turned back to the man, raising his arms – but the hunter had already gone, scrambling sideways over the surface.

Stone lay flat against the Floor and wormed his way to his sister. Her toes and fingers dug deep in the rock, she was crying and shuddering. Stone was aware of the tightness of his own throat, the trembling of his taut muscles. He wrapped an arm over her thin back, pressing Flower securely against the Floor. 'It's all right,' he whispered. 'They're gone.'

There was a hand on his shoulder. 'Yes, but there must be more of them. And they'll be back –'

Stone twisted his neck, scraping his cheek on the Floor.

A woman – squat, with spadelike fingers – lay against the Floor beside him. She was smiling at him. She lifted her arm from his shoulder, showing him her empty hands. She spoke to them, but Stone couldn't understand. She kept smiling and tried again, and this time her speech was a clatter of clicks and glottal stops; still the words were unrecognizable. The woman tried a third time, and now, suddenly, her words were clear. 'It's all right,' she said. 'I won't hurt you. It's all right. All right. I – Do you understand me?' She grinned at their nods. 'Good. At last.' Her accent was strange, Stone thought, but her words were easily comprehensible. 'My. You've fallen a long way, haven't you? Come into the larva. You'll feel better . . .'

'Into the what?'

She glanced over her shoulder.

Clinging to the Floor, just a short crawl away, was a larva – broad, magnificent, twice the size of *the* Larva which had sustained his family. Its fans, glistening with mucus, faced the Stream defiantly.

And beyond its translucent walls, *within the body of the larva itself*, Stone saw a human.

Stone pressed his fingers into the flesh of the larva, wondering. He was *inside* the larva. The flesh-hull around him yielded, soft, moist, warm. Far above his head the larva's pads waved, and beyond the walls the Stream rushed.

The four of them – Flower, Stone and the two city-women – huddled, their legs pressed together. In the confined space Stone was aware of the scent of humans: a musty warmth he remembered from a childhood spent scurrying across the Floor beneath the safe bellies of his parents.

For the first time in his life he was out of the Stream. His head felt clear, easy, his breathing easy. It was *wonderful*.

Flower-of-Bones said, 'Doesn't it hurt the larva, to have us sit inside him like this?'

'No.' It was the one called *Speaker-to-Upstream* – the one who had come out to save them from the hunters, the one who had thrown the spear. She was squat, like her companion, but not without grace; she wore a suit of woven net-fabric, soft and comfortable-looking, with tools tucked into a belt. 'No, we won't hurt him.' She reached out behind herself and stroked the larva's inner wall with a robust affection. 'This is the larva's stomach lining . . . But it's designed to be open to the Stream, like this. Every stomach needs a lot of surface area, because food is digested through surface.' She poked gently at Flower's belly. 'Your stomach is coiled up inside you – you carry around all that area, stored neatly away. The larva's stomach is opened out – the creature is *all* stomach, really. And its body traps a pocket of the Stream, sheltering it from the current, and filters food particles from it.'

Flower looked uneasy; she squirmed away from where she was sitting.

Speaker-to-Upstream laughed. 'Don't worry; you're much too big to digest. The larva is interested in microscopic fragments – tiny pieces – that's all. But you asked a good question.'

She smiled at Flower, and Stones-of-Ice stared, wishing he'd asked the question.

Speaker said to Flower, 'You must have asked yourself other questions. Haven't you ever wondered what the Stream is *for*?'

'Yes,' Flower said. 'I have.'

The second woman – *Rider-of-Larvae*, Stone remembered – grinned and ruffled Flower's hair. Flower-of-Bones glared at her until she stopped.

'Good for you. But do you have any answers?' Rider asked.

'I've a question. Why did you save us?' Stone demanded.

Speaker smiled. 'Because you were too interesting to let those barbarians eat you up. Look.' Gently she lifted Stone's hand, uncurled his long fingers, and pressed her own hand against his. Her palm was dry, somehow confident. But her fingers had only three joints above the knuckle, while Stone's had six.

He let his fingers fold down over hers.

Speaker said, 'You've come from a long way Upstream, haven't you?'

Rider leaned towards Stone. 'We can tell. And not just because you look different. Even your language has drifted away from ours, significantly. It's really quite precise; we've even put together a map of the Upstream – schematically, anyway – based on language drift . . . You've diverged a long way from us, you see. Since the Crash. The further Upstream the more isolated the communities are, and the more diverse the adaptation. Nothing can pass Upstream – not even information – so adaptations, language distortions, genetic changes, can only propagate Downstream. We're closer to the original form than you are – more of a mix, you see –'

Stone scowled. '*Original form?*' He, and Flower-of-Bones, were the original form. Of course they were; everyone at home had known that. 'What are you talking about?'

Speaker sighed. 'We don't know much about our origins. We know there was a Crash – a ship came here, from *somewhere else*, and fell into this Stream-world . . . Humans were scattered all along the Floor, and left to cling to the rock for their lives. But that's the sum of our knowledge. All we really know is that *humans don't belong here*. That's why we're going Downstream.'

Flower was wide-eyed. 'Downstream? In this larva? How far?'

Speaker touched her cheek. 'As far as it takes. Forever, perhaps.'

Rider said, 'Maybe the Stream doesn't go on forever. How could it be infinite, after all? Perhaps it circles back on itself, like a huge wheel, so that Downstream at last becomes Upstream . . . Think of that.'

'Or,' Speaker said, 'there may be twin singularities – a black hole at the far Downstream, feeding a wormhole which –'

'I don't know what those words mean,' Stone said, embarrassed. He pressed his hands flat against the larva's flesh. *To have tamed a larva* . . . 'Speaker,' he said slowly. 'Can this larva take us Upstream?'

She studied him, the age lines around her eyes softened by the diffuse lichen-light; she wore her hair tied back behind her neck. 'We can't take you home. I'm sorry.'

Flower wriggled past the women and grabbed Stone's hand. Her face was shining. 'Stone, let's stay with them.'

Rider touched their shoulders, embracing them both. 'Come with us; let's fly with this larva into the Downstream. The Upstream's gone . . . but at least we can find out what's at the end of it all.'

'Can we, Stone? Oh, can we?'

Stone stared beyond the larva's thin flesh – beyond the net farm, and into the lost infinity of Upstream.

'I'll always love you,' he whispered.

Then he turned Downstream. And smiled.

THE BLOOD OF ANGELS

The Angel's singing – multitonal, delicate as air-snow – came to him through water still winter-crisp.

Carver opened his eyes. The last few ice crystals embedded in his flesh made his eyelids crackle, and prismatic forms – crystals within the eyeballs – moved across his retinae.

People rained from the frozen surface above him, arms wrapped around their legs, down towards the Shelf floor. There were Angels everywhere, singing, touching the sleeping people.

Lyra's face swam before him, smiling, translucent. The Angel's bare body was still skeletal from last autumn's fast, and her pale bones shone through her flesh. Her hands were moving over his body. He could barely feel her touch; it felt as if layers of chitin had been plated over his dulled senses. She seemed to be caressing him, welcoming him to the new, month-long summer. He was tempted to close his eyes, to relax in her soft attention . . .

He felt her lift away the heavy pack of tools from his waist.

His eyes snapped open. *Something was wrong.*

'Lyra?' His voice was a croak, barely carrying through the chill water.

She smiled; through the ghostly flesh of her neck he could see vocal cords shimmer as she sang in harmony with herself. But she clutched his tool bag – a simple thing of woven weed, attached to a belt of rope.

Beyond her, Angels swam coolly through the defenceless rain of people. The Angels were carrying away tools, clothes, food caches – even weapons: spears, knives of bone.

Carver grabbed Lyra's arm. Sheets of his flesh, frozen,

141

ruined – peeled away from him, exposing new, pink skin. 'Lyra . . . What doing?'

Her flesh was soft, hot; she recoiled from his touch, uncomprehending distress distorting her face.

His brain seemed still to be half-frozen; he struggled to force it to work. Lyra couldn't answer him, of course; Angels had no speech – not even the guttural, verb-free sub-language of the Baskers.

But Angels weren't thieves, either. They'd never been known to steal from True Humans before – especially in the few brief days after the spring thaw, when the sleepless Angels were the first creatures to recover, to begin functioning, with True Humans – and every other Shelf creature – still half-frozen, unconscious, vulnerable.

Unlike people – and Baskers, and Anglers – Angels didn't freeze. They didn't have to sleep through the eleven-month winter; they stayed conscious, entombed in the ice, making up their beautiful songs.

He took his tool kit from her unresisting grasp.

'Baskers!'

It was the voice of Hunter, his wife.

Carver turned in the water. Hunter – squat, muscular, middle-aged, her hair tied back from her brow – swam through the cloud of stirring people. Layers of dead flesh flaked from her limbs, but she was moving purposefully, slapping and pushing the adults to make them wake faster. She carried her spear of chitin and wood. The spear was fouled, stained by smears of something clear, sticky –

Angel blood.

The chill of the spring water sank deep into Carver's bones; he felt as if he would never be warm again.

Hunter saw him staring at her. She pointed past him. 'Baskers incoming! *Move!*'

No-one had killed an Angel – a harmless, beautiful Angel – ever before . . .

The Baskers were coming down on them in a great wall across the ocean. Their huge mouths were clamped shut, and in their wide, clumsy hands they clutched their own crude weapons – shards of chitin, bits of rock – and, he saw, True Human weapons: knives, spears, bows.

Human weapons, stolen for them by the Angels.

Too much was happening, too fast. Carver cast about for a weapon. But the knife at his waist was gone, and the cache of spears and nets he'd helped gather, just before the winter sleep, was vanished.

Stolen by Angels?

He turned to face the Baskers, his fists bunching.

Silhouetted against the ruddy sunlight, a burly female dropped from the ice-coated surface at Carver.

Hair like weed, white and thin, straggled across her broad, flat skull. Her eyes were buried deep in pits of bone. Her limbs were spread wide, her elbows and knees bent, and she clutched a True Human knife – perhaps it was even his own.

He tipped backwards in the water, bringing up his arms and legs.

The Basker's body smacked into his, full on. Nipples like pebbles pressed into his chest, and she scrabbled at his back, nails like claws raking his flesh. Her huge mouth loomed before his face, a translucent cavern, and he could see sunlight through the filtering gills at the sides of her immense throat. That mouth was designed to filter out immense quantities of plankton and krill, as the Baskers swam in their great schools through the Shelf waters . . .

But she wasn't feeding now. If the knife didn't get him, she could simply smother him by wrapping his face and head in that huge, enclosing mouth.

He brought up his knees, trying to prise her away. He had to ignore the looming mouth before him. *The knife. Where was the knife?* Her free hand was still working at his back – he ran his left hand along her bony arm – so the knife must be – *there!*

He felt the blade lunge into his hand; it passed through the webbing between his thumb and forefinger. But there wasn't much pain. Clearly unused to the weapon, the Basker was holding the knife handle awkwardly, too high.

He closed his palm around the knife. The stone blade rasped into his flesh, and he felt his palm grow slick with blood. But he had it, and with a twist – *oh, the pain now* as the blade scraped against bone – he was able to wrench the knife out of her grasp.

The knife slipped away from his bloodied fingers.

The Basker, enraged, shrieked into his face. He could smell foul brine, see scraps of krill clinging to the back of her throat.

Now she had both her legs wrapped around his waist; she tore at his back, and pounded the side of his head. He tried to fight back. But she was out of reach of his legs and knees. Her skin was hard, leathery – still winter-dehydrated – but her muscles, toned by a life of steady swimming, were like boulders.

She was crude, stupid, little more than an animal. It was impossible to believe that Baskers were humans too, cousins of True Humans. But it *was* the truth; every person was born knowing it. And this Basker was *strong*, and she was going to win.

Unless . . .

With his right hand he reached down to the tool bag at his waist. He scrabbled at his back, at the loose knot in the rope belt at the base of his spine. In a few heartbeats, working blind and one-handed, he had it free – and then almost lost the bag altogether, as the Basker-woman pounded his head and back.

He reached out, past the Basker – to an onlooker this must seem like some obscene embrace, he thought distantly – and with his right hand he wrapped the rope belt around his left wrist.

Then he dragged his arms up and over the Basker's head, and down before her face. With a quick motion he wrapped the rope backwards, around her neck – and with all his strength he *shoved*.

The Basker's eyes, deep in the leather mask of her face, stared at him, resentful, dimming. The scrabbling at his back and face grew in intensity, until it was as if independent animals were gouging into him. She coughed, and a huge, obscene mass of half-digested krill erupted from that cavernous neck and spewed into his face.

But he held on. And *so did she,* obviously unaware that he depended on the leverage she was giving him by clinging to his waist with her legs. He felt the rope saw through the dehydrated flesh at her neck. Her blood stained the water before his face; it tasted sharp and salty.

Then her arms fell away, limp. That huge mouth, the distended caves of cheeks, lost their shape.

He had to peel her locked legs away from his waist. He pushed the corpse away from him. Sheets of pain creased his back, face and hand.

Bloodied, gasping, still winter-weak, he stared around.

Baskers moved through the rain of people, clubbing at heads and chests at will. Blood billowed through the water. Carver saw a splinter of rock – held in a broad Basker fist – slice open the chest of a squirming child; the other fist reached into the chest and pulled aside white, gleaming ribs, exposing organs like pale worms.

It was a slaughter.

The Baskers couldn't be after food – they didn't eat True Human food, let alone Human *flesh*.

Could it be that the Baskers simply wanted to *destroy* the Humans?

He heard the distant, thin voice of Hunter; she had moved out of the battle-cloud.

'Flee! Flee!'

Carver grabbed at his tool bag and began to swim, pain lancing through his joints. Around him, other surviving Humans – adults, a few children – emerged from the cloud of death, dulled, many wounded, bemused.

He looked back once. The Baskers still worked at unresisting bodies, pounding and gouging in a frenzy, their motions indistinct in the blood cloud.

And beyond them, a school of Angels sported through the water. They sang and played, oblivious of death.

*   *   *

Twenty True Humans survived, of over fifty. And of the twenty, only six were children.

They fled across the Shelf, seeking out their hunting grounds at its lip.

Hunter and Carver had borne one child of their own – a boy, who had failed to revive after a winter's hibernation, three or four seasons earlier. They had mourned the child. Strangely, Carver thought, that period just after the boy's death was the closest they had ever been.

But the world – the endless pressure of hunger, of summers which flew by and winters which closed around them like fists – gave little room to grieve.

Hunter had withdrawn into her own deep, frozen ocean, somewhere inside her head – a place Carver had never been able to reach. Somehow they had not considered having another child. Now, as Carver surveyed the straggling, exhausted, bloodied band of survivors, that choice seemed irresponsible.

For as far as anyone knew, there were no other True Humans, anywhere in all the seas of the world.

Once they saw a school of Baskers. The True Humans dove down to the bare, rocky floor of the Shelf. The Baskers – a hundred or more – cruised overhead in their dull, stolid way. Their huge legs beat in patient formation at the water, and the sunlight illuminated the interiors of their gaping, ballooned mouths as they scoured krill from the ocean.

Lyra, the Angel, followed the True Humans.

Carver saw her behind them, distant, wary, clearly scared and confused. *She doesn't understand what she's done*, he thought. *She really doesn't know what this means.*

The other Humans didn't seem to have noticed her. He tried to shoo her away – he even shook his fist at her, silently, trying to scare her off. If the True Humans got hold of her now . . .

But she couldn't understand. She smiled back at him, the bones of her skull shining through her clear flesh, clearly wondering what new game he was playing.

He turned his back on her and swam close to Hunter, his wife.

Oblivious to the True Humans' despair, the world around them blossomed gorgeously, making as much of the brief summer as it could. The residual surface ice was reduced to a thin shell, almost transparent; diatoms, flagellates and algae absorbed the ice-filtered sunlight, filling the ocean like blue-green dust. Polychaete worms, sea butterflies and krill, liberated from their own icy prisons, wriggled through the newly rich waters, gorging.

The richness of the warming waters prompted the quickening of his own thin blood, and filled Carver with an irrational optimism – despite the Baskers' attack. Spring always affected him this way. And yet he knew that the species of plankton scrambling through their brief lives around him were a fraction of the armies which had inhabited the oceans before the Impact.

Carver's optimism dissolved as rapidly as it had coalesced, and exhaustion seemed to congeal around him, like the touch of a premature winter. His empty stomach was an unending ache inside him, and his muscles – overextended, depleted – shivered as he forced his arms and legs to keep moving. But he knew better than to try to slow Hunter, to call for a rest. Exhausted, battered as they were, they had to go on to the lip of the Shelf – to hunt, to gather food; or they would surely die.

Everyone knew the story of the world. True Humans were born with it in their heads.

Once only a fraction of the oceans had been permanently covered with ice. And in some places the oceans had never frozen over at all . . .

Now, things were different. The Earth, thrown onto a wide ellipse by the Impact, swung close to the Sun for only a couple of months each year. Most of the oceans stayed frozen, to their cores, all year round; only in the Shelf regions, the thin ribbons of shallow water around the continents, was there any thawing.

Any room for life.

The food chains had been devastated. Even the plankton had to be modified to enable them to endure the ice – remade by the last humans on dry land, working desperately as the air snowed around them.

At last the humans themselves had returned their own children to the oceans, the last habitable places on Earth.

They had populated the seas with animals and fish, all modified to withstand the winters. But none had survived. There were nothing but human variants left in the oceans now.

Plankton, and human variants.

And the humans had turned on each other.

'Down!'

Hunter's hiss startled him from his reverie.

People settled against the sea floor, letting bottom mud silt around their bodies. Children slid through the mud, squirming close to the adults.

From the corner of his eye Carver saw Lyra shadow their motions, settling to the mud a few hundred yards behind them – pretty, ineffectual, a sexless, childlike hermaphrodite.

Carver peered ahead through the dispersing mud cloud – and saw why Hunter had called a halt. An Angler swam towards them. It was a bloated, mud-orange ball; its limbs were stubs, with hands and feet webbed over and extended into fins. Its lantern glowed sharply on the rod of bone growing out of its skull, and wide nostrils filtered the silty water, Basker-style.

The Angler paused in its waddling path. It dipped forward, its huge mouth closing around some floating fragment of food. A mass in its stomach moved, some bony protuberance bulging across the Angler's distended belly. The stomach contents looked like a child within a womb; perhaps that prey was still alive, Carver speculated.

The Angler's neck barely existed; its massive, distorted face merged smoothly into the sleek mass of its body, and thin tufts of hair clung to its stretched scalp. This was a male,

Carver saw; a small penis nestled in a sprouting of coarse hair beneath the distended belly. Its flesh was thin, still etiolated by long months in a chamber of ice – but the flesh was stretched thin over its stomach.

Through its huge, hinged jaw the Angler could swallow more than its own mass. This creature had already fed, and now it was almost lazing through the shallows, complacent, sleepy, patiently digesting its first meal of the year.

The Anglers lived in the deep, cold, barren waters beyond the Shelf. There was no light down there – no plankton, the only food the silty detritus of the Shelf communities. In the brief spring the Anglers swarmed upwards, over the lip, to feed on the blooming life of the shallows.

And on the Shelf, True Humans awaited them.

Hunter lifted from the mud, slowly, stealthily. Carver marvelled at his wife's economy of movement; her webbed feet seemed almost motionless and she raised barely a handful of mud from the floor. She held her spear before her – a spear still stained with the blood of Angels, Carver saw – and with her free hand she made a circling motion.

Carver and another man – a burly fellow called Healer-of-Wounds – lifted from the mud, trying to copy Hunter's silent glide through the water. Carver worked his way around to the left of the Angler and Healer took the right.

In moments they were in position, the two men and Hunter at three corners of a triangle around the oblivious, sleepy fish-man. Carver held his breath, the intensity of the hunt quickening his pulse.

Sunlight glimmered through the ice above them, illuminating the still, regular tableau.

The fish-man stirred. Hunter raised her right hand.

Carver and Healer burst towards the Angler. They roared and thrashed at the water, exploding with noise and motion.

The fish-man tipped up in the water, its bony light-rod quivering. Its startlingly human eyes seemed to move separately, fixing on the men.

Then it turned and, the flukes of its leg-fins beating so fast they blurred, it hurtled away from the men –

– and straight towards Hunter's spear-point.

Carver watched his wife raise the spear and ram it into the Angler's head, between its eyes. The Angler cried out, its voice deep, faintly human. The momentum of the fish-man caused it to plunge on, thrashing, carrying Hunter; but she'd been prepared for this and she clung onto her spear grimly, using her mass to lever it back and forth inside the Angler's head.

Blood and brain, pale grey, littered the water in a cloud around the struggling fish-man.

Now the other True Humans erupted from their shallow nests of mud and closed on the Angler. They tore at its pulsing flanks with knives, spears, hands and teeth. By the time Carver reached the group, the fish-man had been reduced to a bloodied pulp, barely recognizable, its flesh hanging loose in sheets over its ribs, its four distorted limbs dangling in the water.

At last it was stilled. The huge carcass, lifeless, settled to the bottom, followed by its attendant cloud of True Humans.

Carver ground tough flesh between his teeth as quickly as he could, forcing the food into his empty stomach. Save for traces of krill he'd swallowed during the journey, it was the first food he'd taken since last summer. It tasted *wonderful*.

Healer-of-Wounds climbed into the opened-up carcass. He pushed his feet against the Angler's white-gleaming spine and grasped its ribs; shreds of flesh slithered between his broad fingers. Healer pulled, hard, the huge muscles of his shoulders working; slowly he prised open the fish-man's chest. Organs – pale, swollen – tumbled out of the opened body cavity. A dozen hands descended on the stomach, pulling apart its soft walls with ease.

A body slithered out of the stomach. The flesh was eroded, gouged away by digestive acids.

At first Carver thought it was a True Human. But the shape of the skull, what was left of a huge mouth, were distinctive. This was a Basker – a young adult, judging by its size and weight.

The children descended on the Basker, dragging away loose bits of flesh, chewing on the salty, acid-softened goodies. Carver watched them indulgently, pleased they had found

something to distract them from the horror of the Baskers'
attack.

'Carver.'

It was Hunter's voice, from somewhere away from the feeding group. He drifted away from the carcass. Growing complacent himself now his stomach was filling, he hadn't noticed
she'd gone.

Hunter was close to the bottom, a few yards away – *and
she had the Angel, Lyra.*

Carver hurried to them, his heart racing.

Hunter waited for him, her face set. One broad hand was
wrapped around the wrist of the Angel – gently, Carver saw,
but firmly – and in the other hand she held a scrap of
Angler-meat.

Lyra squirmed, her pretty, glowing face crumpled with fear;
she was trying to sing, but her song was fragmented, dis-
cordant.

Hunter faced Carver. 'Saw her follow.'

Carver was aware of his hands working, pulling at each
other. 'Let go. Harmless. Let go . . .'

'Not harmless. Worked for Baskers.'

But she didn't know what she was doing, Carver wanted
to cry. *And – oh – and she was beautiful!*

All the Angels, with their grace and song, were beautiful,
he thought – the only source of beauty in a grim, dying world.

'They help us,' he said desperately. 'Against Baskers. Next
spring.'

Hunter was still shaking her head. 'Not harmless. Never
harmless again. *Never.*' She held the bit of meat out to Carver.
He took it uncertainly; it was slick and warm in his palm.
'Give. Feed her.'

At first Carver couldn't understand. He held the meat out
to the Angel; Lyra, her face lightening, reached for it eagerly.

Then – with shocking suddenness – he saw it. He snatched
the meat back, ignoring Lyra's disappointment. He faced
Hunter, appalled. '*No.* She not understand. *No.*'

Hunter reached out and took his arm, just as she held the
Angel; she flexed her shoulders and dragged Carver and the

Angel together, until they were face to face. 'She like you. She *trust* you. You give her food. She take to her friends. Feed them all.'

Carver looked into the vapid, pretty, trusting eyes of the Angel – and then into the eyes of his wife. Hunter's face was harder than the rock of the sea bottom, harder than midwinter ice. He saw determination there – a bleak, hard determination *that the species must survive*, at all costs – a determination that had once made humans, trapped on a freezing world, rebuild the very bodies of their children.

Before that will, beauty and music had no power. Carver had no power.

Carver faced the Angel and – slowly, fighting it all the way – he held out the meat to her.

The Angel's soft mouth closed around the meat. She chewed delicately, then swallowed, smiling at him trustingly; he could see the pale mass of meat pass down through her throat towards her stomach.

No pre-Impact human could have survived a single winter on the new Earth; the first freeze would have burst open the human's cell walls.

When people – True Humans and their distant cousins – had returned to the all-but-frozen seas, different groups had adopted different strategies to survive the long months of ice-entombment. The strategies were new to humankind, but had been exploited by animals and larvae in Earth's polar regions as long as life had existed on Earth.

In the bodies of True Humans, ice crystals formed – but in the spaces *between* cells, not *inside* the cells. Baskers, and their close relatives the Anglers, allowed their bodies to dehydrate before the winter entombed them. Where there was no water, no ice could form.

Angels were different. The blood of an Angel was a natural cryoprotectant – an alcohol-based antifreeze. So Angels didn't freeze at all; they supercooled, their blood remaining liquid below freezing point.

But Angels had to fast, before the winter came. It was *very,*

very important that the blood of an Angel was as pure as it could be before the freezing started . . .

Carver knew all this, as he knew his own name, how to swim; True Humans were born with an understanding of the world around them.

And they were born knowing how to destroy Angels.

All through the summer, the Angel Lyra was allowed to stay with the little band of True Humans as they foraged at the lip of the Shelf. And Carver fed her constantly. He watched that delicate mouth close around the delicious morsels – bits of liver, kidney, heart-veins still warm and thick with blood; Lyra's pretty eyes were empty, even as she fed.

Suddenly autumn was on them. The waters, which had glowed with new life only weeks before, turned cloudy and stale as the diatoms, worms and other small animals began to die. The ice over the world thickened perceptibly, turning the Shelf into a place of shadows and murky gloom; deep, chill currents flowed up over the lip, buffeting the True Humans and making them huddle together against the cold.

Lyra – sleek, almost fat – seemed aware of the impending winter. She spent long hours away from the Humans now – Carver knew she must be with her own kind, perhaps mating (Angels were hermaphroditic, and mixed their fluids by kissing) – but she always returned.

When Carver brought her food now, she closed her pretty mouth and tried to pull away. But he gave her the most tender pieces of offal – he even chewed some of the pieces for her, to soften the meat and enhance the flavour.

She could not resist. She smiled at him and swallowed the wonderful, moist morsels.

And, as Lyra sang for him, Carver held out more meat.

Long splinters of ice reached down from the thickening surface crust.

The True Humans swam to a place far across the Shelf – far from the breeding ground of the Baskers who had attacked them. The children turned dull, lethargic, the fluids of their bodies slowing; one by one they gathered their knees to their chests, tucked their arms around their thighs, and closed their eyes.

The tiny bodies drifted to the surface, like bubbles, lodging in the ice.

Cold, his joints stiff, the blood like mud in his veins, Carver faced Lyra for the last time. She looked unnaturally fat – Angels in autumn should be like ghosts, barely more than glassy skin stretched over bone – and she seemed aware of it; her face was creased with unfocussed concern.

But when he held out the food bag to her – when the stench of chewed, ripe offal reached her nostrils – she grabbed it with joy, all thoughts of the future driven from her small mind.

Above the thickened ice-crust, the air started to snow.

When he awoke, Hunter was waiting for him. She held out a sack of stored food. She grinned. 'See. Safe. No Baskers. No Angels.'

Carver pushed his way out of the ice, impatient to be free of winter's dulling grip. He snatched the bag from Hunter and dragged a slab of foul, rotting Basker-flesh from it; he crammed it into his mouth, chewing impatiently.

The water was chill, barren, the surface ice still a thick crust.

He swam off, across the Shelf, towards the Angels' breeding ground. He didn't look back. He ignored his companions, the other True Humans. But he was aware that Hunter stayed close to him, her spear in her hand.

They passed a shoal of Baskers, most of them still fixed in the ice. One, conscious, watched the True Humans approach with dull eyes and slack jaw, and swam off with thrusts of its huge-boned, winter-wasted legs.

An Angel came drifting down from the frozen sky – stiff, limbs held rigid.

Carver hurried to her.

Gently, with stiff, trembling hands, he took her shoulders and spun her around. Long, pale hair lay plastered over the

Angel's face and back, and her flesh shone with the light of the approaching Sun.

There was no awareness in that small mouth, those eyes; no blood moved beneath his hands. Her face was frosted over, crystallized; planes of ice dissected the thin body.

It wasn't Lyra.

Hunter reached past him and poked at the Angel with her spear. A frozen limb shattered and fell away; from a frozen vein, crystals of Angel blood trickled into the water, sparkling.

Supercooled fluids were unstable. They could precipitate instantly around any nucleating particles – like a fragment of food.

Carver studied the segmented torso. As the freezing had spread – cutting through this thin body in great sheets, as the Angel lay in her cave of ice, alone and helpless – what agony she must have endured!

Hunter grunted. 'Good. One less. Now we do again, and again, until no more Angels. And we have kids. Grow strong. And then,' she ran a fingertip along her spear, 'and then we seek the Baskers.'

Carver stumbled away from her, away from the mist of frozen Angel blood, in search of Lyra.

COLUMBIAD

The initial detonation was the most severe. I was pushed into my couch by a recoil that felt as if it should splay apart my ribs. The noise was extraordinary, and the projectile rattled so vigorously that my head was thrown from side to side.

And then followed, in perfect sequence, the subsidiary detonations of those smaller masses of gun-cotton lodged in the walls of the cannon. One after another these barrel-sized charges played vapour against the base of the projectile, accelerating it further, and the recoil pressed with ever increasing force.

I fear that my consciousness departed from me, for some unmeasured interval.

When I came to myself, the noise and oscillation had gone. My head swam, as if I had imbibed heavily of Ardan's wine butts, and my lungs ached as they pulled at the air.

But, when I pushed at the couch under me, I drifted slowly upwards, as if I were buoyant in some fluid which had flooded the projectile.

I was exultant. Once again my Columbiad had not failed me!

My name is Impey Barbicane, and what follows – if there are ears to hear – is an account of my second venture beyond the limits of the terrestrial atmosphere: that is, the first voyage to Mars.

My Lunar romance received favourable reviews on its London publication by G. Newnes, and I was pleased to place it with an American publisher and in the Colonies. Sales were depressed, however, due to unrest over the War with the Boers. And there was that little business of the protests by M. Verne at the 'unscientific' nature of my device of gravitational opacity; but I was able to point to flaws in Verne's work, and to the verification of certain aspects of my book by experts in astronomy, astronomical physics, and the like.

All of this engaged my attention but little, however. With the birth of Gip, and the publication of my series of futurological predictions in *The Fortnightly Review*, I had matters of a more personal nature to attend to, as well as of greater global significance.

I was done with inter-planetary travel!

It was with surprise and some annoyance, therefore, that I found myself the recipient, via Newnes, of a series of missives from Paris, penned – in an undisciplined hand – by one Michel Ardan. This evident eccentric expressed admiration for my work and begged me to place close attention to the material he enclosed, which I should find 'of the most extraordinary interest and confluence with [my] own writings'.

As is my custom, I had little hesitation in disposing of this correspondence without troubling to read it.

But M. Ardan continued to pepper me with further fat volleys of paper.

At last, in an idle hour, while Jane nursed Gip upstairs, I leafed through Ardan's dense pages. And I have to confess that I found my imagination – or the juvenile underside of it! – pricked.

Ardan's enclosure purported to be a record made by a Colonel Maston, of Baltimore in the United States, over the years 1872 to 1873 – that is, some twenty-eight years ago. This Maston, now dead, claimed to have built an apparatus which had detected 'propagating electro-magnetic emissions': a phenomenon first described by James Clerk Maxwell, and related, apparently, to the more recent wireless-telegraphy demonstrations of Marconi. If this were not enough, Maston also claimed that the 'emissions' were in fact signals, encoded after the fashion of a telegraph message.

And these signals – said Maston and Ardan – had emanated from a source *beyond the terrestrial atmosphere*: from a space voyager, en route to Mars!

When I got the gist of this, I laughed out loud. I dashed

off a quick note instructing Newnes not to pass on to me any further communications from the same source.

Fifth Day. Two Hundred and Ninety Seven Thousand Leagues. Through my lenticular glass scuttles, the Earth now appears about the size of a Full Moon. Only the right half of the terrestrial globe is illuminated by the Sun. I can still discern clouds, and the differentiation of ocean blue from the land's brown, and the glare of ice at the poles.

Some distance from the Earth a luminous disklet is visible, aping the Earth's waxing phase. It is the Moon, following the Earth on its path around the Sun. It is to my regret that the configuration of my orbit was such that I passed no closer to the satellite than several hundred thousand leagues.

The projectile is extraordinarily convenient. I have only to turn a tap and I am furnished with fire and light by means of gas, which is stored in a reservoir at a pressure of several atmospheres. My food is meat and vegetables and fruit, hydraulically compressed to the smallest dimensions; and I have carried a quantity of brandy and water. My atmosphere is maintained by means of chlorate of potassium and caustic potash: the former, when heated, is transformed into chloride of potassium, and the oxygen thus liberated replaces that which I have consumed; and the potash, when shaken, extracts from the air the carbonic acid placed there by the combustion of elements of my blood.

Thus, in inter-planetary space, I am as comfortable as if I were in the smoking lounge of the Gun Club itself, in Union Square, Baltimore!

Michel Ardan was perhaps seventy-five. He was of large build, but stoop-shouldered. He sported luxuriant side-whiskers and moustache; his shock of untamed hair, once evidently red, was largely a mass of grey. His eyes were startling: habitually he held them wide open, so that a rim of white appeared above each iris, and his gaze was clear but vague, as if he suffered from near-sight.

He paced about my living room, his open collar flapping. Even at his advanced age Ardan was a vigorous, restless man, and my home, Spade House – spacious though it is – seemed to confine him like a cage. I feared besides that his booming Gallic voice must awaken Gip. Therefore I invited Ardan to walk with me in the garden; in the open air I fancied he might not seem quite so out of scale.

The house, built on the Kent coast near Sandgate, is open to a vista of the sea. The day was brisk, lightly overcast. Ardan showed interest in none of this, however.

He fixed me with those wild eyes. 'You have not replied to my letters.'

'I had them stopped.'

'I have been forced to travel here unannounced. Sir, I have come here to beg your help.'

I already regretted allowing him into my home – of course I did! – but some combination of his earnestness, and the intriguing content of those unsolicited missives, had temporarily overwhelmed me. Now, though, I stood square on my lawn, and held up the newest copy of his letter.

'Then perhaps, M. Ardan, you might explain what you mean by transmitting such romantic nonsense in my direction.'

He barked laughter. 'Romantic it may be. Nonsense – never!'

'Then you claim this business of "propagating emissions" is the plain and honest truth, do you?'

'Of course. It is a system of communication devised for their purposes by Impey Barbicane and Col. Maston. They seized on the electro-magnetic discoveries of James Maxwell with the vigour and inventiveness typical of Americans – for America is indeed the Land of the Future, is it not?'

Of that, I was not so certain.

'Col. Maston had built a breed of mirror – but of wires, do you see? – in the shape of that geometric figure called a hyperbola – no, forgive me! – a *parabola*, for this figure, I am assured, collects all impinging waves into a single point, thus making it possible to detect the weakest –'

'Enough.' I was scarcely qualified to judge the technical possibilities of such a hypothetical apparatus. And besides, the inclusion of apparently authentic detail is a technique I have used in my own romances, to persuade the reader to accept the most outrageous fictive lies. I had no intention of being deceived by it myself!

'These missives of yours – received by Maston – purport to be from the inhabitant of a projectile, beyond the terrestrial atmosphere. And this projectile, you claim, was launched into space from the mouth of an immense cannon, the *Columbiad*, embedded in a Florida hill-side . . .'

'That is so.'

'But, my poor M. Ardan, you must understand that these are no more than the elements of a fiction, written three decades ago by M. Verne – your countryman – with whom I, myself, have corresponded –'

Choleric red bloomed in his battered cheeks. 'Verne indeed now claims his lazy and sensational books were fiction. It is convenient for him to do so. But they were not! He was commissioned to write truthful accounts of our extraordinary voyage!'

'Well, that's as may be. But see here. In M. Verne's account the projectile was launched towards the Moon. Not to Mars.' I shook my head. 'There is a difference, you know.'

'Sir, I pray you resist treating me as imbecilic. I am well aware of the difference. The projectile was sent towards the Moon on its *first* journey – in which I had the honour of participating . . .'

The afternoon was extending, and I had work to do; and I was growing irritated by this boorish Frenchman. 'Then, if this projectile was truly built, perhaps you would be good enough to show it to me.'

'I cannot comply.'

'Why so?'

'Because it is no longer on the Earth.'

'Ah.'

Of course not! It was buried in the red dust of Mars, with this Barbicane inside.

'But –'

'Yes, M. Ardan?'

'I *can* show you the cannon.'

The Frenchman regarded me steadily, and I felt an odd chill grow deep within me.

Seventy-Third Day. Four Million One Hundred And Eighty Four Thousand Leagues.

Today, through my smoked glass, I have observed the passage of the Earth across the face of the Sun.

The planet appeared first as a mar in the perfect rim of the parent star. Later it moved into the full glare of the fiery ball, and was quite visible as a whole disc, dwarfed by the Sun's mighty countenance. After perhaps an hour another spot appeared, even smaller than the first: it was the Moon, following its parent towards the Sun's centre.

After perhaps eight hours the passage was done.

I took several astronomical readings of this event. I measured the angles under which Earth and Moon travelled across the Sun's disc, so that I might determine the deviation of my voyaging ellipse from the ecliptic; and the timing of the passage has furnished me with precise information on whether the projectile is running ahead or behind of the elliptical path around the Sun which I had designed. My best computations inform me that I have not deviated from the required trajectory.

It is little more than a century since Captain James Cook, in 1769, sailed his Endeavour to Tahiti to watch Venus pass before the Sun. Could even that great explorer have imagined this journey of mine?

I have become the first human being to witness a transit of Earth! – and who, I wonder, will be the second?

It took two days for us to travel by despatch-boat from New Orleans to the bay of Espiritu Santo, close to Tampa Town.

Ardan had the good sense to avoid my company during this brief, uncomfortable trip. My humour was not good. Since leaving England I had steadily cursed myself, and Ardan, for my foolishness in agreeing to this jaunt to Florida.

We could not ignore each other at dinner and breakfast, however. And at those occasions, we argued.

'But,' I insisted, 'a human occupant would be reduced to a thin film of smashed bone and flesh, crushed by recoil against the base of any such cannon-fired shell. No amount of water cushions and collapsing balsa partitions would be sufficient to avert such a fate.'

'Of course that is true,' Ardan said, unperturbed. 'But then M. Verne did not depict the detail of the arrangement.'

'Which was?'

'That Barbicane and his companions in the Gun Club anticipated precisely this problem. The *Columbiad*, that mighty cannon, was dug still deeper than Verne described. And it did *not* contain one single vast charge of gun-cotton, but many, positioned along its heroic length. Thus a *distributed* impulse was applied to the projectile. It is an elementary matter of algebra – for those with the right disposition, which I have not! – to compute that the forces suffered by travellers within the projectile, while punishing, were less than lethal.'

'Bah! What, then, of Verne's description of conditions within the projectile, during its Lunar journey? He claims that the inhabitants suffered a sensation of levitation – but only at that point at which the gravitational pulls of Earth and Moon are balanced. Now, this is nonsense. When you create a vacuum in a tube, the objects you send through it – whether grains of dust or grains of lead – fall with the same rapidity. So with the contents of your projectile. You, sir, should have floated like a pea inside a tin can throughout your voyage!'

He shrugged. 'And so I did. It was an amusing piece of natural philosophy, but not always a comfortable sensation. For the second journey we anticipated by installing a couch equipped with straps, and hooks and eyes on the tools and implements, and additional cramp-irons fixed to the walls. As to M. Verne's inaccurate depiction of this sensation – I refer you to the author! Perhaps he did not understand. Or perhaps he chose to dramatize our condition in a way which suited the purposes of his narrative . . .'

'Oh!' I said. 'This debating is all by the by. M. Ardan, it is simply impossible to launch a shell to another world from a cannon!'

'It is perfectly possible.' He eyed me. 'As you know! – for have you not published your own account of how such shells might be fired, if not from Earth to Mars, then in the opposite direction?'

'But it was fiction!' I cried. 'As were Verne's books!'

'No.' He shook his large, grizzled head. 'M. Verne's account was fact. It is only a sceptical world which insists it must be fiction. And that, sir, is my tragedy.'

One Hundred and Thirty Fourth Day. Seven Million, Four Hundred and Seventy Seven Thousand Leagues.

The air will be thin and bracing; it will be like a mountain-top on Earth. I must trust that the vegetable and animal life – whose treks and seasonal cycles have been observed, as colour washes, from Earth – provide me with provision compatible with my digestion.

I have brought thermometers, barometers, aneroids and hypsometers with which to study the characteristics of the Martian landscape and atmosphere. I have also carried several compasses, in case of any magnetic influence there. I have brought canvas, pickaxes and shovels and nails, sacks of grain and shrubs and other seed stock: provisions with which to construct my miniature colony on the surface of Mars. For it is there that I must, of course, spend the rest of my life.

I dream that I may even encounter intelligence! – human, or some analogous form. The inhabitants of Mars will be tall, delicate, spidery creatures, their growth drawn upward by the lightness of their gravity. And their buildings likewise will be slender, beautiful structures . . .

With such speculation I console myself.

I will confess to a sense of isolation. With Earth invisible, and with Mars still no more than a brightening red star, I am suspended in a starry firmament – for my speed is not discernible – and I have only the dazzling globe of the Sun himself to interrupt the curve of heaven above and below me. Has any man been so alone?

At times I close the covers of the scuttles, and strap myself to my couch, and expend a little of my precious gas; I seek to forget my situation by immersing myself in my books, those faithful companions I have carried with me.

*But I find it impossible to forget my remoteness from all of human-
ity that ever lived, and that my projectile, a fragile aluminium tent,
is my sole protection.*

We stayed a night in the Franklin Hotel in Tampa Town. It
was a dingy, uncomfortable place, its facilities exceedingly
primitive.

At five a.m. Ardan roused me.

We travelled by phaeton. We worked along the coast for
some distance – it was dry and parched – and then turned
inland, where the soil became much richer, abounding with
northern and tropical floras, including pineapples, cotton-
plants, rice and yams. The road was well built, I thought,
considering the crude and underpopulated nature of the
countryside thereabouts.

I am not the physical type; I felt hot and uncomfortable,
my suit of English wool restrictive and heavy, and my lungs
seemed to labour at the humidity-laden air. By contrast Ardan
was vibrant, evidently animated by our journey.

'When we returned to Earth – we fell back into the Pacific
Ocean – our exuberance was unbounded. We imagined new
and greater *Columbiads*. We imagined fleets of projectiles,
threading between Earth, Moon and planets. We expected
adulation!'

'As depicted by M. Verne.'

'But Verne lied! – in that as in other matters. Oh, there was
some celebrity – some little notoriety. But we had returned
with nothing: not so much as a bag of Lunar soil; nothing
save our descriptions of a dead and airless Moon.

'The building of the *Columbiad* was financed by public sub-
scription. Not long after our return, the pressure from those
investors began to be felt: *Where is our profit?* – that was the
question.'

'It is not unreasonable.'

'Some influential leader-writers argued that perhaps *we had
not travelled to the Moon at all*. Perhaps it was all a deception,
devised by Barbicane and his companions.'

'It might be the truth,' I said severely. 'After all the Gun Club members were weapons manufacturers who, after the conclusion of the War between the States, sought by devising this new project only to maintain investment and employment . . .'

'It was not the truth! We had circled the Moon! But we were baffled by such reactions. Oh, Barbicane refused to concede defeat. He tried to raise subscriptions for a new company which would build on his achievements. But the company soon foundered, and the commissioner and magistrate pursued him on behalf of enraged debtors.

'If only the Moon had not turned out to be dead! If only we could succeed in finding a world which might draw up the dreams of man once more!

'And so Barbicane determined to commit all to one throw of the die. He took the last of his money, and used it to bore out the *Columbiad*, and to repair his projectile . . .'

My temper deteriorated; I had little interest in Ardan's rambling reminiscences.

But then Ardan digressed, and he began to describe how it was – or so he claimed – to fall towards the Moon. His voice became remote, his eyes oddly vacant.

Two Hundred and Forty Fifth Day. Twelve Million, One Hundred and Twenty Five Leagues.

The projectile approaches the planet at an angle to the sunlight, so Mars is gibbous, with a slice of the night hemisphere turned towards me. The ochre shading seems to deepen at the planet's limb, giving the globe a marked roundness: Mars is a little orange, the only object apart from the Sun visible as other than a point of light in all my three-hundred-and-sixty-degree sky.

To one side, at a distance a little greater than the diameter of the Martian disc, is a softly glowing starlet. If I trouble to observe for a few minutes, its relation to Mars changes visibly. Thus I have discerned that Mars has a companion: a moon, smaller than our own. And I suspect that a little further from that central globe there may be a second satellite, but my observations are not unambiguous.

I can as yet discern few details on the disc itself, save what is known from observation through the larger telescopes on Earth.

However I can easily distinguish the white spot of the southern polar cap, which is melting in the frugal warmth of a Martian summer, following the pattern of seasons identified by Wm. Herschel.

The air appears clear, and I can but trust that its thickness will prove sufficient to cushion my fall from space! ·

'I imagined I saw streams of oil descending across the glass of the scuttle.

'I thought perhaps the projectile had developed some fault, and I made to alert Barbicane. But then my eyes found their depth, and I realized I was looking at *mountains*. They slid slowly past the glass, trailing long black shadows. They were the mountains of the Moon.

'Our approach was very rapid. The Moon was growing visibly larger by the minute.

'The satellite was no longer the flat yellow disc I had known from Earth: now, tinged pale white, its centre seemed to loom out at us, given three-dimensional substance by Earthlight. The landscape was fractured and complex, and utterly still and silent. The Moon is a small world, my friend. Its curve is so tight my eye could encompass its spherical shape, even so close; I could *see* that I was flying around a ball of rock, sus-pended in space, with emptiness stretching to infinity in all directions.

'We passed around the limb of the Moon, and entered total darkness: no sunlight, no Earthlight touched the hidden land-scape rushing below.'

I asked, 'And of the Lunar egg shape which Hansen hypo-thesizes, the layer of atmosphere drawn to the far side by its greater mass –'

'We saw none of it! But –'

'Yes?'

'But . . . When the Sun was hidden behind the Lunar orb, there was light all around the Moon, as if the rim was on fire.' Ardan turned to me, and his rheumy eyes were shining. 'It was wonderful! Oh, it was wonderful!'

We crossed extensive plains, broken only by isolated

thickets of pine trees. At last we came upon a rocky plateau, baked hard by the Sun, and considerably elevated.

Two Hundred and Fifty Seventh Day. Thirteen Million, Three Hundred and Fifty Thousand Leagues.

The nature of Mars has become clear to me. All too clear!

There is a sharp visible difference between northern and southern hemispheres. The darker lands to the south of an equatorial line of dichotomy are punctuated by craters as densely clustered as those of the Moon; while the northern plains – which perhaps are analogous to the dusty maria of the Moon – are generally smoother and, perhaps, younger.

A huge canyon system lies along the equator, a planetary wound visible even from a hundred thousand leagues. To the west of this gouge are clustered four immense volcanoes: great black calderas, as dead as any on the Moon. And in the southern hemisphere I have espied a mighty crater, deep and choked with frost. Mars is clearly a small world: some of these features sprawl around the globe, outsized, overwhelming the curvature.

I have seen no evidence of the channels, or canals, observed by Cardinal Secchi, nor of the other mighty works of Mind which many claim to have observed. Nor, indeed, have I espied evidence of life: no herds move across these rusty plains, and not even the presence of vegetation is evident to me. Such colourings as I have discerned appear to owe more to geologic features than to the processes of life. Even Syrtis Major – Huygens' Hourglass Sea – is revealed as a cratered upland, no more moist than the bleakest desert of Earth.

Thus I have been forced to confront the truth:

Mars is a dead world. As dead as the Moon!

We got out of our phaeton and embarked by foot across that high plain, which Ardan called Stones Hill. I saw how several well-made roads converged on this desolate spot, free of traffic, enigmatic. There was even a rail track, rusting and long disused, snaking off in the direction of Tampa Town.

All over the plain I found the ruins of magazines, workshops, furnaces and workmen's huts. Whether or not Ardan spoke the truth, it was evident that some great enterprise had taken place here.

At the heart of the plain was a low mound. This little hill was surrounded by a ring of low constructions of stone, regularly built, and set at a radius of perhaps six hundred yards from the summit itself. Each construction was topped by an elliptical arch, some of which remained intact.

I walked into this ring, two thirds of a mile across, and looked around. 'My word, Ardan!' I cried, impressed despite my scepticism. 'This has the feel of some immense prehistoric site – a Stonehenge, perhaps, transported to the Americas. Why, there must be several hundred of these squat monoliths.'

'More than a thousand,' he said. 'They are reverberating ovens, to fuse the many millions of tons of cast iron which plated the mighty *Columbiad*. See here.' He traced out a shallow trench in the soil. 'Here are the channels by which the iron was directed into the central mould – from all twelve hundred ovens, simultaneously!'

At the summit of the hill – the convergence of the thousand trenches – there was a circular pit, perhaps sixty feet in diameter. Ardan and I approached this cavity cautiously. I found that it opened into a cylindrical shaft, dug vertically into that rocky landscape.

Ardan took a coin from his pocket and flicked it into the mouth of the great well. I heard it clatter several times against metal walls, but I could not hear it fall to rest.

Taking my courage in my hands – all my life I have suffered a certain dread of subterranean places – I stepped towards the lip of the well. I saw that its sides were sheer: evidently finely manufactured, and constructed of what appeared to be cast iron. But the iron was extensively flaked and rusted.

Looking around from this summit, I saw now a pattern to the damaged landscape: the ovens, the flimsier huts, were smashed and scattered outwards from this central spot, as if some great explosion had once occurred here. And I saw how disturbed soil streaked across the land, radially away from the hill; from a balloon, I speculated, these stripes of discoloration might have resembled the rays around the great craters of the Moon.

This Ozymandian scene was terrifically poignant: great things had been wrought here, and yet now these immense devices lay ruined, broken – forgotten.

Ardan paced about by the lip of the abandoned cannon; he exuded an extraordinary restlessness, as if the whole of the Earth had become a cage insufficient for him. 'It was magnificent!' he cried. 'When the electrical spark ignited the guncotton, and the ground shook, and the pillar of flame hurled aside the air, throwing over the spectators and their horses like matchstalks! . . . And there was the barest glimpse of the projectile itself, ascending like a soul in that fiery light . . .'

I gazed up at the hot, blank sky, and imagined this Barbicane climbing into his cannon-shell, to the applause of his ageing friends. He would have called it bravery, I suppose. But how easy it must have been, to sail away into the infinite aether – for ever! – and to leave behind the Earthbound complexities of debtors and broken promises. Was Barbicane exploring, I wondered – or escaping?

As I plunge towards the glowing pool of Martian air – as that russet, cratered barrenness opens out beneath me – I descend into despair. Is all of the Solar System to prove as bleak as the worlds I have visited?

This must be my last transmission. I wish my final words to be an utterance of deepest gratitude to my loyal friends, notably Col. J. T. Maston and my partners in the National Company of Interstellar Communication, who have followed my fruitless journey across space for so many months.

I am sure this new defeat will be trumpeted by those jackals who hounded my National Company into bankruptcy; with nothing but dead landscapes as his destination, it may be many decades before man leaves the air of Earth again!

'Sir, it seems I must credit your veracity. But what is it you want of me? Why have you brought me here?'

After his Gallic fashion, he grabbed at my arm. 'I have read your books. I know you are a man of imagination. You must publish Maston's account – tell the story of this place . . .'

'But why? What would be the purpose? If Common Man is unimpressed by such exploits – if he regards these feats as a hoax, or a cynical exploitation by gun-manufacturers – who am I to argue against him? We have entered a new century, M. Ardan: the century of Socialism. We must concentrate on the needs of Earth – on poverty, injustice, disease – and turn our faces to new worlds only when we have reached our manhood on this one . . .'

But Ardan heard none of this. He still gripped my arm, and again I saw that wildness in his old eyes – eyes that had, perhaps, seen too much. 'I would go back! That is all. I am embedded in gravity. It clings, it clings! Oh, Mr. Wells, let me go back!'

BRIGANTIA'S ANGELS

'[It was] a peaceful night . . . I went to bed and was awakened by the roar of the wind, the crash of the breakers . . . When it was light I went down to see how it [the machine] had fared and found it scattered about a field . . .'
Bill Frost, *Western Mail*, 1932.

1 THE STORM

The street door opened, and the rattle of the wind almost drowned out his mother's voice.

'Jimmy!'

Jimmy Griffiths was lounging on his bed upstairs, reading his London pamphlets. The draught, piercing the ill-fitting window frames, was making his lamp flame flicker. 'What?'

'It's Bill Frost, here to see you . . .'

Bill Frost? Jimmy pushed his face closer to the murky type of the pamphlets. 'Mother, if he's trying to get me back into his choir again, tell him I'm not interested.'

'It's not the choir, Jimmy,' his mother said uncertainly. 'You'd better come down.'

With an elaborate sigh, Jimmy threw his pamphlets down on the crumpled blanket.

Downstairs his mother stood before the open door, her small, nervous hands buried in her apron. The door from the street opened straight into the parlour, and the wind was intruding into the room like some invisible animal: rattling the brasses on the range, clattering the framed prints from the *Graphic* in their neat rows on the walls, and scattering

September leaves across the polished floor tiles. And the doorway framed the unprepossessing figure of Bill Frost: thin-faced, his lined mouth hidden by a tired moustache, a drab tie knotted tight up against his throat.

'Bill says he couldn't think where else to go,' his mother said.

Bill's eyes were shadowed, like hollows in a log. Despite himself, Jimmy's heart moved. 'Is somebody ill?'

Bill Frost mumbled something, dropping his eyes.

'Bill wants your help,' his mother said.

'Help with what?'

'With his machine.' Her grey eyes seemed to be begging him to go along with Bill, out into the storm. *And why?* – just to avoid a little social awkwardness, no doubt.

Jimmy looked from one to other, a slow, familiar impatience burning in him. Bill Frost was forty-seven years old: a deacon at the chapel, the founder of the local choir, a sound carpenter, and a good neighbour to his parents, he knew. And yet here he was, so suppressed by his own provincial awkwardness that he couldn't even speak for himself. *In God's name, this is 1895. In London, things are on the move. A new century is nearly on us; blood is rising. You wouldn't think so, here on the coast of Godforsaken Pembrokeshire!*

'*What* bloody machine?' Jimmy snapped.

Frost mumbled again, looking down at his cap.

'What?'

'He said,' his mother replied with dogged determination, 'his *flying* machine.'

Bill Frost's cottage was a quarter-mile further up St Bride's Hill from the Griffiths's.

Bill marched stiffly up the path, his anxiety obvious in every movement of his angular body. Buffeted by the air, Jimmy pulled his cap down over his ears and followed.

It was eleven o'clock. There was a quarter-moon, its face criss-crossed by scudding clouds. The trees around Jimmy were huge and invisible and moving in the dark winds, like ancient giants. Behind him, the Hill swept down to Saundersfoot Bay, and from the harbour rose the anxious tolling of a colliery boat bell, the sustained crash of breakers.

After a hundred yards or so Bill turned off the path, making towards Fred Watkins's farm.

'So,' Jimmy shouted across the wind, 'what about this machine of yours, Bill?'

Bill turned his narrow head. 'It crashed. The wheels caught in the top branches of a tree. You know, that big ash at the bottom of Fred Watkins's field –'

'*What* caught in the ash tree?'

'The *wheels*. The machine's wheels.'

Jimmy shivered. He pulled his jacket close around his chest. Unexpectedly, he felt a little scared. *Wheels in a tree? Flying machines?* What kind of closeted lunacy was he walking into?

Bill went on, 'I thought I'd be safe to leave the machine in the field until the morning, but then this wretched wind came up, see.'

Jimmy tried to laugh. 'But it's not actually a *flying* machine. I mean, you haven't made a machine that can really *fly*. Have you, Bill?'

Bill turned his face into the wind. 'Not if it can't clear a bloody ash tree, I haven't.'

They reached Fred Watkins's field. This was wasteland, really: *dorrix*, just weeds and trash. But there *was* something here, Jimmy saw: some kind of machinery – wreckage – scattered over the grass. Silver moonlight glinted from polished, finely-shaped wood, all over the field.

Bill knelt beside one of the larger pieces of wreckage. It was shaped like a small boat, with flaps of wood – hinged somehow – protruding from the sides. 'Thank God,' he said fervently, his words snatched away by the wind. 'We're not too late. I thought the storm might have smashed it all up by now, see.'

Jimmy walked further into the field. There was one other large piece of wreckage: another boat-shape, smaller than the first. Lengths of cable lay scattered across the grass. It looked as if the two boats had been strung together, somehow, by the bits of cable. In the wind, the smaller boat had scraped across the grass, leaving a trail of crushed blades.

Close up, Jimmy saw that the device did indeed have wheels: simple, iron-rimmed wooden discs, fixed to a trolley of crude axles under the smaller boat. And – he bent to see – there were twigs and leaves wrapped around the wheels.

Twigs and leaves, from an ash tree.

'Come on,' Bill said. He got to his feet, brisk and nervous. 'Help me lift it up to the house. If we cover it all with tarpaulin, it should be all right for the night.'

He took hold of one end of the larger boat, the one with the protruding side-flaps. Jimmy took the other end, and they hefted the device off the ground. It was surprisingly light, and Jimmy staggered.

'You go backwards,' Bill shouted to him. 'I'll guide you. Careful, now . . .'

Jimmy, blinded by the rushing air, stumbled awkwardly across the uneven ground.

They reached Frost's cottage; clean anthracite smoke rose from its chimney to be whipped away by the turbulent air.

Jimmy, tripping over a step, allowed the boat to scrape against the side of the house. A side-flap hit the wall, and Jimmy heard the crackle of splintering wood.

Bill Frost cried out, as if in pain. 'Bloody hell, boy, have a care!'

Jimmy felt as shocked by Bill's swearing as by his own near fall. 'It's only one of those flaps, Bill.'

'*Flaps*? Dain it, that's a bloody *wing*, boy. Now, be careful what you're about . . .'

When he got home, Jimmy took a cup of tea up to bed, and returned to his pamphlets.

At around one he heard the door open again, admitting from the storm his father and older brother, George. The two men were working shifts at the local colliery, Bonville's Court. In their shabby jackets and crumpled trousers, they would be wet, cold and weary, having been carried home along the coast rail line by the open coal drams; and now Jimmy heard the weary clatter of their boots as they prepared for their baths.

Jimmy pored over his political pamphlets, drinking in the scent of their cheap ink, trying to escape in spirit from all this grinding poverty, and soul-breaking work, and provincialism. His father thought he was a *rodni*, he knew: strolling about when real men were at their work, down the pits. But it wasn't Jimmy's fault that he, of all of them, was the only one to have the spirit and brains to escape the mines – wasn't his fault, even, that he was 'so bloody *floity*', as his father had endlessly drummed into him. He never had fit into this family.

But, if truth be told, his new job in London, as a publisher's clerk, was no great joy. And – though he would never, *ever* admit as much – he knew he didn't really fit in there either. In London, his Welshness stuck out like a sign pasted to his head, he thought gloomily. But still, there in London he was in the *centre* of things, surrounded by the pulsing, evolving soul of the new age. He had literature from all the major centres of radical London thought: the Social Democratic Federation, Morris's Socialist League, the Fabian Society, and even one thin sheet from the Independent Labour Party. Beyond the cottage's sturdy walls the wind still swirled, like – he thought sleepily – London's eternal storm of information and debate. Jimmy was nineteen years old, and his mind and heart were wide open to that intellectual tempest. He could hardly bear to return, even for a visit like this, to the restricted cage of Pembrokeshire; for him, Saundersfoot was the past, and London the promise of the bright new century.

He doused his lamp and snuggled under his sheets; it was best to be asleep before his brother came up to their shared room. Jimmy had taken leave from work, and he'd told his mother he would visit for another few days. He could always pack his bags and clear off first thing in the morning, and get back to the quick, exciting air of London . . .

But, as he waited for sleep to claim him, he couldn't stop thinking of poor old Bill Frost. A flying machine in Saundersfoot? What had the chap been thinking of?

It was all nonsense, of course. But he remembered, with vague unease, those ash twigs in the machine's wheels.

2 MORNING

At a little after eight o'clock, Jimmy pulled on his jacket and cap and stepped out of the cottage. The storm had blown itself out. The sunlit air was crisp, invigorating, poised between summer's richness and the ice of winter.

Jimmy looked down the wooded limbs of St Bride's Hill, to where Saundersfoot hugged its crescent of beach; the sharp white crests of waves glittered on the wrinkled ocean. The view made for an exhilarating sweep, and for a moment Jimmy imagined himself to be Bill Frost: to be leaving the ground, here halfway up the Hill, like some heavy, cloth-feathered bird; he would rise into the air, heading down the Hill and into the breeze, off like billy ho towards the Bay. For an instant the vision was so real Jimmy felt as if his feet, light and airy, were indeed lifting from the mundane grass like a buckiboo, a dragon.

He smiled at himself. The vision passed, and he set off up the Hill path.

He found Bill working in his garden, in shirtsleeves, braces and cap; he had a pipe jammed in the corner of his small mouth, and he wore his tie neatly knotted up to his throat. Behind Bill, the garden – a neat, unimaginative square of lawn – sloped down the hillside.

'Hello, Bill. I wanted to see if you were all right.'

Bill greeted him with a handshake; his grip was firm, confident, the palm heavily callused. 'I'm glad you came up,' Bill said in his soft, melodic voice. 'Thanks for coming out last night. I know you must have thought I'd gone a bit daft.'

'It was nothing, Bill. I –'

'No, I mean it.' An intensity shone out of Bill's blue eyes now, burning through his shyness; Jimmy, jolted, realized that Bill meant every word with a passion, and there wouldn't be many occasions in his life when Jimmy would be the recipient of such gratitude. 'If you hadn't helped, that wind would have smashed up my machine, and that would have been that.'

Jimmy, embarrassed, tried not to laugh. 'You could have built another.'

'No. I couldn't afford the materials.' He leaned closer to Jimmy, conspiratorial. 'Anyway, it's Edna, you see. She thinks all this business of flying about is a bit daffy. Particularly after that letter from the War Office. Still, it was good of her to get Fred Watkins to let me use his field. Edna's a Watkins herself, you know.' He straightened up, the morning sunlight catching his shock of grey hair. 'As it turned out, thanks to you, the machine is almost intact. There's only that one wing, really, that took a bit of a knock, and the cabling wants fixing, of course. Do you want to come and have a look at it? It's just round here . . .'

Bill wiped his hands on a cloth, and led Jimmy around the corner of the house. And there – close to a small potting shed, in the shadow of straggling raspberry canes – stood the flying machine.

The whole thing was suspended off the ground, on crude wooden trestles. The two boat-like devices Jimmy remembered from last night were arranged one atop the other, their prows pointing in parallel down the Hill. Bill pointed out the machine's components to Jimmy. The *cradle* – the smaller wheeled boat – was at the bottom, near the ground, with the *gondola* – the larger section, with its 'wings' of wood, one smashed – suspended above. Wood gleamed, shaped, planed and polished; the whole thing looked like some elaborate piece of furniture, Jimmy thought.

Bill stepped forward and climbed easily into the cradle, ducking his head to avoid the wings. He smiled at Jimmy around his pipe, his face a little flushed. 'This is how I stood last night, you see, Jimmy. Of course I've got to replace all the cables yet, but you can imagine how it looked, can't you? The wind off the sea felt just right; and it's the wind that lifts up the machine, you see.'

'The *wind*?' Jimmy looked up at the wings uncertainly. The machine seemed so *real* – solid and finished – here in the autumn sunlight. Jimmy dug deep into his soul, searching for a little scepticism. 'What do you do, flap those wooden wings and take off like a bird?'

'Of course not. I told you, it's the *wind* you need. See those tanks up there?'

Jimmy leaned forward and peered up through the gondola's open base, to see a series of cylindrical tanks fixed inside the framework.

'*Hydrogen*,' Bill said softly. 'Just to get me off the ground. Of course I have to pedal a bit too.'

'*Pedal?*'

'And when I'm up, I tilt the wings forward and *tip* into the wind.' He made a swooping motion through the air with his broad hand. 'And off I go like billy ho, just like a seagull, eh?' He sighed. 'And if it hadn't been for Fred Watkins's bloody ash tree I'd have made it clear across the Bay to Stepaside, I tell you.'

Jimmy became aware of his mouth gaping open, as he stared at Bill Frost inside the remains of his flying machine. He had no idea what to say.

Bill eyed him, some of his shyness returning. 'You're *interested* in all this, aren't you, Jimmy?'

'Interested? Ah –'

Bill squinted up at the snapped wing. 'I'll spend some time on her this evening, before the light goes. There's just that wing to fix, and load up the tanks again, and fix those cables . . . She'll be ready for another shot by the weekend, probably. You know, with just another couple of feet – if I'd been a few years younger and a bit less tizzicky – I would have been *over* that bloody ash tree. Well. What do you say?'

Jimmy felt disconcerted. 'What do you mean?'

Again, that painful shyness seemed to descend on Bill, and the carpenter averted his eyes. 'Jimmy, would you like to give me a hand?'

3 THE PATENT

So for the next few evenings, after Bill got back from his employment up at the colliery-owners' folly, Hean Castle, Jimmy worked on the flying machine.

Slowly the machine took shape once more, as Bill laced the cradle and gondola together with his lengths of cable. Jimmy grew fascinated by the machine itself, by the craftsmanship in it, as if it were some kind of sculpture. The surfaces, lovingly fashioned by Frost's strong hands, were polished so deep that the light off the sea seemed to sink into the curved wood; the joints and pegs were as finely worked as if it were a bit of Chippendale. Whether it flew or not, the machine was certainly a bloody beautiful piece of work, Jimmy thought.

Jimmy saw slowly that the machine – or, more fundamentally, the idea of *flying* – was a fixed compass-point in Bill's thoughts. But it wasn't an obsession. Bill was a chapel elder, and he took one evening a week off from his machine to coach his male-voice choir.

No, he wasn't obsessed, or mad. Bill Frost simply wanted to fly.

'*Why*, Bill?'

Bill Frost straightened up from the gondola, kneading the muscles at the base of his spine; the coals of his pipe glowed. 'Why what?'

'Why *fly*?'

With one hand resting against the flank of his machine, Bill looked across the fold of the Bay, to the north. 'Well, I'll tell you, then,' he said. 'It was many years ago. I was quite a young lad still, but already in the trade. I was working up at Hean then, too, as it happens.

'I'd just cut a plank of pine, and I was carrying it, see, across the front of Hean. Suddenly there was a wind – a gust, really, straight up off the Bay. Well, it picked up that plank, with me clinging to it, and lifted us both straight up into the air, I swear by five or six feet or more. And then it let me down, as gentle as you like.'

He turned to Jimmy, his eyes deepened by the gloom. 'So there you are. I've flown once already, you see. And it was such a bloody marvellous feeling, I said to myself, "Why, I want to do that again".' He slapped the solid flank of his machine. 'And that's what this is all about.'

Jimmy shook his head. 'But, Bill, you don't know anything about flying. You don't have any scientific education.'

'Neither did that plank, I reckon,' Bill said. 'And neither do the seagulls that wheel around the Bay. You don't need science to fly. All you need is a wind to lift you, and a way to catch the wind. And I knew I had the hands, the craft to do it.' He smiled. 'So this machine is part seagull, and part furniture, you see. Just like me, I suppose.

'Anyway,' he said, 'I'm as scientific as you like. I've got a Patent, you know.'

'You're joking.'

Bill looked shocked. 'Never. *And* there's my letter from the War Office. Do you want to see?'

It was a real Patent, all right: Number 20,431, dated October 25th, 1894. In the fading light, Jimmy read out the certificate: '"A FLYING MACHINE. William Frost, Carpenter and Builder, Saundersfoot, Pembrokeshire, do hereby declare the nature of this invention to be as follows . . ."'

'I filed it as soon as I had the design,' Bill said. 'The thing itself wasn't even half-built back then.'

'And the War Office?'

'Well, I sent the Patent there. I thought the Secretary of State might make something out of it.'

Bill produced his War Office letter. It was from an Under Secretary, Mr St John Brodrick. Bill was thanked, but, Jimmy read out, '"This nation does not intend to adopt aerial naviga-tion as a means of warfare."'

Jimmy shook his head; he felt a bubble of humour rise inside him, but he was unsure whether he was laughing at Frost, or Brodrick, or himself. 'Bloody English. He had no *arrant*, no right, to speak to you like that, Bill.' Of *course* the English would dismiss a Patent for a flying machine, coming from some unknown mining village in Wales. But there seemed to be real pain etched in Bill's face, as he looked over his letter from Mr St John Brodrick. Suddenly Jimmy felt his mockery of Bill melt away, and resentment at the dismissal of Bill's life work by this London functionary merged with his own uneasy sense of displacement.

He laid a hand on Bill's shoulder. 'Never mind, Bill,' he said. 'Another couple of days and your machine will be winging it around the Bay with the seagulls, just as you say. That will show them.'

And what, an inner voice warned, *will you say to this old fool when the bloody thing won't even leave the ground?*

Bill turned to him, his pipe discarded. 'Yes,' he said evenly. 'This time, it's going to fly with no mistake.'

'Of course you will. And –'

'No,' Bill said sharply. 'Not me. I've been thinking. I'm a bit of a *kroker* now, see, Jimmy. I'm worn out. My legs and lungs just aren't what they were twenty years ago. And I get tizzicky with my chest in the winter . . . No, *I* can't do it; I'll just end up in the ash tree again.'

'I don't understand,' Jimmy said slowly.

'*You're* going to have to fly the machine for me, Jimmy Griffiths.'

4 THE FURNITURE SEAGULL

It was a fine morning, a late September Saturday.

In the middle of Fred Watkins's field, Jimmy Griffiths stood in the lower cradle of the restored flying machine, his feet resting on the two pedals set in the base. He was taller than Bill Frost, and his head kept bumping against the walls of the upper, winged gondola. The two table-leaf wings were tilted upwards on their hinges, folded neatly away against the gondola's gleaming flanks. Rubber pipes snaked up from Bill's home-made feeder tanks into the cylinders of hydrogen gas fixed inside the gondola.

The cradle rested on its wheels – now freed of ash twigs –

and the upper gondola was supported by its trestles, transported from Bill Frost's garden. Bill and George, Jimmy's brother, stood to either side of the trestles, steadying the gondola.

Now the breeze picked up. The machine creaked a little, a deep wooden sound, and there was a smell of wood chippings and polish. The breeze was coming off the sea and straight up St Bride's Hill; looking down over the Hill now, Jimmy could see gulls floating effortlessly over an ocean of crumpled silk.

Jimmy wondered what he was doing here.

Of course he didn't believe that Bill's machine was actually going to work today; and many times in the last few days he had come to regret his sentimental impulse to waste so much time with the carpenter. It had all been a bit of a lark, he supposed.

But now it came to it, he found he didn't have the heart to walk away from Bill and his foolishness – not without *trying*.

Then the machine strained again, as if yearning to be free of this imprisoning ground.

. . . And what if it's true? What if I really am going to fly, today? He remembered his odd, momentary vision of flying, that first morning looking down over the Hill. *Wouldn't it be glorious, though?* He felt a tiny window of doubt open up in his heart, and a small part of him began to wonder – in hope, for Bill's sake – if this bit of furniture really was, impossibly, going to leave the ground.

'. . . You must be bloody tapped, Jimmy Griffiths,' George murmured sourly.

Jimmy looked down at his brother, beside the trestle. George's expression was full of its usual vicious humour, and Jimmy felt immediately absurd.

'If it's so mad, why are you here then?' he said defiantly.

'To watch you make an idiot of yourself, of course.' George sniffed. 'And to carry you home when you bust your bloody leg. Father always said you were a *floit*, Jimmy.'

'*Flighty*, eh,' Jimmy snapped back. 'Well, maybe you're going to be right for once, George.'

But George's stolid face – round, coal-streaked under its battered cap – was like a dark, Earth-bound moon, its sour gravity holding Jimmy forever to the ground. Oh, wouldn't it be wonderful if, just for once, George could be proved spectacularly, finally wrong?

Then, as if in response to Jimmy's silent plea, the machine shuddered in the breeze; Jimmy rattled in the cradle, and had to grip its polished rim . . .

And – unexpectedly, alarmingly – there was a surge, faint and weak, *upwards:* so *delicate* Jimmy wasn't sure if he was imagining it, so *even* it was like being a child again, swept up by his father's arms.

George stumbled forward, suddenly dragged by the machine across the grass. 'Bloody *hell*,' he said, his mouth a round pit in his face.

'What?'

'You've lifted off the trestles, man.' George staggered, his arms straining at the cradle. 'I don't believe it. You're in the bloody *air*, Jimmy.'

'Pedal, Jim!' Bill Frost's tie knot had slipped a few degrees around his neck. He pulled free the gas feeder lines, and Jimmy heard valves close with a snap; then Bill staggered away from the machine. 'You're up! Pedal, man!'

Jimmy gripped the walls of the cradle and pushed at the two paddle-shaped foot-pedals beneath him. The pedals worked wide, creaking fans of shaped wood. The pedals took a bit of effort to get moving, but once the fans were spinning – pushing air down in a wash towards the ground – it got a lot easier, no harder than riding a heavy bicycle.

The machine lurched sideways, to Jimmy's left. His feet slipped off the pedals and he almost fell over the wall of the cradle; its hard rim dug into his ribs, through his jacket.

'Let go!' Bill screamed at George. 'You're pulling him over! Let go!'

George, Jimmy realized, was still hanging onto the side of the cradle, his arms upstretched, his knuckles white. Now George opened his fists and staggered backwards from the machine.

Released, the machine tipped violently the other way, and the cables between cradle and gondola hummed and creaked. For a few seconds Jimmy could do no more than cling on, as the cradle bobbed in the air like a cork on water.

Then, at last, the machine steadied, leaving the cradle twisting from side to side in its nest of cables.

'Pedal, Jimmy! Keep pedalling!' Bill called.

Jimmy pushed at his pedals, and once more the fans creaked into motion. He glanced down. The bottom of the cradle was open, and – through the cradle's open structure, beyond his trouser legs and muddied shoes – he could see a square of sunlit grass: a square *which slid away beneath him.*

He was in the air!

Still pedalling, he peered over the side. It was as if he stood at the top of an invisible staircase, looking down at George. Jimmy felt a surge of triumph. George's dark disc of a face, turned up towards the machine, looked like a doll's face, scoured of all its scepticism, devoid at last of its lifelong ability to tether Jimmy to the ground.

'You're not flying yet, Jimmy Griffiths.' Bill Frost's voice, floating up from the ground, was like a reedy tenor emerging from some invisible choir. 'You've not got enough height. Keep pedalling, boy!'

So Jimmy pedalled, the sweat pooling around his collar. The machine, with its rotating fans and gas cylinders, lifted him easily upwards. And now Jimmy was so high that he could see the whole of Fred Watkins's field in one glance, spread out like a green handkerchief beneath him. Bill and George, and the machine's empty trestles and Bill's bags of tools, were no more than a little cluster in the receding grass, like an abandoned nest.

Suddenly the breeze picked up, bumping against the machine. The wind seemed stiffer, up here away from the grass, and suddenly the machine felt like a fragile thing indeed, bobbing like a thistledown in the air. Jimmy had a rushing vision of the machine as he'd first seen it, smashed and strewn across Fred Watkins's field. Somehow he hadn't considered the possibility of *falling* before; now, though, he thought about it with a vengeance. What if the machine was to tumble out of the air again, now, with him in it?

'The wings, Jimmy!' Bill Frost had cupped toy hands around his tiny mouth; his voice floated up out of the huge landscape. 'You're high enough. Pull the lever!'

The lever. The lever was a length of wood before his face. In a panic, Jimmy pulled at it, hard.

The wings of wood spread out over his head, dropping on their creaking hinges away from the sides of the gondola.

'Now tilt! Tilt them down!'

Jimmy pulled at the lever again, and the wings, stiffly, tipped downwards, pointing their polished leading edges towards the ground.

The machine fell, so suddenly that Jimmy felt his stomach lurch . . . But he wasn't falling *downwards*, he realized; he was falling *across* the air, gliding down like a seagull towards the ground.

Bill Frost was shouting again, but Jimmy remembered what to do. He shoved at his lever, making the wings tilt upwards. They shuddered as they caught at the air, and the cradle twisted in its cables. But the machine rose again, and the air pushed at his face.

The ash tree at the bottom of Watkins's field sailed beneath him, its crown passing safely beneath the cradle's wheels.

'Well,' Jimmy breathed, 'what do you think of *this*, then, George? I'm bloody flying after all.'

He worked at his lever, and the flying machine dipped and soared in the air, just like a stiff furniture seagull. It was utterly quiet up here, as if he were suspended in some bubble of glass: isolated with only his own ragged breathing, the creak of the wings' hinges, the singing of the breeze in the cables.

He rose fifty, a hundred feet, and St Bride's Hill unfolded beneath him like a curving breast. Glancing down, he could see George and Bill scrambling over the Hill after him, small and unimportant, evoking a sharp boyhood memory of wooden soldiers tumbling down a counterpane.

Saundersfoot Bay spread itself beneath him. From up here

the shape of the land was clear. He could see the Bay's crescent of captured sea, with the harbour structures like shadows on the palm of the land's cupping hand. The folded landscape itself seemed complex and dynamic – as if he were looking down at a photograph, a frozen slice out of the life of some immense, ancient organism. Once – he'd read in London – all of Pembrokeshire had been an ocean floor. But time and ice had compressed that old ocean into strata, into layers of rock that had at last twisted up and come busting through the grass and sand like splintered bone, hard and defiant. And, from up here, he saw how all of human history was compressed into thin layers too, overlying the geology. Here the old tribes had walked: the Cambrae, the Ordovices, the Silures, tribes who had bequeathed their names to the geological layers into which later men had split time.

How apt it was, he thought wildly, that he had launched into the air from *St Bride's* Hill! For St Bride was no more than a Christianized memory of Brigantia, the oldest of the Saxon goddesses: *Brigantia*, goddess of the Earth, and spring, and light. Under a thin patina of Christianity, Brigantia was still here, with all her Neolithic grandmothers: he could *feel* it up here, her ancient green soul soaked into the time-sculpted, layered landscape.

He laughed out loud, and the air-bubble around him contained his voice, making it loud in his ears. By leaving the ground he had become something immortal, he thought: an angel of Brigantia!

He lay on the cool grass, laughing, staring up at the clouds and feeling the Earth rotate under him, as light as a thistle-down itself.

The faces of Bill and George loomed over him: two moons, round with wonder, eclipsing the Sun. Jimmy saw envy and pride mixing in Bill's watery gaze.

'How was it, Jimmy? How was it?'

'It was marvellous, Bill,' he said. 'Bloody marvellous. But I can't tell you. You'll have to try it for yourself, tizzicky chest or not.' He was seized by a sudden passion, an echo of his

rediscovery of Brigantia. 'And that ought to show those English with their letters and their War Office. Get Mr St John
bloody Brodrick to come out here, and stand where you stood,
and watch me flying like a seagull, and *then* tell him to write
his letters, eh?'

Bill looked reflective. 'They'll never do that, Jimmy,' he said
gently. 'You know the English think we're all tapped, the
whole lot of us this side of the Severn.' He stroked the flank
of his flying machine. 'Flying is what this is about. That's all.'

'It's *not* all, dain it,' Jimmy said. He got to his feet; he felt
infused by vigour, by a strength pulsing out of the ancient,
sculpted land from which he had flown. 'If the bloody English
won't come to us, then let's go to them,' he shouted. 'Let's
take our flying machines and soar over their heads, blocking
out the Sun! What do you say, Bill? George?'

Bill seemed to shy away within himself, suddenly every bit
the humble local carpenter, the timid church elder.

But George was grinning.

5 THE ANGELS OF BRIGANTIA

The third Marquess of Salisbury, Prime Minister of Great
Britain, was a man of regular habits (so Jimmy Griffiths
learned from his circle of scurrilous friends in London). Each
day Salisbury hurried through the London traffic to catch his
seven o'clock train from King's Cross, up to his residence at
Hatfield. Thus, one Friday in the late spring of 1896, Lord
Salisbury, in his greatcoat, came down the stairs of the Foreign
Office at a little after half past six of the evening. A messenger
threw open the door of a single-horsed brougham; and as
soon as the Prime Minister was on board, the trained horse
started at full speed. And *off* went the brougham: under the
Horse Guards' Arch, along Whitehall, and towards Trafalgar
Square and the bustle of Charing Cross Road . . .

But today was different.

Londoners – clerks and shop assistants and drapers,
hurrying for their trains and omnibuses home from work –

paused on Westminster and Lambeth Bridges, to peer past the ornate walls of Parliament at the odd events taking place in the river.

From a Welsh coal ketch called the *Verbena*, stationed close to Lambeth Bridge, a box of wood rose awkwardly into the air. To the watchers on the Bridges, the object looked like a piece of furniture, unusually propelled upwards. But then – quite unexpectedly – the box sprouted wings; and it dipped towards the water and up again, in the manner of a bird.

It was a *flying machine*, and it carried – people saw, pointing – a *man*, a dour-looking, thin-faced fellow in a cap.

And now, up from the ketch, there rose another machine: and another, and a fourth. Soon the four furniture seagulls were wheeling over the Thames, and their occupants called out to each other in a lilting accent.

The machines formed up into a rough diamond shape, like a flock of wooden geese. And off they soared: over Parliament, past Westminster Bridge, and along Whitehall, dipping and swooping.

Jimmy Griffiths took the lead, with, at his shoulder, his brother George. Behind them flew Teddy Poole, a cockle-picker from Monkstone, and Harold Read, son of a shipbuilder and a power in the Stepaside rugby team.

The heart of London was laid out below Jimmy like a glittering map. The traffic was snarling up, he saw, as the drivers and passengers, of broughams and phaetons and omnibuses, stopped to stare at the crowded sky. There were a hundred, a thousand faces turned up at him like coins, lit with wonder; once again, Jimmy felt the awesome power of *flight* pulsing through his soul.

And there – nearing the top of Whitehall and quite distinctive – was Salisbury's brougham.

He shouted to the others and pointed down. Teddy Poole waved and called back, his voice carrying small and perfect across the upper air: 'Good shooting, boys!'

The four machines circled like kestrels over the brougham.

From a bag at his waist Jimmy pulled out a lump of coal: good Saundersfoot anthracite, glassy and hard, the best coal in the bloody world.

He hurled the lump down at the brougham.

The coal missed the brougham by a dozen feet, so he reached into his bag to haul out another. Soon the anthracite was spattering down onto the road like a dark rain. It was difficult to aim, but Jimmy had the satisfaction of seeing a couple of his shots, at least, clatter against the brougham's polished top. And Teddy Poole, with a whoop, laid one shot *slap* on the horse's exposed thigh; the poor beast whinnied and lurched forward, rattling the brougham like a shoebox.

When his coal was exhausted, Jimmy hauled at his lever and wheeled for one last time over the brougham. He yelled down at the Prime Minister, as loud as he could: ' "This nation does *not* intend to adopt aerial navigation as a means of warfare!" '

Then, laughing, he led his angels of Brigantia away, towards the open spaces of St James's Park.

6 CAPPER'S FLYERS

'Ah, but do you remember that day?' Bill asked.

Jimmy smiled, and lifted his face to the afternoon sun. The Frosts' two goats, tethered at the bottom of Bill's famous garden, nibbled at the grass. The growling noise of Stanley Scourfield's delivery van floated up from the bottom of St Bride's Hill; Jimmy knew it was the butcher's, because that was still the only van in Saundersfoot.

'Yes. Yes, I do. It was bloody marvellous, Bill.'

'Now, you know I'm not a cruel man, Jimmy. But I'd have given a great deal to see the face of that old ass Lord Salisbury as Welsh coal came hurtling out of the sky all around him!' Bill Frost wiped tears from his weakening eyes. Sixty-three years old now, he was still more gaunt and grey than ever. Jimmy saw how the cuffs of Bill's suit were threadbare and patched. Well, Bill had never been flush with money – and he still wasn't, it seemed, despite the success of his invention. 'You don't come home much these days, Jimmy.'

'Well, I've my job in London.'

'Still working on the newspapers?'

'I'm a deputy editor now.' Suddenly Jimmy was aware of how flat – how *English* – he had let his accent become, with time. He pressed on, 'And I've got a family, a wife and a daughter, half grown she is. We live in Ealing, which is –'

'And what about your family here?'

Jimmy sat back in his chair, and looked out over the expanse of St Bride's Hill, down towards the Bay. 'Well, we've taken in Vickerman's pit ponies, to let them graze our garden. This strike's hitting us hard, Bill.'

'It's hurting a lot of folk around here.'

The coal field strike had started a year earlier – in 1910 – when a band of miners at Tonypandy, in the Rhondda, had got themselves locked out after haggling over a price list. Now, thirty thousand men were locked out or on strike, right across South Wales. There had been a lot of trouble – even in sleepy places like Saundersfoot – what with the owners' attempts to bring in blacklegs. The police and troops had been kept busy, and there was even an Army general put in charge of keeping order in the area – 'as if we were all a bunch of bloody Boer farmers,' as Jimmy's father had complained.

'It's hard for George,' Jimmy said. 'He spends his days digging coal off the beach with his mates. George can't put up with this, with idleness. Well, you know George. He never was the most reflective man in the world . . .'

He heard a *thrumming* noise, a soft pulsing that rose from over the crest of the Hill behind them. Jimmy glanced at Bill; the old carpenter merely lifted his face to the light.

Jimmy stood up and walked down the slope to the middle of the garden, and looked back towards the crest of the Hill.

A dozen Army Flyers came soaring over St Bride's Hill towards the Bay, a hundred feet in the air, their polished wings tilting smoothly into the light wind. The large, petrol-driven fans set in the Flyers' bases shushed easily through the air.

From the leading Flyer, a soldier's goggled face returned Jimmy's stare, expressionless.

'There must be trouble in Saundersfoot again,' Bill Frost said.

Jimmy shielded his eyes and squinted up at the machines. 'Those are Capper Flyers,' he said. 'Model E, I think.' Each powerful enough to carry two English soldiers: refined versions of Capper's first fighting craft, themselves a major advance over Bill's prototype design – machines which had swept over the Transvaal in 1899, winning the war against the Boer republics in a matter of months. And now the Flyers carried English soldiers – like khaki-clad angels, with guns mounted in their Flyers' cradles – to subdue Saundersfoot's *leer*: the hungry Welsh miners, that rabble of 'undeserving poor', as even Jimmy's own paper called them.

Jimmy remembered his excitement – his radical, intellectual rage – at the age of nineteen, at the turn of the century, when he'd first left home for London. But it was gone now: all gone. Jimmy was still only thirty-five – younger than Bill Frost had been in the days of their great adventure, he realized – but those moments of flight, when he had soared like a gull, seemed long ago. Now the years, and his responsibilities, had finally bound him to the Earth for ever.

And the twentieth century didn't seem so bloody wonderful, now he was in it.

Jimmy walked up the garden, slowly. He sat down with Bill Frost. 'Sometimes I wonder what would have happened if I hadn't come out to help you, that stormy night. There might be no flying machines yet, eh?' *And would we be better off, I wonder?* 'But I suppose you should still be proud, Bill. Without you . . .'

But Bill had closed his eyes and seemed to have drifted to sleep: perhaps dreaming, Jimmy wondered, of that distant day at Hean Castle when a gust of wind had swept up a pine plank and a frightened, astonished young carpenter.

Behind him, the Capper Flyers swept steadily down St Bride's Hill towards the lights of Saundersfoot.

WEEP FOR THE MOON

The engines coughed into life. The little plane shuddered, then settled into a steady buzz as the props turned. The passenger cabin started to heat up; there was an oily warmth that slowly banished the damp chill.

The AAF Captain huddled into his greatcoat and peered out of the cabin's tiny, grubby porthole. He could barely see the end of the wing through the swirling December fog, and the light of the short English afternoon was already fading.

He shivered.

He took off his wire-framed glasses and polished them on a handkerchief; short-sightedly he sneaked a glance at the plane's only other passenger – a Colonel whose name he'd already forgotten, a solid-looking citizen who was going through an attache case, oblivious to his surroundings.

Fear knotted the Captain's stomach; he clenched his jaw to keep from whimpering like a boy.

Maybe he ought to just up and off this damn plane.

He hated flying at the best of times. And to take off now, in this fog? His orderly mind listed the dangers. Crashing into a tree in the fog. Getting shot down by some Luftwaffe patrol over the Channel. Damn it, getting punctured by English ack ack – the flight was unscheduled, he remembered.

He could just stand up, give his apologies to the Colonel, break for the door . . .

He took a deep breath and pushed himself back into his seat; and he told himself to grow up.

Before he'd joined up a couple of years earlier, he'd got used to getting things done – he'd run his own bands for five years, after all. But in the AAF there was always some desk-pilot to block whatever he wanted to do, and he seemed to spend his whole time fighting just to stand still. Well, this time he'd cut through the red tape by talking his way onto this flight; he was on his way to Paris to set up the band's arrival there, and he was damned if he was going to compromise that for a schoolboy funk.

He closed his eyes and thought about Helen.

It was then that he heard the voice.

'Weep for the moon, for the moon has no reason to glow now,
'Weep for the rose, for the rose has no reason to grow now –'

He recognized the lyric; Eddie Heyman had written it for 'Now I Lay Me Down to Weep', the tune that had become 'Moonlight Serenade'. Al Bowlly used to sing that lyric for Ray Noble, he remembered. Well, it sure as hell wasn't Bowlly now. For a moment his own arrangement of his tune sounded in his ears, with the clarinet lead and the ooh-wah brass . . . Funny how he could hear the singing over the props. In fact, he realized, suddenly he couldn't hear the props at all. Maybe it was something to do with the fog.

'The river won't flow now,
'As I lay me down to weep . . .'

He opened his eyes.

'Hi, bro.'

The Captain turned. In the seat next to him sat his brother Herb . . . Herb? Confused, he looked around the plane's dingy fuselage; but the studious Colonel wasn't to be seen.

'Herb? What the hell are you doing here? I thought you were in the States.'

Herb's thin face split into a grin. 'You aren't glad to see me? Some welcome, my man.'

The Captain's confusion broke up under a wave of affection. 'It was the singing, boy. I could have sworn it was Sinatra;

you threw me off . . .' He reached over and hugged his brother, awkwardly, confined by the plane seats and his greatcoat. Within his embrace Herb felt stiff and strangely cold. Herb was in civvies, a suit under a brown overcoat; the Captain found himself staring. 'Herb, I don't know how the hell you got in here. This is an AAF field. And the damn plane's about to take off; we're on our way to France –'

But the props were still silent. He turned to see if they were still twisting, but the windows had fogged over even more.

Herb put a hand on his shoulder; the Captain was startled by the intensity of the grip. 'Glenn,' Herb said. 'Don't think about the props. Don't think about how I got here.' His voice was heavy, uncharacteristically serious.

'Herb?'

Herb bit his lip, obviously hesitant. Then a thought seemed to strike him, and he sat up in his chair and rummaged through his pockets. 'Damn it.'

'What is it?'

'Glenn, can you bum me a Strike?'

'. . . Sure.' The Captain pulled a crumpled green packet from the inside pocket of his jacket and thumbed out a Lucky Strike for Herb; using one of the Captain's matches his brother lit up and drew a great drag on the cigarette – then exhaled and stared at the Strike, looking oddly disappointed. 'Glenn, are these stale, maybe?'

The Captain frowned. 'New today . . . Herb, what's going on?' Herb was an organized kind of a guy; the Captain couldn't recall a time when he'd been caught short of a smoke. 'Did you dress in a hurry today?'

Herb smiled, somehow sadly. 'Something like that. Let's say I was – equipped – in a hurry.'

'Equipped?'

'Glenn, listen to me.' Again that note of heaviness. 'I've – come – to tell you something.'

'Is something wrong at home?' Panic spurted in him. 'Helen. It's Helen, isn't it?' A few years earlier his wife had been ill enough to be hospitalized. She'd come out; and the experience had brought them closer. But now – 'In God's name tell me, Herb.'

Herb was shaking his head. 'No, it's not Helen. Take it easy. Nothing's wrong with Helen.'

'Then what?'

Herb opened his mouth, hesitated, shut it again. 'I don't know how to tell you, boy.'

'Just tell me, damn it! You're frightening me.'

'Okay.' Herb leaned forward. 'It's you, Glenn. It's news about you. You've got to get off this plane, right now.'

The Captain felt a chill, deep in the place where his darkest, most secret fears lurked, far under all the control, the business. 'What are you talking about?'

'Because the damn thing never makes it.' Herb, clearly mixed up and distressed, couldn't meet Glenn's stare; but his voice stayed steady. 'It's true, Glenn; you have to believe me.

'Nobody finds out what happened. Maybe you're shot down; maybe you just lost your way. But *you never make it to Paris.*'

The Captain sat back, still staring. The silence of the plane started to feel eerie. 'Damn it, Herb, you've sure learned how to scare a man. You're talking like it already happened.'

'Glenn, to me it did. I remember it.' Herb's eyes grew misty. He turned again to his brother. 'I remember it; I read newspapers about it. Damn it, man; I can prove it to you.' He squirmed in his seat and from the pocket of his overcoat he drew an object about the size and shape of a dime novel; it was bound in leather, and set in its upper surface was a piece of glass three inches square. 'Watch,' Herb said strongly. He poked at small lettered squares inset into the leather cover, and to the Captain's amazement the glass square filled abruptly with light; a series of grainy black-and-white images flickered across it, and from somewhere tiny voices spoke, insect music played.

'Herb. What the hell is this?'

'Don't worry about it,' Herb said with a crap-cutting chop of his left hand. 'It's a pocket television. Okay?'

'So where's the tube? Up your sleeve?'

'Yeah,' said Herb sarcastically. 'Now will you forget it and just concentrate on the pictures?'

The Captain leaned forward and peered into the little screen. He saw pictures of himself and the band – mostly old stock, from before the war – images of a plane like the one he was sitting in. There was a commentary he couldn't quite make out. 'It looks like a newsreel,' he said.

Herb nodded vigorously. 'That's just what it is. A newsreel. Hang on to that, Glenn. Now listen to me: this is a newsreel, not of what has happened in the past – *but what will happen in the future.*'

Herb's words seemed to slide away from the Captain's understanding. 'What are you telling me, Herb?'

Now his brother was speaking with a kind of weight, an authority, that was alien to the Herb he'd grown up with. 'Just forget about the whys and hows for a minute, and think about the pictures. What's the story here?'

The Captain peered into the window to the future, trying to comprehend the parade of little figures, the tinny voiceover.

'It's your death, Glenn. Isn't it? They're reporting your death. If you don't get off this plane, it's a fact as real as apple pie; Glenn, it's as real to me as anything else that ever happened. Damn it, the President himself calls a national Miller Day, in July, not long after the end of the war. Not bad for a horn-player –'

'The war ends in July? Next July?' Could it really be as close as that?

Herb tapped another part of the little box and the pictures faded. 'Glenn, I've come back to warn you. I can't make you get off this plane and save your life; you have to do that for yourself . . .'

'Slow up, Herb.' He closed his eyes, tried to find a piece of calmness. 'You're going too fast.'

It couldn't be a trick. Herb wouldn't play a trick like this.

But, of course, this mightn't be Herb.

He opened his eyes again, stared hard at the man beside him. 'Damn it, you sure look like Herb. You talk like him. You even sing like him.'

A cloud of doubt crossed Herb's face. 'I'm not going to lie to you. I'm Herb inside, Glenn. I know myself. I am Herb; that's all I am; that's all I'll ever be. But –' And now Herb himself looked scared, and that frightened the Captain more than anything. 'But,' Herb went on, 'even while we're sitting here I know there's another Herb, back in the States. This minute. I've got his memories, Glenn. If I was smart enough I could tell you what I was doing right now. What he *is* doing right now. Maybe he's eating doughnuts. I was always crazy for doughnuts, wasn't I?' A thought struck him. 'Hey, Glenn, you got any doughnuts?'

The Captain snorted. 'Do I look like I have?'

Herb seemed disappointed. 'Maybe it's as well. I couldn't taste a damn thing when I smoked that Strike . . . I guess I've not been sent here to enjoy myself.'

The Captain wanted to shrink away from this person . . . But this was his brother. He could *feel* it. 'Herb, all of this sounds crazy. You're not making any sense.'

Herb spread his hands and stared at them, as if they were unfamiliar objects. 'No more to me, guy. Glenn, I'm a – like a photograph. Or a movie image.' He nodded. 'Yeah; that's what I am.' He looked scared again. 'But I'm Herb inside.'

The Captain wondered what to say. 'Why are you here? Did someone send you?'

'Yeah.' Herb nodded. 'Men from the future, Glenn; from the next century, a hundred years from now.'

'They made you up and sent you back here? How?'

'Glenn, I'm only Herb. How the hell do you expect me to be able to tell you that?' He pointed at the little television. 'I couldn't even tell you how this thing works.'

The Captain didn't want to smile. 'Then just tell me why you're here.'

'I've told you. To tell you to get the hell off of this plane.'

The Captain sighed; somehow his fear was fading, to be replaced by a kind of irritation. 'Okay, Herb, let's go at this another way. I'm not a general. I'm not the President. I'm not even Walt Disney. I'm a goddamn bandleader. Why the hell would these – these guys from the future – go to all this trouble to save me? What do I do, invent penicillin?'

Herb shook his head. 'You don't believe me, do you? Then you won't believe this next bit.'

'Try me.'

'It's not just you, Glenn. It's the western world; it's Christianity, and democracy. It's to save all of that.'

The Captain snorted in disgust. 'I haven't got time for this.'

Herb held up his hands. 'Believe me, you have. Just listen for a minute. Okay?' He glared back. 'Okay?'

The Captain shook his head. 'One minute, Herb; then I get on with my job.'

Herb started to speak.

'I want you to get hold of this, Glenn,' he began. 'Ideas are *alive*. Have you ever thought that? The good ones seem to come out of nowhere; and they latch on, they grow, they spread. They propagate.

'Think about it. Look at – oh, "Pennsylvania Six Five Thousand". Remember where that came from? Jerry Gray took a riff from, what the hell was it –'

'"Dipsy Doodle",' said Glenn. 'Larry Clinton.'

'Sure. That one little riff was like a seed, see; that's what I'm telling you. And Jerry's head was like the sweet Earth, where that seed took hold and grew.' Herb mimed the action of plants. 'And you, you're like the gardener who picks out the good stuff and cultivates it –'

The Captain laughed. 'What's your job, Herb? Spreading the horseshit?'

Herb smiled, but he kept going. 'Just listen. So ideas are living things. They grow, and compete with each other for space to grow – which is the space between our ears. And the younger ones, the stronger ones, push out the weak.' Herb looked into his brother's face. 'All right?'

The Captain thought about all of that. It made him feel uneasy – not just the sheer craziness of it, but the fact that it reminded him of something else. But he said, 'You've still got my attention. I'm looking forward to you getting to the point.'

'Now,' Herb said patiently, 'the strongest breed of idea, the toughest strain of all, is *music*. You know? There's something fundamental about music, something that sits in your head, underneath all the words, the logic, the business. Like when you can't get a melody out of your head, even when you hate the damn thing –'

'Or you hate the guy who wrote it. Sure.'

'Okay.' Herb sat straighter in his seat. 'Let's leave that for a minute.

'Second thing. Glenn, in a hundred years – in the time of the guys who sent me – the Earth gets Visited.'

The Captain shook his head. 'Herb, you really are talking like a crazy man.'

'You promised to hear me out.'

'I said a minute.'

'Glenn, I'm your brother; you owe me this.'

The Captain frowned, studying Herb's tense, earnest face. There was a light around Herb now, a kind of soft focus which disconcerted the Captain even more. 'Are you my brother?' he asked softly.

Herb said, 'We've discussed this, Glenn. I am. And, at the same time, I'm not.'

'Why would these guys from the future send *you*?'

'Why good old Herb?' A mocking snort cut through the strange aura of saintliness. 'I guess they picked someone who you might listen to. And believe. Who would you rather they picked? The President? Donald Duck?'

The Captain shook his head. 'Tell me what you have to tell me.'

'Visitors,' said Herb.

'From where? Mars? Orson Welles did that before the war, Herb.'

Herb didn't even smile. 'Nobody knows where they came from. They know it wasn't Mars, though; the people there would have died first –'

The Captain blinked. 'There are people on Mars? Martians?'

'No, Glenn; men like you and me. They'll live on Mars, in cities, ah, under glass.'

'You're kidding.' He felt tendrils of fear returning to his heart. 'Did you say people die?'

Herb pursed his lips. 'The Visitors are different from us. Very different. They don't even recognize us; not as living, breathing creatures with souls, anyhow. They think we're – I don't know, cattle maybe. Less than that; like worms in the ground, or the ground itself. Dirt.

'People start dying, Glenn; in great swathes. Like footfalls.'

'Why?'

Herb shrugged. 'The Visitors don't have a reason. They don't need a reason. Glenn, we can't even see them; maybe they can't see us.

'They don't know we're alive. They think ideas are alive.' Herb looked into his face. 'Are you understanding me? The Visitors are like ideas, too. Maybe. Maybe they can talk to the ideas; I don't know . . . Anyway they respond to the biggest ideas, the strongest. And, if you don't happen to have the Biggest Idea in your head, the Visitors will wipe you out without even thinking about it.'

Baffled, frightened, the Captain pulled his greatcoat closer around him. It didn't seem to be getting any darker, funnily enough, but it sure as hell was cold. 'Tell me what it's got to do with me, Herb.'

'Okay.' Herb wet his lips. 'Let me tell you what happens if you get off this damn plane.' He poked at the little television box again, and a fresh newsreel started. Images of bands, of the Captain himself, in uniform and out of it. 'You live,' said Herb. 'You don't get lost in the Channel. The war finishes; the AAF let you out; you go home. You're a war hero.

'The bands form up again. All the old guys are still around. Billy May on the horn. Trigger Alpert. Dorothy Claire. The Modernaires – not the same ones . . .'

The Captain watched the flickering images. Now he saw a montage of towns, of glittering venues, splashed newspaper headlines. It was a tale of success piled on success, but he felt distant, chastened somehow.

Herb said, 'Glenn, you were the biggest before. Right? But, man, after the war you are *huge*. I can't tell you . . .

'You start to step back from the band, though. Jerry Gray does a lot of the arranging –'

'Like before the war.'

'But you keep close to it; nobody else has your ear for the riff, Glenn; and you know it.

'1950, you have your biggest hit yet. "Amazing You".' A compelling little riff wafted out of the television box. The Captain didn't recognize it. 'Sinatra and Day duet on the vocals –'

Glenn couldn't help but smile. 'I get to work with Doris?'

'Still with that unique voicing of yours,' said Herb. 'With the clarinet lead and the sax as a fifth voice in the reeds . . . But you're spreading your wings. You get into song publishing. Personal management. You produce shows on the radio, the television. Man, you've still got that business sense. It's not just your own stuff – you're doing it for everyone else as well. You keep swing alive; you're providing the framework the rest can work in.

'And the world's whistling your songs, man; you're a legend.'

The newsreel images, in colour now, had reached 1960. The Captain, following the fragmented story, learned that he would be worth a lot of money. Ten million; a hundred million maybe. There would be a new writer, a young guy from Texas, name of Holley. The Captain would hear his songs on some crackly old station during a business sweep through the South . . . Inspired by Holley, Miller would decide to get closer to the music again, realizing what he'd been missing with all the business stuff. But he'd changed; he'd learned new things. With his swing over Holley's riffs he became bigger than ever.

And all the bands played on and on . . .

'Your music is the sound of America, Glenn,' Herb said. 'They're still playing "GI Patrol" as they sweep through 'Nam in their helicopter gunships . . .'

'Nam?'

'Vietnam.'

'Where the hell's that?'

Herb shrugged. 'Another war, man; what does it matter?

'It goes on and on. Even after you die in '77, a ripe old seventy-three, in your bed . . .

'Glenn, you come to symbolize something; you, and your music, and your mood. Something that keeps alive and growing; something at the heart of America, and democracy.'

The Captain felt tears prickle; he took off his glasses and dabbed at his eyes. The plane was a myopic blur. Strangely enough Herb still looked quite sharp, a preternatural clarity that added to his aura of unreality. 'Shut up, Herb. Damn it; you always did know how to push my buttons.'

'I'm telling you the truth, man. And when these Visitors come, in a hundred years' time, and they seek out the Big Idea – you know what they find?'

'Tell me.'

Herb slapped his leg. 'Music. Your music.'

'You're telling me they'll still be playing my crummy tunes in the year two thousand and forty four? You expect me to believe that?'

'They are, Glenn; but not just yours. All the other guys, who came after you. You made it possible for them; all the new, brilliant bandleaders. Riddle. Mancini. McCartney. Watts.

'You're the leader, the one with the business sense *and* the ear for what the punters want to hear. To dance to. The music grows. There are people who use the bands the way, I don't know, Beethoven used the symphony orchestra. There's great music, Glenn; the greatest. But, because of you and your instincts, it never loses touch with the people.'

Herb pushed another button on his box, now, and music billowed out of it. Recognizably swing, the Captain realized, but of a depth and complexity that staggered him; the notes seemed to swirl around Herb's unreal, crystal-clear face, against the blurred backdrop of the plane.

Herb said, 'Glenn, after a hundred years it's the American Big Idea; it's sunk in so deep you could never get rid of it. Americans live through the Visit, Glenn; and it's thanks to you . . .'

The Captain replaced his glasses. Strangely he felt disturbed now by Herb's account rather than moved; there was something not quite right about this Big Idea stuff – something that was making him uneasy. He said, 'It's a neat story. Now tell me the other side. What if I don't get off the plane?' He swallowed, forced himself to say it. 'What if I don't live through this?'

Herb took a deep breath. 'What do you want me to say? Instant sainthood, man, if that's what you want.

'The band keeps going; your Army band, I mean. They play France, the rest. But it's not the same.

'After the war the guys try to keep it going.'

The Captain felt morbidly curious. 'Who?'

'Try Tex Beneke.'

He laughed. 'Tex holds down a neat tenor-sax, but he couldn't manage a smile.'

'Sure. But Tex is just the front man. Don Haynes runs the show, behind the scenes.

'But it doesn't work. Don has the business but he just doesn't have your – what, your ear? Your intuition? Tex and Don are like the two halves of you, Glenn, but they don't add up to the whole.

'They fight. Tex wants to move on, try new things. Don wants to keep it just the same as it always was . . .

'It falls apart. Tex leaves; the band starts to break up. The vultures come down, imitators.'

He frowned. 'What vultures?'

'Ralph Flanagan.'

'Who?'

'Ray Anthony. Even Jerry Gray. Imitators; they add nothing new. It's like a long funeral, Glenn. It's dreadful.

'The music stops changing. People remember it, with affection, but the life just goes away.' Herb tapped at his television box and a fresh newsreel started up in the little window. 'Glenn. Look at these headlines. 1946, Christmas. Just two years from now, right? Listen who's retired. Dorsey. Goodman. Teagarden. Les Brown –'

'I can't believe it.'

'It's true, man. Some of them keep trying, but the music

gets too hard. They lose the audience. Kenton, for instance –'

Glenn shook his head. 'You got to produce music they can dance to.'

'You can see that,' said Herb. 'Kenton doesn't have the ear; he loses people.

'The singers take over. Sinatra, Cole. The bands become too expensive to ship around the country, damn it, especially as no-one wants to hear any more.

'People stay home, watch television. There are new kinds of music; the young take it up because there's nothing else. But there's no class to it, no swing. You should hear it, Glenn; it's like jungle drums. People like you and me can't even listen to it.' Herb frowned, sadly. 'Can you imagine that? Parents and kids who can't share their music any more . . .' Now a scratchy image filled the little screen: some guy in a tux talking directly to the camera against a cheap backcloth. Herb brightened. 'Here's something funny, or maybe sad. The Dorseys keep going, in a way. This is their television show; not big, but a show. And you know who starts getting his first breaks on this show? Presley, that's all.'

'Presley? What kind of a name is that?'

Herb shrugged. 'Never mind. Look, Glenn, it all fragments. Splinters. Twenty, thirty years later you wouldn't call it music any more. The kids take drugs to write it; you wouldn't believe it.

'People are sick of it. There's nothing they can understand any more; nothing they can dance to.

'By the end of the century they don't buy music; not en masse, not together. Two hundred million Americans buy two hundred million different songs, it seems like. There's no *identity*, Glenn. That's what you provided.'

'And when the Visitors come –'

'They look for the Big Idea. You know what they find? Islam. Mohammedans; the Arabs.

'Americans – simply die, Glenn. Europe, Australia too . . . a hundred years from now America's a wasteland.'

Herb fell silent again; he snapped off his television and stowed it in his overcoat pocket.

The Captain settled back in the tight plane seat and folded his arms. 'I don't know what to say, Herb.'

'Don't say anything. Just get off the damn plane!'

Miller tried to take it all in. Could it really be true, that ideas were like living things which populated people's heads? And if that were so . . .

Suddenly he realized what had been making him so uneasy about the whole concept.

'Herb,' he said softly. 'These living ideas.'

'Yeah?'

'How much room do they leave for democracy?'

Herb stared at him. 'What are you talking about?'

The Captain rubbed at his temples. 'I think I'm talking about freedom, Herb. About the freedom of the individual. After all, doesn't Mr Hitler think he has a big idea, a living idea?'

'Glenn, this isn't relevant. Forget Hitler. At the bottom of it, we're talking about whether you live or die.'

The Captain looked out at the fog, which seemed to be frozen against the dingy porthole. He found himself wondering just how important that really was. 'What about Helen?'

'If you die?' Herb reached out and touched his brother's arm. 'She does OK, Glenn. Your stuff keeps selling; the estate keeps her comfortable.'

The Captain sat in the odd stillness of the plane. Herb waited patiently. The Captain tried to accept all Herb had told him, tried to imagine this bizarre world of the future, with glass cities on Mars and yet lit up by band music he'd recognize . . . but darkened by the deadly footfalls of the Visitors.

Then he thought of Helen. Of the feel of the trombone in his hands. Of the hordes of khaki-clothed GIs, here in England and the States, who threw their caps into the air and whooped as the trumpets and trombones blasted at them in all their roaring purity, as the saxes welled up below and the rhythm section let loose with those clear, crisp, swinging beats –

Herb studied him. 'Well? Have you decided?'

'There's nothing to decide, Herb. Not if Helen's going to be OK. Remember the statement I put out when I joined up?'

Herb nodded and closed his eyes. ' "I, like every American, have an obligation to fulfil . . ." '

Glenn opened the top few buttons of his coat, pointed to the pips on his shoulder. 'I'm a serviceman, Herb. I have to do my duty, even if it means I risk my life. Just like every American serviceman in this damn war. And, Herb . . . maybe all this "living idea" stuff really could save the world. But, damn it, there's something about it that just isn't *American*.'

Herb narrowed his eyes. 'Glenn, I don't know what to say to that. You know I always looked up to you, for your sense of honour, of duty. But . . . Glenn, you have a duty to all those Americans in the future. The Visitors –'

'Herb, across that Channel there are young Americans who, not six months ago, were preparing to lay down their lives in Normandy . . . And they could still die, before Europe is free. Right now they're expecting me to go over there and bring them some real, live American music. To let them go home for a few hours, in their heads.

'That's where my duty is.' Glenn closed his eyes, let his own words sink in. It was right; he knew it was right. 'That's all there is, Herb.'

Herb held his arm for a long minute. Then he stood up. 'Maybe the future guys were wrong to send me back. I understand, Glenn. I won't argue with you any more.'

The Captain heard the noise of the props return, faintly, as if from a tremendous distance.

'You know,' Herb said as he pulled his overcoat closed, 'I'm not sure what happens now.'

'What do you mean?'

'I know I'm not Herb. Not really. But inside I'm me, with two sets of Herb memories . . . What happens to me now? Will I know about it?'

The Captain stared up at him. He had no idea how to answer. He wanted to get up, hug his brother and calm his fears, but Herb was already heading down the aisle, receding into a darkness the Captain hadn't noticed before. The Captain called after him, 'Herb, wait. Do you want to take these Strikes?'

Herb shrugged. 'I can't taste them anyway. Hey,' he said. Now it was really hard to see him in the gloom. 'They make a movie about you. 1953.'

'Sure they do. Who plays me?'

'You won't believe it.' Herb's voice was faint now, almost drowned by the props.

'Try me.'

'Jimmy Stewart.'

'You're kidding. He's a hero . . . I'm proud.'

'No, Glenn. Stewart should be proud . . .'

'Herb?'

But Herb had left the plane, although Glenn hadn't seen him open the door. And the Air Force Colonel with the attache case was back where Herb had sat, just as if nothing had happened.

The prop noise rose to a growl. The plane bumped forward.

The Captain peered out through the port, looking for Herb; but there was only the fog.

GOOD NEWS

Falco, Reader and the two cops crammed into the rusty elevator cage. They avoided looking at each other's eyes. In the cage's dim light Reader's bald head seemed smooth, almost faceless to Falco.

Falco looked into his heart.

He felt numb, his own emotions as hidden from him as were Martin Reader's. *What the hell am I doing here?* He wished he was back in his office: with its banks of screens, wire feeds and online consoles, with the news floor beyond his windows harshly lit and vibrant, with the ocean of events lapping around him.

They reached the fifth floor. Falco led the party along the landing, to a heavy, scuffed door: it was commonplace, one in a corridor of identical doors, in this nondescript brownstone.

The two cops glanced at each other, and took up positions to either side of the door. They were big men, but they looked nervous; their black tunics were bulky, and Falco wondered if they were wearing vests.

Falco raised his fist, and banged on the door.

He answered. *Him.* He was still in his blue work suit; it was a little after seven in the evening. He smiled when he saw Falco, his eyes warm behind his thick glasses. But then he registered the cops, and Reader, and the smile faded.

Reader spoke first. 'You know why we're here.'

The man stepped forward, coming into the corridor's dim light. His physical size became apparent. The cops flinched.

The older of the cops was a sergeant, around forty-five,

going to paunch. He hissed to Falco, 'Are you sure it's *him*? I mean, this is a big guy. But – can it be *him*?'

Falco tried to keep his voice level. 'Yes. Yes, it's him. Son – did you think you could keep your secret from *me*?'

He was still watching Falco, with a face that had hardly changed since the day a boy from Kansas had walked into Falco's office, nervous, clumsy, overgrown, asking for a job on his paper.

His eyes were empty.

No, Falco thought. *Not empty. He understands.* Falco was barely able to meet that gaze. *Jesus. Already he understands what's happening. And he forgives me.*

Falco felt irritation: unexpected, unwelcome, savage, the first emotion to break through his numbness. *Maybe I don't want to be forgiven.* 'God damn it, boy, let's get this over. Open your shirt.'

Falco watched those huge biceps bunch, under the scuffed suit. *My God. If he really does blow his top –*

But then, with a fast motion of one hand – *impossibly* fast, too fast to follow – he ripped open his shirt, careless of torn fabric. It was like a snake shedding its skin. The colours of the costume he revealed, red and blue and gold, were vivid in the dingy corridor.

The younger cop, staring, said: 'Well, I'll be – it *is* him.' *He sounds like a country boy*, Falco thought. *Maybe he comes from Kansas too.*

The sergeant read a statement of rights. At the end of it, he held out a pair of cuffs. 'No,' Falco said. 'That's not necessary. Cuffs couldn't restrain him anyway. And there are cameras outside, damn it; leave him his dignity.'

'He's right,' the junior cop said. 'I guess if he doesn't want to come with us – why, he could fly right out the damn window – it'd take a nuke to shoot him down . . .'

'Shut up, Clancy.'

But *he* was smiling at the sergeant, evidently forgiving him too. He held out his wrists. The cuffs snapped on, the noise sharp in the enclosed corridor.

The cops led the way to the elevator; the man walked

between them, calm, his head high, his cape rustling over his shoulders. In Falco's eyes, made rheumy by too many years of blotchy type and vdu screens, the bright colours of the costume melted and ran.

Reader took the stairs, with Falco. 'Well. It's over. He's submitting himself to the due process of law.'

'He doesn't have to.' Falco heard his own voice crack. 'That kid was right. He could bust out, be a hundred miles away in a second.'

'Of course. But he won't, will he? Not *him*.' He patted Falco's shoulder, with a hand gloved in soft leather. 'That's why we love him, I suppose.'

The word startled Falco. 'What?'

'Oh, you mustn't be ashamed. We all feel the same, about *him*!'

'He's never done us any harm, damn it.'

'He may have *intended* no harm.' Reader sighed, and Falco couldn't tell how sincere he was. 'That's what makes this so painful.'

'What's in this for you, Reader?' Falco snarled. 'Why prosecute him? Why do you want to play Judas?'

For the first time there was a flicker of real emotion on the smooth face, a lift of an eyebrow, a flash of irritation. 'Don't you understand anything? My role in this is *quite* different.' He stared at Falco, from within glassy blue eyes. '*You* figured out his secret identity; *you* led the police here. You're his editor, damn it. *You're* the Judas.'

They emerged from the brownstone, into the glare of TV lights.

The charges were complex, brought by Readercorp at both state and federal levels. They concerned a break-in at a lab belonging to Readergen, a subsidiary of Readercorp. The charges centred around wilful damage to property, theft, industrial espionage, and restrictions of trade.

Justice Hynes, appointed to the case, decided that a Grand Jury hearing wouldn't be appropriate. Any jurors couldn't help but be biased by the intensive media coverage. Instead there would be a pre-trial, in open court. The purpose was to establish if the prosecuting attorney had enough evidence to take the case to a higher court for full trial.

While the court assembled, Martin Reader's words and image filled newsprint, screens, the fizzing online nets.

'*What is a hero?*

'*Look: I'm chairman and CEO of Readercorp. A major industrial grouping. And so I have powers, which I have to use with discretion. It's not always clear what's the right thing to do. And in some situations there is no action without undesirable consequences ... In a morally ambiguous world like ours, how can heroes function?*'

The pre-trial was televised.

The whole thing's a circus, Falco thought. *Calvary on TV*. Of course he watched it all, several channels at once, on the bank of small screens in his office. And his own paper ran yards of reportage, analysis and comment.

The court was small, modern, panelled with oak. A Stars and Stripes hung limp in one corner of the room. The seats were of moulded plastic, and looked too small for *him*; but he sat patiently, his huge shoulders hunched over, his hands still cuffed, his costume a splash of primary colour in the sombre tones of the court. He submitted to everything he was asked to do, but he wouldn't say anything. Not a word. His attorney even had to register his plea, of not guilty. Falco had the impression the decision on which way to plead had come from the attorney, not the client.

Martin Reader whispered: '*Look: a superhero can avert a car crash. Fine; most people would applaud that as "good". But what is his view of the motor industry, which sells us cars designed to exceed sensible speed limits? What about wider dilemmas, for instance the conflict between the right to freedom of movement and environmental damage? Can a hero hold a view on such things? Should he? Does he have any entitlement to act, if he does?*

'*Which would be the right side for a superhero to "choose" in a revolution? What would a superhero's position be on euthanasia, overpopulation?*

'*Like everyone else's, my heart skips a beat when I see that streak of red and blue in the sky. But I have reservations. For, even when he restricts his intervention to situations which are, on the face of it, morally unambiguous, he is damaging us. Because, somewhere within us, we know that next time we need take that little bit less care, be that little bit less perfect . . . He is a crutch for us. At best.'*

The prosecuting attorney was called Stock – a woman, athletically slim, mid-forties. Telegenic. Over the days of the pre-trial she built her arguments with skill.

Stock called *his* parents to the stand. Miserably, liver-spotted hands shaking, the old farming couple told the world, for the first time, of the strange origin of their child. Their adopted child.

Reader's smooth face filled screens, whispering.

'His intentions are benevolent. I don't deny it. But now that his "secret identity" has been exposed in open court, we know what we always suspected: that he is not human. He landed on Earth, in a rocket-ship in a field in Kansas, as a baby: in a ship that had carried him from the wreckage of his native world.

'He – it – is alien. And by "saving" us against our will, this alien takes away our dignity as humans.'

Falco felt his own blood pump, in response to Reader's words. *Every word is calculated,* Falco thought. *He knows the impact of every syllable. Reader is speaking to some hidden part of me. The part which betrayed him. This is why I did it.*

The TVs, the papers sprawled over Falco's desk, were like antennae. And Falco sensed a slow shift in the public mood.

A shift, against *him.*

It didn't surprise anybody when Justice Hynes recommended referral to a full trial.

It took two months to assemble the court. *He* was kept in a secure unit, on a military base in Omaha. *Secure.* Falco knew, everyone knew, that there wasn't a cage on Earth that could restrain him, if he didn't want to be restrained. But he submitted to his captors, his passiveness shaming those assigned to guard him.

One of his guards quit his job and sold his story to tabloid TV.

His costume had been taken away. He was given prison

issue clothing. He submitted to that, too. He didn't need food, he said, although he was provided with three meals a day. But he needed sunlight.

The guard described him walking in the cramped yard, his face turned up to the Sun like some muscular flower.

The trial was televised.

The prosecution's key piece of evidence was the testimony of Lester Stiggins, CEO of Readergen.

Stiggins was a small, round man, sweating under the brilliant lights; but in his flat Boston accent he spoke calmly and well. Convincingly. 'Readergen is a wholly-owned subsidiary of Readercorp,' Stiggins said. 'We specialize in genetic engineering: research and development, and commercial exploitation. We were working on fragments of a complex organic molecule which had been discovered in a meteorite . . .'

'Are organic materials common in meteorites?'

'Yes. Organics are common throughout the universe. But such substances are mostly formed, we think, by inanimate processes – the action of radiation, and so forth – rather than by the processes of life, here on Earth.'

'But there was something different about this fragment.'

'Yes. It's unusual to find molecular strands of such length and complexity. We thought they were fragments of some equivalent of DNA. We suspected that this particular material *did* have biologic origin.'

'You're saying you found fragments of the DNA of an alien life form?'

'A DNA analogue,' Stiggins said carefully. 'Yes.'

'Where did you think this "DNA analogue" might have come from?'

Stiggins smiled and turned his round head. 'From the same planet, or origin, as *him*.'

'Witness is looking at the defendant,' Stock said briskly. 'What made you think that?'

'It was the simplest hypothesis. *His* world, wherever and whatever it is, is the only home for life we know about, outside Earth.'

'Did you try matching your sample against the defendant's genetic type?'

'We tried to contact him. But he wouldn't respond.' Stiggins shrugged. 'It was his right, I suppose, not to give samples. We certainly couldn't *force* him.'

'So what did you do?'

'We continued to work on our meteorite sample. After a while –'

'Yes?'

'We began to believe we could reconstruct the DNA-analogue.'

'*Reconstruct* it?'

Falco, watching, had to smile; Stock's performance as an actress – building almost unbearable tension out of material she must already know by heart – was consummate.

'You mean, you could grow alien life forms?'

'I wouldn't say that,' Stiggins said carefully. 'But we might have been able to retrieve some characteristics.' Stiggins ticked off points on his small, neat fingers. 'First of all there is energy conversion. We know – or we believe – that the defendant draws his powers from the Sun.'

'Plants take energy from sunlight, don't they?'

'Through photosynthesis, yes.' Stiggins smiled. 'But you don't see too many flying trees. If it's true that *he* draws from the Sun, it must be by some high-capacity transfer process we don't yet understand. Perhaps there is an agent which links the fusing core of the Sun to his body – an agent to which the cooler outer layers of the Sun are transparent. A neutrino flux, perhaps, or dark matter, which –'

Stock cut short his speculation. 'What do you think, Dr Stiggins, of the *morals* of siphoning off huge amounts of solar energy – mankind's main energy reserve – for personal use?'

Stiggins shrugged. 'I don't approve. How could I? We don't know what damage is being done, to the Sun. Readergen's research, by comparison, was controlled; directed towards the general betterment of mankind.'

'How so?'

'Imagine a fuel cell drawing its power seamlessly from the

Sun. No more oil-burning, or nuclear power . . . And we might have gone further.'

'Yes?' Stock prompted.

'Imagine a world free from hunger, a world in which every human could draw sustenance from the Sun. We could perform great engineering feats – *with our bare hands* – even travel to other worlds . . .'

Falco watched the faces of the jury. They were entranced. *Stiggins has been well coached*, Falco thought.

'What stopped your research, Dr Stiggins?'

'*He* did.'

'Let the record show that the witness is indicating the defendant.'

He had arrived in Readergen's central labs, in the middle of a working day. Stiggins had been called immediately. Lab workers and site guards had clustered around that extraordinary figure in red, blue and gold, buzzing as ineffectually as flies.

He'd gathered up the fragments of meteorite, from the various experiments, instruments and stores, and wrapped them in his cape.

'We couldn't stop him, of course.'

'Did he say what he was doing?'

'He told us he couldn't allow our research to continue. He was going to take the material away, destroy it. He said that the exploitation of the DNA-analogue would be catastrophic. There would be wars, that super-powers used without moral control would be tools of destruction. He said he felt responsible. If not for his own presence on Earth, his activities, we wouldn't have known the significance of the DNA-analogue. He said he felt he should stop us before the damage was done.'

Suddenly, Falco found himself wondering if this 'DNA-analogue' had ever existed. Were even *his* powers capable of telling, remotely, if such a thing were real?

What if this was all a set-up, by Reader? An entrapment?

'That sort of doubt doesn't constitute entitlement,' Stock said. 'By what *right* did he enter your premises?'

'He had no right. He removed Readercorp property, legitimately acquired.' A trace of anger entered Stiggins's voice, for the first time, audible through the tinniness of the small TV speakers. 'And he had no right to *stop our work*. Regardless of the technological application, the increase in scientific understanding we might have achieved ... But he wouldn't let us proceed. We weren't mature enough as a species. He said.'

'*The judgement of an alien*. Doctor, how did that make you feel?'

Stiggins's watery eyes, behind his glasses, gleamed with hatred.

Falco felt a stab of understanding, of empathy with this man.

This is why I betrayed him.

In the end, Falco realized, the details of the case hardly mattered. Reader, other commentators, the sub-text of the case itself: all of these things spoke to something primal, subrational, in people. In the jurors, the judge; in himself.

The conviction was inevitable. Unanimous.

The judge said he was making legal history, setting a precedent that mightn't be repeated for a thousand years – not until mankind left Earth, and reached the stars.

A superhero was too dangerous to be allowed to exist.

The sentence was going to have to be self-administered.

Jesus, Falco thought. *Self-administered. What a situation; how absurd.*

He, of course, submitted to the judgement, without comment.

Every screen in Falco's office, every screen in the world, was filled with Pacific blue sky, cirrus clouds; Falco imagined thousands of lenses turned up to the sky over Hawaii, like a glass forest.

Martin Reader called Falco. He wanted Falco to come to his home and watch the show with him. 'I've a proposition you may be interested in,' Reader said obliquely.

Falco told Reader he wasn't leaving his office. Not today. Reader could join him there, though.

To his surprise, Reader agreed.

A quarter-hour later, Reader was sitting in Falco's visitor's chair. He sipped Scotch whisky from a flask he'd brought; he rested his small metal cup delicately on the piles of newsprint on Falco's desk. The blue of the TV screens shone over his ageless face.

Beyond the glass walls of Falco's office, the news floor was silent; the paper's staff were huddled around TV monitors. There *was* no other news today.

'What a spectacle,' Reader murmured. 'It is rather like waiting for the return of astronauts – the blossoming of parachutes against clear skies ... I wonder who, of all the watching billions, will be the first to spot that streak of red, blue and gold, descending from orbit?'

Falco chewed on an unlit cigar. 'Why the hell's he doing this?'

'I'm sure you understand, if you look into your heart,' Reader said.

'Suppose you tell me.'

Reader leaned forward, his pale eyes intense. 'Because even now, *in extremis*, he is acting in our interest. Or so he believes. Perhaps we will be improved, marginally, by the experience of killing him. Maybe when our blood lust has dispersed, we will reflect – as did the crowds below Calvary, perhaps.' He waved a gloved hand, dismissive. 'To him, his death is worth such a price.'

The screens showed their mosaic of blue sky fragments, as empty as dreams, flickering, the focus wavering.

Reader went on, 'But we humans have killed our gods before: Osiris was torn to pieces beside the Nile; Prometheus was chained to a stone while vultures tore at his entrails; Balder was nailed to a tree, and flowers grew where his blood fell ...' That waxy smile again. 'And we have nailed gods to other trees. And what have we learned?'

'You can't argue that *he* has anything in common with Christ.'

'*Of course he has,*' Reader said gently. 'Oh, Falco – don't you understand any of this? Look: like Christ, a hero has moved among us, *and yet he was not of us.* Both he and Christ came from humble origins. *He* is the adopted son of a simple farmer. Christ lived in a remote, difficult province of Rome, the adopted son of a *naggar* – that's the Aramaic word – a crafts-man. And he has acquired a Christ-like moral authority, through his actions and heroic purpose. The parallels are obvi-ous; why do you think he's so popular? ... These are the bones of myth, Falco.'

Falco stared at him; Reader sipped his whisky with blood-less lips.

'You're crazy,' Falco said. 'Is that what this is about? Are you trying to start a religion? And what do you want of me?'

Reader's eyes gleamed, his eyes reflecting the blue shards of the screens. 'This is a beginning. But much remains to be done.

'Every successful religion must absorb within it the avatars, the primordial images, which have come to us from prehis-tory, and which speak to our souls. We have the Seed: the little spaceship which landed, as if blown on the wind, in Kansas's fertile fields. The oldest avatar, and most potent, is the Mother ... Well, we have a mother here – the grey-haired old lady from Kansas – as well as the lost true mother on his home planet – and there is also the farm, which nurtured the Child. *He* himself is the Saviour, who rescues us poor humans – literally, during his lifetime, and figuratively, in the future. And, with those extraordinary abilities, he is the God-Incarnate ...

'Seed, Mother, Child, God-Incarnate, Saviour – yes: these are indeed the raw materials, Falco, from which one may construct a human religion.'

Falco studied Reader's unnaturally smooth face; there were no drops of sweat on his bald pate, despite the close heat of the office. 'And what do you think *he* would have thought of all this?'

'*He* does not matter any longer. Don't you see that? Nor did

Christ, after his death. *The world is ready*, Falco. The established religions are tired, schismed, tainted with blood. We need something fresh. A new god. And you can be a part of His manufacture, Falco.'

Now there was shouting from the screens. Falco and Reader turned.

There was something in the sky, the focus of a million jostling lenses: a streak, plasma-white; a vertical bolt of light.

He was flying down from space, at orbital velocities, into the heart of the ancient Hawaiian volcano system. *Into the middle of the Pacific Plate. Where the basalt crust of the Earth is thinnest* . . . It was thought he'd penetrate the mantle to a depth of maybe fifty miles, before the friction of the compressed silicates slowed him.

He would survive for days – weeks, perhaps. But at last, cut off from the Sun, he must weaken. The pressure would crush him, embed him.

Falco asked: 'Why are you destroying him, Reader?'

'I am *not* destroying him. I am completing his birth.

'Consider this. If my analogy with the story of Christ is to be followed: *how is the tale to be finished?* Should he die of old age, his powers expended? *Him* – decrepit? Perhaps he should be destroyed by some physical force – a weapon, or a stronger alien. But what resonance would that have for us? Can't you see that the only way in which the myth can be completed is if he is betrayed by his followers – *by us*, Falco? *We* have to drive him to his death.

'At the arrest, you asked me if I was Judas. No.' Reader smiled at Falco. 'You are Judas, of course. And I – I am St Paul.'

The plasma bolt arced down, vertically, into the Earth. *Perhaps it looked like this in the sky over Kansas when he arrived, as a child, in his spaceship*, Falco thought.

'What is it you want me to do for you, Reader? Place features in my paper? Write a book, maybe?'

'No. Haven't you understood yet, Falco? A *Gospel*. I want you to write a new Gospel . . .'

Plasma light swamped the cameras, glaring, before dispersing.

SOMETHING FOR NOTHING

We drifted beside the alien ship. Bluish stars streamed towards us at half the speed of light.

'Fantastic,' Harris rumbled. 'Nothing I like more than something for nothing.' His massive frame floated upside down before a computer terminal.

George and I had our noses jammed up against a viewport. 'Yes, fantastic,' breathed George. I turned and stared at his gaunt profile. 'A windfall for the whole human race,' he said.

'I don't believe it,' I said. 'You two haven't agreed on any damn thing since the three of us climbed into this box six months ago –'

But Harris was glaring at George's skinny neck. 'What's the human race got to do with my overtime payments?'

And that was it. George fluttered away from the port; Harris loomed over him. 'Wasting processing time on trivialities . . .'
'. . . time and a half or double time . . .' And so it went.

Of course, Harris had a point – it was just the viciousness of his argument. We were the fastest humans in history. Thanks to Einstein time passed thirteen percent slower for us than for the folks back home.

'We're like Apollo 11,' mused George. 'Entering unexplored velocity realms . . .'

'There's no precedent in law for overtime payments under relativistic time dilation conditions,' boomed Harris. 'I'm keeping a speed log on the computer, and if you're thinking of deleting it –' He waved a huge fist.

'Always looking for something for nothing, aren't you?' George sneered.

And so on. Sometimes I wondered if we'd all survive the
trip . . .

A warning buzzed. The argument paused and we grabbed
handholds. Our ship was a monstrous magnetic bell topped
by a lifepod. A small fusion bomb went off inside the bell,
and the floor slammed against our feet.

When I turned back to the port, we'd jerked a little closer
to our rendezvous. Our ship worked – we'd managed to catch
up with the mysterious alien as it arced past the solar system
– but it was like riding a plummeting lift, and it had had us
at each other's throats since the first month.

I rubbed my bruised feet. George and Harris got back to
their argument. What a life, I thought gloomily, and got a
coffee.

We prepared for rendezvous, still bickering. Sol was a redshifted blur an eighth of a light year away. The alien ship was
no bigger than our lifepod. It looked smoothed by age, like
an old brain. We secured a line.

George flapped gingerly around what looked like a port in
the melted-looking hull; Harris headed for what had to be a
drive tube.

And me? Remember Mike Collins – the sap who'd stayed
in orbit while Neil and Buzz got the glory on the Moon? I'm
a historian and linguist; I wouldn't get to leave the ship unless
real life aliens opened the hatch and shook George by the
hand – or maybe the throat. When they didn't I took time out
to clean the coffee percolator. It's amazing how the grounds
collect.

I heard George panting as he worked. Then he gasped. I
saw him tumble awkwardly into space as a panel lifted out
and aside from the alien hull. 'Ha!' George exulted. 'Did you
get that?'

'Yeah,' I said. 'Congratulations.'

'There was a magnetic lock embedded in the hull. A prime
number code. Designed to be opened by intelligence, not by
accident.'

From around the curve of the vessel Harris muttered: 'But you managed it. So where did they mess up?'

'Do you want to repeat that?' George snapped.

'What do you see in there?' I said hastily.

George poked a torch inside the hatchway. 'No life. A single cabin about the size of ours. Airless, empty except for three items. An array of what look like crystal cubes – a data bank? A sort of flask set on a pillar. And something like an old-fashioned cathode ray tube, set into a control panel. It's all got the smoothed-over look of the ship's exterior. Stand by . . .'

His feet followed him into the hatch. 'Take it easy, George . . .'

'I can confirm this is a drive tube,' Harris growled. His instruments were arrayed around a circular mesh set in the hull. 'It's an ion drive. Nothing fancy. This is a high voltage grid, and it's operating now. The acceleration's about half of a thousandth of a gee.'

I tried a joke. 'So don't get shaken loose.' I got ignored.

Harris collected up his instruments in silence. Harris was our professional astronaut; he had flight experience going back to the last days of the old space shuttle. And the point of a flight for him was the money, the fame and what they would buy him. 'Do you want to think about that acceleration for a while?' he asked coldly.

'Ah –'

'It looks like there's a couple of attitude jets around the hull,' he said. He swept confidently over the alien's starlit curves.

I finished with the percolator and turned reluctantly to the computer.

After a couple more hours they finished their EVA and drifted stiffly back into the cabin. Until you try it, it's hard to appreciate how tough it is to work in weightless conditions. Even Harris, the paragon, looked shaky. And as for George – well, he was just a physicist. His face was a mask over his coffee nipple.

Neither of them remarked how good the coffee tasted since I'd cleaned the perk, but I didn't let it bother me.

'I've worked out the consequences of the alien's acceleration,' I said to Harris. 'He's blasting sideways, deflecting. He's
turning in a circle half a million light years wide.'

Harris grunted and closed his eyes, still breathing hard.
Obviously my toil at the terminal had confirmed what he'd
known instinctively all along. I was so glad.

George eyed me, still ashen. 'That means nothing. It's too
big. Think of it in real terms. How big's the galaxy?'

'Ah – maybe a hundred thousand light years across.'

'So your turning circle's five times the size of the galaxy.'
He got, if anything, paler. 'It's manoeuvring round the galactic
core.'

Harris' eyes snapped open. 'You're crazy.'

George shook his head weakly. 'No. We assumed the alien
came from a nearby star. From within our galaxy, at least. It
was a reasonable guess.

'But we were wrong. It's cutting through our galaxy, on its
way – somewhere else.' He swallowed. 'And it's in the middle
of a course correction to avoid the core. It all fits in.'

'A course correction on that scale,' Harris said acidly,
'would take maybe a million years.'

'I know,' George said miserably. 'How could anyone think
on that scale? It's appalling.'

Harris looked as if he wanted to spit, but you don't spit in
zero gee. Instead he dumped his coffee and went to a terminal.
He called up a three-dimensional extrapolation of the alien's
path; the orange line snaked backwards from our present position and south out of our galaxy.

'What did you mean, "it fits in"?' I asked George. 'Fits in
with what? What did you find out over there?'

He cuddled his coffee cup like a teddy bear. 'You know
the flask I mentioned? On top of a small pillar?'

'Yeah.'

'Guess what I found inside.'

'Don't be stupid, George,' Harris muttered absently.

'It was a quarter full of potassium 40. And filled up with
the radioactive products of potassium 40. See? Oh, God.'

'You've lost me, George,' I said.

'I think it's a clock. At the start of the voyage I think it was full of potassium 40. The amount it's decayed tells us how long the ship's been travelling. It must have travelled for about two half-lives of the potassium.'

My scalp crawled. 'Which adds up to –'

'About two point six billion years.'

I shook my head. 'I can't get that into perspective, George.'

'Don't try,' he said dolefully. 'That little ship's been travelling for half the lifetime of the Earth.'

'I hate it. How could they think so big?'

'Ha!' Harris snapped. 'Here's the proof that this is just another line of crap.' He'd expanded the scale on his display; the alien's projected path stirred galaxies like bees. Now it lanced through what looked like a bubble in a Swiss cheese. 'This is the nearby universe,' Harris said. 'Nearby on a scale of billions of light years anyway. The galaxies aren't spread out uniformly; there's this bubble-like structure, hollows surrounded by clusters and filaments of galaxies . . .'

'It's fantastic,' I breathed. 'How come?'

George made to answer, but Harris cut in dismissively: 'Cosmology. The Big Bang, the Big Crunch, all of that. Who cares? The point is that if baldy over there is right the alien's two billion year flight must have taken him right through at least one bubble – this one here. See?'

He hauled himself over to George. He had a way of using his physical presence as a weapon. 'You'll concede I know something about ion drives. They've been my living for twenty years.'

He forced a nod out of George.

'Ion drives are efficient – but they still need reaction mass. You've always got to spit something out the back to move forward.' He waved towards the viewport. 'To cross a void like that, the alien would have needed a fuel tank a thousand miles wide. I can't say I noticed it. Did you?

'Damn it, after a billion years half the hull metal should have evaporated –'

George squeezed his eyes shut and said nothing. His lips were white.

After a little more pointless cruelty Harris climbed into his sleeping sack, smirking with his triumph. George looked as if he was asleep where he drifted.

I thought of how these arguments blew up out of nowhere. Something created from nothing.

I cleared up the coffee cups.

Our next interpersonal crisis came a couple of days later.

I watched from my safe distance as George hunched over the artifact that looked like a cathode ray tube. He tweaked its controls gingerly. He made notes on little labels which he stuck to the control panel. Soon the alien console was covered with bits of his spidery writing.

Harris drifted in, a microblaster in his hand.

George flapped at him, excited. 'Harris, I've been doing some experiments –'

'So have I.' Harris grinned slyly. 'Watch.' He raised the blaster and carved a piece out of the nearest wall.

George gurgled and launched himself across the cabin, a jumble of limbs. 'You've no right – you've no right –' He clung to Harris' arm. Harris ignored his feathery mass. 'Take a look,' he said calmly.

The wall was repairing itself. Fibres extended across the scar and twisted together; the resulting patch softened down and fused. It was like watching bones knit.

George let go. Harris said: 'Think what a piece of this would be worth back on Earth. If we can get hold of some of the commercial rights –'

George bristled. 'Harris, you can't just hack bits off this ship.'

Harris patted a suit pocket. 'I already have.' He laughed in George's face.

I said quickly: 'This explains a lot. Why the ship looks smoothed-over – it must have been patched thousands of times. This is how it's survived two billion years.'

Harris sneered. 'You'd still need raw material.'

George remembered his discovery; he recovered his excitement. 'Yes, that's what I've found out.'

Harris ignored him and adjusted his blaster.

'Back off, Harris,' I said. 'Let him show what he's got.'

Harris shrugged theatrically. He mimicked George's reedy voice. 'Yes, George, let's see what you've found.' And he made himself comfortable, braced against an interior strut of the alien ship. Right in the middle of the place George had been working. George waited for him to move. Harris just folded his arms.

George had to climb past him. I saw his expression.

He made sure the monitor camera could see him. He pointed to the ray tube. 'This is a sort of micro-teleportation device,' he said.

Harris yawned.

'Mass enters the device here – via this feed – as a beam of neutrons. Mass comes out by this feed here, as a beam of what are called W-particles.

'The mass that comes out is about ninety times what goes in.'

While we thought about that he went on: 'The extra mass is passed out for further processing: reaction mass for the ion drive, repair material for the hull, and so on –'

Harris got ready to say something very unpleasant. I got in first. 'Run that again, George. You're saying ninety times as much mass comes out as goes in.'

'Right,' he said calmly.

'At the risk of sounding stupid – doesn't that violate the conservation of mass? Shouldn't that be impossible?'

George tried to scratch his cheek. His hand bumped into his faceplate. The astronaut watched him clinically.

'It's a little involved,' George said. 'In about fifteen minutes a free neutron in that tube will decay – it breaks up into a proton, and electron and an antineutrino.'

'And mass is conserved.'

'Sure. But before those products are formed the neutron emits a W-particle, which instantly breaks up into the electron and the antineutrino.'

'So?' It's hard to believe Harris could get so much spite into one syllable.

'The W has about ninety times the electron's mass. No mass conservation, right? A paradox.

'But it makes no difference. Usually. The lifetime of the W is so brief that – ' He struggled to stick to English. 'It's within the uncertainty limit of quantum mechanics.'

I hate that word 'quantum'. 'You're saying that the W disappears so quickly that it doesn't really matter.'

He struggled with that. 'Well, no, not really,' he said unhappily. 'But I can't think of a better way of putting it. The point is, the aliens have found some way of catching the W's before they evaporate.'

'So they create mass,' I said.

'So George is a cracked teapot,' said Harris. 'Come on. That bull boils down to something for nothing.' The practical man sneered at the scientist. 'It's impossible.'

I couldn't resist it. 'I thought you were quite keen on something for nothing. I mean, your overtime – '

George chortled. Harris' face darkened. 'Mass can't appear from nowhere,' he said stubbornly.

George actually patted his head. I winced. We'd pay for this later. 'Very good,' George said cockily. 'I believe that the mass that's extracted here must be disappearing from somewhere else in the universe, in other quantum events. As I said, it's a sort of micro-teleportation, a few grammes a day. No need for huge fuel tanks.

'In fact – ' He had to reach round Harris to get to his sticky labels. 'I think these are controls for moving the "sink", the point in space from which the matter would come. You'd put it in a matter-rich place, say the heart of a star.' His face clouded. 'But I'm making slow progress with the controls. There are a lot of safeguards. You wouldn't want the sink within the structure of the ship, for example.'

'Well, you keep at it, George,' Harris said icily. 'And make sure you put your pretty labels on places where I can hack this gizmo out and take it home.'

George smouldered. 'Look, Harris – '

'Isn't it time for your break, Harris?' I put in quickly.

He checked his watch. 'Yeah. Thanks.' And he closed his

eyes and snuggled down to sleep, right where he was. George clambered round his massive body, jerking with frustration.

I sighed. Do you suppose Mike Collins had all this trouble with Neil and Buzz?

I stared at a video screen full of numbers. I was trying to make sense of the electromagnetic patterns George had recorded within the last of the three alien artifacts, the crystal arrays. To be perfectly honest it wasn't much consolation for finding the ship lifeless.

'I don't think it's my field anyway,' I said to George. We floated in our sleeping sacks sipping coffee; it was the end of one of their EVA cycles. The cabin was peaceful in the absence of Harris who was still packing up. 'I don't think it's text. As much as anything, it reminds me of a map of the structure of DNA.'

'That fits in,' he said gloomily. Knowledge seemed only to oppress him.

'With what?'

'An idea I've been forming about the ship's purpose. Have you thought about that?' He let go his coffee cup and struggled out of the sack. In his underpants he looked like a bag of bones. He began to work at one of the computer terminals.

I gathered my thoughts. 'Not much,' I admitted. 'These people weren't much beyond us in technology. The micro-teleport device and the healing walls are within our understanding at least. And they didn't have faster-than-light travel, for instance.'

'And yet they thought big,' George said. 'A billion years big. Harris says it would have taken the probe a thousand years just to get up to speed.

'But why? Where is it headed?' He'd called up a projection of the alien's path. The orange line arced through the smoke-like bubbles and filaments of the large scale universe. 'Where were they sending a record of their equivalent of DNA – a record of what was most uniquely themselves?'

'That's just my guess about the DNA, George,' I warned.

'Look at this,' he said. Right at the edge of the visible

universe was a dull blue blob. The orange line pierced it. 'A quasar,' breathed George. 'A relic of the universe's birth.'

I shrugged inside my sack. 'So, it's a quasar probe.'

His eyes were large and unhappy. 'But not just any quasar. There's a theory that one day we'll identify a quasar as the site of the original Big Bang. And maybe of the Big Crunch, if it comes – the death of everything, the final collapse of the universe.'

I goggled. 'Could that quasar be it?'

George shrugged. 'Maybe they knew something we don't. 'They're a billion years dead,' he said forcefully. 'But they had ambition. I believe they did their best to send a piece of themselves to the end of everything. Who knows? Maybe they thought something could survive, in some way.'

I nodded slowly.

He wrapped his hands together. 'I believe we've no right to interfere with this ship. We should respect the builders' memory. We can't let Harris hack off bits and take them home –'

His eyes widened. 'Where is Harris?'

And he hustled to the suit cupboard.

Here we go again, I thought. I struggled out of my sack.

Harris was using his microblaster. He was slicing out the micro-teleportation device, severing cables and supports in a rough sphere. The alien ship was trying to repair itself but Harris could move faster. He hummed as he worked.

George crashed in. 'You bastard –'

Watching from the lifepod, I shouted into their ears. 'Take it easy. Hold off for a while, Harris.' He kept humming and cutting. 'There's no rush. Let's talk it through.'

Eventually he shrugged. 'Okay.' He turned off the blaster and settled into his usual place, slap in the middle of George's work area. 'Let's talk.' He played with the blaster, just to keep the temperature up.

George hung in the centre of the cabin for a long while, breathing deeply. Then – remarkably controlled, it seemed to me – he wormed his way round Harris to the control console of the teleport device. He faced Harris, his hands behind his back on the console. 'I can't agree that you should do this,' he began.

Harris' tone was sweet. 'Who's going to stop me? You?'

'This ship's not ours to take apart. It's immoral.' George's voice was deadly even. I noticed his arms moving slightly but I couldn't see what his hands were doing.

Harris' eyes pinned George like a cat's. He was enjoying this. 'Immoral? Listen, the people who built this thing are long dead. Even their descendants must be gone, their sun folded up or nova'd. What do they care?'

'Would you smash up a gravestone to build a wall?'

Harris grinned. 'Maybe. This isn't immorality. It's immortality. For all of us, when this thing's on display in the Smithsonian –'

And so it went on. Round and round, in diminishing circles, for hours. We'd had months of practice at this sort of scene. As time wore on, however, I noticed George doing a higher proportion of the talking. He argued patiently, reasonably – and totally uncharacteristically.

Harris started to look uncomfortable. He was sweating, and occasionally scratched his chest and armpit. But of course there was no question of him moving from his chosen position –

– until he gave a surprised gurgle, clutched at his chest, and folded up. George grabbed him.

Blood came from Harris' mouth in great globes that stuck to the inside of his faceplate.

We wrapped Harris' body in an improvised flag and pushed it into space. I said some words. Well, he'd been a hero, once.

We began the painful process of deceleration. The first grinding fusion explosions were the worst. It would take over a year of this to get us home.

George and I drifted side by side. The cabin was embarrassingly large. We watched as the alien ship – and Harris – disappeared into the structure of the large scale universe.

'Well, he got what he wanted,' George said. 'Immortality.

He's heading for the Big Crunch with the alien ship; he might be all that's left of humanity when the end comes. He'll be the most famous man in the universe. What more could he ask?' He giggled. 'Do you think we should send his overtime payments after him?'

'It can't have been easy overriding the safeguards,' I said drily.

His head swivelled towards me. 'What safeguards?'

'On the controls of the mass sink – the other end of the micro-teleport. You weren't supposed to be able to bring it inside the ship.'

He quickly checked that the cabin monitors were off. 'Do you want to think about what you're saying? I mean, it's possible I overrode some safeguards in my tinkering but –'

'Of course,' I went on doggedly, 'the hard part was keeping Harris in one place long enough for the mass loss to become significant. You handled that final scene very well. I didn't think you had so much understanding of people.'

'What is this? What mass loss? Harris' heart failure was unfortunate, but the stress of the voyage –'

'The teleport device could provide just a few grammes a day, you said. Just a few grammes would be enough for the alien ship, if they came from a star's heart.

'Just a few grammes were enough for you. From Harris' heart.'

He grinned like a skull. 'Prove it.'

The warning sounded and the floor began to slam again.

IN THE MANNER OF TREES

The port of the *Richard P Feynman* opened with a sigh, and the cool air of WhatAPlace wafted into Stoner's head. She walked down the ship's ramp and onto a belt of earth that had been scorched to a deep, black crispness by the *Feynman*'s landing jets, and then further out to where the grass grew undisturbed.

Flowers curled around her boots. The sunlight, the breeze made her uniform feel stiff and formal.

Behind a bush there was a child: dirty, bald, naked, and with a swollen belly . . .

'Oh, drink in that sun.'

Stoner, startled, turned. Dryden and Wald, her two crew-members, had followed her out of the ship, and now Dryden, the life scientist, short and plump, was turning her round face up to the sun. 'Isn't that great, after months of canned air?'

Stoner turned back to the bush. The child had gone; Stoner blinked, seeking to retrieve the afterimage.

Wald, the expedition's physical sciences specialist, pulled his thatch of red hair away from his forehead. 'You can feel the peacefulness seep into you. WhatAPlace . . . they named it well.'

Stoner turned around slowly, appraising the area. The ship sat like a metal egg in a landscape shaped like an upturned hand; the 'palm' was furred by clumps of bushes (no trees, she noticed), while rock formations a little further away, gleaming white in the pale sunlight, encircled the ship like curled fingers. Stoner was surrounded by a jumble of shapes and colours; there was a feeling of newness, of freshness, as if the land had only recently been assembled.

Wild flowers waved in the breeze.

Birds sang, almost in harmony.

Fluffy clouds scudded overhead.

Clouds, birds, flowers. Stoner hated planets like this; they were always the most dangerous kind. 'Something's not right.'

Wald sighed. 'Like what, Captain?'

'I thought there was a child. Peeking out of that bush over there.'

Dryden, hands on hips, studied her sceptically. 'Come on, Captain; the WhatAPlace colony was lost five centuries ago, and we're the first ship to visit since. How could there be a child?'

Stoner closed her eyes and concentrated. 'Definitely a human face,' she said slowly. 'Caucasian. Female, I guess, about five years old. No hair, no clothes, and with a swollen stomach – malnourished, perhaps.'

Dryden snorted. 'If this kid ever existed, how could she be malnourished? There's food in abundance.' She pointed. 'Those are multifruit bushes. From seed to fruit-bearing in a month. The region's covered in them.'

Stoner, irritated, said frostily, 'Are you implying I'm seeing things?'

Dryden's face bore its customary mocking frown. 'Oh, come on, Stoner, lighten up.'

Stoner swivelled a midwinter glare at her. 'I'll lighten up when I have some answers.'

'Answers to what?'

'Like what was it that scraped the first colony off the surface of this "wonderful place". Which is what we were sent to find out; remember?' She jabbed a finger at Dryden. 'But for starters I'll settle for knowing why there are no trees. And why, if I was seeing things with that child, all the multibushes are stripped of fruit. Or hadn't you noticed that either?'

Dryden looked around, surprised.

'In the meantime,' Stoner said, beckoning Wald, 'we'll see if we can't find that kid. And we'll go armed at all times,' she finished.

'For Christ's sake, Stoner,' Dryden protested.

'At all times.'

Wald, placid and accepting, slid to his feet.

They couldn't find the child. They found the site of the original colony, though.

The colony had been established in a clearing which covered ten acres. Lines in the ground, overgrown now, marked the sites of buildings. But the lines were crazed and broken; again Stoner had the odd impression that the landscape had been cracked apart, the pieces jumbled at random.

The colony's single ship, an old-fashioned GUT drive intra-system vessel, had been broken to pieces; creepers and clumps of flowers curled around slivers of hull-metal.

Stoner, standing amid the splayed-out corpse of the ship, shivered. 'Whatever hit them, hit them hard and fast. They weren't given the chance to build again.'

Wald wrapped his arms around his thin torso. 'Well, that's one interpretation.'

Stoner stared at him.

'Maybe they just . . . blended in.'

'What are you talking about, Wald?'

'Captain, look around. This is a near-optimal world. Stable seasons. No native pathogens.' Wald indicated the multi-bushes, the terrestrial grasses which carpeted the colony site. 'Earth vegetation has taken hold as vigorously as you could hope for. I think the settlers let their colony decay, and simply moved out into the landscape.'

'And the smashed-open ship?' Stoner said coldly.

Wald shrugged. 'I think the colonists did that themselves. Maybe they never wanted to leave. Maybe they were happy here. Captain, you're too ready to see disaster and threat in everything.'

There was a rustling, a scampering of feet like a small animal's.

'You heard that?' Stoner hissed.

'Yes. I wonder if – Captain.' Wald pointed. 'Look.'

At the edge of the colony clearing, about a hundred yards

away, a small, brown figure plucked fruit from a bush, crammed it into a wide mouth.

Stoner held herself as still as she could, barely daring to breathe.

The child, bare, filthy, bald, forced fruit into her mouth, scarcely chewing before swallowing. Her legs seemed disproportionately long and slim, enabling her to reach right over the bush.

'Well, at least we know why the bushes are stripped bare,' Wald whispered. 'It's as if she's starving. And look. Her belly's swollen.'

'Yes, but it doesn't make sense. Look at the fat around her legs, her backside. And isn't that belly a little low for malnutrition?'

Wald nodded. He said slowly, 'She doesn't look more than five . . . but it's almost as if she's pregnant –'

The child straightened up, startled like a deer. For a crystalline instant she looked directly at Stoner and Wald; her face was round, smooth and empty, her eyes the blue of the sky.

Then she turned and bounded away among the bushes.

'Come on; we have to catch her!' Stoner hurled herself across the metal-strewn meadow; she heard Wald panting close behind her. Within a few seconds Stoner reached the edge of the clearing; the flat leaves of multibushes scraped at her uniformed legs, and the long, damp grass seemed to pluck at her feet, tiring her rapidly.

The little girl raced through a thicket, screaming like a bird; and from the thicket a shock of children burst and scattered. None looked older than five, but even the youngest scurried over the ground faster than Stoner could run.

The children swarmed over the landscape away from Stoner and Wald, disappearing from sight.

Stoner gave up. She stopped and bent over, resting her hands on her knees, and sucked in the spring-like air of What-APlace. Wald drew up beside her and flopped to the ground, strands of red hair plastered by sweat against his forehead.

'We've lost them,' Wald said.

'Yeah.' Stoner's heart was pumping, making it difficult to speak. 'What did you make of them?'

Wald nodded. 'Human. No doubt about that. Ordinary-looking children.'

'Well, reasonably.' Stoner straightened up and scowled. 'All of a type, with those long legs and bald heads. All girls; did you notice that?'

'It was hard to tell.'

'From toddlers up to five-year-olds, I'd say. And a lot of them with those strange, swollen tummies.'

'Not all of them,' Wald said.

'I think we've opened up more questions than we've answered. Like, where are the older girls? And the little boys?'

'. . . And the grown-ups,' Wald murmured.

'You still think this is some rustic idyll, Wald?' Stoner peered around the empty landscape, her eyes narrow. Somehow it looked different, from the new position they had reached. 'Wald . . .'

'What is it?'

'That rock formation over there.' She pointed.

'What about it?'

'. . . Is that in the same place as it was earlier?'

Wald snorted, an uncharacteristic noise that reminded Stoner of Dryden. 'How could it have moved?'

'I don't know.' Stoner bit her lip. 'The light looks different.'

Wald studied the outcropping of white rock indifferently for a few seconds, then turned his smooth face up to the sun and closed his eyes.

Stoner felt a surge of impatience. 'You're supposed to be the geologist. Check it out,' she snapped. 'But first let's get back to the ship. We need to think of a way to catch those kids.'

For three WhatAPlace days they hunted the children over the grassy landscape, without success.

In the end, Dryden set a trap. The life scientist used the ship's galley to synthesize highly spiced foods, and had them scattered in little packets around a clear stretch of grass a quarter mile from the ship. There was melon laced with ginger and sugar, and mushrooms baked in garlic vinegar . . . Stoner couldn't help nibbling from the packets as she laid them around the clearing.

Before dawn the three of them lay down in clumps of grass, surrounding the baited area. Stoner hefted an ultrasonic pistol – it was set to stun – and tried to ignore the food scents, the cool grassy dampness which seeped through the fabric of her uniform.

Just before dawn – at a moment when the sky shone brighter than the land – a girl looked around a bush.

Stoner held her breath.

The girl's head whipped this way and that, her eyes as bright as the sky, her mouth open. She was tall and slim. She crept forward on gazelle legs, leaving glowing prints in the dew. Now two more children, smaller, one with swollen and pendulous stomach, stole after the first.

The girls fell on the food packets, burying their faces in synthesized fruit; the soft liquid sounds of their feeding carried to Stoner.

She raised her pistol, sighted on the temple of the nearest child, and fired. The girl slumped forward, as if falling quietly asleep. The other children looked up briefly, their mouths smeared with spices from Earth. Then they too fell into the grass, their eyes sliding upwards.

They named the children, arbitrarily, Paula, Petra and Pamela. Paula was the first, tallest girl; Petra was the one with the swollen belly. They all seemed aged between four and five Earth years, and were superficially alike, with their long legs, low, bald brows and wide blue eyes. But Stoner and the rest soon learned to tell them apart.

They confined the children to a cabin of the ship. They turned the walls transparent so that the girls would not feel imprisoned; but the strange environment clearly disturbed them, and they alternated between huddling together at the centre of their cabin, eyes moist and staring, and scampering around the floor, wailing and bouncing from the walls.

They were voraciously hungry.

While Dryden worked in her lab with skin and smear samples, Stoner and Wald brought the children food: basketfuls of multifruit, whatever the ship's galley could turn out. Stoner watched Pamela ram a synthetic peach into her mouth, whole; she could see it progress unchewed down the child's throat. It was like watching a snake feed. After a few hours there were bits of food, skins, pits and other debris – and urine and excrement – scattered like a carpet over the floor, and Stoner, despairing of keeping the children clean in any conventional sense, set up a regime of sluicing out the cage-cabin twice a day.

Stoner and Wald spent frustrating hours talking to the children, reading to them, showing them Virtuals. The girls enjoyed the Virtuals, as long as the flow of food to mouth wasn't interrupted; but as soon as the images disappeared the children would resume their restless wanderings around the cage.

The children never seemed to sleep.

After two days of this Stoner stood with Wald, wearily watching the girls through the clear cabin wall. Petra seemed in distress; she was lying in a foetal position, curled around a pile of fruit she was forcing into her mouth, and she stroked her distended belly in dismay. 'Do you think she's hurt?' Stoner asked.

'Maybe. It's hard to tell. They're more like animals than people; they seem to respond instinctively, and then only to basic stimuli. Pain, hunger.'

'But they're undoubtedly human.'

'Oh, yes. But with inhuman appetites,' Wald said. 'They must eat their bodyweight in food every day.'

'I guess that's right.' Stoner studied Petra with concern. 'Maybe some of our food has hurt her.'

Wald shrugged. 'It's more likely that she ran into a wall, isn't it? They don't seem to remember where the walls are, even after colliding with them a dozen times.'

'No.' Stoner ran a hand over the smooth outer surface of the cabin wall. 'Remind me to reset the texture later, to something softer. And maybe I'll program in some kind of colour coding. I don't want them to feel they're in a cage, but I don't want them hurting themselves either.' She touched Wald's shoulder. 'Come on. I think they've enough food for a few minutes. Let's get some air.'

Outside the *Feynman* the sun was dipping towards the horizon. The hollow in which the ship rested was a pool of darkening shadows, although the encircling fingers of rock still shone with sunlight. 'So,' said Stoner, 'how's your hypothesis of a sylvan paradise coming along?'

Wald scuffed at the grass with the toe of his boot. 'I don't understand the children,' he admitted. 'But I'm not convinced they're unhappy. Perhaps we should release them. Dryden is going to find out all she needs from the samples she's taken already.'

Stoner frowned, squinting at the rocks. 'Maybe,' she said absently. 'But we still haven't got close to the big questions. Like, why haven't we found anybody over the age of five? . . . Wald, did you check out those rocks, as I asked you?'

Wald's face was impassive. 'Sure.'

'And what did you find?' Stoner snapped.

'I filed my report,' Wald said. 'Do you want me to recite it? What can I tell you? Those are plutonic formations – coarse igneous rocks, formed at great depths in the crust. Captain, rocks are rocks. The details are in the log.'

'Look at that formation over there,' said Stoner, frustrated. 'The one shaped like an outstretched hand. Doesn't that look different to you?'

'How?'

Stoner stared at the formation, unsure. Weren't the shadows a little sharper, more severe? 'Wald, have we got a log image of the area when we landed?'

'Sure.'

'Will you check it out? I think –'

'Wald! Captain! I think you'd better get in here.' Dryden's voice, from within the ship, was sharp but controlled.

Stoner turned and ran, her hand on the ultra pistol at her waist. 'What is it? What's happened?'

They found Dryden inside the children's cabin, squatting amid food debris with tightly folded arms. Pamela and Paula scurried nervously around the walls, cramming fruit into their mouths; Petra, pale, shivering, sat close to Dryden. Surgical instruments lay scattered over a cleared area on the floor. There was blood on Dryden's bare forearms, her instruments; and blood was sprinkled over Petra's feet and calves.

Stoner stood in the doorway, staring. 'What the hell's happened?'

Dryden looked up, her eyes wide and moist. She opened up her arms. A baby, pink, slim, shining with amniotic fluid, lay cradled there, kicking feebly. 'It's Petra,' Dryden said quietly. 'She's given birth.'

The new child – they called her Patricia – grew fast. After a day she was crawling, after two days walking: unsteady as a foal, but already competing with the rest for fruit. Petra, the four-year-old mother, tried to feed the child fragments of food, but, though Dryden stemmed an initial haemorrhage, Petra weakened steadily. Soon she lay in a corner of the cabin, able to feed only on the food the crew members brought to her.

Dryden emerged from the cabin and stood with the others, wiping her hands. 'There's nothing I can do for her. It has to be something in the food we supplied. I'm restricting the others to multifruit from now on.'

Stoner rubbed her temples. It was all happening too fast; there didn't seem time to think it through. 'Parthenogenesis?'

Dryden shrugged. 'That's what we saw. That's what my studies of them show, too. We thought they were girls. They're not; they're closer to hermaphrodites, with a full complement of human reproductive equipment contained in each little body. I estimate they'd be fertile about the age of two, and able to – ah, bud – twice a year thereafter, for as long as they live. Guess what.' She faced them impassively. 'Pamela and Paula are pregnant now, too.'

'Now we know why they are so hungry all the time,' Wald said wonderingly, his face pressed to the clear wall of the cabin.

'Why, Dryden?' Stoner demanded.

'Why what?'

'Why did the original colonists build their kids this way? So they could breed like – what, like rats? What's the point?'

Dryden stared at the children, her round face drawn and empty; all her cynicism and sharpness, Stoner thought, seemed to have been knocked out of her by this experience. 'I don't know. I still don't know enough about their biology. For instance, they've clearly adapted to the conditions here, in the hundreds of their generations since the abandonment of the colony. See the long legs, the baldness – the reduction in intelligence.'

'Yeah.' Stoner scowled. 'But how can natural selection be occurring in a population of hermaphrodites?'

'Dryden.' Wald's voice was deep, troubled. 'Look at Petra.' Something about the stillness of Petra, the awkward way she lay on the rubbish-strewn floor, told Stoner without room for doubt that the brief life had gone out of the child-woman. Stoner was surprised to find a morsel of grief in her heart.

'I'll see what I can do for her,' Dryden said.

Stoner held Dryden's arm. 'No. Look at the others. I think we should watch what happens.'

The other girls, including the baby, had gathered around Petra's still form; even forsaking food they muzzled and snuffed at Petra, and pulled at the limp limbs. They were smiling, vacantly.

With a sudden, soundless explosion, Petra's body burst.

Stoner gasped and took an involuntary step back.

At first the skin blackened and splintered away, and then the deeper layers, the tissue, organs and bones. There was no blood, nothing to indicate that this shell had so recently been a human body. The three girls pulled at the fragmenting body, causing it to shatter faster, and soon it was as if they were playing in a mound of autumn leaves; the girls rubbed the blackened stuff over their skin and into their mouths and hair, laughing out loud.

It was the first time Stoner had heard laughter on What-APlace.

*   *   *

Stoner sat with Wald at the foot of the ship's ramp. The sun, at its noon high, bathed Stoner's limbs with a warmth from which she shrank.

Grass lapped tranquilly about a fist-shaped swelling of rock directly ahead of her. The formation seemed close enough now for her to see every niche, every crevice. She stared suspiciously at it.

Dryden emerged from the ship, wiping her hands on a towel. She threw herself to the ground and turned her round face up to the warmth of the sky. 'Well, at least we know how genetic material is passed on,' she said.

Stoner wrapped her arms around her knees. 'Through the disintegration?'

'You said they breed like rats,' Dryden said. 'Maybe. But they die like bacteria. A bacterium, on death, bursts, releasing a cloud of DNA into the air. Others, of the same and related species, are able to absorb the genetic material directly. That's how the cells of the WhatAPlace children behave. And as a consequence evolution, selection, happen rapidly; there's a wide variety of genetic material available for new generations, just floating in the air. You know, it's not completely without parallel, in mythology. Once, warriors would drink the blood of slain heroes, hoping to absorb their strengths ... And it's an efficient way to go about reproduction.'

Stoner scowled. 'Is it?'

'Sure. None of the messy, uncertain, limited business we have to put up with.'

Wald rested his head against the hull. 'In the manner of trees,' he said dreamily.

Stoner's mind was following a lot of unpleasant tracks. And she couldn't take her eyes off the rocks. The grass was stirring around the base of the fist formation, now. She snapped, 'What?'

'I don't think I'd like to live without sex,' Wald said. 'But someone, in the nineteenth century I think, once asked if it wouldn't be better if humans propagated in the manner of trees. Wouldn't there be less suffering?'

Stoner shook her head irritably. 'Let's put together what we've got. The stranded colonists, before their final disappearance, turned their children into baby factories. Fertile at the age of two. No need for sex; tiny gestation periods; no nursing dependency. Dryden, why do bacteria need to breed so efficiently?'

'So that the species can survive, in a desperately hostile environment,' Dryden murmured. 'An environment in which individuals have to breed fast. Before they are destroyed.' She looked around, bemused, at the sunny face of WhatAPlace. 'Is this a place where humans must breed like bacteria, in order to survive?'

A shadow fell across Stoner's face, cast by the rock outcropping ahead of her. Could the sun be dipping already?

... But it was only noon.

There was a tremor in the earth.

Stoner turned to Wald. '"Rocks are rocks",' she said bitterly. 'What the hell was that, Wald?'

Wald was sitting up. 'If it's any consolation, I think I've figured out why there are no trees,' he said.

Stoner stared at the fist-shaped rock formation. The turf around its base was being torn, now, like ice parting before the prow of an icebreaker: the rock was cruising towards them, through the earth.

The fingers of rock around the ship were closing. The three humans stared at each other wildly, the pieces of the puzzle moving around in their heads.

'It must happen every couple of months,' Wald said. 'Something old and plutonic, something vast, emerges from the ground. The surface is torn to pieces. The bushes have time to reestablish, but the trees can't grow quickly enough ...'

'Just like the kids don't have time to grow to adults before they have to breed ... so the colonists, before they were crushed, turned them into bacteria.' Stoner scrambled to her feet; the ground shook violently now, as if to throw them off. 'I think we should get out of here.'

*   *   *

The ship lifted, gleaming in the sunlight like a jewel.

The sunlit half of the world was a storm of rock, churning water and shattered turf. Shadows a thousand feet long raced across the land. Everywhere humans swarmed, millions of them, screaming and dying and breeding.

PILGRIM 7

The bombs flowered across the eastern seaboard a hundred miles beneath the Mercury, banishing the brightness of morning.

Wally Schirra's first reaction was resentment. *Why me? Why the hell did the world have to blow apart during my flight? Why not Shepard's, or Carpenter's, or – ideally – during that asshole Presbyterian John Glenn's?*

Now, he thought grimly, *now no-one will know how damn well I've flown this damn thing.*

It was only when the doors opened in the sky and the Earth – *changed* – that he felt the touch of fear.

He'd seen sky doors once before.

At the top of a high blue climb, with Korea lost in the mists of the curving Earth beneath his F–86 . . . there the doors were, just waiting. As if they were watching.

He'd heard other pilots, in drunken moments, mention similar sightings. *Just hangin' in the sky, as if they're waiting for something to happen . . .*

Schirra was a Navy aviator. He wasn't interested in such things then, and he wasn't now. The doors could wait and watch all they liked, as long as they didn't come in the way of his checklist.

Wally Schirra entered orbit on 3rd October 1962, a little before 8:30 EDT. He was thirty-eight years old.

The launch, atop the shining Atlas-D, was as soft as a baby's kiss – smoother and less noisy than the centrifuge trainers, in fact. He lay on his back as the dial climbed to six g. Then, with a soundless impact, he sailed into weightlessness. The absence of pressure points under his back and legs made the cramped cabin seem a little more roomy. As if he were a genuine aviator, rather than a China doll packed in Styrofoam. With a distant thump the escape tower sailed into space, and the green JETT TOWER light gleamed. Schirra told Deke Slayton, his capcom at the Cape, 'This tower is a real sayonara.'

'You have a go from Control Centre,' Slayton told him.

'You have a go from me. It's real fat.'

Slayton asked innocently, 'Are you a turtle today?'

Schirra grinned. *Klutz*. It was his job to run the gotchas, not Deke's. He switched out of the radio circuit and spoke into his Vox tape recorder. 'You bet your sweet ass I am,' he said, according to the Turtle Club constitution.

Gotcha back, Deke.

Schirra stared through his window at the receding Earth. Just as Shepard and the others had reported before him there was no sensation of separateness from Earth, of being some spooky kind of astral traveller. He was only a hundred miles up, damn it, sailing above the Earth in this titanium thimble; the landscape below didn't look so different than from thirty or forty thousand feet.

Then the discarded Atlas-D sailed into view, rotating like a baton between the Mercury and Earth. The Atlas wasn't much more than a balloon kept rigid by its fuel load. Somehow it was seeing that eighty-foot silver cylinder drift around like a toy that brought home to Schirra the strangeness of his new environment.

But he wasn't really interested. There was work to do.

He told Deke Slayton, 'I'm in chimp mode and she's flying beautifully.' Chimp mode, a little zinger at those who liked to puncture the astronauts, to point out that a monkey could fly a Mercury. Yeah. Well, the later MA models, like his own Sigma 7, the MA–8, had joysticks for working the five-pound attitude thrusters, a genuine window you could sight the horizon through, and even a hatch you could open from the inside, instead of being packed in and out of the capsule like a TV dinner.

Spam in a can.

He had a thirty-five mil cine-camera for taking photos of the Earth; he jammed it in his little window. The boffins wanted images of fold mountains, fault ridges, volcanic fields, meteorite impacts, so they could compare them with features on other planets.

It was at the end of the second orbit, when he was over the Americas again, that he saw the doors open up in the sky.

He wasn't fazed. And he didn't mention it to Deke. *Not on my mission*, Schirra thought grimly. Even on Vox, this kind of thing got out. Look at Glenn and his god-damn fireflies. Following his checklist, he let the roll of the capsule carry his view past the patient mass of Earth and back to the sky doors. Schirra turned his camera off; he didn't want any pictures of damn UFOs.

The doors were six neat rectangles set against the black, empty sky, with a kind of pink light shining through, from – somewhere else. Schirra had no way of judging their size. They could have been ten feet across, or ten miles, or ten thousand miles.

When the capsule rolled away from the doors he turned on his camera again.

Later he went into drifting mode. Drifting, conserving fuel, was one of the main goals of his six-orbit mission profile. The idea was to try out the techniques that would be needed on the longer-duration missions to come, to the Moon and beyond. 'I'm having a ball up here drifting,' he told John Glenn at Port Arguello. Every few minutes he had to link up with a new capcom. He looked at the tubes of paste that made up his lunch. 'Enjoying it so much I haven't eaten yet,' he said.

No damn doors were going to get in *his* way.

The flight was going like a dream. *Operational precision. The text-book flight.* His pulse never climbed much above a hundred ten, and his blood pressure showed a perfect one twenty over eighty. The capsule around him sounded like a little workshop, with the cameras, fans and gyros whirring. He took to ignoring the view when his windows showed him the looming

sky doors; he stared out at the Earthscape, as if that were all
that existed.

But then, even the Earth changed, betraying him.

At first he couldn't make sense of the sparks of light climbing
out of Cuba. They were hard to see against the morning sea-
scape – it was still only around eleven thirty by EDT – and
they moved slowly but steadily, like determined fireflies.

Out of Cuba . . .

Red Cuba, ninety miles off the Florida coast. Khrushchev
had said that if the US hit Cuba he'd bomb American bases
in Europe. Hadn't stopped Kennedy trying, of course, with
the Bay of Pigs fiasco his reward. And this year there had
been rumours of a nuclear build-up on the island. The CIA
had U2 pictures, it was said, of missiles at Casilda Port, of
warheads at San Cristobal, of MRBM launchers at Diego.

Looks like the rumours are right, Schirra thought.

The sparks seemed to take a long time on their thousand-
mile climb to the Eastern seaboard, but it could only have
been minutes.

Schirra imagined more sparks sailing over the Pole.

Slayton kept up with routine business for him – Deke even
ran the turtle gag again – but his voice betrayed his tension.
But Schirra felt calm, and he responded evenly. Deke knew
what was happening, and so did he; but in the last few minutes
it was going to be business as normal, damn it. His pulse, his
blood pressure weren't flickering, he knew.

Operational precision.

Light, everywhere. Deke's voice turned to a mush of static.

This is it, Wal. The final gotcha. When he'd shot down the
first of his two MiGs, in the skies of Korea, Schirra had met
the eyes of the young enemy pilot – from a distance, and just
for a second, as the MiG fell away – but it was enough for a
human contact that had felt to the younger Schirra like a stab
in the heart. That was the first time it had occurred to Schirra
to wonder how it would feel, when his own time came. And
how it would come to him.

*   *   *

The detonations looked like droplets, splashes of light and smoke sprinkled silently into the big bowl of atmosphere. Dutifully Schirra peered through his periscope at the glowing landscape, and pointed his cine-camera out of the capsule's engraved window. The little hand-held camera, meant to assist with the exploration of new worlds, was going to record the death of his own.

Smoke rose up through the atmosphere in great plumes from the burning cities and forests, spreading across the top of the atmosphere as if coming up against a great glass ceiling. Soon those clouds would merge, he realized, and then he wouldn't even be able to see the surface; he'd be lucky, when the time came, to hit the ocean. Any ocean.

By the time the plummeting orbit of the Mercury – his third around the Earth – carried him through another forty-minute sunset, he could see fires outlining the continents on the nightside.

That was when he started to think of Jo, stuck in a world that was burning up under him.

He wanted to shut down his thoughts. 'Got to maintain an even strain,' he said to himself. He glanced over his instrument panel. Thanks to his drifting there was plenty of hydrogen peroxide manoeuvring fuel left. There'd be enough reserve in his tanks for fifteen, twenty orbits or more. He could stay up here for a day and a half, if he felt like it. He looked down at his checklist, close-typed sheets in the greenish glow of the cabin's fluorescents. This mission might never mean anything to anyone else – damn it, without contact with the ground he'd be lucky to make it through the atmosphere – and even if he did he wouldn't have a hope in hell of making his rendezvous with the *Kearsage*.

He shook his head, feeling his hairline rasp against the rubber collar of his pressure suit. To hell with it all. He'd do this by the book, just as if he was going home to an intact world, a hero's welcome in Oradell, New Jersey, and Jo.

Schirra worked patiently through his checklist. He filmed everything he saw, allowed the slow roll to sweep his view past the nightside of Earth. There were burning points of light

even in the wastes of the darkened Pacific, now. He continued
to shut off the camera as he rolled around past the odd, meaningless view of the sky doors.

Six orbits, straight down the line, all his mission objectives
hit, just as he'd been training for, for so many months. And
he'd bring the damn thing down as close as he could to the
mark, off Bermuda. If there was no-one there to meet him, if
no-one ever knew how he'd done – he, Walter M. Schirra,
would know it for himself.

Maybe that would be enough.

It was then, when he'd reached a kind of grim acceptance
of his lot, that the continents started sliding around, throwing
everything up in the air for Wally Schirra again.

The doors changed. They were opening wide over the tor-
mented Earth.

Despite himself, Schirra was forced to study the doors.
They'd grown during the capsule's last couple of rolls, or
maybe had come closer to the Earth. The doors weren't standing off, like in Korea. He felt a surge of resentment towards
them; he felt as if the doors were strangers intruding on the
death of a parent. *Is this what you came to see, assholes? Maybe
Korea wasn't violent enough for you. Maybe you want to watch us
blow each other to bits, huh?*

The doors looked a hell of a lot more real than before. They
were rectangular slabs of pink light, casting purple highlights
off the sleeping ocean below him. The reflections gave the
ocean a texture, like skin; he could pick out the wake of some
ship, a feather laid across a shadowed cheek.

The Sigma 7 was going to pass under the doors, between
the doors and the ocean.

Abruptly the window filled with light. Squinting, he peered
out of his window. The pink glow had emerged from behind
the doors, now. It came down at the ocean in wide, square
beams, like shafts of stained-glass sunlight in a dusty church,
touching the Earth. But beams didn't make sense, because
there was no atmosphere to carry dust. Right? So how could
he see the beams themselves?

Schirra couldn't have evaded the pink beams if he'd wanted to.

Pink-purple light filled his cabin, glinting from the dials, from the wires and air-feeds connected to his suit, banishing the dingy undersea glow of the cabin's fluorescents. It seemed to shine through the walls, not just through the ports.

Schirra tried to keep still, not to cower in his pressure suit. He held his breath and clutched the cine-camera against his chest, in one gloved hand. As an afterthought he pulled down his visor, isolating the suit's air circuit.

The kitchen-sounds of the little cabin, the whir and clunks of the fans and inverters, died away. The moment stretched; Schirra felt as if he were embedded in this thick light, like some insect. He counted off. 'Oh . . . kay . . . Oh . . . kay . . . Oh . . . kay . . .'

The pink glow died, leaving the dirty-green of the fluorescents dingy by comparison. The kitchen noises faded back up to normal, no stranger than if he'd turned up the volume on some TV. Schirra was aware of his blood pulsing rapidly but firmly; his breath was regular, even. He was grimly satisfied. He wanted to be damn sure that none of his fear would show up in the biomedical scans on some hypothetical return to Earth.

He pushed back his visor and squinted into his periscope.

He was over the dayside again. The doors had vanished – closed up and gone, taking their beams of light with them. Schirra pushed back from the periscope and reached for his checklist and his grease-pencil. He pushed away any speculation, the last traces of fear, and forced himself to concentrate. He'd lost maybe fifteen minutes out of his schedule. Well, he could make that up readily enough. He'd been careful to leave plenty of white space in his checklist for a start – he'd wanted a profile he could achieve – and he could always skip a meal, or compress a rest period. And –

'Pilgrim 7. Pilgrim 7. This is the Cape.' The radio crackled in his ears, jolting him stiff in his seat. At first he couldn't recognize the voice . . . or rather, he *could* recognize it, but it didn't make sense. 'Pilgrim 7, this is the Cape. Do you read?'

The voice was clipped, even, but Schirra could hear anxiety in its heavy tones.

'. . . John? John Glenn?'

There was an audible sigh on the line, noises in the background. 'John here, Deke.' *Deke?* 'Good to hear your voice. You were out of contact for an orbit and a half; even the telemetry went down. And –'

'What the hell's going on, Glenn? You're at Arguello, not the Cape.'

There was silence at the other end of the line. Damn it, Schirra thought, it had *sounded* like the Cape. He remembered the explosion of relief when Glenn himself had got through the ionization blackout on his return from orbit.

'Deke?' Glenn's voice was hesitant. 'How are you feeling? Has something gone wrong?' Glenn paused. 'Listen, we're not feeding this out; it's just you and me, buddy.' *Patronizing asshole.* 'Maybe there's something wrong with your air supply. Deke, have you tried isolating your suit circuit? And –'

Again, here he was with his Deke.

John Glenn wasn't capcom at the Cape. John Glenn was capcom at Port Arguello, California.

In fact, John Glenn was a mound of irradiated ash at Port Arguello, California.

Wasn't he?

Irritated, baffled, Schirra pushed his face to his periscope. The sight of the blasted dayside was almost going to be a comfort now, a confirmation that he wasn't going crazy – that the war really had struck – despite the confusing babble in his ears.

. . . But he was denied that comfort.

No smoke, no flame, no lingering, blackening mushroom clouds. The Mercury sailed over a sunlit, mid-morning coastline. He could see the grey mottle of towns, white feathery ship-wakes; a few high clouds lay like lace over the whole diorama.

Nothing wrong with that. Except, it wasn't a coastline he recognized. And, where was the nuclear war?

Apart from that, everything was fine.

'Deke? I've got Flight here. The Flight Director,' Glenn explained carefully. 'And Kraft thinks –'

'Zip it,' Schirra muttered. 'I've got some thinking to do. And don't call me Deke.'

He stared into the periscope, conscious of his mouth dangling.

It took him a couple of orbits to work it out, to pull together a picture in his own head of this new Earth, or wherever-the-hell-he-was. Successive capcoms called plaintively to him as he passed over them. He ignored them. He sketched maps of the new coastlines on the back of his checklist with his grease-pencil.

Half the Earth was covered by ocean. More than half. An immense, empty Pacific stretched two hundred degrees around the globe.

The continents had gone.

They had been replaced by a single, huge landmass. It stretched (as far as he could see) from pole to pole, surrounded by the bloated Pacific. The supercontinent was shaped like a fat letter 'C'. Away from the coasts the supercontinent was arid and given over to yellow-red desert. Far to the south, right on his horizon, the glint of polar ice lightened the layer of atmosphere: a huge icecap engulfed the southern third of the supercontinent.

The open mouth of the 'C' shape was filled by another ocean, which must itself have been the size of the Atlantic. This sea straddled the Equator, and cities glittered like jewels in the bays around its shore. The air over the cities was hazy with industrial gases, and Schirra could see bridges across the bays, stitchings of stone and iron. The wakes of boats and ships fanned around the ports.

There were more cities on the outer edge of the 'C' shape, on its western shore; they spread along the complex seaboard away from the Equator, north and south into the temperate latitudes. Schirra filmed it all with his cine-camera. From the Mercury the western coast looked much like California.

The cities, and surrounding hinterlands of cultivation, pushed a little way into the interior desert; the supercontinent was bordered by neat rectangles of fields, like a quilt edging. But the immense desert areas were almost empty – although here and there lakes glimmered in the sun, and Schirra caught glimpses of more towns near the lakes. Road and rail lines cut like wounds across the desert. There were metallic splashes which must be fuel installations or mines. Plane contrails feathered across the sky, far below him.

Nowhere was there any sign of the war.

Where were the schoolmap continents? Where was America, for Christ's sake?

Schirra stared at his maps. Some of the topography looked kind of familiar. Like, the southern half of the C-continent looked as if it could have been a jigsaw of cut-out continents: there was Africa, with South America snuggling its nose into the Gulf of Guinea, and Antarctica and Australia had been slid around and pushed together into the mass. In the north, Schirra thought he could make out the eastern half of North America – couldn't that circular depression be Hudson Bay? – all pushed up against Western Europe. But the west coast of North America, and much of Asia, would have to be underwater, immersed in that great globe-girdling ocean.

Maybe it was wishful thinking. Or maybe his continents *were* there, their familiar shapes struggling to emerge from beneath this layer of strange landscape, the alien Pacific.

It was all a perfectly logical and plausible world. It just wasn't his.

Over the place where America ought to be, he opened his radio line. 'Hey, Glenn,' he said.

There was a crackle. 'Pilgrim 7,' Glenn replied cautiously.

'This is "Deke". I've got some questions.'

Schirra heard muttering off. Didn't that prig Glenn know enough to keep his hand over his mike, when discussing whether a fellow astronaut had lost his beans?

'Go ahead, Deke,' Glenn said at last. He sounded like a schoolmaster, or a doctor. 'What do you want to know?'

Schirra thought for a moment.

'History,' he said. 'And geography.'

* * *

The eastern coast of the landmass – the inner curve of the 'C' – was called Europe. Schirra didn't bother with the jumbled-around country names, some of which he recognized and some not. The inner sea was the Mediterranean. The west coast, the outside of the 'C', was America.

There had been a Columbus here. He'd taken a huge caravan west across the central desert, half-expecting to walk off the edge of the world.

New Jersey existed, but not Oradell, his home town. There was a Jo. But –

'But,' John Glenn said slowly, reluctantly, 'you're not Deke Slayton. Are you, Deke? I mean –'

Schirra sighed. 'No, John, you Presbyterian pooch. I admit it. I'm Walter M. Schirra, Jr, of the USN.'

Schirra was beginning to work out what had happened. Glenn, though, was still in the dark. He plodded through the logic like a schoolkid. 'This is John Glenn,' he said. 'And I'm capcom for your mission – for Deke Slayton's mission, in the Pilgrim 7.'

Christ, Schirra thought. *You'd think they'd take this klutz off the air.* 'Not any more,' he said. 'This is Wally Schirra in the Sigma 7. And Deke is – was – my Cape capcom.'

Glenn sighed audibly. 'Then where's Deke?'

Slayton hadn't been able to fly at all, in Schirra's world. Heart fibrillations, discovered after he'd joined the programme.

'I don't know,' Schirra said simply. 'Maybe he's okay, some-where.' A thought struck him. 'Where's Jo?'

Glenn paused, evidently checking with somebody. 'At home. With Wally Schirra,' he added heavily.

Insulated by the surroundings of the capsule, familiar from a hundred simulator rides, Schirra had felt bemused by all that had happened – the war, then no war, the sliding conti-nents . . . Now, though, something touched him.

Not that he couldn't see the funny side. *The final gotcha. I'll never top this one.*

'John,' he snapped. 'I've some more questions. How's your geology?'

*   *   *

Continental drifting was a respectable theory, but not univer-
sally accepted by geologists – or so Glenn relayed to Schirra.
Schirra imagined telephone lines buzzing with strange conversations ('He's asking *what*?'). There might be currents in the
mantle; the continents might float this way and that like rafts,
bumping and jostling. Maybe their single supercontinent
hadn't always been this way; maybe once it had consisted of
different pieces which had drifted together.

Yeah.

Schirra stared down at the changed, seamless world.
Maybe if you dug down deep enough, he wondered, there
would be a fine layer of ash, some of it still radioactive-
hot . . .

As he passed over 'America' on his next orbit, his sixth,
Schirra described the position of the continents in his world:
Africa and South America and Antarctica split apart and scattered around the southern hemisphere . . . He asked Glenn
if there had been a time when the world had looked like
that.

It took Glenn another orbit to get answers from his telephone panel of specialists. Yes, such an era was possible. The
guesses ranged from two to three hundred million years . . .
into Glenn's future.

They'd all been moved into the past. The whole population
of the Earth, to somewhere close to the Permian-Triassic boundary, from what Schirra remembered of his high school geology. Moved by little green men from beyond the sky doors,
Schirra supposed, to get them away from the devastation of
the war. To save the species. They'd been watching, since
Korea and perhaps before, maybe drawn by the light of Hiro-
shima and Nagasaki. Waiting for the spark.

Everything had been reconstructed, as near as it could be
to the world that had been destroyed. Of course there must
have been changes. Schirra wondered what had happened
to the Chinese – to the Californians, for Christ's sake. And,
somewhere, Israelis and Arabs must be fighting over some
other portion of land, just as sacred and eternal as Palestine
had been. But no-one seemed to know about it, except him

... and, presumably, the unfortunate copy of Deke Slayton who should have been up here instead of him. Maybe by being in space, he'd been missed out, somehow.

Schirra thought it over. For some reason, being moved hundreds of millions of years into the past was more disturbing, philosophically, than moving into the future. Why should that be?

He laughed at himself. What the hell difference would it make? It would surely cause him a hell of a lot less trouble than the fact that, here, there was another Walter M. Schirra, as large as life, married to his wife.

He sighed, and told Glenn he was ready to come down.

The retrorocket package shoved him into his moulded seat, hard, with a few seconds' worth of six g.

The atmosphere bit at the capsule. The retros were strapped over the heatshield; Schirra watched the hull glow red, the package straps break and fly past his window. He remembered when they thought Glenn's heatshield had come loose, that he might burn up. (Maybe that hadn't happened, here.) He watched the dial creep up – six, seven, eight g. He tensed his calf and stomach muscles to counteract the g-forces. He counted out: 'Oh ... kay ... Oh ... kay ...'

He was kicked in the back again. The main chute blossomed against blue sky.

He splashed down ten miles from the *Kearsage* – from a *Kearsage*, anyway – in the new Pacific, off the coast of 'America'. Not bad, for the first landing on an alien planet. 'Good enough for Government work,' he muttered.

He'd got through most of his checklist, in spite of everything. He wondered if the other Deke Slayton had had the same checklist. According to procedure, he marked the positions of the dials and switches on his control panel with his grease-pencil.

Now he should lie here and wait for the copters to lift the capsule to the *Kearsage*.

He looked at his cine-camera, and thought about the images it contained. He imagined spending the rest of his life explaining away a world which didn't exist any more, a war which had been negated.

On impulse, he pulled the safety pin from the capsule's escape hatch, punched the three-inch detonator button. The explosion as the hatch blew out was too damn loud in the enclosed cabin.

The sea air was fresh, salty, full of sunlight; it banished the greenish gloom of the cabin. He could hear the blades of a copter, only minutes away.

He undid his chest strap, lap belt, shoulder harness and knee straps. He disconnected the sensor wires trailing from his suit, took off his helmet, and rolled the suit's inner rubber neck up around his throat, sealing the suit.

He clambered out of his form-fitting chair and struggled through the hatch. He brought his cine-camera with him. The capsule looked like a misshapen bell, lolling in the water. Yellow marker dye stained the water for ten feet around the Mercury. The lower half of the capsule was scorched black by the reentry, but you could still see the Sigma 7 design, and the US flag.

On the horizon was the *Kearsage*. It was still recognizably a carrier but its profile, flattened by distance, was subtly changed.

Schirra used his weight to haul at the capsule, made it rock until the sea lapped into the cabin.

It sank fast. 'Too fast,' Schirra said to himself as he struggled in the water in his heavy spacesuit. 'Bad design by those McDonnell assholes.'

The copter dropped him a horse collar. He let himself be hauled up, returning the curious stares of the airmen with a grin. 'Turned out fine,' he told them.

The airmen couldn't take their eyes off the US flag sewn to his suit. Maybe he should have ripped it off before he got picked up.

But that wasn't the worst, he reflected. By losing his capsule, they'd think he'd screwed the pooch, just like poor old Gus Grissom. Well, he'd have to live with that. He'd always know the truth.

Schirra grinned. He was going to enjoy meeting the other Schirra. They could pull some gotchas like the world had never seen.

He leaned out of the copter and dropped the cine-camera into the rotor-thrashed surface of the sea. It sank, disappeared.

A few minutes later they were over the *Kearsage*.

ZEMLYA

Yuri Gagarin made ready to fly to Venus.

The Proton booster was a slim black cylinder. The three supporting gantries had tipped back on their counterweights, so that the rocket stood at the heart of a gaunt, open flower of metal. Beyond the launch pit, the flat Kazakhstan steppe had erupted into its brief spring bloom, with evanescent flowers pushing through the hardy grass.

And all around Gagarin there were faces: the faces of technicians and engineers, turned to *him*, as the steppe flowers turn to the Sun. Faces shining with awe. Even the *zeks*, the political prisoners in their drab uniforms, had been allowed to see him today.

Gagarin, in his orange pressure suit and white ribbed helmet, smiled on them all. It was just as it had been in 1961, three years ago, when he had become the first human to journey into space. Gagarin felt a surge of elation, of command; he basked in the warm attention.

Gagarin stepped up to the launch pit. He looked up at the six flaring strap-on boosters which clustered around the slim first stage. His *Zemlya* spacecraft was fixed to the top of the Proton, shrouded by a cone of white-painted metal. White condensation poured off the rocket, rolling down its heroic flanks; and ice glinted on the metal, regardless of the warmth of the Sun.

At the base of the rocket, Leonov and Korolev waited for him.

Alexei Arkhipovich Leonov was dressed in his formal uniform as an Air Force Lieutenant-Colonel, and Gagarin saluted his superior officer. 'I have been made ready, and now I am reporting that I am ready to fly the *Zemlya* mission,' he said.

Leonov, stocky and muscular, grinned at Gagarin and clapped him on the shoulder. 'Yuri,' he said. 'It is a fine day.'

'Yes,' Gagarin said. 'It is a fine day to fly.' Leonov had been Gagarin's double, his backup on this mission. Leonov's day would come next year, when he would walk in space from a two-man Voskhod craft.

Sergei Pavlovich Korolev, the Chief Designer, stepped forward to Gagarin. Korolev's eyes burned with energy. But he was stooped, and his skin looked paper-thin; he was an old man, swathed in his heavy overcoat. He said, 'I wish you a pleasant flight, a fine landing, and a safe return to Earth.'

Gagarin looked down over the small group of men gathered in the amphitheatre-like flame pit. He said, 'The whole of my life seems to be condensed into this one wonderful moment. Everything that I have been, everything I have achieved, was for this.' He lowered his head briefly. 'I know I may never see the Earth again, my wife and my fine children, Yelena and Galya. Yet I am happy. Who would not be? To take part in new discoveries, to be the first to journey beyond the embrace of Earth. Who could dream of more?'

He turned, and climbed into the elevator which would lift him to the capsule.

Complex emotions coursed through Alexei Arkhipovich Leonov: awe, envy, pity, love. 'Your courage is not in question, Yuri,' he said softly. He watched until Gagarin had risen into rocket vapour.

The heat of the young, strengthening Sun scattered the last of the primordial interplanetary dust.

Light broke over Venus.

The planet's surface was cooling. A thin crust hardened over molten, churning rock.

Unlike Earth, there were no distinct tectonic plates here, no fault lines. Rather, vulcanism continued everywhere, as the radioactive heat of the interior poured out into space. The new land was tortured into huge igneous structures: spider-web patterns of cracks hundreds of kilometres across, collapsed volcanic domes, a mountain range that swept halfway around the planet.

Outgassed water vapour cooled and condensed. Droplets of liquid water trickled down to fill the lowlands and impact basins.

Seas gathered. A clear nitrogen atmosphere mantled around Venus.

Energy poured into the atmosphere from many sources: the Sun's ultraviolet light and particle wind, the flash and crackle of lightning, auroral electrons, interior radioactivity, the shock waves of falling planetesimals.

All these sources fabricated organic molecules, which rained into the seas.

In the deep new oceans, life swarmed, half a billion years before its first stirring on Earth.

But the young Sun grew hotter and brighter, still seeking its ultimate Main Sequence stability.

Zemlya's protective shroud cracked open. Sunlight flooded Gagarin's cabin. Fragments of ice, shaken free of the hull, glittered around the craft like snow.

Zemlya swivelled in space. Gagarin saw the skin of Earth, spread out beneath him like a glowing carpet, as bright as a tropical sky.

Gagarin smiled. The frustration of three years of speeches and tape-cutting ceremonials fell from him; at last he was flying again.

He travelled through a single orbit of the Earth. There were clouds piled thickly around the equator, reaching up to him. The continents on Earth's night side were outlined, thrillingly, by chains of city lights. Over central Africa there was a flash of lightning, somewhere beneath the clouds, like a light bulb exploding under cotton wool.

Where he passed, he relayed revolutionary messages. 'Warm greetings from space to the glorious Leninist Young Communist League,' he said. 'Everything that is good in me I owe to our Communist Party and the Young Communist League. This date is one on which mankind's most cherished dreams come true, and also marks the triumph of Soviet science and technology.'

When he flew once more over the baked-clay heart of the Soviet Union, the control centre told him he should prepare for the ignition of his last rocket stage: the Block-D, his interplanetary engine.

It turned out to be another twelve-hour day for Sergei Pavlovich Korolev.

From the launch, he was driven home to his apartment in Moscow by chauffeured limousine. The KGB guards outside his door nodded to him. Korolev glared back. They wore the same colour uniform as his guards at the Kolyma gold mine, the Gulag charnel house where he had endured a year's hard labour after being caught up in one of Stalin's purges against suspected Bonapartists.

But now, of course, these men were here to protect him from the world, rather than the other way round.

Nina, his wife, came to the door to greet him, with a glass of hot tea. As they always did, they sat at the foot of the stairs, and discussed the day's events. Korolev described to her the latest budgetary conflicts, the equipment failures, the scarcity of resource, the low quality of equipment and men available.

And they talked of Gagarin.

Korolev was only fifty-eight. But his health was failing, he knew. The years he had spent in labour camps and prison had damaged him fundamentally. He did not know how long his determination could continue to fuel his weakening body.

Korolev knew that his own name was unknown in the greater world beyond the Soviet Union: even after all these years, all these triumphs. And that web of obsessive secrecy had gathered itself, too, around the new Gagarin flight.

But the motives, the secrecy, even the past – none of it mattered. The spacecraft, his robust little Vostoks, embodied the dream of Korolev's life.

But what Gagarin was attempting now was astounding, beyond even Korolev's imagination. As he sat with his wife, he thought of that brave aviator, that delicate construct of human flesh and blood and bone, in the metal carapace Korolev had built for him.

As the Sun brightened, water evaporated into the atmosphere of Venus, trapping heat. The oceans shallowed rapidly. Life was forced onto the chaotic, encroaching continents, and an explosion of species sought to find a means of survival.

A hectic intelligence emerged.

It was forced immediately into a brutal technological race. Living creatures burrowed into the ground, building complex shelters, hoarding water, fending off the heat.

The abandoned surface died. The seas boiled, pouring water vapour and carbon dioxide into the air.

There was a final dawn, a last sunset. Then the clouds hid the stars.

At last even the carbonate rocks of the sea beds disintegrated, releasing still more carbon dioxide. The last water vapour was driven out of the air, leaving Venus scorched and dry.

The Sun ceased to evolve – pumping twice as much sunlight over Venus as was incident over Earth – and Venus achieved a sterile stability.

Vulcanism continued, and no part of the land was allowed to grow old. The volcanoes coughed sulphur dioxide, and the clouds turned to acid. The lower levels of the air were like a lethal ocean, dense and sluggish.

The last of the planet's life burrowed deeper into rock.

Zemlya – Earth – was, like the proposed Voskhod, a derivative of Korolev's successful one-man Vostok spaceship.

Zemlya consisted of two modules. The entry module was a sphere three metres wide. Its hull was coated with thick ablative heatshield, and strips of metal foil which would reflect the Sun's fierce heat.

The instrument module – fixed to the base of the sphere by tensioning bands – looked like two pie dishes welded together. It bristled with thermal radiation louvres. Once in space, large solar-cell wings had unfolded from its walls. The module was crammed with water, tanks of oxygen and nitrogen, and chemical air scrubbers.

The instrument module omitted the big TDU–1 retrorocket system used to return a Vostok from Earth orbit. Gagarin had no need of a reentry rocket, for his sphere would be flung directly into the atmosphere of Venus. The walls of his entry module contained the flotation collar which would enable the craft, after its descent, to float on the sluggish surface of Venus's world-girdling oceans – those seas of carbonated water, or perhaps of oil – while he awaited the arrival of further Soviet supply ships, and eventual rescue by future cosmonauts in more advanced craft, yet to be specified by the Korolev Design Bureau.

Gagarin's cabin was a cosy nest, lined with green fabric. His couch occupied much of the space in the cabin. Behind his head there was an escape hatch, and there were three small viewing ports recessed into the walls of the cabin.

Gagarin tested his manual control system in pitch, yaw and roll, using the hand controller to his right. The craft was turned about its centre of mass by steering jets fed from compressed gas storage bottles. He monitored the usage of fuel, which was satisfactory. He checked the response of the craft using a stop-watch and his *Vzor* optical orientation device, a system of mirrors and optical lattices mounted in a porthole before him, which would enable him to navigate across the solar system.

Gagarin drifted out of his couch and exercised; he had been given an ingenious regime based on rubber strips, which he could perform without doffing his pressure suit. He monitored his pulse, respiration, appetite and sensations of weightlessness; he transmitted electrocardiograms, pneumograms, electroencephalograms, skin-galvanic measurements, and electro-oculograms, made by placing tiny silver electrodes at the corners of his eyes. He recorded his observations in a log-book and on tape. He washed, opening up zippered panels in his pressure suit, for there was no room to discard the suit entirely.

In his windows he saw how Earth receded rapidly, folding

over on itself. Gagarin exclaimed ecstatically. He was the first man in all of history to observe the Earth from without, complete and entire. It looked beautiful and fragile, an ornament against the black void, and he tried to convey some of this to the ground.

In the abandoned valleys of Venus, the temperature passed the boiling points of many metals, and exotic chemistry began. The turgid atmosphere was stained by complex compounds, boiled out of the rocks: salts, metal halides, chalcogenides. The vapours were transported into the higher, cooler air, and salt crystals – cubes and whiskers – accreted out over the cooler uplands. The crystals, sprouting over millions of years, dug into rock cracks and broke open the surface like a salty frost, leaving a fractured, gleaming rubble.

The mountain tops of Venus shone, as if painted with metal.

The compounds deposited included antimony sulphoiodide, tungsten trioxide, germanium telluride and caesium germanium chloride. These were ferroelectrics, capable of passing electric currents and storing bits of magnetic polarization.

A natural electrical network was growing over the mountain tops of Venus. Charges flowed in complex, unpredictable patterns.

In response to external stimuli – storms, the punching impacts of the last planetesimals – patterns of magnetic polarization were laid down, and modified.

Nikita Sergeyevich Khrushchev stood behind his desk, and glowered at Korolev. 'Listen to me,' he shouted. 'You will complete this Voskhod, Chief Designer. You will launch it on time.'

Korolev tried to control the weary shaking in his legs. 'Comrade Khrushchev. I am trying to explain. We are behind schedule. Our resources have been devoted to the *Zemlya* project.'

Khrushchev's mood switched, as it so often did, to a sly bullying. He waggled a fat finger in Korolev's face. 'You do not deceive me, Sergei Pavlovich, and you should not attempt it. I know you hoped that this *Zemlya* flight might be sufficient to buy me off. Let us sacrifice one man, one brave man, in this reckless jaunt to Venus, and proceed with our *real* work.

Yes? But it will not do, Sergei Pavlovich. It will not do!'

Korolev regarded Khrushchev with disgust. Khrushchev's peasant ignorance was so great, Korolev suspected bitterly, that he understood nothing, truly, of where these men, the cosmonauts, were going. Perhaps Khrushchev thought the six Vostoks had landed on some ledge in the sky, above the flat Earth.

Korolev had delivered the systems which had launched the first satellite, and Gagarin, the first man in space, satisfactorily ahead of the Americans. And now Korolev was reaching out to another world, to Venus.

But for Khrushchev it was never enough.

Korolev feared for the future of his programmes.

'Comrade Khrushchev,' he said now. 'Perhaps you do not understand. Here is how I must do this thing, this stunt. I have only the Vostok, which is a one-man ship. To fit in two or three men, I must remove the ejection seat, and eliminate the reserve parachute. The ship will sustain a single day in space. I must add a solid-fuel rocket to the base to make the landing survivable. There will be no launch escape system. If I carry three men, I cannot even give them pressure suits. Each launch is a terrible risk, without engineering or scientific justification. And –'

'I care nothing for your justifications! I cannot wait the several years until your wonder ship, the Soyuz, is ready to fly out of its paper nest. Not while the Americans make ready to fly their Gemini. I need results, Sergei Pavlovich!'

Khrushchev started to thump the desk with his fist.

Gagarin studied Venus through his *Vzor* telescope. The face of the planet was brilliant white, the clouds shining in the light of the nearing Sun. The grey shading seemed to deepen at the planet's limb, giving the globe a three-dimensional effect, a marked roundness. Venus was a little round pearl, utterly featureless.

To Gagarin, it was clear that the planet was a blank, on which the mind of man could project its desires; the reality lay beneath the clouds, undiscovered, waiting for him.

The receding Earth took on the appearance of a remote

cave: warm, well-lit, but an isolated speck on a black, hostile hillside. In the blue mouth of the cave, he saw the faces of his wife and daughters turned up to him, diminishing, becoming ever less important.

But now Gagarin had ventured far outside the cave.

The padded walls of his cabin were just centimetres from his gloved fingers. Beyond that, there was *nothing*, for millions of kilometres. When he closed his eyes he saw flashes of light, meteoric streaks sometimes, against the darkness. He knew this must be some radiation effect, perhaps the debris of exploded stars coursing through him. His soft human flesh was being remade, shaped anew.

In his uneasy sleep, he receded to his own oceanic past, his childhood. He saw again the German tanks moving past the wooden houses of his home town of Klushino, heard the planes of the Soviet Air Force droning overhead.

Drifting between sleep and wakefulness as between worlds, Gagarin sang hymns to the motherland.

The flickerings of intelligence would not be extinguished.

In a final, desperate gamble, the last sentient minds enfolded themselves in the ferroelectric caps of the mountains, storing themselves in the complex crystal lattices there.

The final, deepest shelters collapsed under the ferocious weight of the atmosphere. The organic molecules of the last corpses coagulated in the oven heat.

But a new, chthonic awareness dawned across the planet.

It probed out with subtle electromagnetic senses. It dug into the heart of the rocky world whose skin it infested, and felt the mass of its heavy nickel-iron core. It reached out to the Sun, the giant fusing ball which tugged the planet on closed paths around its equator. It sensed other worlds: the huge, homogenous gas spheres on the rim of the Solar System, and the rocky worlds closer to the Sun, which moved with jewel-like precision around their miniature orbits.

And, as a human's eye may be caught by the flight of a bird, the iron mass of Earth's core tugged at the electromagnetic senses of the new chthonic mind.

*   *   *

Leonov stormed into Korolev's office. He had a document with him, a glossy booklet; he threw it down on Korolev's desk. 'What is this, Chief Designer?'

Korolev put aside his pen and picked up the booklet. It was in English, evidently a publication of the United States Information Service. It was full of large type, simple trajectory diagrams, and artists' representations of a desolate, baked landscape; its cover bore an image of a fragile, boxy craft with solar-panel wings sailing past a cloudy world.

Leonov paced, magnificent and awesome in his Air Force uniform.

'I cannot read English,' Korolev said.

'The pictures are sufficient, are they not, Sergei Pavlovich? This is an account of *Mariner* 2. An American spacecraft, unmanned, which flew past Venus in 1962.'

'How did you get this?'

'From an American, who met Gagarin in Paris last year. It does not matter.' Leonov leaned forward, with his massive fists resting on Korolev's desk. 'And what did this American probe tell us of Venus? Did it detect the lush jungles, the seas of water, the lakes of oil of which our scientists speak?'

Korolev sighed. 'It found a desert. Baked hard. An atmosphere a hundred kilometres thick, of carbon dioxide, exerting a pressure scores of times Earth's. And temperatures of hundreds of degrees.'

'There is no water, no oxygen?'

'None.'

Leonov thumped the desk. 'Then how will Yuri survive, damn you? Is his capsule strong enough to resist such pressures?'

Korolev shrugged. 'It is possible. It is not easy to send a craft with a submarine's hull all the way to Venus, Alexei Arkhipovich. Even with our new Proton, the weight penalties . . .'

Some of the anger seemed to drain out of Leonov. He sat down, opposite Korolev. 'Sergei Pavlovich, why *Zemlya*?'

'Because the Americans are going to Mars,' Korolev said

simply. 'They intend to send two new *Mariner* craft there this year. We know that we cannot compete with the Americans' delicate electronics. We must, for now, concede Mars.'

Leonov did not look shocked at this admission of weakness. 'And Venus?'

'We must play to our strengths, Alexei Arkhipovich. We are still in advance of the Americans in our ability to loft heavy masses to orbit, and beyond. It will take a massive, plated craft to penetrate the air of Venus and set down on its surface.' Korolev smiled. 'Venus is a Soviet planet, Alexei Arkhipovich. Dour, heavy, difficult, responding only to brute force. But we have that force.'

Although, he thought, we have already launched seven unmanned probes to Venus, all of which failed.

'Must we send a man?' Leonov demanded.

'Ah, but if he should succeed, Alexei Arkhipovich. If he should succeed! It would be a cosmic victory over the United States, a feat that would resound through the ages.'

'And if he dies? If Yuri sails past Venus in his misdirected ship, or falls to his death on those rocky plains? What then?'

Korolev tapped a brown-card file on his desk. 'We have plans. We will say that the ship was a Zond. A mere unmanned craft, an experiment.'

'And Yuri?'

'We will wait a decent interval – until 1967, or 1968. Yuri will disappear into training, perhaps for my new Soyuz programme. And he will be lost, before he journeys into space again. Perhaps he will fall to Earth in his beloved MiG–15.' Holding Leonov's gaze, Korolev caressed the file. 'It is all here, Alexei Arkhipovich. We have prepared. It has been done before. Future generations will read in their reference books of Zond 1, and of the MiG–15 which fell into the birch forest. No-one will know of *Zemlya*.'

Leonov balled up the American leaflet and threw it across the room. 'Chief Designer, these webs of deception shame you. There is no difference between Comrade Khrushchev and his politics, and you and your rockets. You are mirror images, driven by your twin ambitions, your pride and folly.'

Korolev was stung. 'You should be cautious in your remarks, Alexei. You know little of my past.'

'You sent Gagarin to this planet, this hell-hole, *knowing* what the Americans had learned of conditions on its surface.'

'I know what the Americans claim. But this *Mariner* is only a single probe, which flew by a *world*, in mere hours. How can we rely on its data? Perhaps your jungles and oil lakes are there after all, Alexei Arkhipovich. How can we know? Is it not worth risking a life, one life, to determine such a thing?'

'No, it is not, and you do not think so either, Chief Designer.'

'Perhaps. But he knew,' Korolev said softly.

'Yuri?'

'Yuri *knew*, of this *Mariner* data. And yet he travelled anyway, Alexei Arkhipovich.'

Leonov stared at him for long seconds. Then he dropped his head to his hands. 'As would I,' he murmured. 'As would I, of course.'

'I know it, Alexei Arkhipovich.'

Earth was intriguing.

It was the same mass as Venus, and roughly the same composition, yet – because of its greater distance from the Sun – its nature was very different.

A thin layer of nitrogen and oxygen coated its surface, and liquid water was stable there. A weak, complex, evanescent life shimmered within that blue film.

Then there was a change, quite sudden. Metal packets were hurled beyond the transparent air of Earth, to fall back again. Electromagnetic energy – perhaps signals, perhaps probes – pulsed across space, touching even Venus.

Something analogous to curiosity stirred in the planet-wide mind.

More metal packets came limping, on minimum-energy transfer paths, towards Venus. They fell back to Earth, or missed Venus by thousands of times the planet's diameter.

But now a new packet, more massive than the others, climbed out of the dimple of Earth's gravity well. Perhaps this would reach its goal.

The chthonic awareness waited through the flicker of geologic time it would require for the metal packet to complete its transit.

Zemlya plunged into the sunlit face of Venus.

At the ship's portholes Gagarin saw flames, at first filmy, and then thickening into intense fire. The ablative coating of the sphere was burning away, carrying off the deadly heat.

Four hundred kilometres above the ground, he felt the first caress of weight.

The acceleration mounted on his chest. It reached six, seven, eight times gravity. It was much more painful than at the launch; during the long flight his sturdy body had become etiolated.

There was a surge – a peak in the acceleration that made him grunt – and then, for a moment, the pressure subsided. Under automatic control, *Zemlya* was shifting its centre of gravity, skipping across the top of the atmosphere like a stone over an ocean. By this means *Zemlya* would extend its entry, shedding its hyperbolic velocity without subjecting Gagarin to crushing deceleration.

It was, he thought, a marvellous design.

The ship plunged more directly into the air. The pink, fiery glow faded.

He heard a bang, above his head. That was the opening of the parachute compartment. And a lid on the outside hull blew off, to expose atmospheric sensors.

Gagarin, inside his charred sphere, gazed out at the air of Venus.

Zemlya was bathed in a yellow glow, that brightened and darkened periodically. The capsule was spinning under its parachute, and so that cyclical brightening must be the Sun, reduced to a glare behind a diffuse haze.

Suddenly the haze thinned out, and the visibility extended. Gagarin found himself looking down on a layer of cloud, thick and unbroken, a pale, washed-out yellow. The clouds were fluffy, Earthlike.

Zemlya dropped through the clouds.

And then, suddenly, he saw the surface, dimly visible through the murky air.

Gagarin made out a ridge, hundreds of kilometres long, leading up to a plateau. To his right, shadowy cones loomed. They were mountains, perhaps volcanoes. *Zemlya* was drifting towards the mountains, he saw, floating like a fat metal balloon in some sluggish current.

The mountain peaks shone, as if their summits were coated with layers of glass, sharply delineated.

It was a desolate, baked landscape. Despite himself, Gagarin felt a sharp stab of disappointment that the Americans had been proven correct, after all. There were no oceans here, of carbonated water or of oil. But Gagarin felt no fear; Korolev's hull would protect him.

Zemlya was heading for the rough summit of one of the peaks. It was broken up with large, jagged rocks. He saw some evidence of winds: dust streaks, scouring, flattened dunes.

The ground rocked upwards, spinning towards him.

The landing was hard and loud. At the impact, Gagarin groaned.

Zemlya, downed, settled a little on its left side. The hull creaked.

Gagarin lifted his heavy head, and peered through his windows.

The light was dark, reddish, but no worse than an overcast day on Earth. He could not see the Sun at all; there was only an ill-defined glare, almost baleful, spread across half of the cloud bank that covered the sky.

The ground on which *Zemlya* rested looked like clay that had been baked, carelessly, in an oven that was set too high: it was cracked, fractured. The light was strong enough for some of the rocks to cast a sharp shadow. His orange chute had come down close to the capsule, and was spread over the rocks.

Crystals of some salt littered the ground; they bristled from every crack in the rock, aggressive, complex, like tiny antennae.

The hull emitted a metallic groan.

Gagarin lay back in his couch, resting his strained neck.

Perhaps some day a future cosmonaut – in a spaceship built like a tank – would find the remnant of his *Zemlya*, flattened as if by a great footfall, and wonder at the foolishness of the human who had ventured here in such a fashion: his foolishness, and valour. Gagarin grinned. They would erect a statue to him, a hundred kilometres high, and his name would live forever!

The cabin grew dark.

The salt crystals had grown up around the ship, like a forest of glass. They were impossibly long, and they probed at the scorched windows like fingers.

Behind Gagarin's head, there was a noise like a hammer blow. He turned his head. The escape hatch had buckled.

The cabin imploded.

A hail of crystal light whirled in, enfolding Gagarin.

Salt crystals drizzled out of the air, depositing layers of ferroelectrics over the wreckage of Zemlya. Geologic perceptions millions of years deep were adjusted, absorbing the new material.

It was a new stimulus, this notion of reaching out physically to the sister planets. Intriguing.

Tentative plans were made.

Leonov listened to Gagarin's recorded voice.

The present generation will witness how the free and conscious labour of the people of the new socialist society turns even the most daring of mankind's dreams into reality. To reach into space is a historical process which mankind is carrying out in accordance with the laws of natural development . . .

'Did he know that no-one could hear him?'

Korolev said nothing.

'Must we do this, Chief Designer? Must we proceed, for-ever, onwards into space?'

'Yuri thought we must,' Korolev said.

'Yes,' Leonov said. 'Yuri believed it all. Everything they would have us say, about the triumph of socialism leading us to the stars, where our transforming destiny awaits. He believed it. It is why he was a hero. Why we loved him.'

'And perhaps,' Korolev mused, 'he was right. Perhaps despite ourselves we will reach through, beyond the rockets and the politics and the rhetoric, to a new reality. Perhaps we will be transformed. Is that possible, Alexei Arkhipovich?'

Leonov shivered.

Before him, glowing like the mouth of a crowded cave, lay the blue Earth. He sensed the compact mass of the planet's iron core, studied the thin film of life which coated its surface.

The subtle shadows of the glittering, crystalline ships from Venus crossed the crowded lands, the oceans, the shrinking caps of ice.

He imagined the alarms clamouring across the planet, the lids of ageing missile silos gaping open, the huge nuclear submarines breaking the surface of the seas. Already, the first sparks were climbing up towards him, like wasps threatening an elephant.

He reached out a hand, and those small lights died.

On the evanescent surface of Earth, human generations had worn away.

Artifacts orbited the planet, looking inwards; but no longer did humans travel beyond the air, or send their complex metal packets to other worlds. With the deaths of Korolev and Leonov, something else had died, he saw.

But now, all over the planet, there were faces turned up to him, as steppe flowers turn to the Sun. Faces shining with awe.

Yuri Gagarin smiled on them all. He descended, on crystalline pillars of light.

MOON SIX

Bado was alone on the primeval beach of Cape Canaveral, in his white lunar-surface pressure suit, holding his box of Moon rocks and sampling tools in his gloved hand.

He lifted up his gold sun-visor and looked around. The sand was hard and flat. A little way inland, there was a row of scrub pines, maybe ten feet tall.

There were no ICBM launch complexes here.

There was no Kennedy Space Center, in fact: no space programme, evidently, save for him. He was stranded on this empty, desolate beach.

As the light leaked out of the sky, an unfamiliar Moon was brightening.

Bado glared at it. 'Moon Six,' he said. 'Oh, shit.'

He took off his helmet and gloves. He picked up his box of tools and began to walk inland. His blue overshoes, still stained dark grey from lunar dust, left crisp Moonwalk footprints in the damp sand of the beach.

Bado drops down the last three feet of the ladder and lands on the foil-covered footpad. A little grey dust splashes up around his feet.

Slade is waiting with his camera. 'Okay, turn around and give me a big smile. Atta boy. You look great. Welcome to the Moon.' Bado can't see Slade's face, behind his reflective golden sun-visor.

Bado holds onto the ladder with his right hand and places his left boot on the Moon. Then he steps off with his right foot, and lets go of the LM. And there he is, standing on the Moon.

The suit around him is a warm, comforting bubble. He hears the hum of pumps and fans in the PLSS – his backpack, the Portable Life Support System – and feels the soft breeze of oxygen across his face.

He takes a halting step forward. The dust seems to crunch beneath his feet, like a covering of snow: there is a firm footing beneath a soft, resilient layer a few inches thick. His footprints are miraculously sharp, as if he's placed his ridged overshoes in fine, damp sand. He takes a photograph of one particularly well-defined print; it will persist here for millions of years, he realizes, like the fossilized footprint of a dinosaur, to be eroded away only by the slow rain of micrometeorites, that echo of the titanic bombardments of the deep past.

He looks around.

The LM is standing in a broad, shallow crater. Low hills shoulder above the close horizon. There are craters everywhere, ranging from several yards to a thumbnail width, the low sunlight deepening their shadows.

They call the landing site Taylor Crater, after that district of El Lago – close to the Manned Spacecraft Center in Houston – where he and Fay have made their home. This pond of frozen lava is a relatively smooth, flat surface in a valley once flooded by molten rock. Their main objective for the flight is another crater a few hundred yards to the west that they've named after Slade's home district of Wildwood. Surveyor 7, an unmanned robot probe, set down in Wildwood a few years before; the astronauts are here to sample it.

This landing site is close to Tycho, the fresh, bright crater in the Moon's southern highlands. As a kid Bado had sharp vision. He was able to see Tycho with his naked eyes, a bright pinprick on that ash-white surface, with rays that spread right across the face of the full Moon.

Now he is here.

Bado turns and bounces back towards the LM.

After a few miles he got to a small town.

He hid his lunar pressure suit in a ditch, and, dressed in his tube-covered cooling garment, snuck into someone's back yard. He stole a pair of jeans and a shirt he found hanging on the line there.

He hated having to steal; he didn't plan on having to do it again.

He found a small bar. He walked straight in and asked after a job. He knew he couldn't afford to hesitate, to hang around figuring what kind of world he'd finished up in. He had no money at all, but right now he was clean-shaven and presentable. A few days of sleeping rough would leave him too dirty and stinking to be employable.

He got a job washing glasses and cleaning out the john. That first night he slept on a park bench, but bought himself breakfast and cleaned himself up in a gas station john.

After a week, he had a little money saved. He loaded his lunar gear into an old trunk, and hitched to Daytona Beach, a few miles up the coast.

They climb easily out of Taylor.

Their first Moonwalk is a misshapen circle which will take them around several craters. The craters are like drill holes, the geologists say, excavations into lunar history.

The first stop is the north rim of a hundred-yard-wide crater they call Huckleberry Finn. It is about three hundred yards west of the LM.

Bado puts down the tool carrier. This is a hand-held tray, with an assortment of gear: rock hammers, sample bags, core tubes. He leans over, and digs into the lunar surface with a shovel. When he scrapes away the grey upper soil he finds a lighter grey, just under the surface.

'Hey, Slade. Come look at this.'

Slade comes floating over. 'How about that. I think we found some ray material.' Ray material here will be debris from the impact which formed Tycho.

Lunar geology has been shaped by the big meteorite impacts which pounded its surface in prehistory. A main purpose of sending this mission so far south is to keep them away from the massive impact which created the Mare Imbrium, in the northern hemisphere. Ray material unpolluted by Imbrium debris will let them date the more recent Tycho impact.

And here they have it, right at the start of their first Moonwalk.

Slade flips up his gold visor so Bado can see his face, and grins at him. 'How about that. We is looking at a full-up mission here, boy.'

They finish up quickly, and set off at a run to the next stop. Slade looks like a human-shaped beach ball, his suit brilliant white, bouncing over the beach-like surface of the Moon. He is whistling.

They are approaching the walls of Wildwood Crater. Bado is going slightly uphill, and he can feel it. The carrier, loaded up with rocks, is getting harder to carry too. He has to hold it up to his chest, to keep the rocks from bouncing out when he runs, and so he is constantly fighting the stiffness of his pressure suit.

'Hey, Bado,' Slade says. He comes loping down the slope. He points. 'Take a look.'

Bado has, he realizes, reached the rim of Wildwood Crater. He is standing on top of its dune-like, eroded wall. And there, planted in the crater's centre, is the Surveyor. It is less than a hundred yards from him. It is a squat, three-legged frame, like a broken-off piece of an LM.

Slade grins. 'Does that look neat? We got it made, Bado.' Bado claps his commander's shoulder. 'Outstanding, man.' He knows that for Slade, getting to the Surveyor, bringing home a few pieces of it, is the finish line for the mission.

Bado looks back east, the way they have come. He can see the big, shallow dip in the land that is Taylor, with the LM resting at its centre like a toy in the palm of some huge hand. It is a glistening, filmy construct of gold leaf and aluminium, bristling with antennae, docking targets, and reaction control thruster assemblies.

Two sets of footsteps come climbing up out of Taylor towards them, like footsteps on a beach after a tide.

Bado tips back on his heels and looks at the sky.

The sky is black, empty of stars; his pupils are closed up by the dazzle of the sun, and the reflection of the pale brown lunar surface. But he can see the Earth, a fat crescent, four times the size of a full moon. And there, crossing the zenith, is a single, brilliant, unwinking star: the orbiting Apollo CSM, with Al Pond, their Command Module pilot, waiting to take them home.

There is a kind of shimmer, like a heat haze. And the star goes out.

Just like that: it vanishes from the sky, directly over Bado's head. He blinks, and moves his head, stiffly, thinking he might have just lost the Apollo in the glare.

But it is gone.

What, then? Can it have moved into the shadow of the Moon? But a little thought knocks out that one: the geometry, of sun and Moon and spacecraft, is all wrong.

And anyhow, what was that heat haze shimmer? You don't get heat haze where there's no air.

He lowers his head. 'Hey, Slade. You see that?'

But Slade isn't anywhere to be seen, either; the slope where he's been standing is smooth, empty.

Bado feels his heart hammer.

He lets go of the tool carrier – it drifts down to the dust, spilling rocks – and he lopes forward. 'Come on, Slade. Where the hell are you?'

Slade is famous for gotchas; he is planning a few that Bado knows about, and probably some he doesn't, for later in the mission. But it is hard to see how he's pulled this one off. There is nowhere to hide, damn it.

He gets to where he thinks Slade was last standing. There is no sign of Slade. And there aren't even any footsteps, he realizes now. The only marks under his feet are those made by his own boots, leading off a few yards away, to the north.

And they start out of nothing, it seems, like Man Friday steps in the crisp virgin Moon-snow. As if he's stepped out of nowhere onto the regolith.

When he looks back to the east, he can't see the LM either.

'Slade, this isn't funny, damn it.' He starts to bound, hastily, back in the direction of the LM. His clumsy steps send up parabolic sprays of dust over unmarked regolith.

He feels his breath getting shallow. It isn't a good idea to panic. He tells himself that maybe the LM is hidden behind some low ridge. Distances are deceptive here, in this airless sharpness.

'Houston, Bado. I gets some kind of situation here.' There isn't a reply immediately; he imagines his radio signal crawling across the light-seconds' gulf to Earth. 'I'm out of contact with Slade. Maybe he's fallen somewhere, out of sight. And I don't seem to be able to see the LM. And –'

And someone's wiped over our footsteps, while I wasn't looking.

Nobody is replying, he realizes.

That stops him short. Dust falls over his feet. On the surface of the Moon, nothing is moving.

He looks up at the crescent Earth. 'Ah, Houston, this is Bado. Houston. John, come in, capcom.'

Just silence, static in his headset.

He starts moving to the east again, breathing hard, the sweat pooling at his neck.

He rented an apartment.

He got himself a better job in a radio store. In the Air Force, before joining NASA, he'd specialized in electronics. He'd been apprehensive that he might not be able to find his way around the gear here, but he found it simple – almost crude, compared to what he'd been used to. They had transistors here, but they still used big chunky valves and paper capacitors. It was like being back in the early '60s. Radios were popular, but there were few TVs: small black and white gadgets, the reception lousy.

He began watching the TV news and reading the newspapers, trying to figure out what kind of world he'd been dropped in.

The weather forecasts were lousy.

And foreign news reports, even on the TV, were sent by wire, like they'd been when he was a kid, and were often a day or two out of date.

The Vietnam war was unfolding. But there'd been none of the protests against the war, here, that he'd seen back at home. There were no live TV pictures, no colour satellite images of soldiers in the mud and the rain, napalming civilians. Nobody knew what was

*happening out there. The reaction to the war was more like what he
remembered of World War Two.*

*There really was no space programme. Not just the manned stuff
had gone: there were no weather satellites, communication satellites.
Sputnik, Explorer and all the rest just hadn't happened. The Moon
was just a light in the sky that nobody cared about, like when he
was a kid. It was brighter, though, because of that big patch of
highland where Imbrium should have been.*

On the other hand, there were no ICBMs, as far as he could tell.

His mouth is bone-dry from the pure oxygen. He is breathing
hard; he hears the hiss of water through the suit's cooling
system, the pipes that curl around his limbs and chest.

There is a rational explanation for this. There has to be.
Like, if he's got out of line of sight with the LM, somehow,
he's invisible to the LM's radio relay, the Lunar Communications Relay Unit. He is linked to that by VHF, and then by
S-band to the Earth.

Yeah, that has to be it. As soon as he gets back in line of
sight of the LM, he can get in touch with home. And maybe
with Slade.

But he can't figure how he can have gotten out of the LM's
line of sight in the first place. And what about the vanished
footsteps?

He tries not to think about it. He just concentrates on loping
forward, back to the LM.

In a few minutes, he is back in Taylor Crater.

There is no LM. The regolith here is undisturbed.

Bado bounces across the virgin surface, scuffing it up.

Can he be in the wrong place? The lunar surface does have
a tendency to look the same everywhere . . . Hell, no. He can
see he is right in the middle of Taylor; he recognizes the shapes
of the hills. There can't be any doubt.

What, then? Can Slade have somehow gotten back to the
LM, taken off without him?

But how can Bado not have seen him, seen the boxy LM
ascent stage lift up into the sky? And besides, the regolith
would be marked by the ascent stage's blast.

And, he realizes dimly, there would, of course, be an abandoned descent platform here, and bits of kit. And their footsteps. His thoughts are sluggish, his realization coming slowly. Symptoms of shock, maybe.

The fact is that save for his own footfalls, the regolith is as unmarked as if he's been dropped out of the sky.

And meanwhile, nobody in Houston is talking to him.

He is ashamed to find he is crying, mumbling, tears rolling down his face inside his helmet.

He starts to walk back west again. Following his own footsteps – the single line he made coming back to find the LM – he works his way out of Taylor, and back to the rim of Wildwood.

Hell, he doesn't have any other place to go.

As he walks he keeps calling, for Slade, for Houston, but there is only static. He knows his signal can't reach Earth anyway, not without the LM's big S-band booster.

At Wildwood's rim there is nothing but the footfalls he left earlier. He looks down into Wildwood, and there sits the Surveyor, glistening like some aluminium toy, unperturbed.

He finds his dropped carrier, with the spilled tools and bagged rocks. He bends sideways and scoops up the stuff, loading it back into the carrier.

Bado walks down into Wildwood, spraying lunar dust ahead of him.

He examines the Surveyor. Its solar cell array is stuck out on a boom above him, maybe ten feet over the regolith. The craft bristles with fuel tanks, batteries, antennae and sensors. He can see the craft's mechanical claw where it has scraped into the lunar regolith. And he can see how the craft's white paint has turned tan, maybe from exposure to the sunlight. There are splashes of dust under the vernier rocket nozzles; the Surveyor is designed to land hard, and the three pads have left a firm imprint in the surface.

He gets hold of a landing leg and shakes the Surveyor. 'Okay,' he calls up. 'I'm jiggling it. It's planted here.' There was a fear that the Surveyor might tip over onto the astronauts when they try to work with it. That evidently isn't going to happen. Bado takes a pair of cutting shears from his carrier, gets hold of the Surveyor's TV camera, and starts to chop through the camera's support struts and cables. 'Just a couple more tubes,' he says. 'Then that baby's mine.'

He'll finish up his Moonwalk, he figures, according to the timeline in the spiral-bound checklist on his cuff. He'll keep on reporting his observations, in case anyone is listening. And then –

And then, when he gets to the end of the walk, he'll figure out what to do next. Later there will be another boundary, when his PLSS's consumables expire. He'll deal with those things when they come. For now, he is going to work.

The camera comes loose, and he grips it in his gloves. 'Got it! It's ours!'

He drops the camera in his carrier, breathing hard. His mouth is dry as sand; he'd give an awful lot for an ice-cool glass of water, right here and now.

There is a shimmer, like heat haze, crossing between him and the Surveyor. Just like before.

He tilts back and looks up. There is old Earth, the fat crescent. And a star, bright and unwavering, is crossing the black sky, directly over his head.

It has to be the Apollo CSM.

He drops the carrier to the dirt and starts jumping up and down, in great big lunar hops, and he waves, as if he is trying to attract a passing aircraft. 'Hey, Al! Al Pond! Can you hear me?' Even without the LM, Pond, in the CSM, might be able to pick him up.

His mood changes to something resembling elation. He doesn't know where the hell Apollo has been, but if it is back, maybe soon so will be the LM, and Slade, and everything. That will suit Bado, right down to the lunar ground he is standing on. He'll be content to have it all back the way it had been, the way it is supposed to be, and figure out what has happened to him later.

'Al! It's me, Bado! Can you hear me? Can you . . .'

There is something wrong.

That light isn't staying steady. It is getting brighter, and it is drifting off its straight line, coming down over his head.

It isn't the CSM, in orbit. It is some kind of boxy craft, much smaller than a LM, descending towards him, gleaming in the sunlight.

He picks up his carrier and holds it close to his chest, and he stays close to the Surveyor. As the craft approaches he feels an unreasoning fear.

His kidneys send him a stab of distress. He stands still and lets go, into the urine collection condom. He feels shamed; it is like wetting his pants.

The craft is just a box, on four spindly landing legs. It is coming down vertically, standing on a central rocket. He can see no light from the rocket, of course, but he can see how the downward blast is starting to kick up some dust. It is going to land maybe fifty yards from the Surveyor, right in the middle of Wildwood Crater. The whole thing is made of some silvery metal, maybe aluminium. It has a little control panel, set at the front, and there is someone at the controls. It looks like a man – an astronaut, in fact – his face hidden behind a gold-tinted visor.

Bado can see the blue of a NASA logo, and a dust-coated Stars and Stripes, painted on the side of the craft.

Maybe fifty feet above the ground the rocket cuts out, and the craft begins to drop. The sprays of dust settle back neatly to the lunar soil. Now little vernier rockets, stuck to the side of the open compartment, cut in to slow the fall, kicking up their own little sprays.

It is all happening in complete silence.

The craft hits the ground with a solid thump. Bado can see the pilot, the astronaut, flick a few switches, and then he turns and jumps the couple of feet down off the little platform to the ground.

The astronaut comes giraffe-loping across the sunlit surface towards Bado.

He stops, a few feet from Bado, and stands there, slightly stooped forward, balancing the weight of his PLSS.

His suit looks pretty much a standard EMU, an Apollo Extravehicular Mobility Unit. There is the usual gleaming white oversuit – the thermal micrometeorite garment – with the lower legs and overshoes scuffed and stained with Tycho dust. Bado can see the PLSS oxygen and water inlets on the chest cover, and penlight and utility pockets on arms and legs. And there is Old Glory stitched to the left arm.

But Bado doesn't recognize the name stitched over the breast. WILLIAMS. There is no astronaut of that name in the corps, back in Houston.

Bado's headset crackles to life, startling him.

'I heard you, when the LFU came over the horizon. As soon as I got in line of sight. I could hear you talking, describing what you were doing. And when I looked down, there you are.'

Bado is astonished. It is a woman's voice. This Williams is a goddamn woman.

Bado can't think of a thing to say.

He didn't find it hard to find himself a place in the community here, to gather a fake id around himself. Computers were pretty primitive, and there was little cross-checking of records.

Maybe, back home, the development of computers had been forced by the Apollo project, he speculated.

He couldn't see any way he was going to get home. He was stuck here. But he sure as hell didn't want to spend his life tuning crummy 1960s-design radios.

He tinkered with the Surveyor camera he'd retrieved from the Moon. It was a much more lightweight design than anything available here, as far as he could tell. But the manufacturing techniques required weren't much beyond what was available here.

He started to take camera components to electronic engineering companies.

He took apart his lunar suit. In all this world there was nothing like the suit's miniaturized telemetry system. He was able to adapt it to be used to transmit EKG data from ambulances to hospital emergency rooms. He sent samples of the Beta-cloth outer coverall to a fibreglass company, and showed them how the stuff could be used for fire hoses. Other samples went to military suppliers to help them put together better insulated blankets. The scratch-proof lens of the Surveyor camera went to an optical company, to manufacture better safety goggles and other gear. The miniature, high-performance motors driving the pumps and fans of his PLSS found a dozen applications.

He was careful to patent everything he 'developed' from his lunar equipment.

Pretty soon, the money started rolling in.

'Maybe I'm dreaming this,' Williams says. 'Dehydration, or something . . . Uh, I guess I'm pleased to meet you.'

She has a Tennessee accent, he thinks.

Bado shakes the hand. He can feel it through his own stiff pressure glove. 'I guess you're too solid for a ghost.'

'Ditto,' she says. 'Besides, I've never met a ghost yet who uses VHF frequencies.'

He releases her hand.

'I don't know how the hell you got here,' she says. 'And I guess you don't understand this any better than I do.'

'That's for sure.'

She dips her visored head. 'What are you doing here, anyway?'

He holds up the carrier. 'Sampling the Surveyor. I took off its TV camera.'

'Oh. You couldn't get it, though.'

'Sure. Here it is.'

She turns to the Surveyor. 'Look over there.'

The Surveyor is whole again, its TV camera firmly mounted to its struts.

But when he looks down at his carrier, there is the TV camera he's cut away, lying there, decapitated.

'Where's your LM?' she asks.

'Taylor Crater.'

'Where?'

He describes the crater's location.

'Oh. Okay. We're calling that one San Jacinto. Ah, no, your LM isn't there.'

'I know. I walked back. The crater's empty.'

'No, it isn't,' she says, but there is a trace of alarm in her voice. 'That's where my LM is. With my partner, and the Payload Module.'

Payload Module?

'The hell with it,' she says. 'Let's go see.'

She turns and starts to lope back to her flying craft, rocking from side to side. He stands there and watches her go.

After a few steps she stops and turns around. 'You want a lift?'

'Can you take two?'

'Sure. Come on. What choice do you have, if you're stuck here without an LM?'

Her voice carries a streak of common sense that somehow comforts him.

Side by side, they bound over the Moon.

They reach Williams's flying machine. It is just an aluminium box sitting squat on its four legs, with vernier rocket nozzles stuck to the walls like clusters of berries. The pilot has to climb in at the back and stand over the cover of the main rocket engine, which is about the size of a car engine, Bado supposes. Big spherical propellant and oxidizer tanks are fixed to the floor. There is an S-band antenna and a VHF aerial. There is some gear on the floor, hammers and shovels and sample bags and cameras; Williams dumps this stuff out, briskly, onto the regolith. Williams hops up onto the platform and begins throwing switches. Her control panel contains a few instruments, a CRT, a couple of handsets.

Bado lugs his heavy tool carrier up onto the platform, then he gets hold of a rail with both hands and jumps up. 'What did you call this thing? An LFU?'

'Yeah. Lunar Flying Unit.'

'I've got vague memories,' says Bado. 'Of a design like this. It was never developed, when the extended Apollo missions were cancelled.'

'Cancelled? When did that happen?'

'When we were cut back to stop when we get to Apollo 17.'

'Uh huh,' she says dubiously. She eyes the tool carrier. 'You want to bring that thing?'

'Sure. It's not too heavy, is it?'

'No. But what do you want it for?'

Bado looks at the battered, dusty carrier, with its meaningless load of rocks. 'It's all I've got.'

'Okay. Let's get out of here,' she says briskly.

Williams kicks in the main rocket. Dust billows silently up off the ground, into Bado's face. He can see frozen vapour puff out of the attitude nozzles, in streams of shimmering crystals, as if this is some unlikely steam engine, a Victorian engineer's fantasy of lunar flight.

The basin of Wildwood Crater falls away. The lift is a brief, comforting surge.

Williams whoops. 'Whee-hoo! What a ride, huh, pal?' She takes the LFU up to maybe sixty feet, and slows the ascent. She pitches the craft over and they begin sailing out of Wildwood.

The principles of the strange craft are obvious enough to Bado. You stand on your rocket's tail. You keep yourself stable with the four peroxide reaction clusters, the little vernier rockets spaced around the frame, squirting them here and there. When the thrust of the single big downwards rocket is at an angle to the vertical, the LFU goes shooting forwards, or sideways, or backwards across the pitted surface. Williams shows him the hand controls. They are just like the LM's. The attitude control moves in clicks; every time Williams turns the control the reaction rockets will bang and the LFU will tip over, by a degree at a time. The thrust control is a toggle switch; when Williams closes it the lift rocket roars, to give her a delta-vee of a foot per second.

'These are neat little craft,' Williams says. 'They fly on residual descent stage propellants. They've a range of a few miles, and you can do three sorties in each of them.'

'Each?'

'We bring two. Rescue capability.'

Bado thinks he is starting to see a pattern to what has happened to him.

In a way, the presence of the camera in his carrier is reassuring. It means he isn't crazy. There really have been two copies of the Surveyor: one of which he's sampled, and one he hasn't.

Maybe there is more than one goddamn Moon.

Moon One is the good old lantern in the sky that he and Slade touched down on yesterday. Maybe Slade is still back there, with the LM. But Bado sure isn't. Somehow he stumbled onto Moon Two, the place with the Surveyor, but no LM. And then this Williams showed up, and evidently by that time he was on another Moon, Moon Three, with its own copy of the Surveyor. And a different set of astronauts exploring, with subtly different equipment.

As if travelling to one Moon isn't enough.

He thinks about that strange, heat-haze shimmer. Maybe that has something to do with these weird transfers.

He can't discuss any of this with Williams, because she hasn't seen any of the changes. Not yet, anyhow.

Bado clings to the sides of the LFU and watches the surface of the Moon scroll underneath him. There are craters everywhere, overlaid circles of all sizes, some barely visible in a surface gardened by billions of years of micrometeorite impact. The surface looks ghostly, rendered in black and white, too stark, unmoving, to be real.

He knew he was taking a risk, but he took his lunar rocks to a couple of universities.

He got laughed out of court. Especially when he wouldn't explain how these charcoal-dark rocks might have got from the Moon to the Earth.

'Maybe they got blasted off by a meteorite strike,' he said to an 'expert' at Cornell. 'Maybe they drifted in space until they landed here. I've read about that.'

The guy pushed his reading glasses further up his thin nose. 'Well, that's possible.' He smiled. 'No doubt you've been reading the same lurid speculation I have, in the popular science press. What if rocks get knocked back and forth between the planets? Perhaps there are indeed bits of the Moon, even Mars, to be turned up, here on Earth. And, since we know living things can survive in the interiors of rocks – and since we know that some plants and bacteria can survive long periods of dormancy – perhaps it is even possible for life to propagate itself, across the trackless void, in such a manner.'

He picked up Bado's Moon rock, dubiously. 'But in that case I'd expect to see some evidence of the entry of this rock into the atmosphere. Melting, some glass. And besides, this rock is not volcanic. Mr Bado, everyone knows the Moon's major features were formed exclusively by vulcanism. This can't possibly be a rock from the Moon.'

Bado snatched back his rock. 'That's Colonel Bado,' he said. He marched out.

He gave up, and went back to Daytona Beach.

The LFU slides over the rim of Taylor Crater. Or San Jacinto. Bado can see scuffed-up soil below him, and the big Huckleberry Finn Crater to his left, where he and Slade made their first stop.

At the centre of Taylor stands an LM. It glitters like some piece of giant jewellery, the most colourful object on the lunar surface. An astronaut bounces around in front of it, like a white balloon. He – or she – is working at what looks like a surface experiment package, white-painted boxes and cylinders and masts laid out in a star formation, and connected to a central nuclear generator by orange cables. It looks like an ALSEP, but it is evidently heavier, more advanced.

But the LM isn't alone. A second LM stands beside it, squat and spidery. Bado can see that the ascent stage has been heavily reworked; the pressurized cabin looks to be missing, replaced by cargo pallets.

'That's your Payload Module, right?'

'Yeah,' Williams says. 'The Lunar Payload Module Laboratory. It got here on automatics before we left the Cape. This is a dual Saturn launch mission, Bado. We've got a stay time of four weeks.'

Again he has vague memories of proposals for such things: dual launches, well-equipped long-stay jaunts on the surface. But the funding squeezes since '66 have long since put paid to all of that. Evidently, wherever Williams comes from, the money is flowing a little more freely.

The LFU tips itself back, to slow its forward velocity. Williams throttles back the main motor and the LFU starts to drop down. Bado glances at the numbers; the CRT display evolves smoothly through height and velocity readings. Bado guesses the LFU must have some simple radar-based altimeter.

Now the LM and its misshapen partner are obscured by the dust Williams's rocket is kicking up.

At fifty feet Williams cuts the main engine. Bado feels the drop in the pit of his stomach, and he watches the ground explode towards him, resolving into unwelcome detail, sharp boulders and zap pits and footprints, highlighted by the low morning sun.

Then vernier dust clouds billow up around the LFU. Bado feels a comforting surge of deceleration.

The LFU lands with a jar that Bado feels in his knees.

For a couple of seconds the dust of their landing cloaks the LFU, and then it begins to settle out around them, coating the LFU's surfaces, his suit.

There is a heat-haze shimmer. 'Oh, shit.'

Williams is busily shutting down the LFU. She turns to face him, anonymous behind her visor.

There wasn't much astronomy going on at all, in fact, he found out when he looked it up in the libraries. Just a handful of big telescopes, scattered around the world, with a few crusty old guys following their obscure, decades-long projects. And all the projects were to do with deep space: the stars, and beyond. Nobody was interested in the Solar System. Certainly in nothing as mundane as the Moon.

He looked up at Moon Six, uneasily, with its bright, unscarred north-west quadrant. If that Imbrium meteorite hadn't hit three billion years ago – or in 1970 – where the hell was it now?

Maybe that big mother was on its way, right now.

Quietly, he pumped some of his money into funding a little research at the universities into Earth-neighbourhood asteroids.

He also siphoned money into trying to figure out what had happened to him. How he had got here.

As the last dust settles, Bado looks towards the centre of Taylor Crater, to where the twin LMs stood.

He can make out a blocky shape there.

He feels a sharp surge of relief. Thank God. Maybe this transition hasn't been as severe as some of the others. Or maybe there hasn't been a transition at all . . .

But Williams's LM has gone, with its cargo-carrying partner. And so has the astronaut, with his surface package. But the crater isn't empty. The vehicle that stands in its place has the same basic geometry as an LM, Bado thinks, with a boxy descent stage standing on four legs, and a fat ascent stage cabin on top. But it is just fifteen feet tall – compared to an LM's twenty feet – and the cabin looks a lot smaller.

'My God,' Williams says. She is just standing, stock still, staring at the little lander.

'Welcome to Moon Four,' Bado whispers.

'My God.' She repeats that over and over.

He faces her, and flips up his gold visor so she can see his face. 'Listen to me. You're not going crazy. We've been through some kind of – transition. I can't explain it.' He grins. It makes him feel stronger to think there is someone else more scared, more shocked, than he is.

He takes her through his tentative theory of the multiple Moons.

She turns to face the squat lander again. 'I figured it had to be something like that.'

He gapes at her. 'You figured?'

'How the hell else could you have got here? Well, what are we supposed to do now?' She checks the time on her big Rolex watch. 'Bado. How long will your PLSS hold out?'

He feels embarrassed. Shocked or not, she's cut to the chase a lot more smartly than he's been able to. He glances at his own watch, on the cuff next to his useless checklist. 'A couple of hours. What about you?'

'Less, probably. Come on.' She glides down from the platform of the LFU, her blue boots kicking up a spray of dust.

'Where are we going?'

'Over to that little LM, of course. Where else? It's the only source of consumables I can see anywhere around here.' She begins loping towards the lander.

After a moment, he picks up his carrier, and follows her.

As they approach he gets a better look at the lander. The ascent stage is a bulbous, misshapen ball, capped by a fat, wide disk that looks like a docking device. Two dinner-plate-sized omnidirectional antennae are stuck out on extensible arms from the descent stage. The whole clumsy-looking assemblage is swathed in some kind of green blanket, maybe for thermal insulation.

A ladder leads from a round hatch in the front of the craft, and down to the surface via a landing leg. The ground there is scuffed with footprints.

'It's a hell of a small cabin,' she says. 'Has to be one man.'

'You think it's American?'

'Not from any America I know. That ascent stage looks familiar. It looks like an adapted Soyuz orbital module. You know, the Russian craft, their Apollo equivalent.'

'Russian?'

'Can you see any kind of docking tunnel on top of that thing?'

He looks. 'Nope. Just that flat assemblage at the top.'

'The crew must have to spacewalk to cross from the command module. What a design.'

An astronaut comes loping around the side of the lander, swaying from side to side, kicking up dust. When he catches sight of Bado and Williams, he stops dead.

The stranger is carrying a flag, on a pole. The flag is stiffened with wire, and it is clearly bright red, with a gold hammer-and-sickle embroidered into it.

'How about that,' Williams whispers. 'I guess we don't always get to win, huh.'

The stranger – the cosmonaut, Bado labels him – takes a couple of steps towards them. He starts gesticulating, waving his arms about, making the flag flutter. He wears a kind of hoop around his waist, held away from his body with stiff wire.

'I think he's trying to talk to us,' Williams says.

'It'll be a miracle if we are on the same frequency. Maybe

he's S-band only, to talk to Earth. No VHF. Look how stiff his movements are.'

'Yeah. I think his suit is semi-rigid. Must be hell to move around in.'

'What's with the hoolahoop?' Bado asks.

'It will stop him falling over, in case he trips. Don't you get it? He's on his own here. That's a one-man lander. There's nobody around to help him, if he gets into trouble.'

The cosmonaut is getting agitated. Now he hoists up the flag and throws it at them, javelin-style; it falls well short of Bado's feet. Then the cosmonaut turns and lopes towards his lander, evidently looking for more tools, or improvised weapons.

'Look at that,' Bado says. 'There are big funky hinges, down the side of his backpack. That must be the way into the suit.'

Williams lifts up her visor. 'Show him your face. We've got to find some way to get through to this guy.'

Bado feels like laughing. 'What for?'

The light changes.

Bado stands stock still. 'Shit, not again.'

Williams says, 'What?'

'Another transition.' He looks around for the tell-tale heat-haze flicker.

'I don't think so,' Williams says softly. 'Not this time.'

A shadow, slim and jet-black, hundreds of feet long, sweeps over the surface of Taylor Crater.

Bado leans back and tips up his face.

The ship is like a huge artillery shell, gleaming silver, standing on its tail. It glides over the lunar surface, maybe fifty feet up, and where its invisible rocket exhaust passes, dust is churned up and sent gusting away in great flat sheets. The ship moves gracefully, if ponderously. Four heavy landing legs, with big spring-load shock absorbers, stick out from the base. A circle of portals glows bright yellow around the nose. A huge bull's-eye of red, white and blue is painted on the side, along with a registration number.

'Shit,' Bado says. 'That thing must be a hundred feet tall.'

Four or five times as tall as his lost LM. 'What do you think it weighs? Two, three hundred tons?'

'Direct ascent,' she says.

'Huh?'

'Look at it. It's streamlined. It's built for landing on the Moon in one piece, ascending again, and returning to Earth.'

'But that was designed out years ago, by von Braun and the boys. A ship like that's too heavy for chemical rockets.'

'So who said anything about chemical? It has to be atomic. Some kind of fission pile in there, superheating its propellant. One hell of a specific impulse. Anyhow, it's that or antigravity –'

The great silver fish hovers for a moment, and then comes swooping down at the surface. It flies without a quiver. Bado wonders how it is keeping its stability; he can't see any verniers. Big internal flywheels maybe.

As the ship nears the surface dust comes rushing across the plain, away from the big tail, like a huge circular sandstorm. There is a rattle, almost like rain, as heavy particles impact Bado's visor. He holds his gloved hands up before his face, and leans a little into the rocket wind.

The delicate little Russian lander just topples over in the breeze, and the bulbous ascent stage breaks off and rolls away.

In the mirror of his bedroom he studied his greying hair and spreading paunch.

Oddly, it had taken a while for him to miss his wife, Fay.

Maybe because everything was so different. Not that he was sorry, in a sense; his job, he figured, was to survive here – to earn a living, to keep himself sane – and moping after the unattainable wouldn't help.

He was glad they'd had no kids, though.

There was no point searching for Fay in Houston, of course. Houston without the space programme was just an oil town, with a big cattle pasture north of Clear Lake where the Manned Spacecraft Center should have been. El Lago, the Taylor housing development, had never been built.

He even drove out to Atlantic City, where he'd first met Fay, a

*couple of decades ago. He couldn't find her in the phone book. She
was probably living under some married name, he figured.*

He gave up.

*He tried, a few times, to strike up relationships with other women
here. He found it hard to get close to anyone, though. He always
felt he needed to guard what he was saying. This wasn't his home,
after all.*

*So he lived pretty much alone. It was bearable. It even got easier,
as he got older.*

*Oddly, he missed walking on the Moon more than anything else,
more than anything about the world he'd lost. He kept reliving those
brief hours. He remembered Slade, how he looked bouncing across
the lunar sand, a brilliant white balloon. How happy he'd seemed.*

The silver ship touches down with a thump, and those big
legs flex, the springs working like muscles.

A hatch opens in the ship's nose, maybe eighty feet from
the ground, and yellow light spills out. A spacesuited figure
appears, and begins rolling a rope ladder down to the surface.
The figure waves to Bado and Williams, calling them to the
ship.

'What do you think?' Bado asks.

'I think it's British. Look at that bull's-eye logo. I remember
war movies about the Battle of Britain . . . Wherever the hell
that's come from, it's some place very different from the
worlds you and I grew up in.'

'You figure we should go over there?' he asks.

She spreads her hands. 'What choice do we have? We don't
have an LM. And we can't last out here much longer. At least
these guys look as if they know what they're doing. Let's go
see what Boris thinks.'

The cosmonaut lets Williams walk up to him. He is hauling
at his ascent stage. But Bado can see the hull is cracked open,
like an aluminium egg, and the cosmonaut's actions are
despairing.

Williams points towards the silver ship, where the figure
in the airlock is still waving at them.

Listlessly, the cosmonaut lets himself be led to the ship.

Close to, the silver craft looks even bigger than before, so tall that when Bado stands at its base he can't see the nose.

Williams goes up the ladder first, using just her arms, pulling her mass easily in the Moon's shallow gravity well. The cosmonaut takes off his hoop, dumps it on the ground, and follows her.

Bado comes last. He moves more slowly than the others, because he has his tool carrier clutched against his chest, and it is awkward to juggle while climbing the rope ladder.

It takes forever to climb past the shining metal of the ship's lower hull. The metal here looks like lead, actually. Shielding, around an atomic pile? He thinks of the energy it must take to haul this huge mass of metal around. He can't help comparing it with his own LM, which, to save weight, was shaved down to little more than a bubble of aluminium foil.

The hull shivers before his face. Heat haze.

He looks down. The wreckage of the little Russian lander, and Williams' LFU, has gone. The surface under the tail of this big ship looks unmarked, lacking even the raying of the landing. And the topography of the area is quite different; now he is looking down over some kind of lumpy, sun-drenched mountain range, and a wide, fat rille snakes through the crust.

'How about that,' Williams says drily, from above him. Her voice signal is degraded; the amplifier on the LFU is no longer available to boost their VHF link.

'We're on Moon Five,' he says.

'Moon Five?'

'It seems important to keep count.'

'Yeah. Whatever. Bado, this time the geology's changed. Maybe one of the big primordial impacts didn't happen, leaving the whole lunar surface a different shape.'

They reach the hatch. Bado lets the astronaut take his tool carrier, and clambers in on his knees.

The astronaut closes the hatch and dogs it shut by turning a big heavy wheel. He wears a British Union Flag on his sleeve, and there is a name stitched to his breast: TAINE.

The four of them stand around in the airlock, in their competing pressure suit designs. Air hisses, briefly.

An inner door opens, and Taine ushers them through with impatient gestures. Bado enters a long corridor, with nozzles set in the ceiling. The four of them stand under the nozzles.

Water comes gushing down, and runs over their suits.

Williams opens up her gold sun visor and faces Bado. 'Showers,' she says.

'What for?'

'To wash off radioactive crap, from the exhaust.' She begins to brush water over her suit arms and legs.

Bado has never seen anything like such a volume of water in lunar conditions before. It falls slowly from the nozzles, gathering into big shimmering drops in the air. Grey-black lunar dust swirls towards the plug holes beneath his feet. But the dirt is ingrained into the fabric of his suit legs; they will be stained grey forever.

When the water dies they are ushered through into a third, larger chamber. The walls here are curved, and inset with round, tough-looking portholes; it looks as if this chamber reaches most of the way around the cylindrical craft.

There are people here, dozens of them, adults and children and old people, dressed in simple cotton coveralls. They sit in rows of crude metal-framed couches, facing outwards towards the portholes. They stare fearfully at the newcomers.

The astronaut, Taine, has opened up his faceplate; it hinges outward like a little door.

Bado pushes back his hood and reaches up to his fishbowl helmet. He undogs it at the neck, and his ears pop as the higher pressure of the cabin pushes air into his helmet.

He can smell the sharp, woodsmoke tang of lunar dust. And, overlaid on that, there is a smell of milky vomit: baby sick.

The Russian, his own helmet removed, makes a sound of disgust. '*Eta oozhasna!*'

Williams pulls off her Snoopy flight helmet. She is maybe forty, Bado guesses – around Bado's own age – with a tough, competent face, and close-cropped blond hair.

Taine shoos the three of them along. 'Welcome to *Prometheus*,' he says. 'Come. There are some free seats further around here.' His accent is flat, sounding vaguely Bostonian. Definitely British, Bado thinks, probably from the south of England. 'You're the last, we think. We must get away. The impact is no more than twelve hours hence.'

Bado, lugging his tool carrier, walks beside him. 'What impact?'

'The meteorite, of course.' Taine sounds impatient. 'That's why we're having to evacuate the colonies. And you alternates. The Massolite got most of them off, of course, but –'

Williams says, 'Massolite?'

Taine waves a hand. 'A mass transporter. Of course it was a rushed job. And it had some flaws. But we knew we couldn't lift everybody home in time, not all those thousands in the big colonies, not before the strike; the Massolite was the best we could do, you see.' They come to three empty couches. 'These should do, I think. If you'll sit down I'll show you how to fit the seat belts, and instruct you in the safety precautions –'

'But,' Williams says, 'what has this Massolite got to do with –' She dries up, and looks at Bado.

He asks, 'With moving between alternate worlds?'

Taine answers with irritation. 'Why, nothing, of course. That's just a design flaw. We're working on it. Nonlinear quantum mechanical leakage, you see. I do wish you'd sit down; we have to depart . . .'

Bado shucks off his PLSS backpack, and he tucks his helmet and his carrier under his seat.

Taine helps them adjust their seat restraints until they fit around their pressure suits. It is more difficult for the Russian; his suit is so stiff it is more like armour. The Russian looks young, no more than thirty. His hair sticks up in the air, damp with sweat, and he looks at them forlornly from his shell of a suit. '*Gdye tooalyet?*'

The portholes before them give them a good view of the lunar surface. It is still Moon Five, Bado sees, with its mountains and that sinuous black rille.

He looks around at their fellow passengers. The adults are unremarkable; some of them have run to fat, but they have incongruously skinny legs and arms. Long-term adaptation to lunar gravity, Bado thinks.

But there are also some children here, ranging from babies in their mothers' arms up to young teenagers. The children are extraordinary: spindly, attenuated. Children who look facially as young as seven or eight tower over their parents.

The passengers clutch at their seatbelts, staring back at him.

Bado hears a clang of hatches, and a siren wails, echoing from the metal walls.

The ship shudders, smoothly, and there is a gentle surge.

'Mnye nada idtee k vrachoo,' groans the Russian, and he clutches his belly.

As the years wore on he followed the news, trying to figure out how things might be different, back home.

The Cold War went on, year after year. There were no ICBMs here, but they had squadrons of bombers and nuke submarines and massive standing armies in Europe. And there were no spy satellites; nobody had a damn clue what the Russians – or the Chinese – were up to. A lot of shit came down that Bado figured might have been avoided, with satellite surveillance. It slowly leaked out into the paper press, usually months or years too late. Like the Chinese nuking of Tibet, for instance. And what the Soviets did to Afghanistan.

The Soviet Union remained a monolith, blank, threatening, impenetrable. Everyone in the US seemed paranoid to Bado, generations of them, with their bomb shelters and their iodine pills. It was like being stuck in the late 1950s.

And that damn war in Indochina just dragged on, almost forgotten back home, sucking up lives and money like a bloody sponge.

Around 1986, he felt a sharp tug of wistfulness. Right now, he figured, on the other side of that heat-haze barrier, someone would be taking the first steps on Mars. Maybe it would be his old buddy, Slade, or someone like John Young. Bado might have made it himself.

Bado missed the live sports on TV.

*   *   *

In free fall, Taine gives them spare cotton coveralls to wear, which are comfortable but don't quite fit; the name stitched to Bado's is LEDUC, and on Williams's, HASSELL.

Bado, with relief, peels off the three layers of his pressure suit: the outer micrometeorite garment, the pressure assembly and the inner cooling garment. The other passengers look on curiously at Bado's cooling garment, with its network of tubes. Bado tucks his discarded suit layers into a big net bag and sticks it behind his couch.

They are served food: stodgy stew, lukewarm and glued to the plate with gravy, and then some kind of dessert, like bread with currants stuck inside it. Spotted dick, Taine calls it.

There is a persistent whine of fans and pumps, a subdued murmur of conversation, and the noise of children crying. Once a five-year-old, all of six feet tall, comes bouncing around the curving cabin in a spidery tangle of attenuated arms and legs, pursued by a fat, panting, queasy-looking parent.

Taine comes floating down to them, smiling. 'Captain Richards would like to speak to you. He's intrigued to have you on board. We've picked up quite a few alternate-colonists, but not many alternate-pioneers, like you. Would you come forward to the cockpit? Perhaps you'd like to watch the show from there.'

Williams and Bado exchange glances. 'What show?'

'The impact, of course. Come. Your German friend is welcome too, of course,' Taine adds dubiously.

The cosmonaut has his head stuck inside a sick bag.

'I think he's better off where he is,' Bado says.

'You go,' Williams says. 'I want to try to sleep.' Her face looks worn to Bado, her expression brittle, as if she is struggling to keep control. Maybe the shock of the transitions is getting to her at last, he thinks.

The cockpit is cone-shaped, wadded right in the nose of the craft. Taine leads Bado in through a big oval door. Charts and mathematical tables have been stuck to the walls, alongside pictures and photographs. Some of these show powerful-looking aircraft, of designs unfamiliar to Bado, but others show what must be family members. Pet dogs. Tools and personal articles are secured to the walls with elastic straps.

Three spacesuits, flaccid and empty, are fixed to the wall with loose ties. They are of the type Taine wore in the airlock: thick and flexible, with inlaid metal hoops, and hinged helmets at the top.

Three seats are positioned before instrument consoles. Right now the seats face forward, towards the nose of the craft, but Bado can see they are hinged so they will tip up when the craft is landing vertically. Bado spots a big, chunky periscope sticking out from the nose, evidently there to provide a view out during a landing.

There are big picture windows set in the walls. The windows frame slabs of jet-black, star-sprinkled sky.

A man is sitting in the central pilot's chair. He is wearing a leather flight jacket, a peaked cap, and – Bado can't believe it – he is smoking a pipe, for God's sake. The guy sticks out a hand. 'Mr Bado. I'm glad to meet you. Jim Richards, RAF.'

'That's Colonel Bado.' Bado shakes the hand. 'US Air Force. Lately of NASA.'

'NASA?'

'National Aeronautics and Space Administration . . .'

Richards nods. 'American. Interesting. Not many of the alternates are American. I'm sorry we didn't get a chance to see more of your ship. Looked a little cramped for the three of you.'

'It wasn't our ship. It was a Russian, a one-man lander.'

'Really,' Richards murmurs, not very interested. 'Take a seat.' He waves Bado at one of the two seats beside him; Taine takes the other, sipping tea through a straw. Richards asks, 'Have you ever seen a ship like this before, Colonel Bado?'

Bado glances around. The main controls are a conventional stick-and-rudder design, adapted for spaceflight; the supplementary controls are big, clunky switches, wheels, and levers. The fascia of the control panel is made of wood. And in one place, where a maintenance panel has been removed, Bado sees the soft glow of vacuum tubes.

'No,' he says. 'Not outside the comic books.'

Richards and Taine laugh.

'It must take a hell of a launch system.'

'Oh,' says Richards, 'we have good old Beta to help us with that.'

'Beta?'

'This lunar ship is called Alpha,' Taine says. 'Beta gives us a piggyback out of Earth's gravity. We launch from Woomera, in South Australia. Beta is a hypersonic athodyd –'

Richards winks at Bado. 'These double-domes, eh? He means Beta is an atomic ramjet.'

Bado boggles. 'You launch an atomic rocket from the middle of Australia? How do you manage containment of the exhaust?'

Taine looks puzzled. 'What containment?'

'You must tell me all about your spacecraft,' Richards says.

Bado, haltingly, starts to describe the Apollo system.

Richards listens politely enough, but after a while Bado can see his eyes drifting to his instruments, and he begins to fiddle with his pipe, knocking out the dottle into a big enclosed ashtray.

Richards becomes aware of Bado watching him. 'Oh, you must forgive me, Colonel Bado. It's just that one encounters so many alternates.'

'You do, huh.'

'The Massolite, you know. That damn quantum-mechanical leakage. Plessey just can't get the thing tuned correctly. Such a pity. Anyhow, don't you worry; the boffins on the ground will put you to rights, I'm sure.'

Bado is deciding he doesn't like these British. They are smug, patronizing, icy. He can't tell what they are thinking.

Taine leans forward. 'Almost time, Jim.'

'Aha!' Richards gets hold of his joystick. 'The main event.' He twists the stick, and Bado hears what sounds like the whir of flywheels, deep in the guts of the ship. Stars slide past the windows. 'A bit of showmanship, Colonel Bado. I want to line us up to give the passengers the best possible view. And us, of course. After all, this is a grandstand seat, for the most dramatic astronomical event of the century – what?'

The Moon, fat and grey and more than half-full, slides into the frame of the windows.

The Moon – Moon Five, Bado assumes it to be – looks like a ball of glass, its surface cracked and complex, as if starred by buckshot. Tinged pale white, the Moon's centre looms out at Bado, given three-dimensional substance by the Earthlight's shading.

The Moon looks different. He tries to figure out why.

There, close to the central meridian, are the bright pinpricks of Tycho, to the south, and Copernicus, in the north. He makes out the familiar pattern of the seas of the eastern hemisphere: Serenitatis, Crisium, Tranquillitatis – grey lakes of frozen lava framed by brighter, older lunar uplands.

He supposes there must be no Apollo 11 LM descent stage, standing on this version of the Sea of Tranquillity.

The Moon is mostly full, but he can see lights in the remaining crescent of darkness. They are the abandoned colonies of Moon Five.

Something is still wrong, though. The western hemisphere doesn't look right. He takes his anchor from Copernicus. There is Mare Procellarum, to the western limb, and to the north of that –

Nothing but bright highlands.

'Hey,' he says. 'Where the hell's Mare Imbrium?'

Richards looks at him, puzzled, faintly disapproving.

Bado points. 'Up there. In the north-west. A big impact crater – the biggest – flooded with lava. Eight hundred miles across.'

Richards frowns, and Taine touches Bado's arm. 'All the alternate Moons are different to some degree,' he says, placating. 'Differences of detail – '

'Mare Imbrium is not a goddamn detail.' Bado feels patronized again. 'You're talking about my Moon, damn it.' But if the Imbrium impact has never happened, no wonder the surface of Moon Five looks different.

Richards checks his wrist watch. 'Any second now,' he says. 'If the big-brains have got it right – '

There is a burst of light, in the Moon's north-west quadrant.

The surface in the region of the burst seems to shatter, the bright old highland material melting and subsiding into a red-glowing pool, a fiery lake that covers perhaps an eighth of the Moon's face. Bado watches huge waves, concentric, wash out across that crimson, circular wound.

Even from this distance Bado can see huge debris clouds streaking across the lunar surface, obscuring and burying older features, and laying down bright rays that plaster across the Moon's face.

The lights of the night-side colonies wink out, one by one.

Richards takes his pipe out of his mouth. 'Good God almighty,' he says. 'Thank heavens we got all our people off.'

'Only just in time, sir,' Taine says.

Bado nods. 'Oh, I get it. Here, this was the Imbrium impact. Three billion years late.'

Richards and Taine look at him curiously.

It turned out that to build a teleport device – a 'Star Trek' beaming machine – you needed to know about quantum mechanics. Particularly the Uncertainty Principle.

According to one interpretation, the Uncertainty Principle was fundamentally caused by there being an infinite number of parallel universes, all lying close to each other – as Bado pictured it – like the pages of a book. The universes blurred together at the instant of an event, and split off afterwards.

The Uncertainty Principle said you could never measure the position and velocity of any particle with absolute precision. But to teleport that was exactly what you needed to do: to make a record of an object, transmit it, and recreate the payload at the other end.

But there was a way to get around the Uncertainty Principle. At least in theory.

The quantum properties of particles could become entangled: fundamentally linked in their information content. What those British must have done is take sets of entangled particles, left one half on their Moon as a transmitter, and planted the other half on the Earth.

There was a lot of technical stuff about the Einstein-Podolsky-Rosen theorem which Bado skipped over; what it boiled down to was that if you used a description of your teleport passenger to jiggle the transmitter particles, you could reconstruct the passenger at the other end, exactly, from the corresponding jiggles in the receiver set.

But there were problems.

If there were small nonlinearities in the quantum-mechanical operators – and there couldn't be more than a billion billion billionth part, according to Bado's researchers – those parallel worlds, underlying the Uncertainty Principle, could short-circuit.

The Moon Five Brits had tried to build a cheap-and-dirty teleport machine. Because of the huge distances involved, that billion-billion-billionth nonlinearity had become significant, and the damn thing had leaked. And so they had built a parallel-world gateway, by accident.

This might be the right explanation, Bado thought. It fit with Captain Richards's vague hints about 'nonlinear quantum mechanics'.

This new understanding didn't make any difference to his position, though. He was still stranded here. The teleport devices his researchers had outlined – even if they'd got the theory right, from the fragments he'd given them – were decades beyond the capabilities of the mundane world Bado found himself in.

Reentry is easy. Bado estimates the peak acceleration is no more than a couple of G, no worse than a mild roller-coaster. Even so, many of the passengers look distressed, and those spindly lunar-born children cry weakly, pinned to their seats like insects.

After the landing, Alpha's big doors are flung open to reveal a flat, barren desert. Bado and Williams are among the first down the rope ladders, lugging their pressure suits, and Bado's tool carrier, in big net bags.

Bado can see a small town, laid out with the air of a military barracks.

Staff are coming out of the town on little trucks to meet them. They are processed efficiently; the crew of the *Prometheus* gives details of where each passenger has been picked up, and they are all assigned little labels and forms, standing there in the baking sunlight of the desert.

The spindly lunar children are lowered to the ground and taken off in wheelchairs. Bado wonders what will happen to them, stranded at the bottom of Earth's deep gravity well.

Williams points. 'Look at that. Another *Prometheus*.'

There is a launch rail, like a pencil line ruled across the sand, diminishing to infinity at the horizon. A silver dart clings to the rail, with a slim bullet shape fixed to its back. Another Beta and Alpha. Bado can see protective rope barriers slung around the rail.

Taine comes to greet Bado and Williams. 'I'm afraid this is goodbye,' he says. He sticks out a hand. 'We want to get you people back as quickly as we can. You alternates, I mean. What a frightful mess this is. But the sooner you're out of it the better.'

'Back where?' Bado asks.

'Florida.' Taine looks at them. 'That's where you say you started from, isn't it?'

Williams shrugs. 'Sure.'

'And then back to your own world.' He mimes stirring a pot of some noxious substance. 'We don't want to muddy the time lines, you see. We don't know much about this alternating business; we don't know what damage we might do. Of course the return procedure's still experimental but hopefully we'll get it right.

'Well, the best of luck. Look, just make your way to the plane over there.' He points.

The plane is a ramjet, Bado sees immediately.

Taine moves on, to another bewildered-looking knot of passengers.

The Russian cosmonaut is standing at Williams's side. He is hauling his stiff pressure suit along the ground; it scrapes on the sand like an insect's discarded carapace. Out of the suit the Russian looks thin, young, baffled, quite ill. He shakes Bado's hand. '*Do svidanya.*'

'Yeah. So long to you too, kid. Hope you get home safely. A hell of a ride, huh.'

'*Mnye nada k zoobnomoo vrachoo.*' He clutches his jaw and grins ruefully. '*Schastleevava pootee. Zhilayoo oospyekhaf.*'

'Yeah. Whatever.'

A British airman comes over and leads the Russian away.

'Goddamn,' Williams says. 'We never found out his name.'

He got a report in from his meteorite studies group.

Yes, it turned out, there was a large object on its way. It would be here in a few years' time. Bado figured this had to be this universe's edition of that big old Imbrium rock, arriving a little later than in the Moon Five world.

But this rock was heading for Earth, not the Moon. Its path would take it right into the middle of the Atlantic, if the calculations were right. But the margins of error were huge, and, and . . .

Bado tried to raise public awareness. His money and fame got him onto TV, even, such as it was. But nobody here took what was going on in the sky very seriously anyhow, and they soon started to think he was a little weird.

So he shut up. He pushed his money into bases at the poles, and at the bottom of the oceans, places that mightn't be so badly affected. Somebody might survive. Meanwhile he paid for a little more research into that big rock in space, and where and when, exactly, it was going to hit.

The ramjet takes ten hours to get to Florida. It is a military ship, more advanced than anything flying in Bado's world. It has the bull's-eye logo of the RAF painted to its flank, just behind the gaping mouth of its inlet.

As the ramjet rises, Bado glimpses huge atomic aircraft, immense ocean-going ships, networks of monorails. This is a gleaming world, an engineer's dream.

Bado has had enough wonders for the time being, though, and, before the shining coast of Australia has receded from sight, he's fallen asleep.

They land at a small airstrip, Bado figures somewhere north of Orlando. A thin young Englishman in spectacles is there to greet them. He is wearing Royal Air Force blue coveralls. 'You're the alternates?'

'I guess so,' Williams snaps. 'And you're here to send us home. Right?'

'Sorry for any inconvenience you've been put through,' he says smoothly. 'If you'll just follow me into the van . . .'

The van turns out to be a battered diesel-engined truck that looks as if it is World War Two vintage. Williams and Bado with their bulky gear have to crowd in the back with a mess of electronic equipment.

The truck, windowless, bumps along badly-finished roads.

Bado studies the equipment. 'Look at this stuff,' he says to Williams. 'More vacuum tubes.'

Williams shrugs. 'They've got further than we have. Or you. Here, they've built stuff we've only talked about.'

'Yeah.' Oddly, he's forgotten that he and Williams have come from different worlds.

The roads off the peninsula to Merritt Island are just farmers' tracks, and the last few miles are the most uncomfortable.

They arrive at Merritt Island in the late afternoon.

There is no Kennedy Space Center.

Bado gets out of the van. He is on a long, flat beach; he figures he is a way south of where, in his world, the lunar ship launch pads will be built. Right here there will be the line of launch complexes called ICBM Row.

But he can't see any structures at all. Marsh land, coated with scrub vegetation, stretches down towards the strip of beach at the coast. Further inland, towards the higher ground, he can see stands of cabbage palm, slash pine and oak.

The place is just scrub land, undeveloped. The tracks of the British truck are dug crisply into the sand; there is no sign even of a road near here.

And out to the east, over the Atlantic, he can see a big full Moon rising. Its upper left quadrant, the fresh Imbrium scar, still glows a dull crimson. Bado feels vaguely reassured. That is still Moon Five; things seem to have achieved a certain stability.

In the back of the truck, the British technician powers up his equipment. 'Ready when you are,' he calls. 'Oh, we think it's best if you go back in your own clothes. Where possible.' He grins behind his spectacles. 'Don't want you –'

'Muddying up the time lines,' Williams says. 'We know.'

Bado and Williams shuck off their coveralls and pull on their pressure suits. They help each other with the heavy layers, and finish up facing each other, their helmets under their arms, Bado holding his battered tool carrier with its Baggies full of Moon rocks.

'You know,' Bado says, 'when I get back I'm going to have one hell of a lot of explaining to do.'

'Yeah. Me too.' She looks at him. 'I guess we're not going to see each other again.'

'Doesn't look like it.'

Bado puts down his carrier and helmet. He embraces Williams, clumsily.

Then, on impulse, Bado lifts up his helmet and fits it over his head. He pulls his gloves over his hands and snaps them onto his wrists, completing his suit.

Williams does the same. Bado picks up his tool carrier.

The Brit waves, reaches into his van, and throws a switch.

There is a shimmer of heat haze.

Williams has gone. The truck has vanished.

Bado looks around quickly.

There are no ICBM launch complexes. He is still standing on an empty, desolate beach.

The Moon is brightening, as the light leaks out of the sky. There is no ancient Imbrium basin up there. No recent impact scar, either.

'Moon Six,' Bado says to himself. 'Oh, shit.'

Evidently those British haven't ironed out all the wrinkles in their 'experimental procedures' after all.

He takes off his helmet, breathes in the ozone-laden ocean air, and begins to walk inland, towards the rows of scrub pine.

On the day, he drove out to Merritt Island.

It was morning, and the sun was low and bright over the ocean, off to the east, and the sky was clear and blue, blameless.

He pulled his old Moon suit out of the car, and hauled it on: first the cooling garment, then the pressure layer, and finally the white micrometeorite protector and his blue lunar overshoes. It didn't fit so well any more, especially around the waist – well, it had been fitted for him all of a quarter-century ago – and it felt as heavy as hell, even without the backpack. And it had a lot of parts missing, where he'd dug out components and samples over the years. But it was still stained grey below the knees with lunar dust, and it still had the NASA logo, his mission patch, and his own name stitched to the outer garment.

He walked down to the beach. The tide was receding, and the hard-packed sand was damp; his ridged soles left crisp, sharp prints, just like in the lunar crust.

He locked his helmet into place at his neck.

To stand here, as close as he could get to ground zero, wasn't such a dumb thing to do, actually. He'd always remembered what that old professor at Cornell had told him, about the rocks bearing life being blasted from planet to planet by meteorite impacts. Maybe that would happen here, somehow.

Today might be the last day for this Earth. But maybe, somehow, some piece of him, fused to the glass of his visor maybe, would finish up on the Moon – Moon Six – or Mars, or in the clouds of Jupiter, and start the whole thing over again.

He felt a sudden, sharp stab of nostalgia, for his own lost world. He'd had a good life here, all things considered. But this was a damn dull place. And he'd been here for twenty-five years, already. He was sure that back home that old Vietnam War wouldn't have dragged on until now, like it had here, and funds would have got freed up for space, at last. Enough to do it properly, by God. By now, he was sure, NASA would have bases on the Moon, hundreds of people in Earth orbit, a couple of outposts on Mars, plans to go on to the asteroids or Jupiter.

Hell, he wished he could just look through the nonlinear curtains separating him from home. Just once.

He tipped up his face. The sun was bright in his eyes, so he pulled down his gold visor. It was still scuffed, from the dust kicked up by that British nuclear rocket. He waited.

After a time, a new light, brighter even than rocket light, came crawling down across the sky, and touched the ocean.

GEORGE AND THE COMET

There was no jolt, no sharp transition from what I had been to what I have become. I didn't wake up to find I had changed. Awareness faded in, like a slow dissolve.

I was lying on my back. I felt odd. I am – was – a big man; I played a lot of rugby when I was younger . . . But now, lying there, I felt small and light, as if I might blow away.

I stared up at a sky that was very strange indeed. Half of it was covered by a diseased Sun – vast, red, bloated, its surface crawling with blisters of fire and dark pits. – And, directly over me, there burned a moon (I thought at first), a sphere emitting shining gases which streamed away from the Sun.

That was no moon, I realized suddenly. It was a comet. What the hell was going on?

A face drifted into view: a monkey's face, a mask of fur surrounding startling blue eyes. The monkey said, 'Can you hear me? Do you remember who you are?'

I closed my eyes. So. Obviously I was at home in my Islington flat, having a bad night following a bad day.

I was thirty-two, a middle manager in a software house. After a day of being chased from above and below I often found it difficult to switch off; I would spend hours without sleep, finally falling into that uneasy state between sleep and wakefulness, adrift amid lurid dreams.

So I knew what was happening . . . But I couldn't remember what I had done yesterday. I couldn't even work out what day of the week it had been.

Meanwhile there was a distraction, a sharp pain in my cheek.

Reluctantly I opened my eyes. The ailing Sun, the comet were still there, and I became aware that the branches of some huge tree hung over me. My monkey friend hung from a branch by one hand and foot. Its body was delicate – quite graceful-looking – except that its skin looked about three sizes too large; it was looped like a furry cloak around the shoulders and legs.

The monkey's breath smelt sweet, like young wood. And it was pinching my cheek.

I lifted an arm to brush its hand away, and I was struck again by a feeling of insubstantiality. My hand blurred across my vision, paw-like and covered in a pale fur. I tried not to worry about it.

'I know what you're thinking,' the monkey said, its voice tinny. 'But it isn't a dream. It's real, all of it. I spent a week trying to wake up out of it; you may as well accept –'

'Piss off,' I squeaked.

Squeaked . . . ? My God, I sounded like Donald Duck. I rubbed my jaw and found a face that was small and round and covered in a wiry fur.

'Have it your own way,' the monkey said. It reached out its four limbs and all that loose skin stretched out in sheets, so that the creature looked like a cute, furry kite. Like a gymnast it spun around its branch once, twice, and then let go and went gliding out of my view.

I'd seen something like that at a zoo, years ago. A flying lemur with an exotic name. Colugo?

Why dream about a talking lemur?

Then again, why not?

I jammed my eyes shut.

But the world wouldn't go away. And meanwhile I was getting uncomfortable; whatever I was lying on was scratchy, like straw, and the backs of my legs prickled.

With a sigh I opened my eyes. The great Sun was still there, a dome of fiery pools and pits of darkness, like some industrial landscape. The pits mottling the surface looked like photos I remembered of real sunspots.

I spread my hands below me – I found twigs and leaves –

and sat up. I moved easily enough, although I felt as if I were wearing some heavy coat which snagged in the twigs.

I held my right hand in front of my face.

The hand was small and narrow, with two fingers and a thumb; hard, flat nails tipped the fingers and, although the palm was bright pink, the back of the hand was coated with mud-brown fur. There was webbing between the fingers – I could see light through the veined membranes – and more webbing, or skin, fell away from my forearm in great untidy folds. The webbing was covered with a fine fur which lay in neat, smooth streamlines, like a cat's. I lifted my arms and saw how the sheets of skin stretched down to my splayed, spindly legs; I wasn't surprised to find another pane of flesh connecting my legs too.

When I dug my nail into the webby stuff I felt a sharp pain. So this shabby cloak was part of me.

I was a monkey too. The king of the swingers, the jungle VIP. I laughed – but stopped at the squeaky scratch which emerged from my throat.

I was sitting in the topmost branches of a tree. The tree filled the world; I peered down through the branches towards a ground lost in a translucent green gloom.

There was a rustle of leaves; delicate as a sparrow my monkey friend landed before me. Its sail flaps collapsed in folds. Its face was small and delicate, with a long snout, flaring nostrils and a tiny mouth. 'My God,' it said. 'I've just realized.'

'What?'

'You speak English! My God, my God.'

'So?'

'But, don't you see – It might have been ancient Etruscan.' It sniffled and wiped away a tear with one furry hand. 'Then again, perhaps it was all planned this way.'

I considered closing my eyes again. 'I wish I knew what you were talking about.'

'I'm sorry.' It looked at me with moist, human eyes. 'My name is George; George Newbould. I was in London. I think I remember 1985. AD,' it added helpfully.

I opened my mouth – and closed it again. 'My name's Phil

Beard. But the date –' 1985? 'I don't understand. What date is it?'

It – he, I conceded – he absently scratched at one pointed ear. 'So you agree this isn't a dream?'

'I don't agree any such –' I shook my head, frustrated. 'Just tell me. Have I been in some kind of accident?'

He grinned, showing rows of flat teeth. 'You could say that. Look, Mr Beard, I don't know any more than you do. But I've been, ah, awake, a few days longer, and I've made some guesses. I used to be a teacher, you see – General Science at a middle school – so I know a little about a lot, and –'

'Perhaps we could go over your CV later.'

'All right. I'm sorry. I think we've been reconstructed.'

I pulled at a flap of skin. 'Reconstructed how? Anyway, I didn't need reconstructing. I wasn't ill, or dead . . .'

'You ask how . . . I'd guess from some fragment of DNA; a fingernail clipping, or a tooth in some fossil layer, perhaps. Like a clone.'

Fossil layer? I looked up at the swollen Sun, shivering.

'That's why we don't have clear memories of what we did before, you see. The real Phil Beard threw away that nail clipping and carried on his life. The new Beard is a clone with a vague Beard-ness but without specific memories. As to who did this, I can't even guess.' He tilted his face up to the sky; comet light picked out the bones around his eyes. 'After all this time, there might not be humans any more. Maybe the ants took over the world. Or maybe life as we know it – I mean, life based on our sort of DNA – is extinct altogether; maybe a whole new order, silicon-based, has arisen to replace us, and –'

'George –' I tried to keep my voice level. 'How did I get to be a fossil? Where are we? What year is it?'

He jerked his thumb at the sky. 'I think that's the Sun. Our Sun, I mean. It's gone red giant. You want a date? Five billion years, AD. Give or take,' he added.

I rubbed my furry chin. 'So it's five billion years after 1985. The Sun has turned into a red giant, the human race is long since extinct, and future super-creatures have reconstructed me as a small, furry edition of Batman.'

He looked at me out of the side of his face. 'That's about the size of it. You don't believe it, do you?'

'Not a word,' I said.

He shrugged and stretched out his sails. 'Suit yourself.'

'Hey. Wait for me,' I said. I tried to stand up, but my balance was funny and I toppled forward into the leaves. 'What do you do, flap?'

'No, you glide. You control the angle of the sail stuff with your thumbs. See?'

And so, by the light of the ancient Sun, George and I sailed through the branches of our tree.

The tree bore fruit. I mooched through the upper branches of the tree, nibbling experimentally. The best was a bitter-sweet red berry. I tried the fist-sized leaves; they were bland and tasteless, but the younger specimens bulged with water; I crushed them into my mouth and felt cool liquid trickle down my throat. George said that it had rained once, and that he had managed to catch fresh water in a cup of leaves.

Some of the greener twigs were thinner than bamboo and quite flexible, and George had woven a box-shaped cocoon for himself. By shoving leaves into the gaps between the twigs he had made the walls fairly opaque. At first I laughed at this shanty. 'George, you don't need any protection.' I flapped my sail sheets dramatically. 'It's warm and there's never more than a soft breeze. And there's no one else here . . . Is there?'

'That's not the point. Mr Beard, I'm a schoolteacher from West London. I'm not used to the lifestyle of a flying lemur. I feel safer with walls and a roof.'

I scoffed.

. . . But, when I started feeling sleepy, I made automatically for George's crude shelter. As I entered he glanced up from his task – he was making a bow from a branchlet and a liana-like trailer, patiently goading his clumsy hands through the intricate work – and then looked away, without speaking.

I made for the darkest corner of the hut and wrapped my sails around me.

When I awoke George had finished his bow. He had wrapped its string around a short length of stick; now he was experimentally rolling the stick back and forth with the bow string. Silhouetted against the dim, green light his movements were graceful, almost sensual. I felt a strange itch deep beneath the skin of my groin.

It occurred to me that I ought to be terrified. Can you fall asleep inside a dream?

But fear still hadn't hit me. And in the meantime that tickle in my groin had turned into another kind of ache; man or lemur, there's no mistaking the feeling of a full bladder. I pushed my way out of my corner, rubbing sleep from my eyes, and climbed out of the hut.

Then my problems started.

The penis of a flying lemur is nothing to show off in the changing room. Even when erect. I spent five minutes just trying to find the damn thing. Then I could barely hold it; I hosed into space, feeling hot liquid course over my hands.

As for the rest – well, I had a fur-covered backside and leaves for lavatory paper. And no running water.

But lemurs have their moments . . .

When I'd done I launched through the leaves of our world-tree, feeling the wind cup in my skin-sails; if I could catch a breeze I could hang in the air like a seagull, surrounded by comet light and the scent of growing wood.

The Sun hung in the sky, vast and ill. There were no days, no nights here.

George had a theory about that too. 'I don't think we're on Earth. I think they –'

'Who?'

'The Builders, the people who reconstructed us . . . I think they built this place for us.'

'Then why didn't they give us a day and a night?'

He poked one finger into a wide nostril. 'I don't think it occurred to them. You see, eventually – long after our day –

solar tides slowed the Earth; at last the Sun stopped crossing the sky. No more day or night.'

'But the Builders must have known we're from a time when the Earth still turned.'

'But it was long ago to them. Mr Beard, a lot of people of our time thought that, let's say, Alexander the Great was contemporary with Julius Caesar. In fact centuries separated them . . .'

'It was that long ago?' I shivered, and the furs over my arms stood on edge. I brushed them down absently. George stared at the way my small biceps worked; then he caught himself and looked away, embarrassed.

'Why couldn't they just land us back on Earth?' I asked. 'Maybe after all this time Earth isn't habitable, do you think? The greenhouse effect, the ozone layer – '

George laughed and flapped his sails. 'Mr Beard, I fear the ozone layer, or the lack of it, is one with Nineveh and Tyre.'

'With what?'

'Never mind. The Sun has exhausted its hydrogen fuel and has swollen into that great, swimming globe above us. When the outer layers grazed the Earth's orbit the planet – or whatever blasted ruin was left – spiralled towards the core. Soon it flashed into a mist of iron, along with Mercury, Venus, Mars . . . All gone.'

I stared up at the Sun. 'Makes you think, doesn't it, George?'

'Yes. We're a long way from home.'

Hour succeeded changeless hour.

I clambered through the branches into the depths of our tree. As I entered green twilight the fur on my back prickled; but the tangle of branches seemed empty. No birds, no insects even. I wondered how this tree sustained itself. Was a single-organism ecology possible?

I reached the bottom level of the branches; about fifty feet above a featureless earth I clung upside down from a ceiling of wood. Fat branches led like an inverted road network to a single, massive trunk some hundred yards away.

I scampered along the branches towards the trunk.

The trunk was about six feet across. (George and I appeared to be about a foot long – not that it was easy to tell.) The bark was thick, riven by crevices wide enough for my little hands, and I clambered down easily. When I reached the roots I got to my hind legs, clinging to the trunk timidly; then, like a simian Neil Armstrong, I pushed one foot away from the roots and into the mulch. Brown, curling leaves as large as my wingspan crackled under my feet. Under the top layer the mulch was soft, decaying and even warm, as if the ground were some vast compost heap.

I took a few experimental steps – and, with a squeak, fell flat on my face. I got up and fell again, backwards this time. To my infuriation my lithe little body just wouldn't walk upright. I had to scamper on all fours, like the beast I had become.

I raged around the clearing, sail flaps billowing; I tore at dead leaves and hurled them into the air, screeching my frustration.

At last I lay with my back to the trunk, panting, bits of ripped leaf clinging to my fur.

There was a rushing sound, somewhere far above: rain, I guessed, pattering against the upper branches. After a few minutes fat droplets seeped through the woven ceiling and splashed over my upturned face. The water tasted fresh and leafy.

There were no signs of other tree trunks, animal tracks, plants – nothing but a plain of leaves fading in the dimness under a branch canopy. I brushed away leaf fragments, picked a direction and set off, hopping and hovering stoically.

After about a hundred yards I could barely see the tree trunk. I felt small, helpless and lost.

I hurried back to the trunk and clung to its skirts of wood.

At length I tried again. This time I stopped every ten yards to make a marker, a heap of leaves and mulch taller than I was. After some minutes of this my line of cairns led off, quite straight, into the arboreal gloom.

The trunk was out of sight again.

Panic hit me. But I didn't go back; I buried myself in the compost and folded my sails around my head, and when I felt surer I clambered out and pressed on, deeper into the shadows.

I was glad nobody was watching.

There was no way of measuring time down there, of course, but some hours must have passed before I found the second trunk. It hove out of the gloom twenty or thirty yards to the right of my line of cairns. I hurried to it, thinking at first that I had circled and come back to my starting point; but there were no markers here, no sign that the forest surface had been disturbed.

Timidly I clambered up to the branch world.

The bloated Sun was hidden by the tree world, as was the core of the comet; but comet streamers, twisting faster than before, filled the sky with a glow like exploded moonlight.

So I had walked over the horizon. But the branches were empty. No lemur-people; no super-aliens . . .

No answers.

I descended, swiping at the leaves with frustration.

On the ground I set off again, extending my trail of cairns. Some hours later another trunk appeared, this time some distance to the left of my trail. I hurried to it.

A line of leaf cairns, flattened by rain, led away into the darkness. I had returned to my starting point; I had walked around the world.

I spent much of the next few days repeating this exercise; soon cairns trailed pointlessly around the world.

I was marooned on a globe no more than half a mile across. The world bore a single tree, with twin trunks set opposite each other like poles. And, supported by the trunks, a shell of branches encased the world.

George was intrigued by all this. He wondered how gravity was maintained. Black holes at the core of the planet . . . ?

I wasn't interested. I went for long, searing glides through the branches, trying to work off my tension.

I had found the bounds of my prison. It contained only

George and myself. And there was no way out, no one even
to tell me why I was here.

I dug my nails into tree bark and screamed.

I spat berry seeds and chewed stems. 'Admit it, George. Your
theory that we were cloned from fingernails is a crock.'

He sighed; he was hunched over his latest device, a slab of
wood into which he was drilling a pit with a sharpened stick.
'Maybe it is. What do I know?'

'If I was a clone I'd be a physical copy but a separate individual. I'd be a man with no memories of the Phil Beard of
1985. But in fact I'm still Phil Beard, trapped in the body of a
damn monkey.' I shook my sails. 'See?'

'Maybe the Builders used techniques we can't even guess
at,' George whispered. 'Maybe souls leave fossils too, in some
invisible sediment layer.'

I frowned. 'So they reconstructed minds and bodies – separately – and put them together? Is that what you're saying?'

'I suppose so.'

I jumped up, waving my tiny fists at him. 'But why us,
George? Why me?' He dropped his head to his chest, not even
trying to answer as I capered before him. 'And why make
monkeys, George? Why not give us human bodies; why not
reconstruct London instead of some damn jungle?'

He rubbed at his snout, leaving a glistening streak on his
palm. 'Actually I've a theory about that.'

'I bet you do.'

He lifted his head. 'Distance in time, Mr Beard ... You
see, only a few per cent difference in DNA coding separates
humans from the rest of the primates: chimps, gorillas. And
I would guess that only a few per cent distinguishes humans
from even the earliest primates.'

'Since when were flying lemurs the first primates?'

'Not lemurs, but an animal similar in structure and ecology.
That's the theory, at any rate. You see, the "lemurs" developed
hands and visual coordination to help with their gliding. Later
they used their grasping fingers to build tools.'

I shook my head. 'Let me get this straight. The Builders,

seeking to house our – soul fossils – tried to reconstruct human DNA. But they got it wrong.'

'Over ninety per cent right, actually. It was a good job. We are very remote in time.'

I screamed and jumped about the tree top, rattling my arms. 'But you're still guessing, aren't you, George? I've been all around this damn little world; there's nobody here except you and me, and you don't know anything, do you, George?' I hurled leaves and twigs into his face. 'You don't know! You don't know!'

He wrapped his arms over his face and rocked backwards and forwards.

Suddenly my anger imploded, leaving a shell of self-disgust. 'George, George.' I squatted in front of him and pulled at his arms. 'Come on out.'

He lifted his arms so that they framed his tearful face. 'I'm sorry.'

'It's me who's sorry, George.'

'I miss my wife.'

I felt my jaw drop. 'I never knew you were married.'

He shrugged and buried his face again.

'Kids?'

He shook his head.

Hesitantly I stroked at his arms. The skin was warm and soft, and the lay of the fur seemed to guide my palms.

I felt that itch in my groin again.

I snatched my hand away. 'My God, George. You're a female, aren't you?'

He nodded miserably. 'Just another little slip by the Builders. As if I didn't have enough troubles.'

I edged away from him. 'George, this changes the whole basis of our relationship.'

He unwrapped his arms and picked up his crude tools. 'I don't want to talk about it,' he said, and he resumed his patient drilling.

I flung myself through the branches of the world-tree, willing away the ache beneath my belly.

*　　*　　*

George filled the pit in his piece of wood with bits of dry leaf from the forest floor. Then he wrapped the string of his bow around a thin stick, stood the stick in the leaves, and moved the bow back and forth, patiently, making the stick spin in the leaves.

I watched, sleepily. 'Just think,' I said. 'It's all gone.'

'What?'

'Beethoven. Mozart. There's nobody but us to remember.'

He wiped at his brow and peered up at the shining comet. 'But we do remember. I think that's why we've been brought here. I think we're at a unique moment in the history of the Solar System; and we've been brought back. As witnesses.'

'. . . And what about all the music we never heard, all the books we never read . . . Gone, as if they never existed.' I felt brittle; my words were a kind of shell around a cold loneliness. 'And all the other stuff, the junk that filled our heads from day to day. The Church of the Latter Day Saints. The Inland Revenue. All gone. My God, George, nobody else in all creation remembers "Born Too Late" by The Ponytails.'

'Even I don't remember it,' he said, still spinning his stick.

'Let the Builders try reconstructing The Ponytails.' My snout twitched. 'At least I know I'm not insane. Nobody could possibly dream up The Ponytails. George, I can smell the damnedest –'

A thread of smoke rose from the pit of leaves. 'I've done it,' George breathed.

For a long, frozen moment we both stared. Then George threw his sails around the smouldering heap and blew; smoke billowed around his face. Frantically I fed dead leaves into the embryonic fire, cursing as my nubs of fingers crushed the stuff.

A single flame licked at a leaf.

We howled and danced.

Then it started to rain.

I stared up in disbelief. A squat, malevolent cloud had drifted across the Sun's red face, and the first drops were thumping against the leaves. For a few seconds the burning leaves hissed; then our little hearth was smothered, and only scraps of soggy foliage were left.

George just folded up.

I turned my streaming face up to the sky. 'Why are you doing this? We were long dead. Why didn't you leave us be?'

Of course there was no answer; and at that moment I knew that this was real, that I was here forever, that there would never be an answer.

What happened next is . . . vague.

I tore through my world in a mist of rage. I kicked apart George's fire, smashed holes in our hut. I bit, scratched and tore at the world-tree, hurting it in a hundred tiny, futile ways. I dropped to the forest floor and shoved over my longitudinal trails. I rolled in the mulch, howling and tearing my flesh.

Then, bloody, trailing mulch, I hauled myself back to the treetop. I flipped around a branch – the dying Sun, the hated world-tree, the comet, all whirled about me – and I let go and flew high into the air. For a few seconds, at the top of my arc, I hung with mouth wide and limbs outstretched, suspended between leaf-ball world and Sun; the comet filled my eyes, shining more brightly than ever.

I pulled my sails close around me.

The wind of my fall plucked at my fur, and I wished beyond hope to be dashed against the ground.

Once more I lay on my back, staring up at a swollen Sun. George's face hovered over me, anxious and concerned.

I tried to smile at him. Something caked around my mouth – blood? – crackled. 'It didn't work out, did it, George?'

He shrugged, seeming embarrassed. 'You're too light, Mr Beard. I'm sorry. Your terminal velocity wasn't nearly high enough. Although you made enough noise when you came crashing through the foliage.'

I struggled to sit up; George bent over me and slipped his arms under my shoulders. 'I'm sorry to cause you such trouble, George.'

'I'm glad you're awake again.' He squatted beside me and tilted up his head; his face looked like a coin in the red and silver light. 'I think it's abo⸱t to happen; I didn't want you to miss it.'

'What's about to happen?'

'What we were brought here to see. For days that comet has been getting brighter. I think we're approaching a critical point . . .'

He brought me berries, and we sat side by side in the leaves and branches, staring up at a comet which billowed like a flag in a breeze.

It came quite suddenly.

The comet head swelled – and then exploded; silver fire poured around our tree world. We cried out and threw ourselves into the leaves, peeking from under our sails at a sky gone mad.

Within minutes the blaze faded, leaving only wisps glowing pink in the light of the Sun. Where the comet's head had been a handful of glowing rocks drifted. And already the glorious tail, shorn of the nucleus which had fuelled it, was dispersing.

George and I crept closer together, shivering. I said, 'What the hell was that?'

'The death of a comet,' George whispered. 'The Sun has already destroyed the planets; now it is pouring out enough heat to flash the comets to steam. Soon a shell of water molecules will collect around the Sun. Water lines were seen in the spectra of red giants by astronomers in our time . . .' He pulled his cloak-sail tight around him. 'It's the last death of the Solar System, you see, Mr Beard. That's what the Builders brought us to witness: to mark in our own way.'

Now only muddy sunlight obscured the stars – but here and there I could see objects bigger than stars, patches of red and green like distant toys. I pointed them out to George. 'What do you suppose they are? More observers?'

George shrugged. I stared at the enigmatic forms, wondering what strange, baffled creatures, clumsily reconstructed as we had been, were cowering beneath the violent sky.

'Anyway,' George said, 'what do we do now?'

I shrugged and picked at a leaf. 'How long before the Sun swallows us too?'

He frowned. 'I don't think that will be a problem. We must be shielded somehow. Otherwise the sunlight that boiled that comet would have scorched this little world dry. So perhaps we've got years. Centuries, even. I don't suppose the Builders will care what we do.'

I sniffed; it seemed colder without the comet glow. 'I guess the first thing is to fix the house.'

'We can do a lot with fire, you know,' George mused. 'We can harden wood for a start. Make better tools. And perhaps we can go down to the surface, try to clear through the mulch to the bedrock. There might be metal ores.'

'Yes . . . And we ought to think about finding some substitute for paper. Bark, or chewed wood. We'll write down what we know before it dies with us.' I pointed at the discs in the sky. 'One day our kids will travel out there and meet the Builders' other victims. Maybe they will confront the Builders themselves. And they have to be able to tell our story.'

George scratched his ear. 'What kids?'

'I think we have something to discuss, George.'

It wasn't easy. All those sails kept getting in the way. And the first time it was more like relieving an itch.

And, my God, it was embarrassing.

But it got better. And I couldn't believe how fast the kids grew.

INHERIT THE EARTH

The thin voice, drifting through cloudy waters, caused Luke to jerk to half-wakefulness. Feebly he raised his head from the mud. The vision of his one good eye was blurred, darkened, but he could make out the fat, rectangular shape of a Boater, floating just before him; and beyond the Boater Luke could see the ranks of his Clan, all around him. The Walkers' spines were lodged comfortably in the silty mud of the Bottom, and their tentacles sucked at the nourishing fluid which washed over them.

So, he thought sourly, which holy Feast had they stopped to celebrate this time? The Pilgrimage seemed to be the last thing on their tiny heathen minds whenever Luke wasn't driving them on; what a burden they were.

Still ... their presence, surrounding him, was very comforting.

Then he looked a little harder and saw that the Walkers were all, as far as he could see, turned towards him, their huge eyes wide with sorrowful respect. Mother of God, he thought dimly. Not so comforting after all, maybe.

Luke let his neck sag until his head bumped once more against the Bottom. The mud beneath his trunk was piled thick with his own dung, but he could see the twin rows of his Walking spines pinned to the mud. All the spines bore the scars of age, and no less than five of the fourteen were snapped or otherwise bent to uselessness. Now he became aware of the sorry state of the tentacles which lined the top surface of his horizontal trunk. Only four of the seven felt strong enough to support themselves – the others hung beside him or drifted, limp, in the currents – and of the good four, one felt congested.

What a mess, he thought.

'In nomine Patris

'Et Filii

'Et Spiritu Sancti . . .'

Latin! A priest? Luke dipped his front tentacle forward and called, 'Father?'

The monotonous flow of Latin cut off suddenly, and the little Boater scurried away from Luke's head, evidently startled. The Boater was about half Luke's length; his underside was coated with chitin and his upper side bedecked with rows of swimming gills and a pair of long, supple feeding arms. Two huge, black spherical eyes, bobbling on short stalks, stared back at Luke.

'Yes, my son. It's me. Father John. I'm here, Luke.'

'What's –' Luke began, but his tentacle broke up into a fit of helpless coughing. 'What's wrong? Why have these lazy articles stopped?'

'Now, Luke, let's be patient. The Pope has been sitting on his Island for a long time now, and we've been looking for him for almost as long – or so it feels sometimes. He can probably afford to wait for us a little while yet.'

'But why . . . ? Is somebody ill?'

'Yes, Luke,' the priest said solemnly.

'It's me, isn't it?' Luke asked, wondering, fear beginning to uncurl. '. . . Am I dying, Father John?'

'Be calm,' Father John said. 'Soon your troubles here will be over, and you'll be received into the Eternal light of His grace –'

'You were giving me the Last Rites,' Luke said. To his shame the throats of his other tentacles began to mewl, like cubs. Luke felt as if the Bottom had opened up beneath him, revealing only darkness, nonexistence. He gripped mud with his spines, as if clinging to life itself . . . And there, unexpected, resting in the dung between his spines, was the Clan's precious statue of the Virgin Mary, a crude sphere of sand welded together by Roller-spittle; Luke stared at the holy sculpture with relief, a brief Hail Mary sounding in his head. 'I don't want to die,' he told the Virgin.

'He has conquered Death,' the priest said softly; but his words were hollow to Luke.

'I've lived a good life, Father. Haven't I?'

'I know you have and He knows. Now, come; let's pray together.'

'Yes. Yes –'

Soon the familiar, ancient words were lapping over Luke's awareness like childhood mud, and gradually his fear dissipated; but as his thoughts softened, comfortably, towards sleep, one jagged, glaring edge remained, impossible to ignore.

Despite his words to the priest, as he had stared into the Valley of Death during these moments of rationality it had not been a fear of damnation, or an awareness of his own failings in the eyes of the Lord, which had frightened him so.

It had been *doubt*.

As he sank into sleep Luke swore that if God granted him any more life he would use it to pursue those doubts until they were scraped out of his soul.

Somewhat to his own surprise the deadening, enervating weakness which had settled on Luke's system for so long did seem to lift a little. He offered up prayers of gratitude as he raised his head to gaze at the beauty of the rippling Surface above him and of the red, stationary globe that was the Sun.

When he felt well enough he asked Michael, one of the less annoying of the recent youngsters, to send for Father John. Luke extended all his functioning tentacles towards the priest as the little Boater settled to the mud. 'Welcome back, Father. Thanks for bringing me comfort. Will you eat?'

'I'd be delighted, Luke.' Father John murmured a rapid Grace; then, his eyes bobbing against each other, the priest settled to the mound of encrusted faeces beneath Luke and proceeded to munch contentedly.

'Father, we've been together a long time,' Luke began. 'My

Clan have been part of your parish since I was barely out of the mud myself.'

'Since the days of your predecessor Thomas, in fact,' the priest said indistinctly, his feeder-claws digging between Luke's spines. 'Good old Thirteen-Spined Tom; what a rascal he was . . . Long may we remain such friends.'

'We will, as long as I'm alive,' Luke said. He added ruefully, 'For whatever comfort that's worth, in the circumstances. I know about the gossip going around my younger Clanfolk. That only Walkers can make good Catholics. I'll have none of it. That way lies schism and conflict.'

'Good for you, Luke,' the priest said. 'It's a comfort to me to know that your faith is as strong as ever.'

That jarred Luke, and guilt flushed through his system.

'Actually, Father,' Luke said, 'that's why I asked to see you. Faith.' He told the priest as honestly as he could of the doubts which had assailed him.

The priest's tone was mellifluous. 'I think you're worrying yourself about nothing,' he said. 'We're all frightened of death. Even the Lord on the Cross cried out, "Why have You forsaken me?" That's not the same as a loss of faith.'

Luke felt himself tremble. 'I'm sorry, Father, but it isn't just that. I know what I felt, in my heart of hearts, in that extreme moment. I looked for my faith – and it wasn't there.'

The priest's eyestalks shot out from between Luke's two front spines and turned to stare at each other. 'Would it help if I heard your Confession?'

'Thank you, Father, but I doubt it. Anyway, I don't think you'd have the time. You see, I've been a good Catholic all my life; I've followed the teachings of the Scriptures, and the Clan have done the same for generations before me, even before the Pilgrimage. Now, suddenly, I find myself asking – what proof do we have that all this is true? How do we know if the Lord – if humans, even – ever really existed? When you get down to it, we only have the Pope's word for it; and it does all seem a bit unlikely.'

The priest's eyestalks knotted loosely.

Luke, touched by concern, said swiftly, 'I don't mean to be

blasphemous, Father John. I'm sorry if I'm shocking you.'

'Luke, Luke.' The priest clicked his eyeballs together. 'It's a pity old Tom isn't around to knock some sense back into you. How could a mere *fantasy* have lasted through five billion years?'

Luke felt his tentacles grow stiff with exasperation. 'But what *evidence* do we have that Catholicism really is five billion years old? What if the world emerged from nothingness – say, a hundred generations ago?'

The little Boater rose from the Bottom, his gills whirring. Prissily he wiped his feeder-claws on the edge of his lower carapace, scraping away Luke's dung. 'I'm sad to see you like this, Luke, but I don't understand what I can do to help you. Perhaps you will call for me again when you are ready to put aside all these words and look into your heart.'

'Father. Wait. Please . . .'

Luke had come to a decision. 'I've got to get rid of these doubts,' he said. 'I've been talking to some of the youngsters. They're not all a bad lot, you know, even though they called a halt to the Pilgrimage while I slept . . .'

Long ago, the Clan's legends related, the Pope had sailed through the sky beyond the Surface. Then the Pope had fallen out of the sky, built his fabled Island, and – by helping the forefathers of the various species to develop awareness and understanding – had restored Catholicism to a heathen world.

The stories said that the Pope's Island was to be found at the edge of the world, in the unknown seas away from the Sun. So, for generations, the Clan – and its clouds of symbiotes and darting, tiny fish – had followed those legends on a holy Pilgrimage to the Island.

Now they had come to a halt.

Luke said, 'They say they won't move until I'm well again. They say. You know what the truth is, Father. They won't budge another spine's width until they've got me safely buried. This is the end of the Pilgrimage for me.'

The Boater said, 'The youngsters are concerned for your health, Luke.'

Luke rattled his spines impatiently. 'I know they are, Father, but I want to go on. I've spent my life on this journey; and – who knows? – it might only be a little further.

'Father, I want to see the Pope before I die. If anyone can resolve my doubts, surely he can. I want you to help me.'

The Boater's eyestalks turned to each other briefly. 'The youngsters say there is some tough countryside ahead, Luke. Too tough for silly old fools like you and me, at any rate.'

'I don't give a damn, if you'll pardon, Father. I might make it. Who knows? And I won't have the bother of shepherding the whole wretched Clan; I'll leave them here and go on alone . . . although I'll have some of the Clan help me. The best of the youngsters: Michael, Margaret perhaps. If I don't survive the trip – well, I'm in the silt of my life already, Father . . . Join me. Please. You've been my lifelong companion in faith; please join me now, in my darkest hour.'

The priest hovered, hesitating still.

Michael and Margaret thought the expedition was a stupid idea too; but, apparently out of fondness – or, worse, pity, Luke thought sourly – they agreed to come. So the four of them – the three Walkers and the unhappy Boater priest – set off from the dense encampment of the Clan.

Their progress across the Bottom was limited chiefly by Luke's own painfully slow pace. The Boater priest darted behind them, munching on drifting faecal snacks. As they travelled, Luke's aural membranes were washed with the patient murmur of Michael and Margaret as they whispered memorized fragments of Scripture to each other. And every time they awoke they prayed together that they would reach the mysterious Island of the Pope himself before they slept again.

'Of course I'm glad I came along,' Margaret said.

'Then stop complaining,' Luke grumbled, wincing at the stiffness in the joints of spine and trunk as he scraped across the unfamiliar Bottom.

'I wasn't complaining. I just said we'd make quicker progress if we didn't have to carry that stupid Virgin Mary along with us. Why not leave Her here? We can collect Her on the way back.'

Luke defensively licked his precious lump of sand and Roller-spit. 'We'd never find Her again.'

Margaret said, 'Then you should have left Her behind in the first place, you daft old fool.'

Michael came sliding with enviable grace over to Luke. 'Stop teasing him, Margaret. The older folk find these things a comfort.'

'Thanks a lot,' Luke muttered.

'Older folk indeed,' Father John said. The priest's membranes hissed with good-natured annoyance. 'Old Thirteen Spines didn't make do with one measly Virgin. Did he, Luke? In those times we had to lug along six Crucifixes, four statues of the Sacred Heart *and* a full set of Stations of the Cross. All nibbled out of the best Burrower dung.'

'Quite right, Father,' Luke said. 'And we'd have it all still if it hadn't been pinched by those Eaters.'

'Yes, what a bunch of pagans,' the priest said. 'Do you know, Luke, I've never met an Eater yet who could grasp the concept of the Holy Trinity. And –'

'I just find the whole situation ironic,' Margaret said brashly. 'Here we are on a quest to restore Luke's faith, and yet he brings along the most perfect symbol of the unresolved questions that lie at the heart of our religion.'

Luke mouthed the Virgin uncertainly. 'What do you mean? What's wrong with Her?'

Michael sighed. 'She's talking about the debate on the form which humans took. I mean, the statue you're carrying is based on guesswork, really, from clues in the Scriptures.'

'I thought it was all settled,' Luke said, confused. 'Humans must have been ... well, round. Every animal eats and breathes through surfaces. And the bigger you are, the more surface you need. We have solved this problem by having a lot of external surface, by being covered in threads, sheets, spines, gills, loops. The humans had all their surfaces wrapped up inside them.'

'Yes,' Michael said patiently, 'they were simpler externally, but a sphere is the simplest shape of all. What if they were a bit less simple? What if they were – I don't know – shaped like Father John up there, but without the gills? It's perfectly possible.'

'Right,' Margaret said vigorously. 'I mean, what do we really know about the humans?'

'We know Christ was a human,' Father John said quietly.

Michael waved his tentacles thoughtfully. 'I'm glad I don't mix with the folk you do, Margaret. That stuff's a little too heady for me. *I'm* still confused about why we have to hear Mass in Latin.'

The priest was doing slow somersaults in the water above them, his feeder-claws snapping idly at the Surface. 'Now there we do have an answer. The Second Vatican Council was declared heretical when Pope Paul IX decreed that –'

Luke wasn't listening. He had to remind himself that it was his own doubts which had inspired this jaunt in the first place. Still, though, he found Margaret's words shocking. He licked his statue tenderly. 'I don't think I care what you kids say,' he said slowly. 'To me this is how She looked. And that's all that matters. Isn't it?'

'I don't know, Luke,' the priest called in his fluting voice. 'Is it? Perhaps if I knew the answer to that, I wouldn't be neglecting my parishioners to come on this damn silly expedition.'

When Luke got too tired the other Walkers would nestle close to him, supporting him so that he could keep moving, while the little priest hovered above dropping succulent fragments of food close to his weary mouths.

The colour of the Bottom changed: a gritty sand, sickly yellow, replaced warm brown mud. The water itself changed; even to Luke's depleted senses it had become cold, thin, spiced with unfamiliar flavours. It wasn't comfortable, but it was all a sign that they were making progress.

Things, for a while, went well.

*   *   *

The Eater was immense, four or five times the size of the Walkers and utterly dwarfing the poor, terrified priest.

It came drifting out of the distance to loom over them. Huge flukes beat, while a circular mouth set in a head the size of two Boaters opened and closed, dilating.

The expedition froze, the Walkers trembling together and the Boater priest cowering against the Bottom.

The Eater inspected them with one huge, scarred eyeball. Then the beast rumbled a crude profanity and descended towards Luke; to the Walker, staring up, it was like watching a mouth close over him.

The priest fled in a flurry of gills. The other Walkers, Michael and Margaret, hurried across the sand ... but Luke held his ground, cowering into a ball against the dirt.

The Eater's shadow was like death descending.

Margaret returned to his side, all her throats keening with terror. 'Luke, get out of here. He'll kill you!'

Luke's head rotated helplessly. 'The Virgin Mary,' he said. 'He's after Her. Not me. They like the dung, you see ...'

'He'll bite you in half to get to Her,' Margaret cried. 'Luke, *please –*'

Luke closed his eyes and settled more closely around the little statue, Hail Marys ringing in his head.

Then Margaret rammed him.

He rolled across the sand, his useless spines flapping painfully. When he came to rest he opened his good eye and looked back.

Margaret lay against the sand with her spines spreadeagled, her head rotating helplessly, as the Eater descended on her, hissing through its dilating maw.

The Eater's immense bulk crashed to the Bottom, hopelessly crushing Margaret. From beneath the cruel flange of the beast two pathetic, golden-brown spine tips protruded; Luke, unable to move or even to cry out, watched them twitch ... Once, twice.

Then, mercifully, it was over.

The Eater, mumbling Grace, lifted. It belched fragments of

carapace from its circular maw and, with a shuddering beat of its long tail, moved away and out of sight.

The sunlight returned to the scrap of sea bed on which lay scattered the remains of Margaret ... and the undamaged globe of the Virgin Mary.

Michael scraped a grave from the sand, and the priest intoned a simple service.

At times like this, Luke thought, the strength or weakness of his faith was beside the point. For faith, in the face of such meaningless tragedy, was all he had.

The death of Margaret seemed to have drained the resolve out of him.

But a small fragment of determination remained lodged in his soul. He was going to find the Pope.

He nestled against the strong, warm shoulders of his good young friend and concentrated on dragging his spines across the strange mud, watching his long shadow cross the Bottom before him.

Father John, high in the water, saw it first. His voice came down to the Walkers, thin and scared. 'Dear Lord – Dear Lord –'

Michael looked up, startled; Luke tried to raise his head as his four mouths laboured at the thin water.

The little priest came tumbling end over end from the Surface; at last he settled against the Bottom and lay there on his belly, his gills working feebly.

Luke painfully slid across the sand to him. 'The Island,' he said gruffly. 'You can see it, can't you?'

'Yes,' said Father John.

Everyone knew that the Pope's Island, the only Island in the World, reared above the water, breaking the Surface itself. And so, as they approached the Island, Luke found himself climbing a slope. It was quite shallow but almost beyond Luke. His sight and hearing seemed to recede from him; it was as if he swam in some inner sea, insulated from the world he had known.

The little priest bravely swam up to the Surface, poked a tentative eyestalk through the thick, stiff meniscus.

Michael shivered beside Luke. 'We can't go on, and we can't stay here long; the water's almost too thin to breathe. Even if the Pope is there, he won't know we're here.'

'Oh, I think he knows.' The Boater priest retracted his eyeball from the world above the Surface and floated down to the huddled Walkers.

Luke raised his head. 'He's there? The Pope? He's there?'

Father John drifted before Luke's head. 'Yes, Luke, he's there. We've found him.'

Luke's tentacles quivered. *The Pope . . .* Actually whenever he'd thought of the Pope, he realized suddenly, he'd always imagined a huge, sterner version of Thirteen-Spined Thomas. 'Father, tell me. What does he look like?'

Father John's gills flapped. 'He's nothing like any of us. He's immense; I looked up, lifting back my eye, but could not see to the top of him. He's made of something that shines, red and gold in the light of the Sun.'

'What shape is he?'

'I don't know, Michael. Like a huge Boater set on end, maybe.' The priest's voice was close to breaking, suddenly; the courage was visibly draining from him. 'It was wonderful, Luke, like a vision from Heaven. Like something made out of water itself.' Clumsily he made the Sign of the Cross with a feeder-claw and subsided to the Bottom, muttering prayers.

Michael turned to Luke. 'What shall we do?'

Luke sighed. 'Wait, I suppose.'

He closed his eyes and began a Rosary, counting the Hail Marys on the crusty grains of the Virgin.

Suddenly the Surface erupted in a noisy explosion of light and tiny bubbles. All three of the Pilgrims cowered back from the swirling motion in the water. Luke, staring with his good eye, could see that there were many creatures here, before him; it was like a school of tiny fish – but whirling about each other more rapidly than any fish.

Then, miraculously, Luke saw a figure condense out of the water where the fish shoal had been. It was difficult to see – virtually transparent, and with blurred, ever-changing outline – but the overall shape was clear enough. There was the horizontal trunk, the seven pairs of spines embedded in the sand, the seven tentacles waving above, the shapeless plug of a head.

Luke heard Michael gasp. 'It's a Walker. The fish have made themselves into a Walker.'

Now the creature bent all its tentacles towards Luke in the Walkers' universal gesture of friendship.

'Yes,' Luke said softly. 'He's making us welcome.'

Stiffly he moved his four functioning tentacles forward, mouths closed, to match the mock creature's stance; and beside him Michael did the same.

The voice of the Pope-Walker was thin and high, but its words were clear. 'Hello,' it said. 'I'm not used to visitors.'

'We're pilgrims,' Luke said, feeling his head droop between his front spines.

'Pilgrims?' The Pope-Walker's ghostly tentacles wriggled in amusement. 'Pilgrims. Two tiny crab-things and a swimming dust-mote. However it's what's in your hearts that counts, I suppose.'

The Pope was studying Luke. 'You're ill, pilgrim,' it said softly.

'I know that,' Luke snapped. 'I have questions . . .'

The Pope-Walker's head rolled complacently around its axis of neck. 'Questions, eh? Typical. And I suppose you want answers. Where is your faith?'

'Why should we accept your faith?' Luke snapped, ignoring the gasps of protest from the priest who cowered behind him. 'You brought Catholicism to us, from out of the sky. Or is that another fable, like the Messiah Himself?'

'You're not as bitter as you sound, pilgrim. Oh, the Messiah is no fable. At least I don't think He is . . . I've given this a lot of thought, over the years I've been stuck here. You see, I might be right about Him. On the other hand I could be two Hail Marys short of a full Rosary. It's hard to tell, isn't it?

'Little pilgrim, I can't make you believe what I say, any more than I could answer the questions of the humans who used to visit me. Some of *them*, you know, wouldn't even accept an AI as Pope. Ah, what a debate that was. Nearly caused a schism. The Jesuits who built me wanted to place the burden of faith on the believer, you see. You're not a Jesuit, are you? What a Cross they were to bear . . . Sanctimonious rabble. If you have faith, it is because of what is within you, not what is within me. For you see,' the Pope-Walker rambled on sadly, 'there is nothing within me.'

Luke felt his head droop further as he struggled to make sense of these strange words.

Michael stretched his neck forward. 'What were humans like? Were they round?'

The Pope-Walker wriggled its tentacles in a burst of amusement. 'My mission was human souls, not human bodies. I'm sure their souls were just like yours. Apart from that – who knows?'

Luke rested his head, now, against the gritty sand; the darkness was like the warm mud of his childhood, waiting to reclaim him.

The Pope-Walker's shimmering head hovered before him. 'You haven't much time,' it said.

Luke tried to look up. 'Is it true? The story that the Saviour came among us, five billion years ago?'

The Walker's head filled his vision, soft and comforting. 'What a question. Do you know what a "billion" is, pilgrim? Or even a "year"? A year's about twice your lifespan, as it happens, but I suppose that's beside the point . . .

'Listen to me. When I was built the Sun was hot and yellow. I watched it grow huge, red, cooling. Oh, yes, things changed, slowly.

'After some time, the humans stopped speaking to me. I waited, alone.

'At length, still alone, I decided to come back to Earth.

'The humans had gone. I found a shallow sea, covering the Sun-facing hemisphere. And you lot, who had evidently inherited the Earth.'

Luke said, unsure if he even spoke it aloud, 'Did the humans really exist?'

'Pilgrim, even I don't know any more. Perhaps the humans, the legend of the Christ, were all a dream. How could I be certain? After all this time . . . I wanted to find out. I wanted to find traces of humans. So, working from my Island, I began surveys, drilling, seeking fossils.

'But the strata have been metamorphosed, after five billion years. Whole continents have dissolved back into the body of the Earth. No fossil traces of the humans could have survived such aeons.

'But life can leave other traces. Plants selectively extract a certain carbon isotope. So I searched the deep rocks, the old rocks, for the smear of isotopic carbon which would be the sole memorial of the humans after all this time.'

Dimly, Luke was aware of the priest calling his name with concern, of Michael frantically mouthing his tentacles and limbs; but it was all far from him now, all remote from this place he had reached with the Pope-Walker.

'Luke,' the Pope-Walker whispered to him.

'How do you know my name?'

'Grasp your faith. You do not need to share my doubts.'

'Tell me. Did you find this – carbon?'

The Pope-Walker's eyes were huge before him. 'It would prove nothing . . . Only that life of some form covered the Earth, all those years ago. Not even that humans existed. Certainly not that Christ lived. Luke, resolve one mystery and you reveal more; that is why questions and answers can never lead you to *faith*. Even the humans can never have been *certain* . . .

'The world is full of mystery! Pilgrim, I am intelligent. Far more intelligent than you, or even any human, I dare say . . . Even the Jesuits. But I am not self-aware. You are self-aware, pilgrim, and that is a far greater mystery than anything you might ask of me. Perhaps it is I who should supplicate before you –'

It was no answer, Luke thought; and he wasn't going to get an answer . . . but there was triumph, a kind of joy in the mist-like eyes of the Pope-Walker.

Once more he heard the ancient, holy verses of the Last Rites. The Pope's thin Latin words lingered even as its shimmering face receded, leaving him in muddy, comforting darkness; and he felt his faith settle over him once more, as strong as the spines of his Clan.

Of course the Pope was right. There could *be* no answer, no final answer . . . but somehow it no longer mattered.

Still Father John called his name, as if from a great distance. It was time, Luke knew; and, without regret, he sank into the warmth of the mud.

IN THE MSOB

'Get moving, you old bastard.' Bart went around the room, his white jacket already stained by some yellow fluid, and he de-opaqued the windows with brisk slaps.

It took him a while to figure out where he was. It often did nowadays. So he just lay there. He'd been in the same position all night, and he could feel how his body had worn a groove in the mattress. He wondered if Bart had ever seen *Psycho*. 'I thought –' His mouth was dry, and he ran his tongue over his wrinkled gums. 'You know, for a minute I thought I was back there. Like before.'

Bart was just clattering around at the bedside cabinet, pulling out clothes, and looking for his stuff: a hand towel, soap, medication, swabs. Bart never met your eyes, and he never watched out for the creases on your pants.

'My father was there.' Actually he didn't know what in hell his father was doing up there. 'The sunlight was real strong. And the ground was a kind of gentle brown, depending on which way you looked. Autumn colours. It looked like a beach, come to think of it.' He smiled. 'Yeah, a beach.' That was it. His dream had muddled up the memories, and he'd been simultaneously thirty-nine years old, and a little kid on a beach, running towards his father.

'Ah, Jesus.' Bart was poking at the sheet between his legs. His hand came up dripping. Bart pulled apart the top of his pyjama pants. He crossed his arms over his crotch, but he didn't have the strength to resist. 'You old bastard,' Bart shouted. 'You've done it again. You've pulled out your fucking catheter again. You filthy old bastard.' Bart got a towel and began to swab away the piss.

He saw there was blood in the thick golden fluid. *Goddamn surgeons. Always sticking a tube into one orifice or another.* 'I saw my buddy jumping around, and I thought he looked like a human-shaped beach ball, all white, bouncing across the sand . . .'

Bart slapped at his shoulder, hard enough to sting. 'When are you going to get it into your head that nobody gives a flying fuck about that stuff? Huh?' He swabbed at the mess in the bed, his shoulders knotted up. 'Jesus. I ought to take you down to the happy booth right now. Old bastard.'

Like a beach. Funny how I never thought of that before. It had taken him fifty years, but he was finally making sense of those three days. More sense than he could make of where he was now, anyhow. Not that he gave a damn.

Bart cleaned him up, dressed him, and fed him with some tasteless pap. Then he dumped him in a chair in the day room. Bart stomped off, still muttering about the business with the catheter.

Asshole, he thought.

The day room was a long, thin hall, like a corridor. Nothing but a row of old people. Every one of them had his own tiny TV, squawking away at him. Or her. It was hard to tell. Every so often a little robot nurse would come by, a real R2-D2 type of thing, and it would give you a coffee. If you hadn't moved for a while, it would check your pulse with a little metal claw.

You had to set the TV with voice commands, and he never could get the hang of that; he'd asked for a remote, but they didn't make them any more. So he just had his set tuned to the news channels, all day. Sometimes there was news about the programme. Mostly about the dinky little unmanned rovers that the Agency was rolling around Mars these days, that you could work from Earth, like radio-operated boats at Disney World. Now, that was pure bullshit, as far as he was concerned. But there wasn't even anybody up in LEO nowadays. Not since *Atlantis* tore itself up in that lousy landing, and the Russians let what was left of *Mir* fall back into the atmosphere.

He tried to read. You could still get paper books, although it cost you to get them printed out. But by the time he'd gotten to the bottom of the page he would forget what was at the top; and he'd doze off, and drop the damn thing. Then the fucking R2-D2 would roll over to see if he was dead.

The door behind him was open, letting in dense, smoggy air. Nobody was watching him. Nobody but old people, anyhow.

He got out of his chair. Not so hard, if you watched your balance. He leaned on his frame and set off towards the door.

The day room depressed him. It was like an airport departure lounge. And there was only one way out of it. Unless you counted the happy booth. Funny how it had been a Democrat President who'd legalized the happy booths. A *demographic adjustment*, they called it. He couldn't really blame them, Bart and the rest. *Just too many old bastards like me, too few of them to look out for us, no decent jobs for them to do.*

Sometimes, though, he wished he'd just taken a T-38 up high over the Mojave, and gone onto the afterburner, and augured in on those salt flats. Maybe after Geena had died, leaving him stranded here, that would have been a good time. It would have been clean. A few winter rains dissolving that ancient ocean surface; by now you wouldn't even be able to tell where he'd come down.

Outside the light was flat and hard. He squinted up, the sweat already starting to run into his eyes. Not a shred of ozone up there. The home stood in the middle of a vacant lot. There was a freeway in the middle distance, a river of metal he could just about make out. Maybe he could hitch a ride into town, find a bar, sink a few cold ones. Screw the catheter. He'd pull it out in the john.

He worked his way across the uneven ground. He had to lean so far forward he was almost falling, just to keep going ahead. Like before. You'd had to keep tipped forward, leaning on your toes, to balance the mass of the PLSS. And, just like now, you were never allowed to take the damn thing off for a breather.

The lot seemed immense. There were rocks and boulders

scattered about. Maybe it had once been a garden, but nothing grew here now. Actually the whole of the Midwest was dried out like this.

He reached the freeway. There was no fence, no sidewalk, nowhere to cross. He raised an arm, but he couldn't keep it up for long. The cars roared by, small sleek things, at a huge speed: a hundred fifty, two hundred maybe. And they were close together, just inches apart. Goddamn smart cars that could drive themselves. He couldn't even see if there were people in them.

He wondered if anyone still drove Corvettes.

Now there was somebody walking towards him, along the side of the road. He couldn't see who it was.

The muscles in his hands were starting to tremble, with the effort of gripping the frame. Your hands always got tired first.

There were two of them. They wore broad-rimmed white hats. 'You old bastard.' It was Bart, and that other one who was worse than Bart. They grabbed his arms and just held him up like a doll. Bart got hold of the walker, and, incredibly strong, lifted it up with one hand. 'I've had it with you!' Bart shouted.

There was a pressure at his neck, something cold and hard. An infuser.

The light strengthened, and washed out the detail, the rocky ground, the blurred sun.

He was in a big room, white walled, surgically sterile. He was sitting up in a chair. Christ, some guy was shaving his chest.

Then he figured it. Oh, hell, it was all right. It was just a suit tech. He was in the MSOB. He was being instrumented. The suit tech plastered his chest with four silver chloride electrodes. 'This won't hurt a bit, you old bastard.' He had the condom over his dick already. And he had on his faecal containment bag, the big diaper. The suit tech was saying something. 'Just so you don't piss yourself on me one last time.'

He lifted up his arm. He didn't recognize it. It was thin and coated with blue tubes, like veins. It must be the pressure garment, a whole network of hoses and rings and valves and pulleys that coated your body. Yeah, the pressure garment; he could feel its resistance when he tried to move.

There was a sharp stab of pain at his chest. Some other electrode, probably. It didn't bother him.

He couldn't see so well now; there was a kind of glassiness around him. That was the polycarbonate of his big fishbowl helmet. They must have locked him in already.

The suit tech bent down in front of him and peered into his helmet. 'Hey.'

'It's okay. I know I got to wait.'

'What? Listen. It was just on the TV. The other one's just died. What was his name? How about that. You made the news, one more time.'

'It's the oxygen.'

'Huh?'

'One hundred per cent. I got to sit for a half hour while the console gets the nitrogen out of my blood.'

The suit tech shook his head. 'You've finally lost it, haven't you, you old bastard? You're the last one. You weren't the first up there, but you sure as hell are the last. The last of the twelve. How about that.' But there was an odd flicker in the suit tech's face. Like doubt. Or, wistfulness.

He didn't think anything about it. Hell, it was a big day for everybody, here in the Manned Spacecraft Operations Building. 'A towel.'

'What?'

'Will you put a towel over my helmet? I figure I might as well take a nap.'

The suit tech laughed. 'Oh, sure. A towel.'

He went off, and came back with a white cloth, which he draped over his head. He was immersed in a washed-out white light. 'Here you go.' He could hear the suit tech walk away.

In a few minutes, it would start. With the others, carrying his oxygen unit, he'd walk along the hallways out of the MSOB, and there would be Geena, holding little Jackie up to him. He'd be able to hold their hands, touch their faces, but he wouldn't feel anything so well through the thick gloves. And then the transfer van would take him out to Merritt Island, where the Saturn would be waiting for him, gleaming white and wreathed in cryogenic vapour: waiting to take him back up to the lunar beach, and his father.

All that soon. For now, he was locked in the suit, with nothing but the hiss of his air. It was kind of comforting.

He closed his eyes.

AFTERWORD

The stories collected here date from 1987 to 1995.

The title story has a long history. I first drafted it in 1987 as a short action-adventure tale which didn't really come off. After editorial comments I redrafted, and the story was accepted by a small press magazine which folded without publishing my tale. I put it aside for a while, then redrafted the story totally in 1990. *Traces* has some elements in common with my *Xeelee Sequence* tales – the GUT drive, for instance – but it isn't part of that universe.

Many reviewers have commented on similarities between *Traces* and Arthur C. Clarke's great story *The Star*. This was unconscious, but *The Star* is one of my favourite stories, by my favourite author, and *Traces* is one of my own favourite pieces.

Lord Byron's poem *Darkness* reads like an apocalyptic vision of the future, but I wondered if it could have some more intriguing explanation. I was inspired to work on this idea, incidentally, by a holiday near Wordsworth's home in the Lake District.

My good friends Rob Holdstock and Christopher Evans, who bought *The Droplet*, had me change the ending to spare George – in the first draft he was killed. I think they were right.

No Longer Touch the Earth was inspired by the notion that if Aristotle had been right about all those crystal spheres in the sky, it would have made no difference to anyone – save a few dusty astronomers – until Scott reached the South Pole. Hermann Göring, star of *No Longer*, shows up again, as a bit-part player in *Mittelwelt*.

A Journey to the King Planet grew out of some speculation I read about anti-matter comets. My first notion was to give anti-ice to those great explorers the Carthaginians, but I couldn't make the ancillary technology plausible. So *Planet* became a proto-steampunk romp, and as such was an important story for me: my first try-out of a mode of writing which would lead to my novels *Anti-Ice* and *The Time Ships*. *Planet* has some elements in common with *Anti-Ice*, but is not part of the same universe. I always liked the spaceship in this story. As a child, I used to draw diagrams and maps of the wonderful ships in the stories I read. You can map space liner *Australia*.

The Jonah Man is a lifeboat story inspired by some speculation about life in a T Tauri star system. For some reason, whale-like creatures – gigantic, placidly feeding – have turned out to be a trope for me (see *Raft* (1991)).

Many commentators have noticed the influence on me of James Blish's great tale *Surface Tension*. I do seem to come up with a lot of scenarios in which humans, miniaturized or otherwise, subsist in a fluid-filled environment. *Downstream* is an example. I get little story inspiration from TV; the information density is just too low. But documentary images of creatures who spend their lives struggling to survive in a fast-moving river sparked off this story. *The Blood of Angels*, inspired by an account of Antarctic survival strategies, is another *Surface Tension* story, if a fairly grim example.

Columbiad is a collision between my meditations on the fate of the modern space programme, during my research for *Voyage*, and my work on Wells and Verne. *Brigantia's Angels* is only barely alternate history: Bill Frost was real, and you can look up his patented Flying Machine, which was just as I describe it. My wife and I took a holiday in South Wales to research this story. *Angels* won the 1995 *Sidewise Award* for short-form alternate history.

My father was a big Glenn Miller fan. *Weep for the Moon* reminds me of him.

Good News is my only small-press publication in this anthology. It came out of my disappointment, as a comics dilettante, at the unimaginative way the death of a certain superhero was handled. I adapted this story for online publication.

Something for Nothing is the oldest story in this collection, and it probably shows. It was my second professional sale. I still like it: it's a gadget story, but with a nice opening-out of scales. The seed for *In the Manner of Trees* was a fragment I came across about the lifecycles of bacteria. I always loved this type of story: the seductive planet, the suspicious hard-nosed Captain. But nobody writes them any more.

Pilgrim 7 grew out of some reading about the Cuban missile crisis: Kennedy breaking off from crisis management to shake hands with a Mercury astronaut. This turned out to be an important story for me; I found I enjoyed researching and writing about the real space programme, and novels and short stories would follow. *Zemlya* is my tribute to the Soviet space programme, particularly their heroic exploration of Venus. The seeds for *Moon Six* were a fragment of speculation about what kind of world we'd have if sf had never existed, and a NASA puff about the spin-off possibilities of an Apollo space suit.

Two visions of the far future: I worked up *George and the Comet* by using an old sf writer's trick – put together two unrelated ideas (in this case, the fate of comets and specu-lations about early primates) and see what comes out of the collision. Anyone familiar with the creatures of the Burgess Shale will recognize some of the inspiration for *Inherit The Earth*. The rest of it is my Liverpool childhood.

In the MSOB came out of nowhere, while I was working on drafts of *Voyage*. It took two hours to write; the first draft was almost perfect. This is unusual, to say the least, and *MSOB* is one of my favourite pieces.

Timelike Infinity
Stephen Baxter

'As cosmic in scope as any epic by Arthur C. Clarke or Greg Bear'
Starburst

First there were good times: humankind reached glorious heights, even immortality. Then there were bad times: Earth was occupied by the faceless, brutal Qax. Immortality drugs were confiscated, the human spirit crushed. Earth became a vast factory for alien foodstuffs.

Into this new dark age appears the end of a tunnel through time, humanity's greatest engineering project in the pre-Qax era. The other end remains anchored in the past – and a small group of humans in a makeshift craft outwit the Qax to escape there through the tunnel. Amazingly, when they arrive in the past, they do not warn the people of Earth against the Qax, though the aliens are sure to follow them back in time. For these men and women from the future are themselves dangerous fanatics in singleminded pursuit of a bizarre quantum grail.

Michael Poole, the architect of the tunnel through time, boldly confronts the consequences of his genius. The battle for Earth's future begins with colossal violence in the eerie light of Jupiter – and ends at TIMELIKE INFINITY – the strange region at the end of time where the owners of the universe, the fabulous Xeelee, are waiting.

ISBN 0 00 647618 X